Author's Note on
The Italian Girl

I originally wrote the story of Rosanna and Roberto seventeen years ago and it was published as *Aria* in 1996, under my old 'pen' name, Lucinda Edmonds. Last year, some of my publishers asked me about my backlist. I told them all the books were currently out of print, but they asked for some copies. Into my cellar I ventured, and pulled out the eight books I'd written all those years ago. They were covered in mouse-droppings and spiders' webs and smelt of damp, but I sent them off, explaining that I had been very young then and I completely understood if they wanted to bin them then and there. To my surprise, the reaction was incredibly positive and they asked me whether I would like to re-publish them.

This meant that I had to begin reading them too, and as any writer who looks back on their work from the past, I opened the first page of *Aria* with trepidation. It was a bizarre experience, because I couldn't remember much of the story, so I became involved just as a reader does, turning the pages faster and faster to find out what happens next. I felt the book needed some updating and re-editing, but the story and the characters were all there. So I set to work for a few weeks and the finished result is *The Italian Girl*. I hope you enjoy it.

Lucinda Riley, January 2014

Praise for *The Light Behind the Window*

'A fast-paced, suspenseful story, flitting between the present day and World War II narrative . . . Brilliant escapism'

Red

'A beautifully written book that secures Riley's authorial status and proves that her golden penmanship is no mere fluke . . . This is the perfect literary novel to move those readers who wish for something more fulfilling than chick-lit, yet just as entertaining, witty and heart-stopping. The language is dramatic yet truthful and Riley has such a delicate touch with mystery and intrigue that it's difficult to predict where the plot is going . . . Riley's descriptive nuances are so evocative a TV drama is bound to be imminent. A literal and literary page-turner'

WeLoveThisBook.co.uk

'Just sink in and wallow'

Kate Saunders, *Saga*

'Yet again, I have been totally entertained by another great story that is well written with an intricate plot that is multi-layered but tied together so well . . . I became really emotionally attached to these characters . . . This novel really is a joy to read, expertly woven together and mixing social history with family dramas and love and relationships – the perfect blend'

RandomThingsThroughMyLetterbox.blogspot.co.uk

Praise for *The Girl on the Cliff*

'[Lucinda Riley] manipulates the strands of her plot with skill'

Independent on Sunday

'An emotionally charged saga . . . Riley is a writer to watch'

Sunday Express

'Lucinda Riley knows how to write a captivating novel . . . it's layered, it's intricate, it's just brilliant . . . a truly brilliant read'

Chick Lit Reviews

'[A] haunting and engrossing new novel . . . superb characterization, atmospheric locations and a well-paced narrative keep the pages turning and the imagination in thrall . . . perceptive, warm and exquisitely wrought, *The Girl on the Cliff* is another triumph for a talented author'

Burnley Express

'An enchanting and mysterious story of hope after loss, populated with warm characters'

Candis

Praise for *Hothouse Flower*

'Atmospheric, heart-rending and multi-layered'

Grazia

'Romantic, revealing and rich in heart-rending emotion and atmospheric detail . . . could well be the pick of Richard and Judy's spring bunch'

Lancashire Post

'The parallel stories have many layers, and the characters are touching and very humane, which makes this page-turner a perfect beach read'

Elle

'This romance novel conjures up the past in an imaginative way'

Star

'It's a great story, full of atmosphere'

Bookbag

The Italian Girl

Lucinda Riley was born in Ireland and wrote her first book aged 24. Her novel *Hothouse Flower* (also called *The Orchid House*) was selected for the UK's Richard and Judy Book Club in 2011 and went on to sell two million copies worldwide. She is a multiple *New York Times* bestselling author and her books have reached number one in a number of European countries. Her stories are currently translated into 28 languages and published in 38 countries.

She lives with her husband and four children in the English countryside and in the South of France.

Also by Lucinda Riley

Hothouse Flower

The Girl on the Cliff

The Light Behind the Window

The Midnight Rose

The Angel Tree

The Seven Sisters Series

The Seven Sisters

The Storm Sister

The Italian Girl

LUCINDA RILEY

writing as

LUCINDA EDMONDS

PAN BOOKS

First published as *Aria* 1996 by Simon & Schuster

This revised and updated edition published 2014 by Pan Books
an imprint of Pan Macmillan
The Smithson, 6 Briset Street, London EC1M 5NR
Associated companies throughout the world
www.panmacmillan.com

ISBN 978-1-4472-5707-3

18

A CIP catalogue record for this book is available from the British Library.

Typeset by Ellipsis Digital Limited, Glasgow
Printed and bound by CPI Group (UK) Ltd, Croydon, CR0 4YY

For my own son, Kit

'Remember tonight,
for it is the beginning of always'

Dante Alighieri

The Metropolitan Opera House, New York

My Dearest Nico,

It is strange to sit down to relate a story of great complexity knowing you may never read it. Whether writing about the events of the past few years will be a catharsis for me, or for your benefit, darling, I'm not sure, but I feel driven to do it.

So I sit here in my dressing room wondering where I should begin. Much of what I will write happened before you were born – a chain of events that began when I was younger than you are now. So maybe that is the place I should start. In Naples, the city where I was born . . .

I remember Mamma hanging out the washing on a line that reached across to the apartment on the other side of the street. Walking down the narrow alleyways of the Piedigrotta, it looked as though the residents were in a state of perpetual celebration, with the different-coloured clothes on washing lines strung high above our heads. And the noise – always the noise – that evokes those early years; even at night it was never quiet. People singing, laughing, babies crying . . . Italians, as you know, are vocal, emotional people, and families in the Piedigrotta shared their joy and sadness every day as they sat on their doorsteps, turning as brown as berries in the blazing sun. The heat was unbearable, especially in high summer, when the pavements burnt the soles of your feet and mosquitoes took full advantage of your exposed flesh to stealthily attack. I can still smell the myriad scents that wafted through my open bedroom window: the drains, which on occasion were enough to turn your stomach, but more often the enticing aroma of freshly baked pizza from Papa's kitchen.

When I was young we were poor, but by the time I took my First Communion Papa and Mamma had made quite a success of 'Marco's', their small café. They worked night and day, serving spicy pizza slices made to Papa's secret recipe, which over the years had become famous in the Piedigrotta. In the summer months, the café became even busier with the influx of tourists, and the cramped interior was jammed with wooden tables until it was almost impossible to walk between them.

Our family lived in a small apartment above the café. We had our own bathroom; there was food on the table and shoes on our feet. Papa was proud that he'd risen from nothing to provide for his family in such a way. I was happy too, my dreams stretching little further than the following sunset.

Then, one hot August night, when I was eleven years old, something happened that changed my life. It seems impossible to believe that a girl not yet in her teens could fall in love, but I remember so vividly the moment I first laid eyes on him . . .

1

Naples, Italy, August 1966

Rosanna Antonia Menici held on to the washbasin and stood on her tiptoes to look in the mirror. She had to lean a little to the left because there was a crack in it that distorted her facial features. This meant she could see only half of her right eye and cheekbone and none of her chin; she was still too short to see that, even standing on her toes.

'Rosanna! Will you come out of the bathroom!'

Sighing, Rosanna let go of the basin, walked across the black linoleum floor and unlocked the door. The handle turned immediately, the door opened and Carlotta brushed roughly past her.

'Why do you lock the door, you silly child! What have you to hide?' Carlotta turned on the bath taps, then pinned her long, dark, curly hair expertly on top of her head.

Rosanna shrugged sheepishly, wishing that God had made her as lovely as her older sister. Mamma had told her that God gave everyone a different gift and Carlotta's was her beauty. She watched humbly as Carlotta removed her bath-robe, revealing her perfect body with its lush creamy skin, full breasts and long, tapered legs. Everyone who came into the café praised Mamma and Papa's beautiful daughter, and said how she would one day make a good match for a rich man.

Steam began to rise in the small bathroom as Carlotta turned off the taps and climbed into the water.

Rosanna perched herself on the edge of the bath. 'Is Giulio coming tonight?' she asked her sister.

'Yes. He will be there.'

'Will you marry him, do you think?'

Carlotta began to soap herself. 'No, Rosanna, I will not marry him.'

'But I thought you liked him?'

'I do like him, but I don't . . . oh, you are too young to understand.'

'Papa likes him.'

'Yes, I know Papa likes him. He's from a rich family.' Carlotta raised an eyebrow and sighed dramatically. 'But he bores me. Papa would have me walking down the aisle with him tomorrow if he could, but I want to have some fun first, enjoy myself.'

'But I thought being married was fun?' persisted Rosanna. 'You can wear a pretty wedding dress and get lots of presents and your own apartment and—'

'A brood of screaming children and a thickening waistline,' finished Carlotta, idly tracing the slender contours of her own body with the soap as she spoke. Her dark eyes flickered in Rosanna's direction. 'What are you staring at? Go away, Rosanna, and let me have ten minutes' peace. Mamma needs your help downstairs. And close the door behind you!'

Without replying, Rosanna left the bathroom and walked

down the steep wooden stairs. She opened the door at the bottom of the stairs and entered the café. The walls had recently been whitewashed and a painting of the Madonna hung next to a poster of Frank Sinatra over the bar at the back of the room. The dark wooden tables were polished to a sheen and candles had been placed in empty wine bottles on top of each one.

'There you are! Where have you been? I've called and called you. Come and help me hang this banner.' Antonia Menici was standing on a chair, holding one end of the brightly coloured material. The chair was wobbling precariously under her considerable weight.

'Yes, Mamma.' Rosanna pulled another wooden chair out from under one of the tables and dragged it across to the arch in the centre of the café.

'Hurry up, child! God gave you legs to run, not to crawl like a snail!'

Rosanna took hold of the other end of the banner, then stood on the chair.

'Put that loop on the nail,' instructed Antonia.

Rosanna did so.

'Now, come help your mamma down so we can see if we have it straight.'

Rosanna descended from her own chair, then hurried to help Antonia safely to the ground. Her mamma's palms were wet, and Rosanna could see beads of sweat on her forehead.

'*Bene, bene.*' Antonia stared up at the banner with satisfaction.

Rosanna read the words out loud: '"Happy Thirtieth Anniversary – Maria and Massimo!"'

Antonia put her arms round her daughter and gave her a

rare hug. 'Oh, it will be such a surprise! They think they are coming here for supper with just your papa and me. I want to watch their faces when they see all their friends and relatives.' Her round face beamed with pleasure. She let go of Rosanna, sat down on the chair and wiped her forehead with a handkerchief. Then she leant forward and beckoned Rosanna towards her. 'Rosanna, I shall tell you a secret. I have written to Roberto. He's coming to the party, all the way from Milan. He will sing for his mamma and papa, right here in Marco's! Tomorrow, we will be the talk of the Piedigrotta!'

'Yes, Mamma. He is a crooner, isn't he?'

'Crooner? What blasphemous words you speak! Roberto Rossini is not a crooner, he is a student at the *scuola di musica* of La Scala in Milan. One day he will be a great opera singer and perform on the stage of La Scala itself.'

Antonia clasped her hands to her bosom and looked, to Rosanna, exactly as she did when she was praying at Mass in church.

'Now, go and help Papa and Luca in the kitchen. There's still much to do before the party and I'm going to Signora Barezi's to have my hair set.'

'Will Carlotta come and help me too?' asked Rosanna.

'No. She's coming to Signora Barezi's with me. We must both look our best for this evening.'

'What shall I wear, Mamma?'

'You have your pink church dress, Rosanna.'

'But it's too small. I'll look silly,' she said, pouting.

'You will not! Vanity is a sin, Rosanna. God will come in the night and pull out all your hair if he hears your vain thoughts. You'll wake up in the morning bald, just as Signora

Verni did when she left her husband for a younger man! Now, get along with you to the kitchen.'

Rosanna nodded and walked off towards the kitchen wondering why Carlotta hadn't yet lost all her hair. The intense heat assailed her as she opened the door. Marco, her papa, was preparing dough for the pizzas at the long wooden table. Marco was thin and wiry, the polar opposite to his wife, his bald head glistening with sweat as he worked. Luca, her tall, dark-eyed older brother, was stirring an enormous, steaming pan on top of the stove. Rosanna watched for a moment, mesmerised, as Papa expertly twirled the dough on his fingertips above his head, then slapped it down on the table in a perfectly formed circle.

'Mamma sent me in to help.'

'Dry those plates on the drainer and stack them on the table.' Marco did not pause in his task as he rapped out the order.

Rosanna looked at the mountain of plates and, nodding resignedly, pulled a clean cloth out of a drawer.

'How do I look?'

Carlotta paused dramatically by the door as the rest of her family stared at her in admiration. She was wearing a new dress made from a soft lemon satin, with a plunging bodice and a skirt which tapered tightly over her thighs, stopping just above her knees. Her thick black hair had been set, and hung in ebullient, glossy curls to her shoulders.

'*Bella, bella!*' Marco held out his hand to Carlotta as he walked across the café. She took it as she stepped down onto the floor.

'Giulio, does my daughter not look beautiful?' asked Marco.

The young man rose from the table and smiled shyly, his boyish features seemingly at odds with his well-muscled frame.

'Yes,' Giulio agreed. 'She is as lovely as Sophia Loren in *Arabesque*.'

Carlotta walked towards her boyfriend and planted a light kiss on his tanned cheek. 'Thank you, Giulio.'

'And doesn't Rosanna look pretty too?' said Luca, smiling at his sister.

'Of course she does,' said Antonia briskly.

Rosanna knew Mamma was lying. The pink dress, which had once looked so well on Carlotta, made her own skin seem sallow, and her tightly plaited hair made her ears look larger than ever.

'We shall have a drink before the guests arrive,' Marco said, brandishing a bottle of jewel-bright Aperol liqueur. He opened it with a flourish and poured out six small glasses.

'Even me, Papa?' Rosanna asked.

'Even you.' Marco nodded to her as he handed everyone a glass. 'May God keep us all together, protect us from the evil eye and make this day special for our best friends, Maria and Massimo.' Marco lifted his glass and drained it in one go.

Rosanna took a small sip and almost choked as the fiery, bitter-orange liquid hit the back of her throat.

'Are you all right, *piccolina*?' asked Luca, patting her on the back.

She smiled up at him. 'Yes, Luca.'

Her brother took her hand in his and bent down to whisper in her ear. 'One day, you will be far more beautiful than our sister.'

Rosanna shook her head vehemently. 'No, Luca, I won't. But I don't mind. Mamma says I have other gifts.'

'Of course you do.' Luca wrapped his arms round his sister's thin body and hugged her to him.

'*Mamma mia!* Here are the first guests. Marco, bring in the Prosecco. Luca, go check the food, quickly!' Antonia straightened her dress and advanced towards the door.

Rosanna sat at a corner table and watched as the café began to fill up with friends and relatives of the guests of honour. Carlotta was smiling and tossing her hair as she stood at the centre of a group of young men. Giulio looked on jealously from a seat in the corner.

Then a hush fell over the café and every head turned towards the figure in the doorway.

He stood, towering over Antonia, then bent to kiss her on both cheeks. Rosanna stared at him. She had never thought to describe a man as beautiful before, but could summon no other word for him. He was very tall and broad-shouldered, his physical strength evident in the muscles of his forearms, which were clearly visible beneath the short sleeves of his shirt. His hair was as sleek and black as a raven's wing, combed back from his forehead to emphasise the finely chiselled planes of his face. Rosanna could not see what colour his eyes were, but they were large and liquid and his lips were full, yet firm and masculine in contrast to his skin, which was unusually pale for a Neapolitan.

Rosanna experienced a strange sensation in the pit of her stomach, the same fluttering feeling she had before a spelling test at school. She glanced across at Carlotta. She too was staring at the figure at the door.

'Roberto, welcome.' Marco signalled for Carlotta to follow him as he pushed through the crowd towards the door. He kissed Roberto on both cheeks. 'I am so happy you have honoured us by coming here tonight. This is Carlotta, my daughter. I think she has grown up since last you saw her.'

Roberto looked Carlotta up and down. 'Yes, Carlotta, you have grown up,' he agreed.

He spoke in a deep, musical voice that caused Rosanna's butterflies to flutter round her stomach once again.

'And what of Luca, and . . . er . . . ?'

'Rosanna?' answered Papa.

'Of course, Rosanna. She was only a few months old when I last saw her.'

'They're both well and . . .' Marco stopped as he glanced beyond Roberto to two figures making their way up the cobbled street. 'Hush, everybody, it's Maria and Massimo!'

The assembled company immediately became silent, and a few seconds later, the door opened. Maria and Massimo stood at the entrance to the café, staring in surprise at the sea of familiar faces in front of them.

'Mamma! Papa!' Roberto stepped forward and embraced his parents. 'Happy anniversary!'

'Roberto!' Maria's eyes brimmed with tears as she hugged her son to her. 'I cannot believe it, I cannot believe it,' she repeated over and over.

'More Prosecco for everyone!' said Marco, grinning from ear to ear at the coup they had managed to pull off.

Rosanna helped Luca and Carlotta pass round the sparkling wine until everyone had a glass.

'A little quiet, please.' Marco clapped his hands. 'Roberto wishes to speak.'

Roberto climbed onto a chair and smiled down at the guests. 'Today is a very special occasion. My beloved mamma and papa are celebrating their thirtieth wedding anniversary. As everyone knows, they have lived here in the Piedigrotta all their lives, making a success of their bakery and amassing a multitude of good friends. They're known as much for their kindness as they are for their wonderful bread. Anyone with a problem knows they will always find a sympathetic ear and sound advice behind the counter of Massimo's. They've been the most loving parents I could have wished for . . .' Roberto's own eyes were moist as he watched his mamma wipe away a further tear. 'They sacrificed much to send me away to the best music school in Milan so I could train to become an opera singer. Well, my dream is beginning to come true. I hope it won't be long before I am singing at La Scala itself. And it's all thanks to them. Let us toast to their continued happiness and good health.' Roberto raised his glass. 'To Mamma and Papa – Maria and Massimo.'

'To Maria and Massimo!' chorused the guests.

Roberto stepped down from the chair and fell into his mother's arms amid much cheering.

'Rosanna, come. We must help Papa serve the food,' Antonia said, and ushered Rosanna out of the room and towards the kitchen.

Later, Rosanna watched Roberto as he talked to Carlotta, and then, when Marco had put records on the gramophone brought downstairs from their apartment, she saw how

Roberto's arms slipped naturally around Carlotta's narrow waist as they danced together.

'They make a handsome pair,' whispered Luca, echoing Rosanna's thoughts. 'Giulio doesn't look pleased, does he?'

Rosanna followed her brother's gaze and saw Giulio still sitting in the corner, watching morosely as his girlfriend laughed happily in Roberto's arms. 'No, he doesn't,' she agreed.

'You would like to dance, *piccolina*?' Luca asked.

Rosanna shook her head, 'No, thank you. I can't dance.'

'Of course you can.' Luca pulled her from her chair and into the crowd of guests who were dancing too.

'Sing for me, Roberto, please,' Rosanna heard Maria ask her son when the record stopped.

'Yes, sing for us, sing for us,' chanted the guests.

Roberto wiped his brow and shrugged his shoulders. 'I will do my best, but it's hard without accompaniment. I shall sing "*Nessun dorma*".'

Silence descended as he began to sing.

Rosanna stood spellbound and listened to the magical sound of Roberto's voice. As it ascended towards the climax and he stretched out his hands, he looked as if he were reaching towards her.

And that was the moment she knew she loved him.

There was thunderous applause, but Rosanna could not clap. She was too busy searching for her handkerchief to wipe away the involuntary tears that had trickled down her face.

'Encore! Encore!' everyone cried.

Roberto shrugged his shoulders and smiled. 'Forgive me, ladies and gentlemen, but I must save my voice.' There was a murmur of disappointment in the room as he resumed his place by Carlotta's side.

'Then Rosanna shall sing "*Ave Maria*",' said Luca. 'Come, *piccolina*.'

Rosanna shook her head violently and remained rooted to the spot, a look of horror on her face.

'Yes!' Maria clapped her hands. 'Rosanna has such a sweet voice, and it would mean much to me to hear her sing my favourite prayer.'

'No, please, I . . .' But Rosanna was swept up in Luca's arms and placed on a chair.

'Sing as you always do for me,' whispered Luca gently to her.

Rosanna looked at the sea of faces smiling indulgently up at her. She took a deep breath and automatically opened her mouth. At first, her voice was small, barely more than a whisper; but as she began to forget her nervousness and lose herself in the music, her voice grew stronger.

Roberto, whose eyes had been preoccupied with Carlotta's ample cleavage, heard the voice and looked up in disbelief. Surely such a pure, perfect sound could not be coming from the skinny little girl in the dreadful pink dress? But as he watched Rosanna, he no longer saw her sallow skin, or the way she seemed to be all arms and legs. Instead, he saw her huge, expressive brown eyes and noticed a hint of colour appear in her cheeks as her exquisite voice soared to a crescendo.

Roberto knew he was not listening to a schoolgirl perform her party piece. The ease with which she assailed the notes, her natural control and her obvious musicality were gifts that couldn't be taught.

'Excuse me,' he whispered to Carlotta, as applause rang round the room. He crossed the café to Rosanna, who had just emerged from Maria's enthusiastic embrace.

'Rosanna, come and sit over here with me. I wish to talk to you.' He led her to a chair, then sat down opposite her and took her small hands in his.

'*Bravissima*, little one. You sang that beautiful prayer perfectly. Are you taking lessons?'

Too overwhelmed to look at him, Rosanna stared at the floor and shook her head.

'Then you should be. It's never too early to start. Why, if I had begun earlier, then . . .' Roberto shrugged. 'I shall talk to your papa. There's a teacher here in Naples who used to give me singing lessons. He is one of the best. You must go to him immediately.'

Rosanna raised her eyes sharply and met his gaze for the first time. She saw now that his eyes were a deep, dark blue and full of warmth. 'You think I have a good voice?' she whispered incredulously.

'Yes, little one, better than good. And with lessons, your gift can be encouraged and nurtured. Then one day I can say proudly it was Roberto Rossini who discovered you.' He smiled at her, then kissed her hand.

Rosanna felt as if she might faint with pleasure.

'Her voice is so sweet, is it not, Roberto?' said Maria, appearing behind Rosanna and placing her hand on her shoulder.

'It's more than sweet, Mamma, it . . .' Roberto waved his hands expressively. 'It is a gift from God, like my own.'

'Thank you, Signor Rossini,' was all Rosanna could manage.

'Now,' said Roberto, 'I shall go and find your papa.'

Rosanna glanced up and saw that several guests were looking at her with the same warmth and admiration usually reserved for Carlotta.

A glow spread through her body. It was the first time in her life that anyone had told her she was special.

At half past ten, the party was still in full swing.

'Rosanna, it's time you went to your bed.' Her mother appeared by her side. 'Go say goodnight to Maria and Massimo.'

'Yes, Mamma.' Rosanna weaved her way carefully through the dancers. 'Goodnight, Maria.' Rosanna kissed her on both cheeks.

'Thank you for singing for me, Rosanna. Roberto is still talking about your voice.'

'Indeed I am.' Roberto appeared behind Rosanna. 'I've given the name and address of the singing teacher to both your papa and Luca. Luigi Vincenzi used to coach at La Scala and a few years ago he retired here to Naples. He's one of the best teachers in Italy and still takes talented pupils. When you see him, say that I sent you.'

'Thank you, Roberto.' Rosanna blushed under his gaze.

'You have a very special gift, Rosanna. You must take care to cherish it. *Ciao*, little one.' Roberto took her hand to his mouth and kissed it. 'We will meet again one day, I am sure of it.'

Upstairs in the bedroom she shared with Carlotta, Rosanna pulled her nightgown over her head, then reached under her mattress and pulled out her diary. Finding the pencil she kept in her underwear drawer, she climbed onto the bed and, brow furrowed in concentration, began to write.

'*16th August. Massimo and Maria's party . . .*'

Rosanna chewed the end of her pencil as she tried to remember the exact words Roberto had spoken to her. After carefully writing them down, she smiled in pleasure and closed the diary. Then she lay back on her pillow, listening to the sounds of music and laughter from downstairs.

A few minutes later, unable to sleep, she sat up. And, reopening her diary, picked up her pencil and added another sentence.

'*One day, I will marry Roberto Rossini.*'

2

Rosanna awoke with a start, opened her eyes and saw it was almost light. She heard the rumbling of the dustcart approaching on its dawn round, then turned over and saw Carlotta sitting on the edge of her bed. Her sister was still wearing her lemon dress, but it was badly crumpled and her hair was hanging dishevelled around her shoulders.

'What time is it?' she asked Carlotta.

'Shh, Rosanna! Go back to sleep. It's still early and you'll wake Mamma and Papa.' Carlotta took off her shoes and unzipped her dress.

'Where have you been?'

'Nowhere,' she shrugged.

'But you must have been *somewhere*, because you're just getting into bed and it's almost morning,' persisted Rosanna.

'Will you hush!' Carlotta looked angry and frightened as she threw her dress onto a chair, then pulled her nightgown down over her head. 'If you tell Mamma and Papa I was in so late, I shall never speak to you again. You must promise me you won't.'

'Only if you tell me where you were.'

'All right!' Carlotta tiptoed across to Rosanna's bed and sat down. 'I was with Roberto.'

'Oh.' Rosanna was puzzled. 'What were you doing?'

'We were . . . walking, just walking.'

'Why did you go for a walk in the middle of the night?'

'You'll understand when you get older, Rosanna,' Carlotta answered abruptly as she moved back to her own bed and climbed under the sheet. 'Now, I've told you. Be quiet and go back to sleep.'

Everyone in the Menici household overslept. When Rosanna arrived downstairs for breakfast, Marco was nursing a terrible hangover at the kitchen table and Antonia was struggling to clear up the mess in the café.

'Come and help, Rosanna, or we shall never be ready to open,' Antonia demanded, as her daughter stood surveying the debris.

'Can I have some breakfast?'

'When we've tidied the café. Here, take this box of rubbish out to the backyard.'

'Yes, Mamma.' Rosanna took the box and carried it through to the kitchen, where her father, looking grey, was rolling pizza dough.

'Papa, did Roberto talk to you about my singing lessons?' she asked him. 'He said he would.'

'Yes, he did.' Marco nodded wearily. 'But Rosanna, he was only being kind. And if he thinks we have the money to send you to a singing teacher on the other side of Naples, then he is deluded.'

'But Papa, he thought . . . I mean, he said I had a gift.'

'Rosanna, you're a little girl who'll grow up to make a

husband a good wife one day. You must learn the gifts of cooking and home-making, not waste your time on fantasy.'

'But . . .' Rosanna's bottom lip trembled. 'I want to be a singer like Roberto.'

'Roberto is a man, Rosanna. He must work. One day, your sweet little voice will help soothe your babies to sleep. That is enough. Now, get that rubbish outside, then come back and help Luca wash the glasses.'

As Rosanna took the box to the dustbins in the yard behind the kitchen, a small tear rolled down her cheek. Nothing had changed. Everything was the same. Yesterday, the best day of her life – when she was somebody special – might as well not have happened.

'Rosanna!' Marco's voice roared from the kitchen. 'Hurry up!'

She wiped her nose on the back of her hand and went back inside, leaving her dreams in the yard with the rubbish.

Later that day, as Rosanna was slowly climbing the stairs to bed, exhausted by long hours of waiting on tables, she felt a hand on her shoulder.

'Why do you look so glum tonight, *piccolina*?'

Rosanna turned and looked at Luca. 'Maybe I'm just tired,' she shrugged.

'But Rosanna, you should be very happy. It's not every young girl that reduces a room of people to tears when she sings.'

'But Luca, I . . .' Rosanna sat down abruptly at the top of the narrow stairs and her brother squeezed in next to her.

'Tell me what it is, Rosanna.'

'I asked Papa about the singing lessons this morning and

he said Roberto was only being kind, that he didn't really believe I could be a singer.'

'Attch!' Luca swore under his breath. 'That isn't true. Roberto told everyone what a beautiful voice you have. You must go to singing lessons with this teacher he suggested.'

'I cannot, Luca. Papa says he hasn't got the money for me to go. I think singing lessons must be very expensive.'

'Oh *piccolina*.' Luca put his arms round his sister's shoulders. 'Why is Papa so blind when it comes to you? Now, if that had been Carlotta, well . . .' Luca sighed. 'Listen, Rosanna, please don't give up hope. Look.' He fumbled in his trouser pocket and pulled out a scrap of paper. 'Roberto gave me the name and address of this teacher too. Never mind what Papa says. *We* will go and see him together, yes?'

'But we have no money to pay, Luca, so there's no point.'

'Don't worry about that yet. Leave it to your big brother.' Luca kissed her on the forehead. 'Sleep well, Rosanna.'

'Goodnight, Luca.'

As Luca made his way down the stairs and through the café, he sighed at the thought of another long night in the kitchen. He knew he should only be grateful he had a more secure future than other young men in Naples, but he found little pleasure in his work. Entering the kitchen, he went over to the table and began chopping a pile of onions, his eyes stinging from the pungent fumes. As he scraped them into the frying pan, he thought about his father's refusal to countenance singing lessons for his little sister. Rosanna had a gift and Luca would be damned if he was going to let her throw it away.

*

On Luca's next afternoon off from the café, he and Rosanna took a bus up to the exclusive neighbourhood of Posillipo, perched on a hill overlooking the bay of Naples.

'Luca, it's beautiful here! There's so much space! Such cool air!' exclaimed Rosanna as they stepped off the bus. She took a deep breath and exhaled slowly.

'Yes, it's very lovely,' agreed Luca, as he paused to gaze out across the bay. The shimmering azure water was dotted with boats, some plying a trade, others resting in their moorings close to shore. Looking straight ahead, the island of Capri floated like a dream on the horizon. Following the curve of the bay to the left, he could see Mount Vesuvius brooding in the distance on the skyline.

'This is really where Signor Vincenzi lives?' Rosanna turned and looked up at the elegant white villas nestled on the hillside above them. 'My goodness, he must be rich,' she added as they started walking up the winding road.

'I believe his house is one of these,' Luca said as they walked past several grand entrances. He finally stopped in front of the last one.

'Here we are – the Villa Torini. Come, Rosanna.' Luca took his sister's hand and led her up the drive to the bougainvillea-covered porch which housed the front door. Hesitating out of nervousness for a few seconds, he finally rang the bell.

The door eventually opened and a middle-aged maid peered out at them.

'*Sī? Cosa vuoi?* What do you want?'

'We have come to see Signor Vincenzi, signora. This is Rosanna Menici and I am her brother, Luca.'

'Do you have an appointment?'

'No, I . . . but Roberto Rossini—'

'Well, Signor Vincenzi sees no one without an appointment. Goodbye.' The door was closed firmly in their faces.

'Come, Luca, let's go home.' Rosanna pulled nervously at her brother's arm. 'We don't belong here.'

From somewhere inside the villa, the sound of a piano drifted through the air. 'No! We've come all this way and we won't return without Signor Vincenzi hearing you sing. Follow me.' Luca pulled his sister away from the front door.

'Where are we going, Luca? I want to go home,' she pleaded.

'No, Rosanna. Please, trust me.' Luca firmly took hold of Rosanna's arm and followed the sound of the music, which led them around the side of the villa. They found themselves on the corner of a gracious terrace decorated with large clay pots filled with dusty-pink geraniums and deep-purple periwinkles.

'Stay there,' whispered Luca. He crouched down and crawled along the terrace until he came to a pair of French windows, which hung open to let in the afternoon breeze. He peered tentatively inside, then ducked back out of sight.

'He's in there,' Luca whispered as he returned to Rosanna's side. 'Now, sing, Rosanna, sing!'

She stared at him in confusion. 'What do you mean, Luca?'

'Sing "*Ave Maria*" – quickly!'

'I . . .'

'Do it!' he urged her.

Rosanna had never seen her gentle brother so adamant. So, she opened her mouth where she stood and did as he had asked.

*

Luigi Vincenzi had just picked up his pipe and was about to take his afternoon stroll in the gardens when he heard the voice. He shut his eyes and listened for a few seconds. Then slowly, unable to contain his curiosity, he walked across the room and out onto the terrace. In the corner of it stood a child of no more than ten or eleven, wearing a washed-out cotton dress.

The child stopped singing as soon as she saw him, fear crossing her face. A young man, obviously a relative of the child judging by his resemblance to her, was standing next to her.

Luigi Vincenzi put his hands together and clapped slowly.

'Thank you, my dear, for that charming serenade. But may I ask what the two of you are doing trespassing on my terrace?'

Rosanna slid slowly behind her brother.

'Excuse me, signor, but your maid would not let us in,' Luca explained. 'I tried to tell her that Roberto Rossini asked my sister to call, but she closed the door on us.'

'I see. May I know your names?'

'This is Rosanna Menici, and I am her brother, Luca.'

'Well, you'd better come inside,' said Luigi.

'Thank you, signor.'

Luca and Rosanna followed him in through the French windows. The spacious room was dominated by a white grand piano positioned in the centre of a gleaming grey marble floor. Bookshelves lined the walls, stuffed untidily with piles of sheet music. On the mantelpiece over the fireplace were numerous framed black-and-white photographs of Luigi in evening dress, his arms round the shoulders of people whose faces looked familiar from newspapers and magazines.

Luigi Vincenzi sat down on the piano stool. 'So, why did Roberto Rossini send you to see me, Rosanna Menici?'

'Because . . . because . . .'

'Because he thought my sister should have proper singing lessons with you,' answered Luca for her.

'What other songs do you know, Signorina Menici?' Luigi asked her.

'I . . . not many. Mostly hymns I sing in church,' Rosanna stuttered.

'Why don't we try "*Ave Maria*" again? You seem to know that very well.' Luigi smiled, sitting down at the piano. 'Come closer, child. I won't bite, you know.'

Rosanna moved towards him and she saw that, although his moustache and curly grey hair made him seem very stern, his eyes sparkled warmly under his thick eyebrows.

'So, you sing.' Luigi sat down and began to play the opening chords of the hymn on the grand piano. The sound was so different from any other piano she'd ever heard that Rosanna forgot to come in at the right moment.

'Have you a problem, Rosanna Menici?'

'No, signor, I was just listening to the beautiful sound your piano makes.'

'I see. Well, please concentrate this time.'

And, inspired by the grand piano, Rosanna sang as she'd never sung before. Luca, standing nearby, thought his heart might burst with pride. He knew it had been right to bring Rosanna here.

'Good, good, Signorina Menici. Now, we shall try some scales. Follow me as I play.'

Luigi led Rosanna up and down the keys, testing her range. He was not normally given to superlatives, but he had to admit that the child had the greatest potential he'd come across in all his years of coaching. Her voice was remarkable.

'So! I have heard enough.'

'Will you teach her, Signor Vincenzi?' asked Luca. 'I have money to pay.'

'Yes, I will teach her. Signorina Menici' – Luigi turned to Rosanna – 'you will come here every other Tuesday at four o'clock. I will charge four thousand lire for one hour.' It was half of what he usually charged, but the brother looked proud, if penniless.

Rosanna's face lit up. 'Thank you, Signor Vincenzi, thank you.'

'And on the days you're not with me, you'll practise for two hours at least. You will work hard and never miss a lesson unless there is a death in the family. Do you understand?'

'Yes, Signor Vincenzi.'

'Good. Then I shall see you on Tuesday, yes? And now you shall leave by the front entrance.' Luigi led Rosanna and Luca through the house to the front door. '*Ciao*, Rosanna Menici.'

The two of them said goodbye, then walked sedately down the drive until they were out of the front gate. Then Luca picked Rosanna up in his arms and gleefully swung her round.

'I knew it! I knew it! He just had to hear your voice. I'm so very proud of you, *piccolina*. You know this must be our secret, don't you? Mamma and Papa might not approve, Rosanna. You mustn't even tell Carlotta.'

'I won't, I promise. But Luca, can you afford the lessons?'

'Yes, of course I can.' Luca thought of the cash he'd been

saving for two years to buy a scooter, which would provide the first step towards his much longed-for freedom. 'Of course I can.'

As they saw the bus approaching, Rosanna gave her brother an instinctive hug. 'Thank you, Luca. I promise I'll work as hard as I can. And one day I will repay you for this kindness.'

'I know you will, *piccolina*, I know you will.'

3

'Take care, Rosanna. The bus driver knows where to let you off, in case you don't remember.'

Rosanna smiled down at her brother from the steps of the bus. 'Luca, you've already told me a hundred times. I'm not a baby. It's only a short journey.'

'I know, I know.' Luca kissed his sister on both cheeks as the bus driver started the engine. 'You have the money safe?'

'Yes, Luca! I'll be fine. Please don't worry.'

Rosanna made her way to a seat at the front of the bus, sat down and waved to Luca through the grimy window as the driver pulled out of the bus station. The journey was pleasant, taking her out of the bustle of the city and up into the freshness of the hills. Rosanna's heart beat a little faster as she left the bus at the correct stop and walked up towards the villa. She rang the bell cautiously, remembering the previous frosty reception, but this time when the door was opened Rosanna was greeted with a smile by the maid.

'Please come in, Signorina Menici. My name is Signora Rinaldi and I'm Signor Vincenzi's housekeeper. He's waiting for you in the music room.' The woman led Rosanna along a corridor to the back of the villa and knocked on a door.

'Rosanna Menici, welcome. Please sit down.' Luigi indicated a chair by a table, on which a jug of iced lemonade was standing. 'You must be thirsty after your journey. Would you like a drink?'

'Thank you, signor.'

'Please, if we're to work together, you must call me Luigi.' He poured them both a glass of lemonade and Rosanna drank thirstily.

'This weather is most uncomfortable.' Luigi mopped his brow with a large checked handkerchief.

'But it's cool in this room,' ventured Rosanna. 'Yesterday, in the kitchen, Papa said it was over one hundred and twenty degrees.'

'Really? That kind of temperature is only for Bedouins and camels. What does your papa do for a living?'

'He and Mamma have a café in the Piedigrotta. We live above it,' Rosanna explained.

'The Piedigrotta is one of the most ancient quarters of Naples, as I'm sure you know. Your papa was born there?'

'All our family were.'

'Then you are true Neapolitans. Me, I'm from Milan. I only borrow your lovely city.'

'I think it's much nicer up here than down there, especially with all the tourists.'

'You work in the café?'

'Yes, when I'm not at school.' Rosanna pulled a face. 'I don't enjoy it.'

'Well, Rosanna Menici, if you cannot enjoy it, you must learn from it. I'm sure you have many English visiting your café during the summer.'

'Yes,' Rosanna agreed. 'Many.'

'Then you must listen to them and try to learn some English. You'll need it in the future. You also learn French at school?'

'I'm top of my class,' she replied proudly.

'Some of the great operas are written in French. If you begin to speak these languages now, it will be easier for you in the future. So, what do your mamma and papa think of their daughter's voice?'

'I don't know. I . . . they have no idea I'm taking lessons. Roberto Rossini told Papa I should come and see you, but Papa said we didn't have the money.'

'So, your brother is paying?'

'Yes.' Rosanna took some lire notes out of the pocket of her dress and placed them on the table. 'Here is enough for the next three lessons. Luca wanted to pay in advance.'

Luigi took the money with a gracious nod of acceptance. 'Now, Rosanna, I wish to know if you enjoy singing.'

Rosanna thought of how special she'd felt after she'd sung at Maria and Massimo's party. 'I love it very much. I'm in a different world when I sing.'

'Well, that at least is a good start. Now, I must warn you that you are very young, too young for me to be sure whether your voice will develop in the right way. We must not strain your vocal cords – we must nurture them carefully, learn how they work and the best way to care for them. I teach a school of singing called Bel Canto. This involves a series of increasingly difficult voice exercises, each designed to learn a specific aspect of singing. When you have mastered these, you'll have studied every possible potential vocal problem before it arises in the music. Callas herself learnt this way. She was not much older than you when she began. You're prepared for this kind of hard work?'

'Yes, Luigi.'

'I must stress that there will be no singing the great arias until you are much older. We'll first become familiar with the stories of the great operas and try to understand the characters. The finest performers are those who not only have wonderful voices, but are magnificent actors too. And don't think that two lessons a month with me will be enough to improve your voice,' he cautioned. 'You must practise the exercises I give you every day, without fail.'

Luigi broke off as he looked at Rosanna's wide eyes and chuckled suddenly. 'And you, Rosanna, must sometimes remind me that you're still a child. Please accept my apologies for frightening you. The beauty of your youth is that we have so much time. Now, we begin.' Luigi stood up and walked over to the piano stool. He patted the space on the seat next to him. 'Come, we will learn which notes are which on the piano.'

An hour later, Rosanna left the Villa Torini feeling deflated. She hadn't sung one single note during her entire lesson.

When she arrived home, exhausted from the heat on the bus and the tension of the afternoon, she headed straight up to her bedroom. Luca, his hands covered with flour, followed her upstairs.

'You found your way back then?'

'I'm here, aren't I, Luca?' She smiled at his concerned face.

'How was it, Rosanna?'

'It was wonderful, Luca. Luigi is very kind.'

'Good. I—'

'Luca!' Marco roared his son's name from the kitchen below.

'I must go. We're very busy.' Luca kissed Rosanna on the cheek and hurried downstairs.

Rosanna lay on her bed, reached for her diary from under her mattress, and began to write. A few seconds later, Carlotta entered the room.

'Where have you been? Mamma wanted you to help but we couldn't find you. I had to wait on tables all afternoon.'

'I've been out . . . with a friend. I'm hungry. Is there anything to eat?'

'I don't know. Go ask Mamma. I'm going out.'

'Who with?'

'Oh, just Giulio,' Carlotta answered, looking bored.

'I thought you liked Giulio? I thought he was your boyfriend?'

'He was . . . I mean, he is . . . Oh, stop asking questions, Rosanna! I'm going for a bath.'

When Carlotta had left the bedroom, Rosanna finished writing her diary and returned it to its usual hiding place. Once she'd done that, she wandered into the kitchenette and poured herself a glass of water from the fridge. She knew that if she went downstairs to find something to eat, Mamma and Papa would find her a job to do. And she was very tired. Creeping along the landing, she opened the door to the iron staircase which led from the apartment to the street below. It was a place she often went when she needed time by herself, even though it looked over the dustbins at the back. Sitting on the top step, she sipped her water and relived every moment of her lesson with Luigi. Even if the hour had been spent learning to read the black notes on the music, not singing them, Rosanna loved Luigi's tranquil home. And the fact that she finally had a secret of her own thrilled her.

She went back into her bedroom and changed into her nightdress. Carlotta was wrapping a shawl round her shoulders, almost ready to leave.

'Have a nice evening,' said Rosanna.

'Thank you.' Carlotta gave her what seemed more of a grimace than a smile and left the room, leaving the smell of her perfume hanging in the air behind her.

Rosanna climbed into bed, pondering how she was going to escape to Luigi's villa every other Tuesday afternoon without being missed. Eventually, she decided she'd make up an imaginary friend. She would call her Isabella and make her parents quite wealthy, as that would impress Papa. She could then visit Isabella every other Tuesday without getting into trouble. As for the practising, she'd have to try to get up an hour earlier every morning and slip into church before Mass began.

Solutions found, Rosanna fell fast asleep.

It was late September. The café had quietened down, the summer tourists had left the city and the stifling heat had mellowed to a pleasant warmth. Luca went outside into the yard and lit up a cigarette, enjoying the balmy evening. Carlotta appeared behind him at the kitchen door.

'Luca, can you spare me a few minutes tonight before the café gets busy? I . . . have to talk to you.'

Luca looked at Carlotta's unusually pale face.

'What's the matter, Carlotta? Are you ill?'

She hovered in the doorway, opened her mouth to reply, then heard Antonia's heavy footsteps coming down the stairs.

'Not here,' she whispered. 'Meet me in Renato's on the Via Caracciolo at seven. Please, Luca. Be there.'

'I'll be there.'

Carlotta returned a wan smile, then left.

A few days later, Rosanna walked through the café and opened the door leading up to their apartment. As she climbed the stairs, she heard Papa shouting in the sitting room. Concerned he might have discovered her secret, Rosanna stopped at the top of the stairs and listened.

'How could you? How could you?' Marco was repeating over and over.

Rosanna heard Carlotta's loud sobbing.

'Can't you see you're making things worse, Marco?' Antonia sounded near to tears too. 'Shouting and screaming at our daughter will not help her! *Mamma mia*, we must try to calm down and think what to do for the best. I'll go and get us all a drink.'

The sitting room door opened and Antonia appeared, her usual high colour drained from her face.

'Mamma, what is it? Is Carlotta sick?' Rosanna asked, following her along the corridor to the kitchenette.

'No, she isn't sick. Go downstairs to your brother, Rosanna. He'll make you some supper.' Antonia's voice was strained and she was breathing heavily.

'But Mamma, please, tell me what's happened.'

Antonia took a bottle of brandy from a cupboard in the kitchen, then turned round and gave her daughter a rare kiss on the top of her head.

'No one is sick, everyone is fine. We'll tell you all about it a little later. Now, off you go and tell Luca that Papa will be down in a few minutes.' Antonia forced a smile and disappeared back into the sitting room.

Rosanna walked through the empty café and into the main kitchen, where Luca was standing at the back door smoking a cigarette.

'Luca, what's happened? Papa's shouting, Carlotta's crying and Mamma looks as if she's seen a ghost.'

Luca took a long pull on his cigarette and exhaled slowly through his nose. Then he stubbed it out with his foot and turned back into the kitchen. 'Would you like some lasagne? There's one just ready.' He walked across the kitchen and opened the oven door.

'No! I want to know what's happened. Papa never shouts at Carlotta. She must have done something very bad.'

Luca served the lasagne in silence. He put two full plates on the kitchen table and sat down, indicating that Rosanna do the same.

'*Piccolina*, there are some things you're just too young to understand. Carlotta has made a bad mistake, and that's why Papa's so angry with her. But don't worry. The three of them will sort it out and all will be well, I promise. Now, eat your lasagne and tell me about your lesson with Signor Vincenzi.'

Knowing she was not going to acquire any further information, Rosanna sighed and picked up a fork.

Rosanna was awoken by the sound of soft sobbing. She sat up in bed, blinking in the grey light of the approaching dawn.

'Carlotta? Carlotta, what's wrong?' she whispered.

There was no reply. Rosanna climbed out of bed and went across to her sister. Carlotta had a pillow over her head in an attempt to drown out the sound of her crying. Rosanna put a tentative arm on her shoulder and an agonised face appeared from under the pillow.

'Please don't cry. It can't be all that bad,' Rosanna soothed.

'Oh . . . it *is*, it *is*. I . . .' Carlotta wiped her streaming nose on the back of her hand. 'I have to marry . . . I have to marry Giulio!'

'But why?'

'Because of something I've done. But . . . oh Rosanna, I don't love him, I don't love him!'

'Then why must you marry him?'

'Papa says I must and it's all I can do. I've lied to him about the . . . oh . . .' Carlotta sobbed again and Rosanna put her arms round her sister's shoulders.

'Don't cry, please. Giulio is a nice man. I like him. He's rich and you'll have a big apartment and you won't have to work in the café anymore.'

Carlotta looked up at her sister and smiled weakly through her tears. 'You have a kind heart, Rosanna. Maybe when I'm married, Mamma and Papa will notice you more.'

'I don't mind. We can't all be beautiful – I understand that,' Rosanna answered quietly.

'Well, just look where my beauty has got me! Maybe you're better off without it. Oh Rosanna, I shall miss you when I leave.'

'And I you. Will you be getting married soon?'

'Yes. Papa will go to see Giulio's father tomorrow. I think we'll be married within a month. Everyone will guess, of course.'

'Guess what?' asked Rosanna.

Carlotta stroked her sister's hair. 'There really are some things you can't understand until you're older. Stay young for as long as possible, little sister. Growing up isn't as much fun as it looks. Now, go back to your bed and sleep.'

'Okay.'

'And Rosanna?'

'Yes?'

'Thank you. You're a good sister and I hope we'll always be friends.'

Rosanna climbed back into bed with a sigh, still understanding nothing.

Four weeks later, Rosanna stood behind Carlotta in a blue satin bridesmaid's dress as her sister made her marriage vows to Giulio.

There was a party afterwards at the café. Although Rosanna knew that this should be the happiest day of Carlotta's life, her sister looked pale and tense, and Antonia not much happier. Marco seemed cheerful enough, breaking open bottle after bottle of sparkling wine and telling his guests of the lovely apartment with two bedrooms that the young couple would live in.

A few weeks after the wedding, Rosanna went to visit Carlotta in her new apartment near the Via Roma. Rosanna stared in awe at the television set in the corner of the sitting room.

'Giulio must have lots of money to have one of those,' Rosanna exclaimed as Carlotta brought in some coffee and they sat together on the sofa.

'Yes, he has money,' Carlotta agreed.

Rosanna sipped her coffee, wondering why her sister seemed so subdued.

'How is Giulio?'

'I hardly see him. He leaves at eight to go to his office and doesn't arrive home until after half past seven.'

'He must have an important position,' Rosanna encouraged.

Carlotta ignored her sister's comment. 'I make supper and then I go to bed. I feel so tired at the moment.'

'Why?'

'Because I'm having a baby,' Carlotta replied wearily. 'You will soon be a *zia* – Auntie Rosanna.'

'Oh, congratulations!' Rosanna leant over and kissed her sister on the cheek. 'Are you happy?'

'Yes, of course I'm happy,' Carlotta replied morosely.

'Giulio must be very pleased that he's to be a papa.'

'Yes, of course he is. So, how are things at home?'

Rosanna shrugged. 'Papa's drinking a lot of brandy and being bad-tempered and always shouting at me and Luca. Mamma is tired all the time and keeps having to lie down.'

'So not much is different then, Rosanna.' Carlotta managed a smile.

'Except I think Mamma and Papa miss you.'

'And I miss them, I . . .' Tears came into Carlotta's eyes. 'Sorry, it's being pregnant. It makes me emotional. Luca still has no girlfriend then?'

'No. But he has no time to have one. He's in the kitchen at eight in the morning and he doesn't finish until very late.'

'I don't understand why he puts up with it. Papa's so rude

to him and pays him so little. If I were Luca, I'd go away and start a new life somewhere else.'

Rosanna was horrified. 'You don't think Luca will leave, do you?'

'No, Rosanna. Luckily for you, and unfortunately for him, I don't think he will,' Carlotta replied slowly. 'Our brother's a very special man. I hope one day he finds the happiness he deserves.'

At the end of May, Carlotta gave birth to a baby girl. Rosanna went to the hospital to see her new niece.

'Oh, she's so beautiful, and so tiny. May I hold her?' asked Rosanna.

Carlotta nodded. 'Of course. Here.'

Rosanna took the baby from her sister and cradled her in her arms. She stared into the baby's dark eyes.

'She doesn't look like you, Carlotta.'

'Oh. Who do you think she does look like? Giulio? Mamma? Papa?'

Rosanna studied the baby. 'I don't know. Have you thought of a name?'

'Yes. She will be called Ella Maria.'

'It's a lovely name. You are so clever, Carlotta.'

'Yes, isn't she?'

The two sisters turned as Giulio came into the room.

'How are you, *cara*?' Giulio kissed his wife.

'I'm well, Giulio.'

'Good.' Giulio sat down on the edge of the bed and reached for his wife's hand.

Carlotta moved her arm swiftly away. 'Why don't you give your daughter a cuddle?' she suggested.

'Of course.' Giulio stood up and, as she passed the baby to him, Rosanna saw the hurt in his dark eyes.

Once her visitors had left, Carlotta lay back and stared at the ceiling. What she had done had been the right thing, she was sure of it. She had a successful husband, a lovely daughter, and had managed to avoid bringing disgrace on herself and her family.

Carlotta turned her head and looked down into the cradle. Ella's dark eyes were wide open, her perfect white skin in contrast to the shock of black hair on the top of her head.

She knew she would have to live with her deceit for the rest of her life.

The Metropolitan Opera House, New York

So, Nico, you have read how I first met Roberto Rossini and how the seeds of the future were sown. At the time that Carlotta married Giulio, I was very young and naive, unaware of much that was happening around me.

For the next five years, I worked hard at my singing. I joined the church choir, which gave me the excuse to practise at home as much as I could. I enjoyed my lessons with Luigi Vincenzi and, as I matured, so did my passion for opera. I had no doubt in my mind what I wanted to do when I grew up.

Throughout that time, it was as though I lived a double life. I knew I'd have to one day tell Mamma and Papa of my secret, but I only hoped the right moment would present itself. And I couldn't risk them stopping me.

Little else in my life changed. I went to school and worked hard at my French and my English. I went to Mass twice a week and waited on tables in the café every day. Other girls in my class were dreaming of film stars and experimenting with make-up and cigarettes, but I only had one dream: to one day sing on the stage at La Scala with the man who had begun it all for me. I thought of Roberto often and believed – hoped – he sometimes thought of me.

Most days, Carlotta would bring her lovely daughter, Ella, to the café to visit us. Looking back, I realise she was terribly unhappy. The vivacity she'd always possessed had left her and the sparkle had disappeared from her eyes. Of course, at the time, I had no idea why . . .

4

Naples, May 1972

'Rosanna, welcome. Please come in and sit down.' Luigi indicated a chair by the enormous marble fireplace in the music room.

Rosanna did as he asked and Luigi sat down in a chair opposite her.

'For the past five years you've been coming to me twice a month. I don't believe you have ever missed a lesson.'

'No, I haven't,' agreed Rosanna.

'And in those five years we have mastered the basics of Bel Canto. We have performed the exercises so often you could sing them in your sleep, yes?'

'Yes, Luigi.'

'We have seen performances at Teatro San Carlo, we have studied the great operas, learnt their stories and explored the personalities of the characters you may one day play.'

'Yes.'

'So, now your voice is a perfectly prepared canvas that is ready to be given colour and shape and turned into a masterpiece. Rosanna' – Luigi paused before continuing – 'I have taught you all I know. I can teach you no more.'

'But . . . but, Luigi . . . I . . .'

He reached over and took her hands in his. 'Rosanna, please. Do you remember when you first came to see me with your brother? And I told you that it was too early to tell whether your gift would grow as you did?'

Rosanna nodded.

'Well, it *has* grown, grown into something that is too rare for me to keep to myself. Rosanna, you need to move on now. You're almost seventeen years of age. You must go to a proper school of music that can give you what I cannot.'

'But—'

'I know, I know,' sighed Luigi, 'your mamma and papa are still unaware of your visits here. I'm sure they hope that when you leave school this summer, you'll find a nice boy, marry and give them many grandchildren. Am I right?'

'Yes, Luigi.' Rosanna winced at his accurate appraisal.

'Well, Rosanna, let me tell you something. God has given you a gift, but with that gift comes hardship, decisions that will be difficult to make. And it's only you who can decide whether you're brave enough to take them. The choice is yours.'

'Luigi, during the past five years I've lived for my lessons with you. It hasn't mattered if Papa has shouted at me, or if Mamma made me wait on tables every night, because I could always think of coming here.' Rosanna's eyes glistened with tears. 'What I want more than anything else in the world is to sing. But what am I to do? My parents have no money to pay for me to go to a school of music.'

'Please don't upset yourself, Rosanna. All I wanted to hear is that you wish with a passion to make singing your future. I am, of course, aware of your parents' financial situation, and that's where I might be able to help you. I'm having a soirée, a musical evening, here in six weeks' time,' Luigi explained. 'All my pupils will be performing. And to this soirée I've invited my good friend Paolo de Vito, who's the artistic director at the great opera house of La Scala in Milan. Paolo is also a director of La Scala's *scuola di musica*, which, as you know, is the best school of music in Italy. I've told Paolo all about you and he's prepared to come all the way from Milan to hear you sing. If he thinks, as I do, that your voice is special, he may be prepared to help you gain a scholarship to study at the school.'

'Really?' Rosanna's eyes lit up with hope.

'Yes, really. And I think you should invite your mamma and papa to my soirée and let them hear you sing too. If they're in a room with people who recognise how talented their daughter is, then I think it may help our cause.'

'But, Luigi, they'll be so angry I've lied to them for all these years. And I don't think they'll come.' She shook her head dejectedly.

'All you can do is ask them, Rosanna. Remember, you're almost seventeen – nearly an adult. I understand you don't wish to distress your parents, but trust Luigi and ask them to come. Promise?'

Rosanna nodded. 'Promise.'

'Now, we've wasted enough time today. We're going to learn one of my favourite arias. You will perhaps sing this at my soirée: "*Mi chiamano Mimi*" from *La Bohème*. It's difficult, but I believe you're ready for it. Today, we shall study the music. Come' – Luigi stood up – 'we have work to do.'

On the bus on the way home, Rosanna sat lost in thought. When she arrived home she went straight into the kitchen to find Luca.

'*Ciao, piccolina*. What's wrong? You look tense.'

'Can we talk?' she asked Luca, and added, 'privately.'

Luca glanced at his watch. 'It's quiet this evening. I'll meet you in our usual place in half an hour.' He winked at her and Rosanna hurried away before either of her parents saw her.

The Via Caracciolo was bustling with cars and tourists as Luca strolled down towards the seafront. He saw his sister leaning over the railing, looking out at the foamy waves, turned a deep navy by autumn shadow. He watched with a mixture of brotherly pride and protectiveness as two men passed her, then turned back to look again. Although Rosanna would never believe she was as pretty as her sister, Luca knew she was turning into a beauty – tall and slim, her childhood awkwardness gradually giving way to a natural long-limbed elegance. Her long, dark hair cascaded around her shoulders, framing her heart-shaped face containing thickly lashed brown eyes. He could refuse her nothing when she smiled at him, and paying for her lessons was the only reason he was still working in the café, doing most of the work while his father sat at a table in the corner, drinking with his cronies.

'*Ciao, bella*,' he said as he reached her side. 'Come, let us have an espresso and you can tell me your problem.'

Luca guided Rosanna to a pavement table in front of a

café. He ordered two coffees and studied his sister's worried expression. 'Tell me, Rosanna, what's happened?'

'Luigi doesn't wish to teach me any longer.'

'I thought you said he was pleased with your progress?' Luca was horrified.

'He is, Luca. He doesn't want to teach me because he says I've learnt all he knows. Luigi has an important friend at La Scala. This friend is coming to hear me sing at a soirée at Luigi's villa in six weeks' time. He may offer me a scholarship to study at a school of music in Milan.'

'But that's wonderful news, *piccolina*! So why do you look so sad?'

'Oh Luca, what shall I tell Mamma and Papa? Luigi wants them to come and hear me sing at the soirée. But even if they did come, they'd never agree to me leaving Naples and going to Milan. You *know* they won't.' Rosanna's lovely brown eyes filled with tears.

'It doesn't matter what they say.' Luca shook his head.

'What do you mean?'

'You're old enough to make your own decisions, Rosanna. If Mamma and Papa don't like it, if they can't appreciate and support your talent, then that's their problem, not yours. If Signor Vincenzi believes you're good enough to win a scholarship to study in Milan, and is bringing an important friend to hear you sing, then nothing must stop you.' Luca reached for her hand. 'It's the news we've both dreamt of, isn't it?'

'Yes.' Rosanna felt her tension slowly easing at Luca's words. 'And it's you I have to thank. All these years that you've paid for me to go to lessons. How can I ever repay you?'

'By becoming the great opera star I've always known you will be.'

'Luca, do you really think it will happen?'

'Yes, Rosanna, I do.'

'And what about Mamma and Papa?' she asked.

'You leave them to me.' Luca tapped his nose. 'I'll make sure they come to hear you sing.'

Rosanna leant across the table and kissed Luca on the cheek, her eyes shining with tears. 'What would I have done without you, Luca? Thank you. Now, I must go home. I'm waiting in the café tonight.'

Rosanna rose from her chair and walked away. Luca gazed across the bay towards Capri, his heart feeling lighter than it had for years.

If Rosanna went to Milan, what was to keep him here?

Nothing. Nothing at all.

5

'Bastard!' Carlotta dissolved into tears as she sank onto the sofa. 'How could you, Giulio?'

'Carlotta, please, I'm sorry.' Giulio looked at her in despair. 'But for five years we've been married and for the past four you haven't allowed me to touch you! A man has needs – *physical* needs.'

'Which you fulfilled with your secretary! I'm sure everyone in your company must know. I'm a laughing stock!'

'No one knows, Carlotta. The affair only lasted a few weeks and it's over now, I swear.'

'And who was it before that? How many other women have you bedded behind my back?'

Giulio walked across to Carlotta. He sank to his knees and took her hands in his. '*Cara*, please, can't you understand? It's you, only you, that I want – have ever wanted. And yet, since the day you married me, I've never felt *you* wanted *me*. You've been' – Giulio shuddered – 'so cold. I think, Carlotta, that you only married me because of the baby. Am I right?'

Carlotta looked at him, then pulled her hands out of his grasp as five years of resentment and misery finally boiled over. 'Yes, you are right. I never loved you; I certainly didn't want to marry you. I could have had anyone! When I think of the life I might have had . . . And here I am wasting my best years with a man I don't even like! And you know the funniest thing of all?' Carlotta stood up, shaking with rage. 'The baby was not even yours. It wasn't even *yours*.'

There was a slight pause before she clapped a hand over her mouth, regretting the words she'd just spoken.

Giulio was staring at her. His face had turned deathly pale. 'Are you telling me the truth, Carlotta? You are telling me Ella is not my child?'

'I . . .' Carlotta could not meet his gaze. She put her head in her hands and began to sob.

Giulio stood up and left the apartment, slamming the door behind him.

Carlotta slumped back down onto the sofa. 'My God, my God, what have I done?' she cried to the silent walls. She'd wanted so badly to hurt him for what he had done to her, for taking the only thing she had left – her pride.

Two excruciating hours later, he returned. As he walked back into the sitting room, she ran to him, sobbing. 'Forgive me, forgive me, Giulio. I was hurt by your affair and I wanted to hurt you. It was a lie, I swear. Of course Ella is yours.'

Giulio pushed her away from him in disgust, his eyes devoid of emotion. 'No, Carlotta, it wasn't a lie. Now I think back, it all fits. I can't believe how blind I've been. The baby was five weeks early, and yet such a healthy size. I knew you were not a virgin the first time we made love, although I never said so. Your unhappy face on our wedding day, the way you shuddered every time I touched you . . . tell me, did you love this other man?'

Eventually, knowing there was no way back, she shook her head slowly in defeat. 'No. It was a terrible mistake, one night of stupidity.'

'Which you decided to make *me* pay for too?' Giulio sat down heavily on the sofa. '*Mamma mia*, Carlotta! I knew you were selfish, but I had no idea you were completely heartless. Who else knows of this?'

'No one.'

'Give me the truth, Carlotta, please. You owe me that at the very least.'

'Luca knew,' she admitted.

'You plotted together, did you?' he spat at her.

'No, Giulio. It wasn't like that. I was desperate. And I thought that, as I was going to marry you anyway—'

Giulio reached out and gripped her arm. 'Were you, Carlotta? I thought you said earlier that you didn't love me, didn't even *like* me, in fact?'

'Ouch! Please, Giulio, you're hurting me. I told you, I didn't mean those things, I—'

'But you *did* mean them, Carlotta.' He let go of her arm suddenly and sighed wearily. 'I'm not a bad man. I've only ever wanted the best for you and Ella. All these years I've worked so hard to try and make you love me the way I loved you. And now I discover my marriage was a sham before it even began!'

'Please, Giulio, please!' she begged him. 'Give me another chance. I *will* make it up to you, I promise. Now I've told you, we can start again without any lies. A clean slate . . .'

'No,' Giulio laughed bitterly, 'there's no way back from

here, Carlotta. While I was out I walked and did some thinking, and I've made a decision. Now that you've finally been honest with me, I want you to pack your things and leave. You can tell everyone you've left your husband because he was cheating on you. No one need ever know the truth. I'm prepared to take the blame for Ella's sake. Even if she's *not* my flesh and blood, I've loved her as if she was. And I don't wish to bring disgrace on her.'

'No, Giulio, please! Where will I go? What will I do?' Carlotta moaned in despair.

'That's no concern of mine anymore. My company has offices in Rome and I will ask for a transfer there as soon as I can.'

'But what of Ella? She thinks of you as her father. She loves you, Giulio.'

'You should have thought of that before you deceived us both.' He turned from her, still shaking with anger and emotion. 'I'm going to bed now. I'm tired. You will sleep in here and when I leave for the office tomorrow morning, you will pack your things and be gone by the time I arrive home.'

Antonia hugged her daughter to her considerable bosom. 'Of course you can both stay with us for a while. You know you need not even ask. Oh Carlotta, my poor child, what is it? What has happened?' She surveyed her daughter with concern. 'You look like a ghost. Do you want to lie down? You can sleep in your old room with Ella, and Rosanna can sleep on the sofa in the sitting room.'

A pale Carlotta nodded wearily. 'Oh Mamma, oh Mamma, I . . .'

Antonia caught sight of four-year-old Ella looking in

distress at her mother. She called out for Luca, who appeared at the door. 'Take Ella down to the kitchen and find her something to eat while I talk to your sister,' she murmured. 'God only knows what has happened.'

Luca looked at Carlotta. Her distraught face told him only one story.

Antonia took out her handkerchief and wiped her brow as she bustled her daughter into the bedroom. 'Dear me, it's too hot to have such problems today.'

'I'm sorry. I won't stay for long.' Carlotta sank onto the bed and Antonia sat down heavily next to her. 'Are you all right, Mamma? You look sick.'

'Yes, I'm fine. It's only the heat. Please, Carlotta, tell me what's happened. You and Giulio have had a bad argument, yes?'

'Yes.'

'You mustn't worry.' Antonia embraced her daughter. 'All husbands and wives argue. Your papa and I used to do it all the time. Now we don't have the energy.' She gave a tight laugh. 'When you've slept a little, you'll feel calmer. Then you can go back to Giulio and make it up.'

'No, Mamma. I can never go back. Giulio and me, we are over. Forever.'

'But why? What have you done?'

Carlotta turned her head away from her mother and began to sob.

Sighing, Antonia heaved herself from the bed. 'Get some rest, Carlotta. We'll talk later.'

Rosanna was surprised to find a small lump in her bed when she returned home from choir practice that evening. Her niece, Ella, was fast asleep in it, so she left the bedroom quietly and walked along the narrow corridor to the sitting room. The door was closed but she could hear her parents talking.

'I don't know what has happened, Marco. She won't say anything. She's downstairs now talking to Luca. Maybe *he* can get some sense out of her. I've tried calling Giulio at their apartment, but there's no reply.'

'She must return to her husband, of course. It's where she belongs. I will tell her that.' Marco sounded furious.

'Please, leave her alone tonight. She's distraught,' Antonia pleaded.

Rosanna pushed the door open. 'What's happened?' she asked.

'Your sister has left her husband and she and Ella will be staying here for a few days. You, Rosanna, can sleep in here on the sofa.' Antonia's breath was coming in short, sharp bursts. She stood up slowly.

'Are you all right, Mamma?' Rosanna said, going towards her.

'I . . . I'm fine.' Antonia stood, staggering a little as she regained her balance. 'I must go downstairs. I need some air.' She fanned herself violently as she lumbered from the room.

'Papa, why has Carlotta left Giulio? I—'

There was a sudden heavy thump from the stairs.

Marco and Rosanna rushed out of the sitting room together and into the corridor. They saw Antonia lying at the bottom of the stairs leading to the café.

'*Mamma mia!* Antonia! Antonia!' Marco hurried down the stairs to his wife's prone body and knelt by it, Rosanna following close behind him.

'Run for the doctor, quickly!' her father screamed at her. 'Get Luca and Carlotta.'

Rosanna hurried through the deserted café and into the kitchen. Luca was standing with his arms round Carlotta, comforting her as she sobbed on his shoulder.

'Hurry! Mamma's collapsed on the stairs! I'm going for the doctor!' Rosanna called before she opened the door and ran off along the cobbled street.

Carlotta and Luca found Antonia lying on the stairs, her head thrown back onto the tiled floor at the bottom. There was blood seeping from a wound underneath her thick hair and her skin was grey, her eyes partially open. Carlotta knelt down next to her and searched for a pulse.

'Is she . . . ?' Marco, standing over his wife, could not finish the sentence. 'Let us try to at least make her more comfortable,' suggested Luca desperately.

Father and son managed to half-carry, half-drag Antonia off the stairs and into the café while Carlotta fetched a pillow for her head.

Rosanna returned with the doctor an agonising fifteen minutes later.

'Please tell me she is not gone. Not my Antonia, not my wife,' Marco moaned. 'Please save her, Doctor.'

Luca, Carlotta and Rosanna watched in silence as the doctor listened through his stethoscope to Antonia's heart, then felt her pulse. When he looked up, they all saw the answer in his eyes.

'I'm so sorry, Marco,' the doctor said, shaking his head. 'I believe Antonia has suffered a heart attack. There's nothing more we can do for her now. We must send for Don Carlo immediately.'

'The priest!' Marco stared at the doctor in disbelief, then knelt down and buried his face in Antonia's lifeless shoulder. He began to cry. 'I am nothing, nothing without her. Oh *amore mio*, my love, my love . . .'

The three children looked on silently, each one of them in shock, unable to move.

The doctor packed his stethoscope back into his bag and stood up. 'Rosanna, go and fetch Don Carlo. We will stay here and make your mamma ready.'

Rosanna gave a whimper, then, clenching her fists to stop herself breaking down completely, she stood up and walked out of the café.

'What's happened? Why is Nonno crying?' Ella appeared on the stairs.

'Come with Mamma, Ella, and I will explain what has happened.' Carlotta climbed the stairs to Ella and steered her young daughter gently back up them.

'Luca, I think it best if you lock the front door of the café until Don Carlo arrives. I'm sure you would not wish for customers now,' said the doctor.

'Of course.' Luca walked shakily towards the front door and turned the key. Marco was now holding his wife's hand in his lap, stroking it as he sobbed uncontrollably. Luca returned and knelt down next to him, putting an arm round Marco's hunched shoulders. Tears began to fall down his own cheeks. He reached out a hand and gently stroked his mother's forehead.

Marco looked up at Luca, the agony visible in his eyes. 'I have nothing without her, nothing.'

*

Two days later, Don Carlo held a private requiem Mass for the family. Then Antonia's body lay overnight in the church she had attended all of her life. The following morning, her friends and relatives filled the church for her funeral. Rosanna sat in the front pew between Luca and Ella, her black lace veil obscuring the coffin containing her mother's body. Marco held Carlotta's hand and wept inconsolably all through the service and at the burial. They made their way back to the café afterwards, where Luca and Rosanna had worked hard to put on a fitting spread for their mamma's wake.

Hours later, when the guests had finally left, the Menici family sat in the café, still numb with shock. Marco sat silently, staring into space, until Carlotta gently helped him up from his chair.

'You two clear up down here,' she ordered. 'I'll take Papa upstairs.'

'Do we open the café tomorrow, Papa?' asked Luca quietly as Marco walked slowly towards the stairs.

He turned round and looked desolately at his son. 'Do as you wish.' Then he followed Carlotta up the stairs like an obedient child.

When Luca reopened the café a day later, Marco did not come down to help him. He remained upstairs in the sitting room, silently staring at his wife's photograph, with Carlotta by his side.

'Another two pizza margheritas and one "special",' Rosanna said as she opened the door to the kitchen and slammed the order onto the spike.

'It'll be at least twenty minutes, Rosanna. I have eight orders ahead of that one,' sighed Luca.

Rosanna grabbed two pizzas and put them on a tray to carry into the café. 'Maybe Papa will come back to work soon. And Carlotta might help us.'

'I hope so, I really do,' grunted Luca.

It was past midnight before Rosanna and Luca were able to sit down in the kitchen and eat their own supper.

'Here, have some wine. We both deserve it.' Luca poured some Chianti into two glasses and passed one to Rosanna.

They ate and drank silently, too exhausted to speak. When they'd finished, Luca lit a cigarette.

'Can you open the door, Luca? Luigi says cigarette smoke is terribly bad for my voice,' asked Rosanna.

'Excuse me, *Signorina Diva*!' Luca raised an eyebrow and went to open the back door. 'Talking of such things, when is your soirée at Signor Vincenzi's?'

'It's in two weeks' time, but I can't see Papa coming now. And anyway, what's the point?' she said, further despair washing over her. 'With Mamma gone and Papa unable to work, I'll be needed here in the café.'

'If he doesn't return tomorrow, I must advertise for some help. I doubt I can persuade Carlotta to wait on tables.'

'Do you know what's happened between her and Giulio?' Rosanna asked. 'With Mamma dead, I would have thought Giulio would have at least come to the funeral to pay his last respects. Poor Carlotta – her husband and now Mamma. She looks like a ghost,' she sighed.

'Yes, she's certainly been punished for making a mistake,' he replied.

'What mistake, Luca?'

'Oh, nothing you need to know about.' Luca ground out his cigarette underfoot and closed the kitchen door.

'I wish everyone would stop treating me like a child! I'm seventeen soon. Why won't you tell me what has happened?'

'Well, if you wish to act as an adult, then you must think of your own future, Rosanna,' Luca countered. 'Mamma's death changes nothing.'

'It changes everything, Luca. Papa will never, *ever* let me go to Milan now Mamma's gone.'

'Rosanna, one step at a time: let's first try to persuade him to come and hear you sing. I think it might do him good to get out and take some pride in his talented daughter.'

'Do you think it's right to be making plans for the future so soon after Mamma has gone?' Rosanna queried guiltily. 'I don't feel like singing.'

'Of course you don't. But you must, Rosanna,' Luca urged. 'All these years you've been going to Luigi and this is your big chance to make your dream come true. Carlotta can manage the café for one night. I'll ask Massimo and Maria Rossini to come and help her.'

'You know, Luca,' Rosanna confessed quietly, 'I think I should feel more sad about Mamma than I do. But I just feel numb, here.' She indicated her chest.

'Of course you do, it's the shock. None of us can believe she's gone. But keeping busy helps, I think. And always remember, Rosanna, that Mamma would want the best for you. Now, I think it's time for us to get some sleep. We have another long day tomorrow. Come, *piccolina*.'

Rosanna followed Luca wearily out of the kitchen.

6

'So, you will perform the aria as if you are singing it in front of the audience.'

Rosanna nodded and walked into the middle of the music room. The soft notes of the piano drifted across to her and she began to sing. When she'd finished, she noticed Luigi staring at her thoughtfully.

'Rosanna, have you a problem?'

'No . . . I . . . why?'

'Because your vocal cords sound as if they are constricted by a python. Come, sit down.'

Rosanna crossed the room and sat on the piano stool next to Luigi.

'Is it your mamma?' he asked her gently.

Rosanna nodded. 'Yes, and also because . . . because . . .'

'Because what?'

'Luigi, it's pointless me singing for your friend at the soirée. I can't possibly go to Milan to study now.' Rosanna let out a sob.

'And why is that?'

'Mamma's gone and Papa will need me to fill her place. Now I've left school, he'll want me to work in the café and take care of him. I can't leave him alone, I can't. I'm his daughter.'

'I see.' Luigi nodded. 'Well then, when you sing here on Tuesday night, you have nothing to lose, do you?'

'I suppose not.' Rosanna found her handkerchief and blew her nose.

'Is your papa coming to hear you?' asked Luigi.

'No, I don't think he will. He hardly comes downstairs to the café anymore.'

Luigi's wise eyes surveyed Rosanna. 'You know, there are some things in life that are beyond our control. Sometimes, we must leave it to destiny. But all I can say is, if you sing as you usually do with me, you may be surprised at the result.' Luigi planted a fond kiss on top of Rosanna's head. 'So, let the fates decide. Now, we go again.'

The following Tuesday, Rosanna took the bus up to Luigi's villa. Ironically, given the heaviness of her heart, it was a perfect balmy evening, the setting sun casting a rosy glow over Naples as she stared listlessly out of the bus window. Carlotta had agreed to run the café for the evening and Maria and Massimo were going to lend a hand. As Rosanna walked up to the Villa Torini, she thought sadly how she was wearing the same black dress she'd worn to her mother's funeral. She doubted she'd see her father in the audience. When Luca had told Papa he was taking him to hear Rosanna sing, he'd ignored his son, not seeming to hear what he was saying.

'Come in, Rosanna.' Luigi greeted her at the front door. He seemed different and very distinguished in his dinner jacket and bow tie. 'You look beautiful,' he said approvingly as he led her into the music room. The French windows were thrown open, held in place by two large floral decorations, and on the terrace beyond stood several rows of seats.

'See.' Luigi guided Rosanna into the centre of the room. 'This is where you will stand to sing. Now, come and meet your fellow performers.'

Six other singers were chatting nervously in the drawing room. They stopped talking as Luigi and Rosanna entered.

'This is Rosanna Menici. She will be singing last. Rosanna, help yourself to refreshments.' Luigi pointed to a table laden with large jugs of lemonade and platters of antipasti. 'I must now go and greet my guests.'

Rosanna sat down in a leather chair in the corner. The other performers resumed chatting to each other, but she was too nervous to join in.

She heard the doorbell ring again and again and the soft murmur of voices as the guests passed the drawing room on their way to the terrace.

Luigi put his head round the door.

'Five minutes, ladies and gentlemen,' he announced. 'Signora Rinaldi will come to collect you. Once you have each finished your performance, you may sit in the audience. Maybe you will learn from each other. Good luck.'

Several minutes later, Signora Rinaldi appeared to usher the first performer out of the room. Soon, the noise from the terrace ceased and Rosanna heard the grand piano begin to play. One after another, her fellow performers disappeared until, finally, Rosanna was alone in the room.

A few minutes later, Signora Rinaldi appeared at the door. 'Come, Rosanna, it is time for you.'

Rosanna nodded and stood up, her palms clammy, her heart thumping. She followed the housekeeper along the corridor until she stood outside the door of the music room, hearing the last performer still singing.

'Signor Vincenzi told me to tell you that your papa and your brother are in the audience.' She smiled fondly at Rosanna. 'You will be wonderful, I promise.'

A wave of clapping signalled the end of the previous performance. Signora Rinaldi opened the door to the music room and gently guided Rosanna inside.

'And now to our last performer. My very special pupil, Signorina Rosanna Menici. Rosanna has been coming to me for the past five years and this is her first public performance. I hope that, once you all hear her sing, you'll appreciate that you have been at the debut of a most remarkable talent. Signora Menici will be singing "*Mi chiamano Mimi*" from *La Bohème*.'

There was polite applause as Luigi went back to his piano stool. A jumble of conflicting thoughts crowded Rosanna's mind as she heard Luigi play the first few bars. She couldn't do this, she had no voice, it wouldn't come . . .

And then, the strangest thing happened. Amongst the blur of faces, she could see her mamma smiling at her, encouraging her, willing her to perform.

You can *do it, Rosanna, you* can . . .

Rosanna took a deep breath, opened her mouth and began to sing.

Luigi was finding it increasingly difficult to read the sheet music in front of him because his eyes were filled with tears. Five years of hard work, and tonight Rosanna and her beautiful voice had come of age, just as he'd always known they would.

*

Paolo de Vito sat in the second row, his eyes closed. Vincenzi had been right about this girl. The voice was one of the purest sopranos he'd ever heard. It had colour, tone, strength, depth; every note of the difficult aria was clear and perfectly judged. And, besides that, the girl seemed to understand what she was singing about. He could feel the raw emotion hanging invisibly in the air, paralysing the audience. Paolo felt tingles running up and down his spine. Rosanna Menici was sensational and he wanted to be the one to give her talent to the world.

Marco Menici stared disbelievingly at the slim figure standing in front of him. Was this really his Rosanna, the shy child who'd always been so easy to ignore? He'd known she had a sweet voice, but tonight . . . why, she was singing in front of all these people as if she had been born to it! If only Antonia could have been here to see her daughter. Marco wiped the tears away from his eyes.

Luca Menici surreptitiously watched Marco's expression and thanked God for helping him persuade his father to come. He too blinked away a tear. The die was cast. He knew nothing could stop Rosanna now.

As the last notes died away, there was silence from the audience. Rosanna stood in a trance as her mamma's face, the face she had sung to for the past few minutes, disappeared. A storm of rapturous applause broke in her ears, then Luigi appeared at her side and together they took bow after bow. The other performers joined them as the audience rose to their feet.

Luigi raised his hands and begged for quiet. 'Thank you for joining us here tonight. I hope our humble performance has brought you pleasure. Drinks will now be served, during which there will be a chance to mingle with our artistes.'

Another burst of applause followed his short speech, then he was surrounded by people clapping him on the back and shaking his hand. Rosanna stood alone, unsure what to do. A waitress offered her a glass of Prosecco. She took a sip and spluttered helplessly as the bubbles fizzed in the back of her throat.

'*Piccolina*, oh Rosanna, you were . . . magnificent!' Luca was by her side. 'You will be such a star one day – I have always known it.'

'Where's Papa? Did he enjoy it? Was he angry that we didn't tell him about the singing lessons?' asked Rosanna anxiously.

'When Signor Vincenzi announced that you'd been coming to him for five years, his face looked like thunder. But now he's heard you sing, well . . .' Luca chuckled. 'He's boasting to everybody that you're his daughter.'

She looked out onto the terrace and saw Marco talking to several people. She realised he was smiling for the first time since her mamma had died.

'Rosanna, I have someone I want you to meet.' Luigi appeared by her side, accompanied by an elegantly dressed middle-aged man. 'This is Signor Paolo de Vito, artistic director of La Scala, Milan.'

'Signorina Menici, it's delightful to meet you. Luigi has told me much about you. And having heard you sing, I have to say he was not exaggerating. Your performance tonight was breathtaking. As always, Luigi has done a wonderful job. He has a nose for special talent.'

Luigi shrugged modestly. 'I can only work with the tools I am given.'

'I think too, my friend, you have a little genius of your own. Would you not agree, Signorina Menici?' Paolo smiled down at her.

'Luigi has been wonderful to me,' Rosanna replied shyly.

'And he tells me your papa is here?' continued Paolo.

'Yes,' answered Rosanna.

'Well, if you would excuse me, I wish to speak to him. Will you introduce us, Luigi?'

Luca and Rosanna watched nervously from the other side of the terrace as Luigi introduced Paolo de Vito to Marco. The three men sat down and Luigi signalled to a waitress to bring more Prosecco.

Rosanna turned away. 'I cannot bear to look,' she said. 'What do you think they're talking about?'

'You know what they'll be saying. After your performance tonight, there's no need for false modesty.' Luca turned his attention to a heavily bejewelled lady and her husband who had come up to congratulate Rosanna on her performance.

Eventually, Luigi stood up and beckoned to Rosanna and Luca to join them.

'Rosanna, *bravissima*!' Marco stood up and kissed his daughter on both cheeks. 'Why did you not tell me you were having singing lessons all this time? If I had known, I would of course have helped. You are a bad girl, eh?' Her papa smiled. 'Well, what's done is done. Signor de Vito has been telling me he thinks you will one day be a big star. He wants you to go to a music school in Milan. He's sure they will offer you a scholarship.'

Paolo shrugged. 'As a director of the school and La Scala, I can take what you might call an executive decision.'

'And what do you say, Papa?' asked Luca anxiously.

'Well, it's all well and good to have such a talent, but I could not let my daughter go alone to such a big city. Who knows what would become of her?' Marco sighed.

Rosanna felt the adrenaline of the evening leave her. She'd been right. In the end, it had all been for nothing. Papa was going to say no.

'So,' Marco continued, 'Signor Vincenzi suggested that someone should accompany you. And of course, I think to myself, who? Who could I trust to take care of my daughter and keep her safe? And then it came to me. Luca, my son, who has paid all these years to help you.'

'You . . . you mean, you'll let me go to Milan if Luca accompanies me?' Rosanna gazed up at her papa in amazement.

Marco nodded. 'Yes. It seems like the perfect solution.'

'But what about you, Papa? We couldn't leave you alone.' Luca was staring at his father as though he had lost his mind.

'But I won't be alone, Luca. Carlotta and Ella are home now. And my daughter insists that she will not return to her husband. So, she can look after her old papa and help in the café. And I will find a replacement for you, Luca. You were a bad cook anyway,' joked Marco. 'And as these two gentlemen have said' – he nodded in the direction of Luigi and Paolo – 'we must try to do everything we can to give your precious gift to the world, Rosanna. So, there we are. Are you happy?'

'Oh Papa! I . . . of course I am! Thank you, thank you!' Rosanna hugged him tightly, still unable to believe the longed-for future was hers to grasp.

'And what about you, Luca? Will accompanying Rosanna to Milan suit you?' asked Luigi.

Luca's eyes shone. 'I can't think of anything that would please me more.'

'Good, good, so that is settled,' said Paolo. 'Forgive me, but I must leave now. I have a post-performance supper with the director of the Teatro di San Carlo in the city.' He stood up and turned to Rosanna. 'I'll speak to my colleagues about you on my return to Milan. If all goes well, then in the next few days you will receive a letter formally confirming you have been granted a scholarship. The term begins in September. I look forward very much to welcoming you to the school and after that, perhaps, La Scala itself. Goodnight, Rosanna.' He took her hand in his and kissed it.

'I can't ever thank you enough, Signor de Vito,' she replied, her voice thick with emotion.

Paolo smiled at her, then walked inside the house with Luigi to the front door. 'You handled that very well, Paolo. I'll always be grateful to you,' said Luigi.

'I've dealt with difficult parents many times.' Paolo grinned suddenly. 'You know, Marco even told me that Rosanna had inherited her voice from him! And I must thank you, Luigi, for entrusting Rosanna to me. I'll do my best to see that her talent is nurtured.'

'I know you will, Paolo. All I ask for is a ticket to her debut at La Scala.'

'Of course. *Ciao*, Luigi.'

Luigi shut the door and was immediately waylaid by the

mother of one of his students. Eventually, he made his way back to the terrace and sought out Luca.

'I have something for you, young man.' Luigi pressed a thick brown envelope into Luca's hands. 'This is for you and Rosanna, to help you with your expenses in Milan. You've been an exceptional brother to Rosanna. And I think, out of your kindness, you *too* have won your freedom, yes?' There was a look of surprise on Luca's face as Luigi patted his shoulder and went to join his other guests.

When the Menici family arrived home in the taxi Luigi had insisted he pay for, Luca went up to his bedroom and shut the door. He opened the envelope and emptied hundreds of lire notes onto his bed. There was also a letter in the envelope, which he unfolded and read.

I kept your money from the first day Rosanna gave it to me. I wanted to teach her for free but I understand pride. I also thought it might help in the future. I'm sure you will use it wisely. Kind Regards, Luigi Vincenzi.

Luca lay back on his bed, his heart bursting with gratitude at such unexpected kindness.

7

Carlotta sat motionless in a chair in the sitting room as her father explained that Rosanna had won a scholarship to a music school in Milan and that Luca was to accompany her.

'It's all worked out perfectly,' smiled Marco. 'Antonia's gone, but you, my favourite daughter, are back to take her place. As you've told me so many times that you won't return to Giulio, you can live here with Ella and help me in the café as your mamma would want you to.'

Marco waited for his daughter's reaction. Carlotta stared off into the distance as if she hadn't heard.

'It is a good plan, yes? For all of us,' Marco encouraged.

Eventually, Carlotta nodded. She had lost a considerable amount of weight and her brown eyes looked huge in her drawn face. 'Yes, Papa. I will stay here and take care of you. As you say, it's my duty. Excuse me, I think I will take a walk.'

Marco watched as Carlotta stood up and left the room. Soon, he hoped, his child would be back to her old self. They would laugh together and he would be for Ella the papa she'd recently lost. Pouring himself a brandy, Marco decided that, under the dreadful circumstances, things had at least worked out better than he had could have ever expected.

Rosanna was searching through a drawer for a clean white blouse when her sister came into the bedroom.

'Congratulations.'

Rosanna looked at her sister apprehensively. She knew Papa had told Carlotta of her move to Milan and was not sure what the reaction would be.

'Thank you.'

'Why did you not tell us of your secret, Rosanna?' Carlotta asked.

'Because . . . I didn't think anyone would approve.'

Carlotta sat down on the bed and patted the space next to her. Rosanna moved towards her nervously.

'You think I'm jealous, don't you, Rosanna? Because you and Luca are soon to be leaving for a new life in Milan, while I stay here and take Mamma's place?'

'Carlotta, Luca and I will come home every holiday and help you, I promise,' Rosanna reassured her.

'It's kind of you to say so, but I think, once you're away from here, you will forget your old life.'

'No, Carlotta! I'll never forget you and Papa and everyone here in the Piedigrotta,' Rosanna replied defensively.

'I didn't mean it like that,' Carlotta said gently. She reached for Rosanna's hand. 'I can't deny I felt at first a little envy when Papa told me, but I'm pleased for you, really. You've been given a chance, and I hope,' she sighed, 'that you're wiser than your big sister and don't mess it up.'

'Carlotta, please don't say that. You're still young too. And you might get back with Giulio.'

'No, Rosanna, I won't,' Carlotta said firmly. 'And I can never marry again as he will never divorce me. You know how such a thing would cause a scandal here. So, what I'm trying to tell you is that it takes one moment of stupidity to ruin your life forever. And I don't want to see you suffer the same as I have because of it.'

'I'm sure I won't,' replied Rosanna, still not sure what mistake it was that her sister had made. 'I'll be careful, I promise.'

'You're a sensible girl, Rosanna, but when it comes to men' – Carlotta smiled wryly and shook her head – 'all women can be stupid.'

'I'm not interested in men, only in singing. Please tell me, what is it that's happened between you and Giulio?'

'I can't tell you now, but maybe some day I will. All I know is that I've paid the price for my stupidity and will continue to do so for the rest of my life,' Carlotta replied sadly.

'And now, on top of everything, you'll have to stay here and care for Papa!' said Rosanna, suddenly overwhelmed with guilt. 'If I wasn't going to Milan, then—'

Carlotta put a finger to her sister's lips. 'Don't think like that. For now, Ella and I need Papa as much as he needs us. Things have worked out well, really.'

'You really don't mind us going to Milan and leaving you here?'

'No. I'm very happy for you, truly. Just promise to take care of Luca for me.'

'Of course,' Rosanna agreed.

'We're so lucky to have a brother like him. And it's good that he's going with you. You've given him his freedom too and that's a wonderful thing. He deserves it.' Carlotta stood up, kissed the top of her sister's head affectionately and left the bedroom.

Rosanna took off her T-shirt and put on her white choir blouse. She was confused by Carlotta's reaction. She'd expected tears, tantrums and jealousy from her fiery sister, not an almost saintly acceptance of her lot, and she felt unsettled by Carlotta's uncharacteristic resignation to her situation. And she couldn't help feeling terrible that, through winning freedom for herself and Luca, the two of them seemed to have sentenced their beautiful sister to a life of unhappiness.

Roberto Rossini waited until he was fully awake before he opened his eyes to the blinding light of a hot August morning in Milan.

Roberto turned over and saw Tamara's pretty face, still in peaceful repose. Tamara was accommodating and they'd had an enjoyable three weeks. But now it must end, as she was becoming far too possessive and had started talking of their future together. The moment women did this, he knew it was time to move on.

He put his hands behind his head and lay watching the clear blue sky beyond the window, thinking of the day ahead. He had a singing lesson this afternoon, then tonight there was a benefit performance at La Scala for a children's charity – he couldn't remember which, but everyone who was anyone in Milan would be there.

Roberto sighed. He'd been singing professionally for the past five years, and, although he was now a soloist with La Scala, he always sang minor roles. There were other opera companies in Europe he had appeared with who had offered him larger parts in their forthcoming seasons, but he wanted more than anything to succeed at La Scala. Caruso, his hero, from his home town of Naples, had made his name there. And it was also in Milan's magnificent opera house that Callas and di Stephano had given some of their finest performances.

Roberto was becoming impatient for the glory he knew his voice and his charisma deserved. Although thirty-four was hardly old for an opera singer, he had only a few more years before his still handsome young features and taut body moved into middle age, and the moment for true greatness at the height of all his powers had passed.

But how could he achieve his goal in time? Roberto knew he had the qualities that, once he'd been given the opportunity, would separate him from the rest. His voice was strong, distinctive and growing richer as he matured. He'd been told often that he possessed great stage presence and knew how to pour emotion into the characters he portrayed. So why hadn't he yet been given the chance to shine in a leading role at La Scala?

When he'd joined the company five years ago, he'd presumed that it would be only a matter of time before he was promoted and given all the great tenor parts he so yearned to make his own. But, since then, roles he was right for in every way had gone to others. Singers who Roberto hardly rated were rising above and beyond him.

Roberto turned away from the sun and groaned. He had to accept that, for all his talent, he had something of a public relations problem with those who employed him. When he'd been at the music school, he'd done himself few favours by sending a stream of distraught female students in the direction of their tutors. His reputation as a Casanova had not endeared him to anyone, and Paolo de Vito, not only a director of the school but also artistic director at La Scala, had heard of his antics.

Last year he'd had an affair with a guest soprano, who'd gone running to Paolo when Roberto had unceremoniously dumped her. He'd had a major dressing-down for that, Paolo pointing out that it wasn't good for La Scala's reputation to have an up-and-coming young soprano swearing never to return.

After the great soprano debacle, a chastened Roberto had apologised to Paolo and promised it wouldn't happen again. He'd desperately tried to discipline himself for the rest of the season, his ambition to succeed at La Scala and to appease Paolo subduing his more hedonistic tendencies.

Roberto had often wondered whether it was purely a clash of personalities, or something deeper. Paolo was a well-known homosexual and Roberto was sure his handsome good looks and success with women were not qualities that would naturally endear him to the maestro, however well he behaved. And he *had* behaved . . . at least, until Tamara had arrived, fresh from Russia. She'd been impossible to refuse.

Roberto rolled out of bed and walked into the bathroom to take a shower. The season at La Scala finished in September. Then he was off to sing in Paris for a couple of months. He would return to Milan in November for the final year of his contract and, if he didn't get the roles he wanted in the new season, he'd vowed to give up and go abroad permanently. Until then, he'd have to sit it out.

*

That evening, Roberto sang to an audience worth several billion lire.

Afterwards, there was a reception in the foyer of La Scala to which the entire opera company was invited. As Roberto sipped a glass of champagne, he decided he'd leave as soon as possible. This kind of event bored him: there were too many over-made-up wives glittering with the fruits of their ageing husbands' wealth.

He watched morosely as the young Spanish tenor, who had given, in his opinion, such a mediocre Otello, was fêted by the Italian Prime Minister and other well-known dignitaries.

'Good evening. I enjoyed your performance tonight.' Roberto heard a female voice behind him and turned without enthusiasm, prepared for a tedious five minutes of being polite.

'Donatella Bianchi. I am pleased to meet you,' ventured the woman.

Roberto shook her outstretched hand. Donatella Bianchi had a head of the most glorious curly, ebony-coloured hair, green eyes that sparkled brighter than the priceless emeralds around her throat, and the most sensational cleavage. Although certainly past forty, she oozed sex appeal. Her long, perfectly manicured fingernails lingered on Roberto's palm for a little longer than necessary.

'I'm pleased to meet you too.' Roberto gave her a genuine smile.

'I've seen you perform many times before. My husband is a very generous patron of the company. And I think you are a very talented . . . performer.'

'You're most kind.' The conversation was outwardly formal, but the eye contact between them was electric.

Donatella reached into her Gucci evening bag and drew out a card. 'Give me a call tomorrow morning, Roberto Rossini. We need to discuss your future. *Ciao*.'

Roberto slipped the card into his pocket as he watched her make her way through the crowd and slip her arm round the considerable waist of a short, balding Italian.

Minutes later, Roberto left. As he walked across the Piazza della Scala, he pondered whether he would give Signora Bianchi a call. Older *paramours* were not usually his thing, but Donatella was obviously no ordinary woman.

And, when he found himself undressing her in his mind as he climbed into bed that night, he knew that, despite his misgivings, he'd pick up the telephone tomorrow and call her.

8

'Do I look okay?'

'Rosanna, you look as you always do – lovely.'

'Oh, you're just saying that, Luca.'

'Listen, *piccolina*, you're only going to your first day at music school, not entering a beauty pageant. Come, or we'll be late.' Luca offered his hands.

Rosanna took them. 'I'm so nervous, Luca.'

'I know you are, but you'll be fine, I promise. Now, we need to go.'

Luca shut and locked the door to their tiny fifth-floor apartment and they began to walk down the many stairs.

'I like our new home, but I hope the lift will be mended soon. I counted seventy-five steps last night,' Rosanna giggled.

'It will keep us fit, and besides, the climb is worth it for the beautiful view we have of Milan.' Luca knew they'd been lucky to get an apartment so centrally located and suspected that Paolo had pulled a few strings to secure it for them.

The two of them reached the downstairs hall and Luca opened the front door. They stepped out onto the wide pavement of the Corso di Porta Romana, narrowly avoiding a collision with the steady stream of pedestrians that flowed busily in both directions. Luca consulted a sheet of paper on which he'd scribbled down the directions that Paolo had given him.

'We could take the tram, but it's so crowded at this time of the morning.' He watched one rattling past at that moment, with passengers spilling out of the open windows. Two young men ran behind it and daringly leapt onto the rear footplate to hitch a ride. 'Signor de Vito says it's only a fifteen-minute walk to the school from here. Well, we'll try it and see if he's correct,' Luca shouted above the hubbub.

'I keep having to pinch myself to believe that today is happening,' said Rosanna, drinking in the atmosphere as they walked along the noisy street, past teeming cafés and shops opening their shutters for business. 'What will you do while I'm at school?'

'I think I'll be a tourist,' Luca said. 'There are so many beautiful old churches in the city and I'll start with those. The Duomo di Milano is only a few streets from here. And I must find a place of worship that's near our apartment. I promised Papa I'd take you to Mass every Sunday.'

As Paolo had predicted, after fifteen minutes or so, the two of them turned left into the Via Santa Marta. 'Look, there's the school.' Rosanna paused on the street corner and turned to her brother. 'There'll be no need to walk me here every morning. I want you to have your own life in Milan too, Luca.'

'I know. And I will. But my first priority is you.' The two of them crossed the road and stood looking at the entrance to the school. Other young men and women were streaming past them, funnelling into the door that led to the hallowed corridors of Italy's most illustrious music academy. 'Well, here we are,' Luca said, smiling at her. 'I'll say goodbye now and meet you back here at five o'clock.'

Rosanna clutched his hand. 'I'm scared, Luca.'

'You'll be fine. Remember, this was our dream.' Luca kissed her on both cheeks. 'Good luck, *piccolina*.'

'Thank you.'

Three hours later, Luca was sitting in a small café writing a postcard to his father, eating crostini and drinking a glass of beer. He'd spent an hour inside the great Duomo, then walked through the Galleria Vittorio Emanuele, marvelling at the exotic shops and the cost of the goods they contained. He'd exited the Galleria into the Piazza della Scala and stood for a while gazing up at the fabled facade of the world-famous opera house, where one day he hoped he would hear his sister sing.

Tonight, he wanted to organise a celebration supper for both of them. Glancing at his watch, he realised he still had a lot to do before he went to collect Rosanna. He finished the remains of his meal, paid the bill and headed off in the direction of their apartment. As he walked, he spotted a small supermarket, its window crowded with hanging strings of dry-cured sausages and wooden crates of fresh vegetables. He went inside and purchased all the ingredients he would need, plus a bottle of Chianti. Emerging into the busy street, and unsure of his bearings, he turned right and found himself in the Via Agnello. Realising he'd taken a wrong turn, he was just about to retrace his footsteps when a church, its spire visible from behind the buildings lining the main street, caught his eye.

Luca decided to take a closer look. He walked in the

direction of the spire along a narrow alleyway until he arrived in a small square. He made his way across it towards the church, hesitating in front of the arched wooden door. To the right of it was a small plaque. Luca struggled to read the words – worn away by the ravages of time – that were written on it.

'La Chiesa Della Beata Vergine Maria – The church of the Madonna', he read out loud.

Luca checked his watch. He still had two hours before he needed to collect Rosanna. Enough time to satisfy an overwhelming urge to take a look inside, so he stepped into the front lobby. Above the door leading inside the church itself was a worn and faded fresco depicting the Virgin Mary cradling the baby Jesus in her arms. He gazed at it for a few seconds, then entered the church. He saw it was deserted and his eyes adjusted to the dimness after the bright sunlight outside.

Luca looked up at the high, arched ceiling, scarred with cracks in the plaster. To his left, a cherub holding up one of the pillars had a chipped nose and half a wing, and the pews in front of him were so worn that the varnish had disappeared altogether. And yet . . . and yet, even though the church looked forlorn and uncared for, Luca was struck by its beauty, its warmth.

The echo of his footsteps rang around the church as he walked further down the aisle. Although it was empty, he felt as if he were not alone. Suddenly feeling dizzy and a little weak, he took a seat in one of the pews and put the shopping bags by his feet.

Luca stared at the statue of the Madonna standing in the centre of the altar. The blue paint of her dress was peeling and her lips had lost their original redness. Luca closed his eyes, crossed himself and began to pray.

When he opened his eyes, a shaft of sunlight was streaming through the stained-glass windows at the front of the church, its rays falling on the statue. The light became brighter. Then in the centre of the light he saw a blurred shape.

Her arms were outstretched. And she spoke to him.

He blinked and she was gone, leaving only brilliant sunlight behind her.

Luca sat still for a very long time. When he finally moved, his body felt light, as though it had lost its gravity. He stood slowly and walked down the aisle to the front of the church. When he reached the altar, he dropped to one knee, tears of joy pouring down his cheeks. Where there'd been uncertainty, there was now purpose; and where there had been emptiness, there was love.

He didn't know how long it was before he felt a hand on his shoulder. He jumped and turned to look up into a pair of wise brown eyes. An old priest smiled down at him and Luca knew instinctively that he had witnessed and understood.

'My name is Don Edoardo. I am *il parroco* of Beata Vergine Maria. If you wish to talk to me, I'm here every morning between half past nine and noon.'

'*Grazie*, Don Edoardo. I wish . . . I wish to make confession.'

The priest nodded, and Luca rose to his feet, the feeling of weightlessness still with him, and followed Don Edoardo to the confessional.

When Luca left the church fifteen minutes later, he knew his life would never be the same again.

An elated Rosanna flung herself into Luca's arms.

'How was it?'

'Wonderful! Terrifying, but wonderful! There are so many beautiful voices, Luca. How will I ever be able to compete? And some of the girls are so mature, even though they're the same age as me. And the clothes they wear! I think some of them must be very rich . . . and my singing tutor, Professor Poli, he's so stern and . . . Luca' – Rosanna stopped and stared at him – 'are you okay?'

'Yes, I've never felt better. Why do you ask?'

'Oh, it's just that you . . . well, you look different somehow. A little pale, perhaps.'

'I promise, *piccolina*, that I am . . .' Luca tried to find a word to describe how he felt. 'Radiant!' He laughed as he steered her across the busy road and they headed home arm in arm. They reached the apartment, short of breath from the stairs, and Luca unlocked the door, mentally noting that the peeling paintwork could do with some attention.

'You go and take a shower before the hot water runs out, Rosanna,' Luca suggested. 'I'm cooking something special for supper tonight.'

Rosanna stared at the small sitting room in delight. Since she'd left that morning, the last vestiges of unpacking had been tidied away. The threadbare sofa in the corner had been covered by a colourful blanket so that it now looked cosy and inviting. The rickety table by the window was disguised with a fringed pink cloth, on which stood a blue and white striped jug of fresh flowers, along with two candles placed in saucers.

'You've worked so hard. Thank you!' she exclaimed. Despite the shabby, pock-marked walls and the grimy windows that Luca hadn't yet had time to clean, the overall impression was cheerful and homely.

'It's a special night – for both of us,' Luca replied from the tiny kitchen, from which the mouth-watering aroma of fresh garlic and herbs was already emanating.

'Yes, Luca, it is,' said Rosanna, her eyes dancing. 'I won't be long, then I'll come and help you.' She retrieved her towel and washbag from her bedroom and, putting the apartment door on the latch, made her way down the dim corridor to the communal bathroom.

Later, after a supper of mushroom risotto and salad that Rosanna pronounced excellent, they sat back nursing their wine glasses and watching dusk fall across the rooftops of Milan.

Rosanna yawned, then smiled at her brother. 'I feel so tired.'

'Then you must go to bed. It's the excitement, I expect.'

'Yes. Do you know, I didn't think it was possible to feel this happy ever again after Mamma died,' she mused.

Luca studied his sister across the table, then shook his head. 'Neither did I, Rosanna, neither did I.'

The wrought-iron gates slid open noiselessly and Roberto drove his Fiat slowly up the tree-lined drive. Negotiating the oversized fountain that played in an ornamental pond, Roberto brought his car to a halt.

Although he'd often passed through Como and had twice picnicked by the lake, he'd never been able to see anything more than the chimneys of the residences that lay cocooned behind their leafy green barricades.

Now in front of him stood a grand palazzo. Its graceful white frontage rose from the ground, the sun glinting off the tiers of neat windows, each one aproned with a balcony fashioned delicately out of wrought iron. In the centre, above the front door, was a circular stained-glass window, framed by an elegant cupola.

Roberto stepped out of his Fiat and shut the door behind him. He walked towards the palazzo and slowly made his way up a staircase to the enormous front door set between pillars of Angera stone. He couldn't see a bell and didn't feel that knocking was the correct way to alert the occupant to his arrival. As Roberto was wondering if there was another entrance, the door opened.

'*Caro*, I'm so glad you could come.'

Donatella was wearing a flimsy white robe. Her hair was wet and her face devoid of make-up. She looked incredible. 'I was showering after a swim in the pool. You're a little early.'

'I . . . sorry, yes.' Roberto gulped, doing his best to avert his eyes from her voluptuous breasts, their fullness barely disguised beneath the robe.

'Follow me.'

Roberto stepped inside and followed his hostess through the large marbled hall and up a sweeping staircase.

Donatella pushed open a door and let Roberto into a huge, high-ceilinged bedroom.

'Here, make yourself comfortable while I dress.' Donatella indicated a sofa by a window and disappeared into another room.

Roberto walked over to the window and stared out across the perfectly manicured gardens, the vast frontage of which led eventually to the shore of Lake Como itself. After a few minutes, he sat down on the deep sofa and let a small sigh escape his lips. Donatella Bianchi and her husband were obviously rich on an epic scale.

'So, *caro*, are you well?' Donatella appeared, clad in a pair of tight white jeans and a black top that accentuated her two best assets.

'I . . . yes, thank you.'

Donatella sat down next to him, her long legs curled under her. 'Good. I'm glad you came today. Champagne?' Donatella reached for the bottle in an ice bucket on the low table. She poured the frothy liquid into two glasses without waiting for a reply.

'Thank you,' Roberto said as she handed him a glass.

'To you and your future,' she toasted.

For the first time in his life, Roberto was at a loss for words. He took a sip of champagne and tried to recover his equilibrium. 'You have a beautiful home,' he managed, then blushed, feeling stupid.

'I'm glad you like it. It's been in my husband's family for more than a hundred and fifty years. But' – Donatella sighed – 'sometimes I feel I live in a museum. We must have a staff of twenty to care for both the palazzo and the grounds.' One of Donatella's long legs uncurled itself from under her and a foot inched towards Roberto's thigh.

'You have no children?' he asked, trying to maintain the conversation.

'No. I've never been the maternal type,' she shrugged, 'and besides, it seems my husband and I . . . we could not conceive a child.'

'Your husband, er, where is he?' Roberto asked nervously as a toe made its way towards his groin.

Donatella sighed and made a mock pout. 'He's in America and has left me all alone again.'

'He travels abroad often?'

'All the time. He's an art dealer. Much of his time is spent in New York or London. I'm here by myself for weeks on end.' She lowered her chin and threw him an unmistakably suggestive glance from under her lashes.

'Can't you go with him?'

'Of course, but I've travelled all over the world, seen so many places, and these days I prefer to stay at home. It's boring to be in a strange city alone while my husband conducts his business. And even *I* can have enough of shopping. So tell me more about you, Roberto Rossini.'

'There's little to tell,' Roberto shrugged.

'I don't believe that for a second. You have a girlfriend?' Donatella fished.

'No, not at the moment.'

'I think you're too modest. You must have a stream of women going crazy for you.' With one practised movement, Donatella rose from the sofa and straddled his knees with her legs. 'I mean, with your beautiful, big voice and your other . . . attractions.' One of her hands inched down his shirt buttons. 'You've had many lovers, yes?'

'I . . .' Caught unawares by her boldness, Roberto found it difficult to form the words. 'A few,' he gasped, becoming more aroused by the second.

'Older women?' Donatella's mouth slid to his neck and kissed it. Her hand, meanwhile, found its target.

'No . . . I . . .'

'Then I will be the first,' she purred triumphantly.

Losing his last vestige of self-control, Roberto buried his fingers in her thick hair as Donatella covered his lips with hers.

*

Three hours later, the two of them retraced their footsteps to the front door of the palazzo.

Donatella smiled as she opened the door.

'This morning has been most . . . enjoyable. Call me tomorrow evening at seven, yes?'

'Yes.'

'Good. Next time we'll talk about your future. *Ciao*, Roberto.'

As he walked unsteadily to his car, he shook his head at the irony.

Roberto Rossini, experienced lover and man of the world, had just been well and truly seduced.

9

Milan, January 1973

Rosanna opened the door to the apartment. 'Luca, Luca! I'm home.'

'In the kitchen, *piccolina*,' he called.

'Luca, I hope you don't mind, but I've brought a friend back from school with me for supper.' Rosanna appeared in the kitchen, her brown eyes sparkling, her cheeks tinged red from the walk through the cold winter air. 'I said you always cook enough for six,' she quipped.

'Of course I don't mind.' Luca smiled.

'Thank you. Abi, this is my brother, Luca Menici.'

'Hello, Luca.' The girl smiled back shyly. 'I'm Abigail Holmes. A pleasure to meet you. Oh, and please call me Abi.' She spoke good Italian with just a trace of an English accent.

'I . . . hello, Abi.' Luca found himself blushing. He stared at Abi and felt his heart rate increase. She was an extremely pretty blonde, with large blue eyes, fine features and the delicate peaches-and-cream complexion of the English.

'Can we help with supper?' asked Rosanna.

Luca tore his eyes away from Abi. 'No. The sauce is

cooked and the pasta will only be another two or three minutes. Go and make yourselves comfortable in the sitting room.'

Abi followed Rosanna out of the kitchen. She sat on the sofa and let out a low whistle. 'Your brother is very handsome, Rosanna. He has the most gorgeous eyes.'

'Do you think so?'

'Yes. Don't sound so surprised.' Abi giggled. 'Does he have a girlfriend?'

'Oh no. He never has had.'

'Why?'

'I don't know, Abi. He's just never been interested in women.'

Luca arrived in the sitting room with a large bowl of pasta.

'Signorine, if you would like to take your seats.'

'*Grazie*, signor.' Abi's eyes twinkled as she sat down at the table next to Rosanna.

Luca served the pasta while Rosanna poured the wine. Then the three of them began to eat.

'You know, you're so lucky, Rosanna,' Abi sighed wistfully.

'Am I?'

'Yes. I mean, this lovely cosy apartment, a brother who cooks like a dream and, most important of all, the freedom to come and go as you please.'

'Abi stays with her aunt whilst she studies at the school,' Rosanna explained to Luca. 'Your aunt is very strict, is she not, Abi?'

'Yes. She treats me as though I were ten. She's English and thinks all Italian men will try to seduce me, even though her own husband is Italian.' Abi rolled her eyes in exasperation. 'I suppose she just feels responsible for my welfare. When I won a place at the school, my parents said I was allowed to take it on the condition that I lived with my aunt.'

'You like Milan?' asked Luca.

'Oh, I love it,' said Abi. 'It's so colourful, so vibrant, especially after dreary old England. Anyway, that's enough of me. So, Luca, what do you do with yourself while Rosanna is at school? Do you work?'

'No, I—'

'Luca spends all his time in a crumbling church just around the corner,' Rosanna interrupted. 'It's his second home.'

'I see.' Abi raised an eyebrow.

'Really, Rosanna. You explain it badly,' Luca chided. 'Beata Vergine Maria is a beautiful fifteenth-century church that's in a terrible state of disrepair. I'm helping the priest there, Don Edoardo, to try and raise funds to restore it to its former magnificence, but,' Luca shrugged, 'it's an uphill battle.'

'Are you . . . I mean, you must believe in God and all that?' asked Abi.

'Yes, of course I do. And Beata Vergine Maria is a very special place. Don Edoardo has told me there have been miracles there, visions of the Madonna herself. I have a little time, so I try to help.' Luca shrugged. 'Something must be done soon, otherwise the stonework and the ancient fresco in the front lobby will be beyond repair.'

'Have you thought of having a recital?' asked Abi suddenly.

'What exactly do you mean?' Luca asked.

'Well, my Aunt Sonia is head of a committee called The Friends of the Milan Opera. I'm wondering whether, if you wrote and asked her nicely, she might be prepared to ask Paolo de Vito if he'd allow a couple of singers from La Scala and a few of the students from the school to perform a recital in the church to raise funds.'

'Abi! That's a wonderful idea.' Luca's face broke into a smile. 'Do you not think so, Rosanna?'

'I do. Especially as it's so close to La Scala. They can only say no, can't they?' she replied.

'Well, you can write a letter to my aunt if I give you her address, then she can put it to her committee next time they meet.'

'Of course. Thank you, Abi, really,' said Luca gratefully.

'Good. That's settled then.' Abi turned to Rosanna. 'And maybe you and I could sing "*The Flower Duet*" from *Lakme*. We've been practising it in class.' She smiled at Luca. 'Of course, my voice is nothing compared to your sister's, but then no voice at the school is.'

'Please, Abi, you're exaggerating.' Rosanna blushed at her friend's praise.

'No, I'm not. You know as well as I do that Paolo goes into a swoon every time he hears you. He comes into classes all the time just to listen to you. I reckon you'll be a solo artiste straight away when you join the company, leaving the rest of us to struggle through the chorus. Remember me when you're a famous diva, won't you?' she teased.

'Abi, of course I'll remember you,' Rosanna laughed.

'There you are, you see,' said Abi, winking at Luca, 'she does know how famous she's going to become!'

'Damn, I've run out of cigarettes,' said Luca. 'Excuse me,

I'll go to the shop on the corner and fetch some,' he said as he rose. 'I'll leave you two to your girls' talk. I won't be long.'

As the door closed behind him, Abi turned to Rosanna. 'You know, I think I could develop a serious crush on your brother. He's so kind and sensitive, on top of those devastating good looks. Mind you, in my experience, men like him usually turn out to be gay. He's not, is he? You said earlier he'd never had a girlfriend.'

'No, Abi!' Rosanna was discomfited by Abi's bluntness: it was a thought she'd had herself but never voiced.

'Don't look so horrified, Rosanna,' Abi said apologetically. 'I just thought I'd ask as it seemed pointless wasting my time on him if you knew for certain he was.'

Blushing, Rosanna changed the subject and Abi took the hint. The pair idly discussed their schedule for the following day until Luca returned with the cigarettes. However, she watched with renewed interest as Abi and Luca chatted easily over coffee, noting the body language and the eye contact between them.

At half past ten, Abi reluctantly got to her feet. 'Thank you so much for supper. I'm afraid I'll have to leave now, otherwise Aunt Sonia will start to worry. When could I come and see your church, Luca? I'd love to visit now I've heard so much about it.'

'Sunday morning? Rosanna and I always attend the nine o'clock Mass there.'

'Okay. Even my aunt can't object to me going out to church! I'll meet you here at eight thirty and we can go together. *Ciao*, Rosanna. *Ciao*, Luca.'

Luca stood up and kissed Abi on both cheeks. 'Goodbye,

Abi. Thank you for your wonderful idea. I'll see you at Mass on Sunday.'

Rosanna saw her friend out, then returned to sit down at the table. 'Did you like Abi?' she asked Luca.

'Very much. I think she'll be a good friend to you, Rosanna. Her heart's in the right place.'

'She's very pretty, isn't she, Luca? I would kill to have her blonde hair. All the boys at school are in love with her.' She was fishing now, remembering her conversation with Abi earlier.

'Yes, I'm sure they are. Now, I'll clear up the dishes, and you must go to bed, *piccolina*.'

'No, I'm not tired. I'll help you wash up.'

'Okay,' Luca acquiesced. He deftly piled up the plates from the table and took them through to the kitchen. Rosanna followed with the wine glasses.

'You wash, I'll dry,' she said.

Brother and sister stood working at the sink in companionable silence. Eventually, Rosanna said, 'Luca, have you . . . have you ever been in love?'

'No, I don't think so. Why do you ask?'

'Oh, no reason. Abi thought you were very handsome.'

'Did she?'

'Yes. You *are* handsome, Luca. I mean, I'm sure girls like you.'

'Rosanna, what are you trying to say?' frowned Luca.

'Just that, well, I know Papa asked you to look after me, but I'm a big girl now. I'm not frightened of being here in the apartment by myself. If you ever wanted to go out in the evenings, then you must.'

'If I want to, I shall,' Luca said, nodding. 'But I'm happy being here with you, *piccolina*.'

'Are you really happy?' Rosanna asked.

'Oh yes,' said Luca. 'Very.'

'I just don't want you to miss out on your own life because of me.'

'Rosanna, the five months we've spent here in Milan have been the happiest of my life. And during that time I've found something that's very important to me.'

'What?'

Luca laughed at her dogged persistence. 'You always did ask too many questions. All I can tell you is that I know where my future lies. When the time is right, I'll tell you. I must have *some* secrets, Rosanna.'

'Of course. I just want you to be happy.'

'And I swear I am. Now, it's time you went to bed. It's late.'

Rosanna threw her arms around her brother. 'Remember I love you very much.'

'And I you,' he said as he kissed her forehead. 'Now, off you go.'

Once Rosanna had closed her bedroom door, Luca too went to his room and lit two small candles in front of the small statue of the Madonna which stood on the makeshift altar. He knelt down, genuflected and began to pray. For the first time since he'd made his decision, he felt his resolve shaken. He begged God to guide him, to explain to him why a young English girl had stirred such unusually strong feelings inside him.

Perhaps, he thought as he rose ten minutes later, it was simply a test. And a test which he would not fail.

10

'Now, ladies, I suggest we get down to business.' Paolo de Vito smiled glacially as he glanced round the table at the eight immaculately dressed women. They were sipping aperitifs in Il Savini and Paolo suspected the lunch bill for the nine of them would cover the cost of an entire term's tuition at the school. He didn't enjoy his monthly meetings with The Friends of the Milan Opera, but these ladies represented some of the wealthiest men in Milan, without whose continuing benevolence both La Scala and the school would struggle.

'Paolo, I've had a sweet letter from a young man asking if we would be prepared to organise a recital to raise funds for La Chiesa Della Beata Vergine Maria,' Sonia Moretti said.

'Really? I thought we were meant to be raising funds for ourselves, rather than a church.'

'Of course, but this case is rather different. Apparently, there's a rare fresco in the church which will be irreparable if something isn't done soon. And this church is very close to the school and La Scala, so it could technically be the company's place of worship. Besides, it would give the students an opportunity to perform in front of an audience in aid of a needy cause. The letter was written by Luca Menici. I believe his sister is a student at the school.'

'Rosanna? She's one of our most talented pupils, along with your niece, Abigail, of course,' Paolo added swiftly.

'I was thinking that we might plan it for this Easter – hold a candlelight recital and ask a couple of members of the opera company to perform alongside chosen pupils from the school,' continued Sonia. 'I've popped in to see the church and it really would make a lovely venue. We ladies could arrange an impressive guest list and the price of the ticket could cover light refreshments.'

'How many people will the church hold?' enquired Paolo.

'Signor Menici says around two hundred. So, how do the rest of you ladies feel about this idea?'

There was a general nodding of perfectly coiffured heads.

Donatella Bianchi leant forward suddenly. 'I was thinking that Anna Dupré and Roberto Rossini might be suitable as the representatives from the company. I know Signor Rossini has a very strong faith and I'm sure he would be happy to help.'

Paolo raised a surprised eyebrow at Donatella's supposition. 'Right. Then I will think of a suitable programme and then decide who we ask to perform it. I agree it's always beneficial to give the students an opportunity to perform and to learn from their professional counterparts.'

'Now that's settled, we must order lunch. I have an engagement at three and so should leave by half past two.' Donatella raised an arm and a waiter appeared immediately at her side. 'I'll have the *carpaccio di tonno*, thank you.'

'So, you will sing at our little recital?' Donatella's fingers trailed down the small of Roberto's naked back. He'd arrived home from Paris two days before and they'd spent successive afternoons in bed at his apartment.

'A recital at a crumbling church? I hardly think that will boost my career.' Roberto turned his head to look at Donatella.

'Maybe you would do it for me?' Her hand slid under the sheets and caressed the inside of his thigh.

'I . . .'

'Please,' she begged, as her hand travelled upwards.

'I surrender.' Roberto groaned and turned over, covering her mouth in kisses.

Afterwards, as she left the bed to take a shower, he lay sated, eyes closed, thinking he'd never known a woman like her.

Their relationship was based purely on sex and it was the best Roberto had ever known. Donatella asked no more of him than his body. She didn't whisper words of love in his ear, or call him at two in the morning. She didn't explode into a tantrum if he didn't say what she wanted to hear. Roberto had recently begun to wonder if he'd finally found the perfect relationship.

Donatella emerged from the shower, wrapped in a towel. Her dark hair was clipped to the top of her head. From a distance she could be in her early thirties, although Roberto knew she was forty-five.

'So, you *will* sing for us at the church? I know Paolo will appreciate it.'

Roberto sighed. 'Yes! I have said I'll do it.'

Donatella removed her towel and began to dress. 'What are you singing this coming season?'

Roberto's features tightened. 'I don't wish to discuss it. As usual, Paolo promised me more than he's given me, so this will be my last season at La Scala. I won't be renewing my contract when it ends next autumn. So, I've decided I'll take one of the many foreign offers I've had.' He sighed heavily. 'Paolo dislikes me. That's all there is to it. I shall never achieve glory at La Scala while he's in charge.'

'*Caro*,' Donatella soothed him. 'I understand what you're saying, but who knows? You have such talent. I'm sure Paolo is only making sure you're ready before he gives you the roles you deserve.' Donatella tidied her hair in a mirror. 'You'll come to me at the palazzo on Thursday, yes? Giovanni is away again in London.'

'Yes,' Roberto acquiesced.

A few minutes later, Donatella opened the front door of Roberto's apartment block and peered out, checking the darkening street. Then she hurried along the pavement towards her Mercedes, unlocked the door and slid into the plush leather seat.

She closed her eyes and let out a sigh of contentment. She'd had many other lovers, of course, most of them younger than her. But Roberto was different. In the past two months, she'd actually *missed* him, counting the days until his return from Paris. This feeling disturbed her, because she'd always seen her previous lovers as disposable. They performed a service, just as any other member of her staff did. She'd been disconcertingly pleased to see him in the past few days. But just now, he'd announced he was thinking of going abroad permanently.

As she started the engine and steered the Mercedes through the busy rush-hour traffic out towards Como, Donatella decided she must use all the weapons at her disposal to make sure he stayed.

Roberto Rossini deserved to be a major star. She would help him, not only because of his obvious talent, but because – Donatella could hardly believe the thought that had popped into her head – she was falling in love with him.

One thing was for certain: she had to keep Roberto in Milan.

'Wonderful news, Rosanna!' Luca passed the letter across the table to his sister. 'It's from Signora Moretti, Abi's aunt. She says her committee has agreed to the idea of a recital at Beata Vergine Maria.'

Rosanna read through the letter quickly. 'Luca, I'm so pleased for you.'

'I must go and tell Don Edoardo. He'll be very happy.'

'Of course. But they say the recital will be at Easter, Luca,' frowned Rosanna. 'We were planning on going home to see Papa and Carlotta.'

'We can go home the day after the recital, Rosanna. I'm sure Papa will understand. This means so much to me. Signora Moretti has said that two members of the La Scala opera company have agreed to perform.' Luca's eyes were shining as he spoke. 'She's suggested we charge fifty thousand lire a ticket. With two hundred or so guests, it'll mean we'll raise almost enough to restore the fresco. But, Rosanna, there'll be so much to do! We'll have to arrange for extra seating, decorate the church with flowers, organise refreshments . . .'

Rosanna watched her brother as he talked animatedly about the work involved. 'Luca, what is it about Beata Vergine Maria that means so much to you? I've never seen you happier than you are this morning.'

Luca looked at his sister, searching for the words. And discovered it was impossible to find them. 'It's hard to explain, Rosanna. It's very special to me, that's all I can say. Now, if you've finished breakfast, I'll walk with you to school. I want to tell Don Edoardo the news immediately.'

Luca waved goodbye to Rosanna as she walked into the school, then quickly made his way to Beata Vergine Maria.

Don Edoardo was hearing confession, so Luca sat in a pew and waited until he emerged from the box and his parishioner left.

'Excellent news!' Luca said as he handed Don Edoardo the letter from Sonia Moretti. 'We shall raise a lot of money, surely?'

'Yes,' the old priest nodded, enjoying the happiness on the face of the young man he'd become so fond of. 'I think your Madonna will be very happy.'

'I hope so.' Luca stared towards the altar. His shoulders sagged and the smile drained from his face. He shook his head. 'Even though, by organising this recital, I'm in some small way helping, sometimes I become so frustrated.'

'I know, Luca, I understand.' Don Edoardo put a comforting hand on his shoulder.

'But I must be patient and wait. It's part of His plan to test me, I'm sure.'

'Well, let us pray together, for a blessing on this church and what we try to do to restore it.'

The two heads, one grey, one dark, bowed together in prayer. Afterwards, Don Edoardo made coffee and they began to plan for the recital.

'We'll need many more chairs, Don Edoardo. There is room for another twenty at the back by the font,' said Luca.

'There are some chairs in the crypt, but they're old and dirty. Have a look, and if they are no good, perhaps we could ask the school to lend us some for the occasion.' Don Edoardo passed Luca a large key. 'There's no electricity down there. Use the oil lamp hanging on the hook by the door. There are matches on the shelf next to the lamp.' He checked his watch. 'I must leave now – I have a bereaved mother to visit.'

When the priest had gone, Luca sat and stared at the statue of the Madonna on the altar. She hadn't spoken to him again since that first wonderful day, but he could feel her calming influence all around him. Eventually, he stood up, walked to the door of the crypt and unlocked it. As Don Edoardo had suggested, he took the oil lamp off its hook and lit it before walking carefully down the creaking stairs, the lamp emanating a shadowy glow. He stood on the bottom step and cast the light around.

The crypt was not big, and was jammed with all manner of discarded junk. A layer of dust covered everything and spiders had been allowed to create elaborate webs undisturbed. As he picked his way carefully through the clutter, he decided that sorting out the crypt would be another task he could complete. He found the wooden chairs Don Edoardo had mentioned and began to unstack them, only to discover that all of them had either a leg missing or no back. He turned round and knelt down to pick up a rotting prayer book from a pile on the floor. As he opened it, the pages disintegrated in his fingers.

Suddenly, the oil lamp went out and the crypt descended

into complete darkness. He ferreted in his pocket for his lighter and reignited the wick, but the lamp went out again almost immediately. As he did his best to stumble back to the entrance, deciding a torch would serve him better, Luca caught his foot on something. Letting out a yelp of pain, he fell with a thump, his ankle taking the brunt of his fall.

Luca lay in the darkness, unable to move until the pain lessened. Something crawled across his hand and he pulled it back quickly. Trying to keep calm, he eventually retrieved his lighter from his trouser pocket and managed to rekindle the oil lamp. Looking down, he saw he'd tripped over the corner of an ancient leather-bound trunk which had been partially hidden by a pile of moth-eaten vestments. Putting the lamp down beside him, he hauled the garments to one side, coughing as a cloud of dust filled the dank air. Gingerly, he lifted the heavy lid off the trunk.

The interior was lined with purple velvet, and as Luca put his hands tentatively inside, they grasped a large, heavy object. He struggled to pick it up and out of the trunk, and shining his lamp upon it, saw an ornately engraved chalice, tarnished by age and neglect. Taking out his handkerchief, he spat on the fabric to moisten it, then rubbed a small spot of the metal to clean it, revealing the lucent gleam of what he was sure must be silver. With a sense of growing excitement, he placed the chalice carefully on the floor beside him, then began to remove the rest of the trunk's contents.

The next item was a prayer book, the pages yellowing and fragile, but, protected from the damp by the thick leather of the trunk, still in one piece. Next out of the trunk was another set of priest's vestments. As Luca lifted them out, he felt something solid wrapped inside. At that moment the oil lamp flickered ominously and, not wishing to be plunged into darkness again, Luca gathered the chalice and prayer book from the floor, and rolled the vestments under his arm. Hooking the wire handle of the lamp over one finger, he groped his way towards the stairs.

In the vestry, Luca laid the vestments on the floor and unfolded them slowly. In the centre of one of the garments he found a small, battered leather pouch, not much larger than his hand. Carefully extracting the contents of the pouch, Luca saw he was holding a small canvas drawing mounted on a crude wooden frame. He stared down at the instantly familiar face.

It was as if the artist had managed to capture her grace, her serenity and her soul. This was how he *himself* imagined the Madonna when he closed his eyes and prayed. The drawing, executed in fine, delicate lines of a reddish-brown colour, was simple, yet so perfect that Luca could not tear his eyes from it.

He stared at it for a long time. Miraculously, having been so well shrouded from light and damp, the drawing itself hardly showed signs of age. Turning the edges of the canvas gently over, taking care to touch it as little as possible, Luca searched for something to give him a clue as to the artist.

Maybe his find was worthless, but Luca nonetheless felt a shiver slide unbidden up his spine. Don Edoardo would be back later and he could show him the drawing and the chalice and see if the old priest knew of their existence. Until then . . . Luca reverently replaced the canvas in the pouch. He stowed the chalice, the prayer book and the drawing inside the sacrament cupboard, then turned the key and locked it.

11

'So, the performers will stand around the altar?'

'Yes.'

'And the grand piano will be placed here?'

'Yes.' Luca watched as the woman prowled round the church.

'And we will serve wine over there by the font? What do you think?'

'It's a good idea, Signora Bianchi,' replied Don Edoardo, surreptitiously raising an exasperated eyebrow at Luca.

'Good. So, everything seems to be under control. Demand for the tickets has been excellent. I think we'll have a full house for our little recital.' Donatella advanced towards the altar and looked in distaste at the tattered altar cloth that had clearly seen better days. 'Have you another piece of material we could use for the evening? This looks rather . . . shabby.'

'No, we haven't another. This is what the recital is all about, is it not, signora? To raise funds for new altar cloths and other renovations,' Don Edoardo reminded her patiently.

'Of course. Well, we can dress the church with candles, and stand flower displays on either side of the statue of the Madonna.'

'Yes,' Don Edoardo agreed once more as he watched Donatella pick up the silver chalice, which had been lovingly polished since Luca's discovery and placed on the altar.

'This is a beautiful piece of workmanship. And very old, I should imagine.' Donatella turned it round in her hands as she studied it.

'Luca found it in the crypt some weeks ago. I've been meaning to get someone to value it – for insurance purposes, you understand – but my mind has been on other things.'

'I see.' Donatella replaced the chalice and glanced at Don Edoardo. 'Although my husband is an art dealer, he has friends who would be well placed to give an opinion on something like this. Shall I ask him to find someone to value it for you?'

'That would be very kind,' agreed Don Edoardo. 'You say your husband is an art dealer?'

'Yes, he is.'

'Then Luca, I think you should go and get the drawing you found.'

Luca made off in the direction of the vestry.

'Signor Menici also found a line drawing,' Don Edoardo explained. 'It may be of no value, but perhaps your husband would take a look at that too?'

'Of course,' Donatella said, nodding.

Luca was soon back with the drawing. 'Here.' He handed it to her carefully.

Donatella stared at the canvas. 'Why, it's such an exquisite sketch of the Madonna,' she exclaimed admiringly. 'You say you found this down in the crypt of this church?'

'Yes, in an old trunk. We checked the records and from the inscription in his prayer book, we are sure it was the property of Don Dino Cinquetti. He was *il parroco*, the priest here, during the sixteenth century.'

'So this drawing could be hundreds of years old? Yet it looks virtually unmarked,' breathed Donatella.

'I think it must be because it was so well protected. It probably hasn't seen any light for three hundred years.'

'Well, I promise I'll take the greatest care of it. Would you wrap the chalice for me?'

Don Edoardo looked uneasy. 'Could your husband not come here to the church to look at both artefacts?'

'He's a busy man, Don Edoardo, and is only home for the next few days before he flies to the United States. You have my word no harm will come to either the chalice or the drawing; and this way I should have an answer for you quickly. I'll take them straight home, where I assure you we have excellent security. Surely you trust me?' Donatella queried.

'Of course, signora,' the old priest murmured in embarrassment.

Giovanni Bianchi stared at the two objects on the table in front of him.

'Where did you say these were found?'

'La Chiesa Della Beata Vergine Maria. Apparently they were packed in an old trunk in the crypt with the belongings of a dead priest. Indications are that the priest lived in the sixteenth century. I thought the chalice might be worth something,' Donatella explained.

'Yes, yes, I'm sure it will be, but this' – Giovanni picked up the drawing – 'this is quite breathtaking. You say the sixteenth century?'

'That's what the priest told me.'

Giovanni pulled a magnifying glass out of his jacket pocket and studied the drawing carefully. When he looked up at his wife, Donatella saw the glint of excitement in his eyes.

'When you look at this, does the face seem familiar?'

'Of course. It's the Madonna,' she replied scornfully.

'So,' continued Giovanni patiently, 'how do you define the image you have in your mind's eye of the Madonna?'

'Through the paintings and drawings I've seen of her, I suppose.'

'Exactly. And who has given us one of the most famous images of the Madonna?'

'I . . .' Donatella shrugged. 'Leonardo da Vinci, of course.'

'Yes. Wait one moment.' Giovanni left the sitting room and returned a few minutes later with the catalogue of the National Gallery, London. He turned the pages until he found what he was looking for. 'There.' Giovanni laid the catalogue next to the drawing on the table. 'Study the face, the detail. There are strong similarities, yes?'

Donatella looked carefully. 'Yes, Giovanni, but . . . I . . . surely it can't be . . .'

'I'll need to make the most careful enquiries, but my instincts tell me this is either the most excellent fake, or we may have discovered a lost Leonardo drawing.'

'You mean, the old priest and the young man have discovered it,' corrected Donatella.

'Of course,' Giovanni agreed hastily. 'I must take this with me to New York. I want a friend of mine to see it. He's an expert in the verification of the great masters. He's also discreet – for a percentage of the profits, that is,' he added slyly.

'Well, I must ask Don Edoardo for his permission before you do that, of course,' countered his wife.

'But surely the priest doesn't need to know just yet? You could tell him that both the chalice and the drawing are being appraised and that I'll have an answer for them in a week's time. And, Donatella?'

'Yes, *caro*?'

'I do not want you telling anybody else about this until we know the truth.'

'Of course.' Donatella registered the gleam of avarice in her husband's eyes. 'I shall do as you ask.'

Ten days later, Donatella visited Don Edoardo at Beata Vergine Maria.

'Good news,' she smiled at him. 'Excellent news, in fact.' Donatella settled herself in a pew.

'Your husband thinks the chalice might be worth something?'

'Yes, it is apparently extremely valuable. My husband says that, at auction, it may go for fifty thousand dollars. That's about thirty million lire.'

'Thirty million lire!' Don Edoardo was stunned. 'I hadn't *dreamt* it would be worth so much!'

'My husband wishes to know what you would like him to do – whether you wish to sell the chalice. If you do, he can arrange for it to go into an auction.'

'I . . . I hadn't considered the possibility of a sale. I will have to talk to my bishop. I'm not sure what he will want to do,' sighed Don Edoardo. 'The Church may well want to keep the chalice in its possession. The decision isn't mine to make.'

'Don Edoardo, please, come and sit down.' Donatella patted the pew next to her. The priest consented warily.

'Please forgive me my impertinence, but what is it your beautiful church requires at the moment?'

'Money, of course, to restore it to its former glory,' he admitted, feeling out of his depth in a conversation of this kind.

'Exactly. Now, may I ask whether you have told anyone of your find?'

'No. I didn't think it necessary until we discovered whether we'd found something of value.'

'I see.' Donatella nodded. 'Personally, I think it's doubtful that, if you tell your bishop, you or this church will see much of the proceeds from the sale of the chalice, even assuming he wishes to sell it.'

'I think, Signora Bianchi, that your assumption is correct,' Don Edoardo agreed uneasily.

'Well now, my husband and I may have come up with a solution. He is prepared to pay you the amount of money he believes the chalice will achieve at auction. The figure I mentioned was thirty million lire. He will then sell the chalice to a private collector. You will have a lot of money to help restore your church and no one need know the truth.'

Don Edoardo stared at her. 'But, Signora Bianchi, surely my bishop will wonder where such a large amount of money came from?'

'Of course. And you'll tell him, and anyone else who asks, that Signor Bianchi was so shocked by the state of the building when he and his wife visited for the recital she had helped organise that he decided to make a large donation there and then.'

'I see.'

'Don Edoardo, I understand you don't wish to do anything dishonest. My husband and I will act in whatever way you wish. But personally, I think that, with your beautiful church in need of so much work, and with the chalice being found here, it may be God's will that it is used for the church's exclusive benefit, no?'

'You may be right, of course, Signora Bianchi. But how could you be sure that no one would ever know?' Beads of sweat pricked Don Edoardo's forehead. Donatella observed them and knew she had her prey firmly in her sights. She went in for the kill.

'You have my word on that. The chalice can be sold privately abroad. My husband has a long list of wealthy private collectors who wish to be discreet. And just think how much work could be accomplished in God's name with the proceeds.'

'I . . . must think.' Don Edoardo sighed deeply. 'I must ask for God's guidance.'

'Of course.' Donatella took a card out of her handbag. 'Why don't you telephone me when you've made your decision?'

'I will. Thank you, Signora Bianchi, for all your help.'

'Really, it was nothing.' She stood up to leave. 'Oh, I almost forgot about the drawing,' she added casually. 'My husband doesn't believe it's valuable. Certainly it is finely drawn, but then the Madonna has been pictured many, many times by the world's most illustrious artists. He doubts this little sketch would generate much interest in comparison.'

'Of course, we assumed that would be the case,' said the priest, with a deferential nod.

'However,' continued Donatella as she buttoned her

immaculately tailored coat, 'I've become quite attached to it, and therefore would like to make you a private offer to buy it for myself. How does three million lire sound?'

Don Edoardo looked at her in disbelief. 'Like a generous sum of money. You're most kind, but I must think about it. I shall be sure to speak to you as soon as I've made my decision.'

'Then I look forward to hearing from you. Good afternoon.' Donatella nodded graciously and swept out of the church.

'Good afternoon, Signora Bianchi,' Don Edoardo murmured to her departing back.

Two days later, Donatella handed her husband a glass of champagne as he entered the sitting room.

'He's agreed?'

'Yes. He telephoned me this afternoon.'

'*Cara*, you've been wonderful,' said Giovanni. 'Now, I must call New York and tell my client the good news. And of course, you must have something for yourself out of the proceeds. Anything you want.'

Donatella eyed her husband, a slight smile curving the corner of her red lips.

'I'll think of something, Giovanni, I promise.'

12

The church was beginning to fill up as Luca helped usher the well-dressed guests to their seats. The candles flickered atmospherically in their holders along the aisle and at the altar, and the scent of the massed arrangements of lilies filled the air.

After Signor Bianchi's offer, Luca had prayed with Don Edoardo for guidance and they had both come to similar conclusions. They had decided this offer was a gift from God. How could it be anything else? If they accepted it, restoration work could begin on the church immediately.

Don Edoardo came bustling up to him. 'I think most of our guests have arrived and our performers are ready. Luca, I thank you from the bottom of my heart. It seems as if, from the day you walked into my church, you've brought nothing but blessings upon it.'

'It's God who brought me here, Don Edoardo,' Luca replied gently.

'I know, and may He bless you also.' He patted Luca's shoulder and made his way down the aisle. Luca followed him and caught the eye of his sister sitting in one of the front pews with the rest of the performers. She gave him a small wave and he winked back. Then Luca saw a familiar tall, dark-haired figure in a dinner jacket hurrying down the aisle. He turned away, fighting back his automatic revulsion. Nothing would spoil tonight for him. Nothing.

Don Edoardo and Paolo de Vito climbed the steps and stood in front of the altar.

'Ladies and gentlemen,' said Don Edoardo, 'thank you for joining us here on this very special night. It is the time of year for celebration: of resurrection, of rebirth, which is what we hope to achieve also for our church. May I say a particular thank you to The Friends of the Milan Opera for making this evening possible. And now Signor Paolo de Vito, the artistic director of La Scala, is here to introduce the programme.'

'Good evening, ladies and gentlemen.' The audience clapped as Paolo addressed them. 'To begin our programme, may I present the students of the *scuola di musica*, singing the sextet from *Lucia di Lammermoor*.'

Paolo left the steps and six students made their way to the front of the church. They arranged themselves before the beautifully dressed altar, and the recital began.

Roberto, however, paid no attention to the setting and hardly listened to the music. He was staring in fascination at Donatella, who was sitting on the other side of the church beside her husband. Roberto wondered if they still made love; he supposed they must do occasionally. It was amazing what money could buy, he thought, as a polite round of applause came from the audience and the first students took their bows.

Roberto found he couldn't help himself and began to undress Donatella mentally. But as he did so, he became aware of a voice so sweet and pure it seemed to naturally belong in a place of worship. And it was a voice he had heard before. It was singing one of his favourite arias: '*Sempre libera*', from *La Traviata*. Abandoning all thoughts of Donatella, Roberto cast his eyes forwards to study its owner.

She had grown several inches taller, but was still as slender as a reed. Her thick, dark hair fell in soft, shining waves below her shoulders. Her skin was pale and almost luminous by candlelight, with only a hint of colour resting on her high cheekbones. Her mesmerising brown eyes expressed every emotion of the aria she was singing. The voice was more mature now, having been trained and developed, but it was the same voice, the voice which had caused him to weep when it had sung '*Ave Maria*' in Naples many years ago. The voice of a little girl who had now become a beautiful woman.

Rosanna sat down with a sigh of relief. Abi squeezed her hand. 'You were wonderful,' she whispered. 'Well done.'

Paolo stood up. 'And now, please welcome our two very special guests from La Scala, Anna Dupré and Roberto Rossini, singing "*O soave fanciulla*" from *La Bohème*.'

Rosanna stared at Roberto Rossini as he began to sing. It was six years since she'd seen him last. As she watched him, her heartbeat increased and her palms became clammy.

She had dismissed the way she'd felt about him all those years ago in Naples as a silly schoolgirl crush, but seeing him now, she knew that the feeling was real and still very much alive inside her. As Roberto's voice joined Anna Dupré's in a glorious crescendo, Rosanna remembered her ambition to sing with him one day, their talents united . . . it was a dream she fervently wished to fulfil.

The recital came to an end and there was loud applause as the artistes took their bows. Don Edoardo stood up and addressed the audience.

'Thank you, ladies and gentlemen, for your presence here tonight, to listen to what has been a most magnificent recital. And now, Sonia Moretti, chairman of the committee, would like to say a few words.'

Sonia joined Don Edoardo at the front of the church.

'Ladies and gentlemen. Thanks to your generosity and that of the artistes of La Scala and students of the *scuola di musica*, this evening has raised almost ten million lire.' Sonia waited until the applause had lessened. 'But there is more. Here I have a cheque for Don Edoardo from Giovanni and Donatella Bianchi. They've been so moved by the sight of this beautiful church that they have decided to make their own personal contribution. Their modesty does not allow me to reveal how much they have donated, but it will go a long way towards restoring Beata Vergine Maria to its former glory. Don Edoardo, please accept the cheque.'

Don Edoardo did so with a humble bow, then turned to the congregation. 'I cannot express my gratitude to Signor and Signora Bianchi. I'm overwhelmed by their generosity. God bless them. Thank you also to each and every one of you for supporting our recital. I hope you will all return after the restoration work is completed, to see what a difference your patronage has made. Wine will now be served at the back of the church for anyone who wishes it.'

As the audience began to rise from the pews, Abi smiled at Rosanna as they walked down the aisle together. 'This evening's been a roaring success. I should think your brother will be over the moon.'

'Yes.' Rosanna's eyes were shining with happiness. 'It's wonderful. Luca will be thrilled.'

'Would you mind if I leave you to go and speak to him and Don Edoardo? I have an idea I want to discuss with him.'

'Of course not. I'll see you later.' Suddenly, a hand touched her shoulder lightly from behind.

'Excuse me for intruding.'

Rosanna turned and looked up into a pair of achingly familiar deep-blue eyes. Her heart began to race against her chest.

'Rosanna Menici?'

'Yes?'

'Do you remember me?'

'Of course I do, Roberto,' she said shyly.

'It's many years since we last met in person, though my mother wrote to tell me of your move to Milan and of your mamma's death. I was very sorry to hear the sad news. How is your papa?'

'As well as can be expected. He misses Mamma very much. Tomorrow, Luca and I are going home to Naples for a week.'

'Then do give him my condolences and best wishes.'

'I will, thank you.' Their eyes locked for a moment, the colour rising in Rosanna's pale cheeks as they stared at each other. Roberto broke the silence.

'So, as I knew he would, Luigi Vincenzi helped you?' he said.

'Yes. He was wonderful. He even arranged for Paolo de Vito to come and hear me sing at a recital in his villa last summer. Paolo offered me a scholarship and so here I am in Milan. And it's all thanks to you, Roberto,' she added softly.

'I did nothing, Rosanna. It's Luigi Vincenzi who should take the credit. And from hearing you tonight, I think he's done an excellent job. I'm sure it won't be long before you're performing on the stage of La Scala.' Roberto smiled down at her, his eyes filled with warmth.

'You sang beautifully too.'

'I'm glad you think so.'

There was another awkward pause between them.

'Well,' said Roberto eventually, 'I'd better do my duty and mingle with the guests. It was so good to see you again, Rosanna. If you ever need any help or advice, you can always find me at La Scala.'

'Thank you, Roberto.'

'Goodbye, little one. Work hard.'

He waved as he walked up the aisle towards the crowd at the back of the church. Rosanna's eyes followed him avidly, until one of the guests, eager to congratulate her, claimed her attention.

A few minutes later, Abi was back at her side. 'I didn't know you knew the bad boy of La Scala.'

'What do you mean?' Rosanna frowned.

'Oh, my Aunt Sonia says that Roberto Rossini has the most terrible reputation with women. He's been through most of the chorus and the soloists. Mind you, I'm not surprised.' Abi shrugged. 'He's completely divine, don't you think?'

'I suppose he is.' Rosanna was still watching Roberto.

'And, by the way he was looking at you, I think you could be his next victim,' Abi teased her.

'Oh no, it isn't like that at all, Abi. We both come from Naples and our parents were good friends. Anyway, he's far too famous to be interested in me. And much older than me too,' she added defensively.

'Honestly, Rosanna, I'm only teasing you. Sometimes you can be so straight.' Abi's face broke into a wide smile as Luca joined them.

'This is indeed a wonderful night, isn't it, Rosanna?'

'Yes. You must be very happy.'

'I am. Thanks to Signor Bianchi's donation, other guests have followed suit. Don Edoardo is still collecting cheques.' Luca's eyes were full of joy.

'I think we should go on to a bar and celebrate,' Abi suggested.

'I'd like that very much, but unfortunately I must stay here and help Don Edoardo clear the church for Mass tomorrow morning.'

'Never mind. Rosanna and I will go for a drink then,' Abi replied.

'Okay, but don't be too late home, Rosanna.'

'No, Luca. *Ciao*.' Rosanna kissed her brother on the cheek.

The two girls said their farewells and left the church.

'I know a place just around the corner where we can get a bottle of wine and something to eat. I'm starving,' said Abi.

The bar was crowded, but they found a table and ordered some wine and two plates of pasta.

'Cheers, as we say in England,' said Abi, holding her glass aloft. 'Here's to wine, men and song,' she laughed.

'Cheers,' copied Rosanna. 'By the way, what was it that you wanted to talk to Luca and Don Eduardo about?'

'Oh, I just thought that now the church is to be restored, it would be wonderful to reinstate a choir. Don Edoardo says they haven't had one for years. I thought I could help, what with my contacts at the school, and they'd need someone to coach the singers, of course.'

Rosanna looked at her friend in surprise. 'But with your schedule at the school, how will you find the time? Besides, you've often said you've no interest in religion.'

'No, but I've definitely got an interest in someone who practises it,' replied Abi artfully.

Rosanna stared at her. 'You don't mean Luca?'

'As a matter of fact, I do. He looked so happy tonight,' Abi continued. 'He really does love that church, doesn't he? But I do wonder what he's going to do with the rest of his life. I mean, he can't live through it forever.'

'You didn't know Luca before,' Rosanna replied defensively. 'He worked for Papa at our café and had no time for a life of his own. And he did it to pay for my singing lessons. If watching the church restored makes him happy, then I'm glad for him.'

'Sorry, Rosanna, I'm not criticising him. Quite the opposite, in fact. As you might have gathered, Luca fascinates me,' Abi confessed. 'He's so different from other men. I mean, most young men of his age have careers, girlfriends. Luca doesn't seem to need those kinds of things.'

Rosanna took a sip of her wine and studied Abi carefully. 'You really like him? In . . . *that* way?'

'Oh yes, I'm afraid I do. Luca is so . . . mysterious. I think there are hidden depths, just waiting to be explored by the right woman. And now I've found a way to see more of him by organising a choir, I've got a better chance to find out what they are. You don't mind, do you?'

Rosanna shook her head and chuckled. 'Abi, you think of nothing but romance.'

'What else is there to think about?'

'Your future as an opera singer, for one thing.'

'Oh, yes, there's that, but I'm a sensible girl, Rosanna. I know I have a decent enough voice, but it's nothing compared to yours. If I'm lucky, I might make it to the chorus, but I'm realistic enough to know that I'm never going to be the next Callas. So, unlike you, who's wedded to her art, I have to think of men to stop me getting depressed when I hear you sing.' Abi gave a mock smile.

'Well, I think you have a lovely voice. You wouldn't be at the school if you didn't. Stop putting yourself down.'

'Get real, Rosanna.' Abi shook her head. 'My aunt is a big noise on the fundraising committee. She's married to a man who's extremely generous to both the opera and the school. You don't think this might just have had something to do with a place being made available to me, do you? In three years' time, while you sweep into your rightful place in the company, it'll be left to my aunt to pull strings and secure me a future at the back of the chorus. To be honest, I don't know whether I want that. Charity, I mean.' A shadow of sadness crossed Abi's face. 'Ah well, being here in Milan is good for my Italian and a little time abroad is what nice English girls should have before they settle down with a suitable husband.'

'Then . . . maybe it's me who's odd.' Rosanna took another sip of her wine.

'In what way?'

'Well, I don't think about men – ever.'

'Really?' Abi raised a sceptical eyebrow. 'When I saw you talking to Roberto Rossini tonight, you didn't look completely immune to his charms.'

'Roberto is different.'

'And why is that?' Abi looked at her intently.

'Because . . . because he is, that's all,' Rosanna sighed. 'Anyway, I don't wish to talk about it. Oh look, here's our spaghetti,' she said, wishing to divert Abi from further questioning.

'Well,' said Abi beadily, raising her fork to attack the steaming bowl in front of her, 'have it your way, but you don't fool me in the slightest, Rosanna Menici.'

Don Edoardo and Luca were surveying the debris that still had to be cleared away.

'Luca, do you remember me?' A hand slapped his shoulder, making Luca jump. He turned round and swallowed hard when he saw who it was.

'Of course. How are you, Roberto?'

'I'm well, very well. It's a small world, isn't it? You're living in Milan too?'

'I'm taking care of my sister here,' he replied stiffly.

'Yes, I spoke to her earlier. She's grown up since I last saw her,' Roberto said. 'And how is your other sister, the lovely, er . . .' Roberto scratched his head.

'Carlotta. She's well. Now, if you'll excuse me, I must help Don Edoardo. Goodnight.' Luca nodded curtly and walked swiftly away.

Registering the snub, and already unsettled by the stirring he'd felt on seeing Rosanna Menici again, Roberto was in a devilish mood. He crossed to stand next to Donatella and surreptitiously laid a hand on her firm behind.

'Take care, someone might see,' she whispered furiously, stepping away from him as though he were carrying the plague.

'But your husband has left, has he not? I saw him walking out of the church earlier. And besides . . .' Roberto leant in towards her and smiled wickedly. 'I want you. Now.'

Fifteen minutes later, Luca found Don Edoardo slumped in a chair in the vestry.

'Go home,' he entreated the old priest. 'There's little left to do here, and you're exhausted. I'll lock up.'

'Thank you, Luca. I will. Could you place these in the sacrament cupboard?' Don Edoardo handed Luca an envelope full of cheques. 'They'll be safer here than with me at my apartment and I shall bank them first thing tomorrow. It's been an extraordinary evening, hasn't it?'

'Yes, it has,' Luca agreed.

'And it's all due to you, my dear friend. When the time comes, you know I'll be recommending you most highly,' he smiled. 'Goodnight, Luca.'

When Don Edoardo had left the vestry by the private back entrance, Luca unlocked the sacrament cupboard and placed the cheques inside a tin box where they kept some lire to buy tea and coffee. Relocking the cupboard, he hid the key, then genuflected and knelt down in front of the small altar Don Edoardo used for private contemplation. He thanked God for tonight, and also for helping him discover the valuable silver chalice. He'd been disappointed when Don Edoardo had told him Donatella's husband had said the drawing was worth very little; if that was the case, it was a pity they couldn't have kept it here in the church. But Don

Edoardo had been so grateful for the money from the silver chalice, he'd felt unable to refuse Donatella Bianchi's personal request to buy the drawing.

Luca sat for a few moments longer in quiet prayer. Eventually, he stood up and, switching the light off, closed the door behind him. Walking along the side of the church towards the front door, he heard a noise from the direction of the altar. Luca turned towards it. Thieves? Heart thumping, he crept forward to investigate.

To one side of the altar, entwined on the floor, were a man and a woman. They were both fully clothed, but what they were doing was all too evident. The man lay on top, and beneath him, the woman groaned in pleasure, her legs curling round his back. The groaning reached a pitch and the man cried out, then collapsed, spent, on top of her.

Too shocked and dumbfounded to confront them, Luca ducked behind a pillar and watched as the couple stood up, straightened their clothes and walked arm in arm down the aisle. He knew exactly who they were.

'*Caro*, that was so very wicked! I will call you on Thursday, yes?'

'Of course.' The man kissed the top of the woman's dark head and they strolled towards the door as though nothing had happened.

The two figures disappeared into the night, leaving a horrified Luca and his desecrated church behind them.

He arrived home much later, his heart in turmoil. To perform such an act *there* . . . the sight had wiped the happiness of the rest of the evening from his mind.

He quietly opened the door to Rosanna's room to check

she was safely in bed. Her light was on, the book she'd been reading still clutched in her hand, although her eyes were closed. Luca walked across the room to turn the light off.

'Luca?' Rosanna opened her eyes.

'Yes, *piccolina*?'

'Wasn't it an incredible evening?' she said sleepily.

'I . . . yes, it was.'

'What's the matter?' She frowned, propping herself up on her elbows. 'You don't look happy.'

'I'm fine. Just tired, that's all. Go to sleep now.'

'Wasn't Roberto wonderful? His voice is so beautiful and he's so handsome.' Rosanna stretched and yawned.

'Rosanna, I don't think Roberto is a good man.'

'That's what Abi said. She said he . . .'

'What?'

'Oh, nothing. Goodnight, Luca.'

'Goodnight.'

Luca switched off the light and made his way to his bedroom.

That night sleep did not come easily. He couldn't forget the dreamy look on Rosanna's face as she had talked about Roberto – the man who had ruined Carlotta's life and now could not even remember her name. Roberto, who had performed an act of sacrilege in his beloved church. Luca's stomach turned every time he thought of it.

Although he tried to convince himself that Rosanna's words had only been an ill-timed coincidence, his instincts told him that Roberto Rossini was not finished with his family yet.

13

'Thank you for meeting me today, Paolo.' Donatella smiled beguilingly as he sat down opposite her. The fashionable restaurant was already humming with well-to-do patrons. '*Aperitivo*? I'll have a Bellini.' She snapped her fingers imperiously to summon the waiter.

'Then I'll join you,' agreed Paolo. 'You are well, Signora Bianchi?'

'Very well. And please, call me Donatella.'

'So' – Paolo was in no mood for small talk – 'what was it you wanted to discuss with me?'

'I have a suggestion to put to you.'

'I see,' Paolo said warily. 'Pray tell me.'

'Recently I have come into a little money – a generous gift from my husband. And you know how I regard the *scuola di musica* as a vital part of the arts here in Milan.'

'It is indeed a breeding ground for new talent and the opera company would be lost without it,' Paolo nodded, wondering where the conversation was headed.

'Exactly. So, I'm thinking of making a generous one-off donation to provide three scholarships for talented pupils

whose parents can't afford the fees. I know at present that you provide an occasional gifted pupil with funds, but that the school's resources are limited.'

'This is true. Exactly how much were you thinking of?'

Donatella named the figure.

'I . . .' Paolo was taken aback. 'That's an extremely large amount.'

'Ah, here are our Bellinis.' Donatella lifted her glass. 'So, will you accept my offer?'

'It really is a most generous gesture. And what would you . . . ?'

'What would I want in return?' asked Donatella. 'Obviously for the scholarship to be named "Bianchi", and' – she paused, fingering the side of her glass – 'for Roberto Rossini to open the new season at La Scala in a leading role.'

Paolo groaned inwardly. He'd known there would be a price. There always was with a woman like Donatella. 'I see.'

'I have followed his career for a number of years now, and I really do think his ability is underused. He has the makings of a star. All my girlfriends agree with me,' Donatella underlined, as if that settled the matter.

'And I too believe Roberto Rossini is a very talented performer. But sometimes, Donatella' – Paolo chose his words carefully – 'there are . . . things that can prevent certain singers from getting the roles their talent deserves. You are right. He does indeed have the vocal and physical ability to make his mark on the opera world, but his personality . . .' Paolo sighed. 'Well, let's just say he doesn't help himself.'

'You mean, you don't like him?' Donatella asked him bluntly.

'No, I assure you that isn't the problem. I mean that I have issues with him as a member of the company. He's unreliable, somewhat immature and, I have to say, selfish on stage. There are a lot of his fellow artistes who find him difficult to work with.'

'But surely all performers can be temperamental? And I know, Paolo, that Roberto Rossini is destined for great things. If not with La Scala, then with some other company. And we wouldn't want that, would we?' Donatella eyed him speculatively.

'I . . .' Paolo tussled with his conscience. He understood the deal only too well. For this one concession, he'd be able to give three young singers the opportunity to be trained. Finally, he took a deep breath. 'It just so happens I have scheduled *Ernani* to open the next season and, in spite of my personal feelings, I have to admit the man in question is perfect for the title role.'

'There, you see, Paolo, it is fate,' she encouraged.

'All right, Donatella,' he sighed. 'Roberto Rossini will open the new season.'

'Wonderful! I'm sure you won't regret it.' Donatella clapped her hands together in obvious delight. 'Just one more thing. You must promise me that Roberto will never know this conversation took place.'

'Of course.'

'Good. Now, shall we order?'

Paolo left the restaurant an hour later. As he walked towards La Scala he wondered how long Roberto Rossini had been having an affair with Donatella Bianchi.

*

Donatella drove home with a satisfied smile playing on her lips. So, it had cost a great deal of money, but it was a small price to pay to keep Roberto in Milan.

Roberto was given a message that he was to see Paolo de Vito in his office after morning rehearsals. Wondering what it was he'd done wrong this time, but deciding he didn't care any longer, he made his way up to the artistic director's office and knocked on the door.

'Come in.'

Roberto opened the door. 'You wished to see me?'

Paolo sat behind his desk, his arms folded. He smiled at Roberto. 'Take a seat, please.'

Roberto did so.

'I'm thinking of casting you as the lead in *Ernani*. It will be the opening production of the season. Are you ready for the role, do you think?'

Roberto stared at Paolo in amazement. He was so shocked he couldn't reply.

'Well?' Paolo looked at him expectantly.

'I . . . why, of course! Since I was a student, it's been my ambition to open the season here in a title role.'

'I'm sure. And I've decided it's time you were given your chance. I believe you have what it takes to become a tenor of the first magnitude.'

'Thank you, Paolo.' Roberto did his best to look humble, but was barely able to contain his mounting euphoria.

'I've told you of my plan now because we still have four months of the old season left, then the summer sabbatical. This will give you time to study the role. In other words, you have seven months to prove to me I'm making the right decision.'

'I swear, Paolo,' Roberto reassured him earnestly, 'I will work like a man possessed.'

'But, Roberto, I must warn you, if you let me down, your future with us will be bleak. From now on, no arriving late, no silly antics on stage. Taking a lead role requires commitment at a level you've never experienced before. I want you to show me you have the maturity to do it. Do you understand me?'

'Paolo, if you give me this opportunity, I promise I won't let you down. Who will be my Elvira?' Roberto enquired.

'Anna Dupré.'

'*Magnifico!* We work well together, I think.'

'Only on stage, I hope.' Paolo raised a warning eyebrow.

'Of course.' Roberto had the grace to blush. 'As a matter of fact, I'm committed at present.'

'Really?' Paolo feigned surprise. 'Let's hope it stays that way, both personally and professionally. Remember, opening the season at La Scala is one of the biggest honours bestowed on any tenor. If you receive the attention you might when you make your debut as Ernani, I can only hope it won't go to your head.'

'Of course not.'

'Well then, that is all,' he nodded.

Roberto stood up and reached across the table to shake Paolo's hand vigorously. 'Thank you, thank you. I shall reward your faith in me, I promise.'

'Good.' Paolo breathed a troubled sigh as Roberto left the room. Then he forced himself to remember that all three parties involved had got exactly what they wanted.

*

Seven months later, Paolo watched from his office window as the seemingly endless convoy of limousines glided across the Piazza della Scala towards the imposing triple arches that formed the grand entrance to the opera house. Uniformed attendants rushed to open the car doors. A fusillade of flashbulbs popped as the passengers stepped out, the female occupants wearing magnificent furs concealing heavy diamond, sapphire and emerald jewellery, their male escorts in immaculate dinner jackets, cummerbunded in richly coloured silk. Television cameras were there to record the most glittering event in the opera calendar, which also heralded the opening of the Milan social season. Police ringed the square, holding back several hundred Milanese all looking expectantly towards the theatre. Even though the December night was cold, with drizzle chilling their bones, at least the notorious fog that could descend on Milan in an instant, blanketing the city and paralysing it, had remained at bay.

Politicians, film stars, models and aristocracy – everyone who was anyone in Italy was here tonight. La Scala's two thousand seats would be filled by the rich and powerful, and, of course, by the *claque* in the upper galleries.

The *claque*, Paolo hated to admit, still existed. It was a system whereby an entrepreneur bought blocks of the cheaper seats and got those to whom he gave them to scream applause at singers who'd paid him handsomely for the privilege, and boo those who hadn't. Paolo was sure Roberto Rossini would have paid up. He just prayed that the rest of the audience would wish to applaud him of their own free will.

Since announcing Roberto as his Ernani, Paolo had watched the feeding frenzy in the media with trepidation. It was rare to have a talented young home-grown tenor who also *looked* the part of the handsome hero, and Roberto had undoubtedly added most of Milan's female journalists to his fan club. He had to admit that Roberto had been a model of dedication and decorum since he'd been offered his big chance. Even Riccardo Beroli, La Scala's famously temperamental conductor, had begun to warm to him.

Paolo straightened his bow tie and checked his watch. He just had time to see Roberto in his dressing room and wish him luck before the curtain went up.

'Come in.' Roberto paused in the middle of an arpeggio as the door opened and Paolo entered the room.

'How are you?'

Roberto grinned. 'My stomach, it feels a little strange, but I'm okay.'

Paolo's eyes fell on a tasteful bouquet of white lilies on the table. 'How lovely. Who are they from?' he enquired.

'Riccardo. He says I can have them on my grave after I've been crucified by the critics tomorrow morning.' Roberto smiled wryly.

'And the roses?' Paolo indicated another far more extravagant bouquet taking up most of the small sofa.

'From a friend,' Roberto replied lightly.

'So, I'm off to receive our honoured guests in the audience. If you fail tonight, you fail in front of the most important people in Italy.'

'Thank you for that reassurance,' said Roberto drily.

'Be brilliant,' Paolo entreated him. 'Prove to me I was not insane to give you this chance.'

'I'll do my best not to let you down.'

'Good. I'll be back in the interval. *In bocca al lupo*, Roberto.' Paolo gave him the traditional good-luck greeting.

'*Crepi il lupo*,' Roberto returned, rolling his eyes heavenwards.

Paolo nodded and left the dressing room.

Roberto put his head on his knuckles, closed his eyes and sent up a prayer.

'Make me the best tonight, God, make me the best.'

The atmosphere of La Scala was never so thrilling as on opening night, reflected Paolo as he sat in the staff box, admiring the graceful tiers of gilded balconies that soared from the floor right up to the glorious curved ceiling with its single, elegant chandelier, the discordant sounds of instruments being tuned drifting up from the orchestra pit. He watched the last members of the star-studded audience flutter into the stalls and take their seats like exotic butterflies coming to rest in a flower garden. He looked to his right and saw Donatella Bianchi, resplendent in a low-cut black velvet gown and glistening diamonds, installed next to her husband in their box. There was a burst of applause as Riccardo Beroli took his place on the conductor's rostrum, bowed to the audience and picked up his baton.

The lights dimmed, the theatre fell silent and the slow, haunting overture of *Ernani* began. Paolo closed his eyes and took a deep breath. It was out of his hands now.

By the interval, Paolo knew what he'd suspected for the past few weeks had been confirmed. The packed bar was buzzing with talk of Roberto, who was producing an astounding vocal performance. Even Paolo had relaxed as he'd watched him command the stage, his magnetism eclipsing the other members of the cast.

'What did I tell you?' Donatella appeared behind him. She was almost purring with satisfaction.

'Yes, he's certainly giving a very good performance.'

'Ah, but it is more, is it not? He has a magnificent stage presence. You must be a happy man tonight, Paolo. We and La Scala have created a new star.'

At the end of the performance, as Paolo watched Roberto take curtain after curtain, bouquets raining down on him, the deafening applause reverberating around the auditorium, he wondered just what they had unleashed on the world.

The Metropolitan Opera House, New York

As you can imagine, Nico, the night Roberto Rossini sang Ernani was to be the turning point of his career. I still wish to this day that I'd seen him; those who did witness it still remember it. Of course, this propelled Roberto from little-known soloist to a star of the first degree. Over the next few years, every time I opened a newspaper or magazine, there was another photograph or interview with him. After his performances, the stage door was mobbed by his female fans. His private life was as well documented as his professional performances, but his seemingly effortless acquisition of beautiful women only appeared to add to his cachet and increase his appeal.

I followed his career with enormous interest. After his triumphant first night, I'd sent him a note to congratulate him, but he never replied. I understood, of course. I was a young student and he was on his way to becoming one of the greatest tenors of his generation. However, it did not stop me dreaming that one day we would sing the great love duets together. Abi and I would often buy tickets for the upper galleries to watch him. Those nights spurred me on to work harder in my singing classes at school.

I look back on the four years I studied in Milan

with great affection. I dedicated myself wholeheartedly to my dream, wishing to justify the faith that had been shown in me by Luca, Luigi Vincenzi and Paolo de Vito. Luca was still involved in his church, watching as it was slowly and painstakingly restored to its former glory. In accordance with Abi's suggestion, he'd re-formed the church choir and, true to her word, Abi had helped him to recruit and train new members. The two of them spent many hours together, working on and discussing their pet project. And I watched their friendship grow with interest. Luca had also taken a part-time job as a waiter in a café round the corner from our apartment, and many nights Abi and I would join him there to eat, drink wine and gossip about our days.

If I sometimes wondered what Luca wanted from his life, or sensed his restlessness, I never voiced my thoughts to him. Maybe I knew in my heart that his future plans might one day take him away from me and I hated to think of that.

During the summer holidays, both Luca and I returned to Naples. I must admit I found it harder and harder to go back home. For a few weeks every July and August, Luca and I lived in a time warp. He cooked in the kitchen and I waited on tables in the café with Carlotta. She rarely asked me about my new life in Milan and, not wishing to upset her, I in turn asked little about her. I could see she was unhappy, unfulfilled; that her life with Papa and Ella was not the one she'd once dreamt of when she was younger. And maybe I didn't want her misery to infect my own positivity for the future. If Luca and I were honest, we were both glad when the summers were over and we were able to escape back to Milan and the life to which we both felt we now belonged.

I was twenty-one years old when I graduated from the scuola di musica. *I won the gold medal for my year, the highest honour the school had to offer. My voice had become my life, and, while other girls of my age were falling in and out of love regularly, romantic interludes played no part in my daily routine. Maybe if they had . . . well, who knows? I was so very innocent, and totally unprepared for what was to happen to me, as you shall hear . . .*

14

Milan, June 1976

'Rosanna, thank you for coming to see me.' Paolo smiled warmly as Rosanna walked into his office. 'Please sit down.'

Rosanna did so.

'Now, I'm sure it will come as no surprise to you to learn that I wish you to join the opera company.'

'That's wonderful news. Thank you, Paolo.' Rosanna's eyes glowed with pleasure.

'Having won this year's gold medal, you are no doubt aware that we at La Scala are hoping for great things from you. The problem is where to place you in the company. Your voice deserves better than the chorus, but' – Paolo shifted some papers around on his desk – 'I'm loath to push you. You're only just twenty-one, with a career ahead of you that might cover forty years. You must gain maturity and experience before we can put you into the roles your voice warrants. Do you understand what I'm saying, Rosanna?'

'Yes, I think so,' Rosanna said, nodding.

'I know you've been approached by other opera companies and I presume you've been offered roles with them?'

Rosanna blushed, wondering how Paolo had heard. 'Yes. Covent Garden and the Metropolitan Opera House in New York have both expressed an interest.'

'Of course, the decision is yours. But, Rosanna, if you stay here with us, Riccardo and I promise to build your future in the way we believe to be best for you. This is our suggestion: that we put you under contract as a solo artiste for the coming season. There are a number of small parts I have in mind for you to sing. But you will not be asked to perform more than two or three times a week. This will give you an opportunity to continue with your singing lessons without putting you or your voice under too much pressure. During this time, Riccardo has agreed to work with you once a week to build and improve your repertoire,' Paolo explained. 'I think it would also be a good idea for you to understudy some of the appropriate leading roles in the season. This will give you a chance to play the parts at cover rehearsals and enable you to get the feel of the stage. However,' Paolo added, 'it's doubtful there will be an opportunity to play the roles for real, for, as you know, the process is to swap principal sopranos from within the company if another is sick. But I think the experience will benefit you enormously when, as I hope will happen shortly, you become a leading soloist. So, how does this sound?' he asked her.

Rosanna couldn't help feeling a twinge of disappointment at Paolo's plans. The Metropolitan Opera House had sent her a recent letter offering her a season that included making her debut as Juliette in *Roméo et Juliette* and Covent Garden had offered equally tempting roles. But Rosanna knew that what Paolo was saying made sense. Besides, this was the man who'd supported her since she was seventeen.

'It sounds just fine, Paolo,' she replied, forcing her mouth into what she hoped was a grateful smile.

Paolo studied Rosanna's face and read her thoughts immediately. 'Rosanna, please don't think we're trying to hold you back, but I've seen too many promising young sopranos pushed into the spotlight before they're really ready. They burn out by the time they're thirty. Your voice is a precious thing, Rosanna, and neither Riccardo nor I wish to push you, or it, too far and too fast. My plan might not be as glamorous as some of the other offers you've had, but you must gain experience and be allowed to make mistakes unseen.'

'Of course.' Rosanna nodded. 'I do understand, Paolo, really I do.'

'And in a year's time, I hope you will make your debut here. I'm thinking of opening next season with *La Bohème*. You would, of course, play Mimi and we might try to entice Roberto Rossini to play Rodolfo.'

Rosanna's eyes lit up. 'Mimi in *La Bohème* has always been my dream.'

'Good. So, all is settled, apart from what we shall pay you,' Paolo continued. 'Again, it will not be as much as you could earn if you were playing the lead at the Met in New York, but believe me, Rosanna, there will be no shortage of money for you in the future. I think the amount of four hundred thousand lire for the season should cover your needs adequately, plus there will be overtime and performance payments. Is that acceptable?'

'Yes, it's more than generous, thank you.'

'And Rosanna, if at any point you feel unhappy, please don't hesitate to come and talk to me. Remember, we're doing this for you as well as us. So, will you accept our offer?'

Little did Paolo know that he had just dangled the perfect carrot. Rosanna was still lost in thoughts of singing *La Bohème* with Roberto Rossini in a year's time. 'Yes. Thank you, Paolo, for everything.'

'Then I'm very happy. And I think you should find some friends and have a drink to celebrate.'

'I will! Oh, I will! Paolo, before I go, could I ask you one thing?'

'Of course.'

'Will Abi Holmes be joining the company? I promise not to breathe a word,' she added.

'She's your close friend, isn't she?'

'Yes.'

'Then I can confirm she will be, so you won't be parted just yet.'

'I'm so pleased for her and for me!' Rosanna clasped her hands together, happy that the picture of her immediate future was now complete. 'Thank you again, Paolo.'

When Rosanna had left his office, Paolo breathed a private sigh of relief. He hadn't been sure whether she would agree to his proposal. And if putting Abi Holmes in the company kept his protégée happy, then he would find a space for her in the back row of the chorus. Rosanna was going to need all the support she could get in the next few years. At present, she was innocently unaware of the seething undercurrent of jealousy and competition that existed backstage between rival singers. Rosanna would have to develop a tough outer shell if she was to take her rightful place at the top of her profession. She had a lot to learn and joining the company would be a rude awakening.

*

'To us!' said Abi.

'To you both,' added Luca.

Three glasses clinked against each other for the umpteenth time that evening. The small table in Rosanna and Luca's apartment was now littered with the remnants of their impromptu celebration, as the two girls toasted the good news.

'I just can't believe Paolo has actually put me in the company!' exclaimed Abi. 'I nearly fainted when he called me in to tell me. I was on the verge of packing my bags, and I know my parents were expecting me home in England at any moment.'

'So you are pleased after all? I thought you didn't care whether you had a career as an opera singer,' said Rosanna.

Abi threw her hands up in a gesture of mock despair as she turned to Luca. 'My God, your sister can be naive at times. Of *course* I wanted a place in the company, but I was protecting myself against rejection, pretending it didn't matter. It's the British way, you know. Not showing your true feelings; stiff upper lip and all that. Unlike you emotional Italians, who wear your hearts on your sleeves. Well' – Abi eyed Luca impishly – 'at least most of you do.'

'And what exactly do you mean by that, young lady?' asked Luca, chuckling gently, for once allowing himself to be drawn into the light-hearted banter.

'My brother, he is the deep horse,' intoned Rosanna in her best English.

'"Dark" horse, actually,' Abi giggled. 'Yes, you are, aren't you, Luca?'

Luca shrugged good-naturedly. 'If you say so, Abi.'

'I do.' She drained the last mouthful of wine from her

glass. 'Pity the bottle's empty. I could have downed plenty more tonight.'

'We've shared two already. Remember what Paolo says about alcohol and your voice,' said Rosanna primly.

'I know, I know,' Abi sighed. 'And I suppose that now I'm a bona fide member of the company, and might possibly have a future as a singer, I have to start taking these things seriously. What a bore!'

Rosanna stifled a yawn.

'Oh look, the little soloist is weary,' Abi teased her. 'Listen, why don't you go to bed and we'll clear up in here, won't we, Luca?'

'If you're sure you don't mind. I must admit I'm a little tired.' A frown of worry crossed Rosanna's brow. 'I hope I'm not getting a cold. I have my first lesson with Riccardo on Monday.'

'Oh, listen to the diva! You see, it's all downhill from here, Luca,' Abi commented with feigned sarcasm. 'And this is only the beginning of her prima donna tendencies: there'll be neuroses over the state of her health, she'll complain about the whiff of cigarette smoke wafting to her delicate nostrils from one hundred yards away, the—'

A cushion from the sofa landed squarely on Abi's chest. 'The diva is going to get her beauty sleep. Goodnight.' Rosanna winked at Abi and left the sitting room.

Luca got to his feet and began ferrying dishes and glasses to the tiny kitchen, while Abi rummaged around in her overnight bag. 'Look what I've found!' she indicated as Luca came back into the room and she waved a bottle of brandy at him. 'I'd forgotten I'd brought it,' she lied smoothly. 'Like some?'

'No, thank you, Abi. I've had quite enough,' Luca replied.

'Don't be so dull, Luca. This is a very special night and I shall be most offended if you won't have a brandy to celebrate with me. Just a small one . . . please?'

'Okay,' he agreed reluctantly.

Luca watched as she filled a tumbler and handed it to him. He raised an eyebrow at the amount.

'I'll drink what you don't want. Cheers,' she said, taking a large gulp and sitting herself down on the sofa.

'To you, Abi. *Bravissima!* I'm very pleased for you,' smiled Luca.

'Are you? I sometimes wonder whether you care for me at all,' she said abruptly.

Luca was taken aback by her words. 'That's a silly thing to say. Abi, you should know that I consider you one of my closest friends.'

'Yes, of course. Sorry.' Abi, realising that she was already dangerously inebriated, changed the subject. 'So, what will you do with yourself now Rosanna has come of age, so to speak? You're being made redundant, aren't you?'

'Well, I think that's an exaggeration. Rosanna will still need support and family around her as she joins the company.'

'Yes, but she's a grown woman now, Luca. Surely, you must have some idea of what you want to do with your future. Will you stay in Milan and continue to work in the café?'

'No. That's just to earn some money. I know exactly what I'm going to do.' Luca sat down on the sofa and took a sip of the brandy.

'Then tell me your plan. I'm dying to know. Open a restaurant, maybe?'

'No,' Luca smiled ruefully, 'definitely not that.'

'Okay, but surely one day you'll want to get married? Have a family?'

'Maybe.'

'Luca, may I ask you a personal question?' Alcohol had given Abi the courage to probe further.

'You can ask, but whether you get a reply or not is a different matter,' Luca said evenly.

'Okay. Well, why, during the years I've known you, have you never had a girlfriend? I mean . . . are you . . . do you . . . prefer men?'

Luca gave a sudden bark of surprised laughter. 'Honestly, the questions you ask! No, Abi. Just because a man doesn't have a woman it doesn't mean he's gay.'

'Then, do you find me attractive?' Abi found herself blurting out.

Luca studied the girl sitting next to him. Her lovely blonde hair fell becomingly around her oval face, her vivid blue eyes sparkled with life. He glanced involuntarily at the long, shapely legs curled up underneath her.

'I think you're very beautiful. I would have to be blind not to notice.'

'Well,' she said slowly, 'if you like my company and you find me beautiful, why have you never tried to—'

'Please! You shouldn't ask me that.' Luca stood up, walked over to the window and looked out at the still busy street. Couples were strolling hand in hand, meandering in the way that people do when they have no particular destination except each other. Luca felt a pang as he silently acknowledged that it was not his destiny to be like them. And if there was anyone he would choose, it was the girl he had grown so fond of . . . *loved,* in fact, sitting on the sofa behind him. He took another sip of his brandy and put his glass down on the windowsill. He knew he must be honest with Abi, and himself, for both of their sakes.

'Luca, you must know how I feel about you, why I became involved with your church choir, why I virtually live at this apartment,' she persisted.

'I'd presumed it was because you're my sister's best friend and because you wanted to help.' Luca turned to look at her.

'Of course, of course,' she reassured him quickly. 'I adore Rosanna, she's very precious to me. And I loved building and coaching the choir too. But surely you must see that there's more to it than that?'

'Abi, please, I don't know what to say.'

There was a short silence as Abi drained her glass. It was now or never.

'Luca, can I now tell you something? Something very private? I . . . I think I'm in love with you.'

Luca stared at her, misery etched on his face.

'God, is that so terrible?' she entreated him.

'No, yes . . . I . . .' He turned away again, his head bowed.

Abi stood up and walked slowly towards him. 'Please, Luca, answer me truthfully. Can you honestly say you don't feel anything for me?'

Abi moved closer until she stood right behind him. Finally he spoke. 'No, I cannot.'

Abi's fingers traced a pattern on his back.

'Then kiss me.'

'No . . . I . . .' He turned round sharply, to find his face tantalisingly close to hers.

She pulled him towards her and put her lips to his. She

could feel his tension easing as she teased his lips open with her own. Her arms wound round him and, finally, he began to respond.

Abi had lived this moment so many times in her imagination, yet the reality was much, much better than she could ever have dreamt.

Then, with a groan, he pulled away. 'Please! Stop!'

'What? Why? I knew what you felt for me. I wasn't imagining it, was I? During these past four years I've had boyfriends, yes, but they meant nothing. In my heart there's never been anyone else. It will always be you, always.' Abi moved forward, but Luca cowered away from her like a cornered animal.

He sank onto the sofa and buried his face in his hands.

'I . . . oh Luca, whatever is the matter? Please, Luca, tell me what it is?'

When he looked up, Abi saw there were tears in his eyes.

He shook his head slowly. 'You won't understand.'

'I will, I promise. If we have the same feelings for each other, then we can work it out, whatever the problem.' She sat down next to him.

'No, Abi, we can't. There can be no future for us. I'm sorry, so very sorry that I have let you believe even for a moment that there might be.'

She inhaled deeply and shook her hair back from her face in an attempt to regain her equilibrium. 'Then you'd better explain why not.'

'All right, I will tell you. Dearest Abi, I will do my best.' Luca too took a deep breath, in preparation to tell her what he must. 'You see, I always wondered when I was younger why I was unhappy. It was as if I was searching for something, something I felt that neither women nor a career could give me. Then I came to Milan with Rosanna and ironically, on the very first day I was here, I discovered what it was.'

'How? Where?'

'I found myself in La Chiesa Della Beata Vergine Maria. While I was there, I saw her.'

'Saw who?' Her lip trembled.

'Maria, the Madonna,' Luca said quietly. 'It sounds strange and ridiculous, I know, but she spoke to me. From that moment on, everything else fell into place and I realised what I must do with my life. So' – he reached for Abi's hand – 'I cannot be with you; I cannot be with any woman or love them. I have given my life to God.'

Abi could only stare at him in stunned silence. Eventually, she found her voice.

'But I believe in God too. Surely that doesn't mean you have to stop loving someone, does it? I thought God *was* love?'

'He is, but, Abi, I must make the ultimate commitment. I've been putting it off until Rosanna finished at the music school. She was my first priority. But very soon I'll be joining a seminary in Bergamo. I'll be there for seven years. I'm going to train to be a priest, Abi. And that's why I can't be with you. There,' he breathed, hardly believing he had finally voiced the words, 'I've said it. I don't expect you, or Rosanna for that matter, to understand, but it's what I want more than anything.'

Such was her shock, Abi was almost overwhelmed by the urge to laugh hysterically. But then, as she gazed into Luca's eyes and studied his gentle face, she saw that this was not a game, or an excuse. It made sense of everything Luca was.

Luca was watching her intently. 'You think I'm crazy, don't you?'

'No, I . . . of course I don't think that. Really I don't,' she reiterated. 'But, Luca, if you become a priest, it means sacrificing all worldly pleasures. Are you really prepared for that?'

'Absolutely.'

'And yet, you can't tell me you feel nothing for me?'

'No,' he agreed, 'I can't. From the first moment I saw you, Abi, I felt something for you that is difficult to describe. And ever since then, you've had a place in my heart. We've grown so close over the past four years.'

'Yes, we have. And perhaps the "something" you can't describe is called "love", Luca.'

'Yes,' he finally agreed. 'I think you are right. But don't you see? You're just one of the tests that God has placed before me. A test which I failed just now.' Luca hung his head miserably.

'I'm not sure whether I'm flattered or insulted.' Abi spoke in a small, hollow voice.

'I'm sorry, that came out insensitively,' Luca said hurriedly, 'but it was meant in the best possible way. You're the first and only woman I have ever loved.'

'So you admit you do love me?'

'Yes, I think I must love you, Abi. I've spent so many nights thinking of you, wanting you, and asking God for guidance. Your presence here so often has made it very hard. That's why sometimes I've seemed . . . aloof maybe,' Luca admitted.

'So . . .' With a heavy heart, Abi realised she was powerless to alter the situation. 'When do you intend to enter this . . . seminary?'

'I've already been through my interviews. If all goes well, I shall leave for Bergamo in six weeks' time, when Rosanna and I return from Naples.'

'I see. Does Rosanna know yet?'

'No. I've been planning to tell her but I didn't want it to spoil her good news.'

'She'll be devastated. You two are so close.'

'No, I don't believe she will be. If she loves me as I think she does, then she'll be happy for me.'

'Maybe,' Abi sighed. 'But forgive me if I can't be happy for you too, at least not for now. There's nothing I can do to make you change your mind?'

The yearning in her voice caught at Luca's heart, but he knew he must remain steadfast. 'No. Nothing.'

She could keep back the tears no longer. 'Then hold me, Luca, please.'

Luca opened his arms and she went into them. Luca stroked her hair, feeling his body stirring as he did so.

'It won't change, you know,' she murmured.

'What?'

'The way I feel about you. What we've shared.'

'Abi, I promise that it will. You're a beautiful girl and very young still. One day, you'll find someone to love you as I cannot. You'll forget all about me.'

She wiped her eyes with the back of her hand. 'Never,' she said. 'Never.'

The following day, Rosanna sat down at the table and listened to what Luca had to tell her. Surprisingly, despite her sadness at the thought of being without him, she felt relief that the mystery of her brother's solitary life was resolved.

'When do you leave?'

'In the autumn, when we return from Naples.'

'Oh Luca, will I be able to visit you in Bergamo?'

'Not for a while, no.'

'I see.'

'You do understand, don't you, Rosanna? Why I have to go?' Luca asked her.

'Yes, as long as it's really what you want.'

'I've wanted it for many years, without even realising it.'

'Then I'm happy for you. But I'll miss you so much, Luca.'

'And I you. But you won't be alone. I think Abi is eager to move in here. You'd like that, yes?'

'Of course, but it won't be the same.'

'You'll be so wrapped up in your new life at La Scala that you'll hardly notice I've gone, *piccolina*.'

'I understand that you must go and find your own way, but that doesn't mean I won't still need you.' Determined not to cry, Rosanna added brightly, 'I wonder what Papa will say?'

'Oh, I think he'll enjoy being able to brag about his son the priest and his daughter the opera singer, so he'll be happy enough.' Luca reached for her hands. 'Rosanna, you know I still love you? That you are the most precious person in my life?'

'Yes, Luca.'

'But I think it's right for me to go now. You too must learn some independence.'

Rosanna nodded sadly. 'Yes, I think you're right. It's time for me to grow up.'

The two months in Naples passed quickly. The café was busy and Rosanna was unable to spend as much time as she would have liked with Luca. As her brother had predicted, when he heard the news, Marco boasted to anyone and everyone that his son was to become a priest. It was this news, rather than his daughter's joining La Scala, that was cause for celebration. Rosanna accepted his apparent lack of interest in her career; it only served to demonstrate how far she'd come from the safe but narrow world of the Piedigrotta. And she didn't expect Papa to understand.

Before she returned to Milan, knowing it might be a while before she could visit Naples again, Rosanna went to see Luigi Vincenzi. They sat outside on his beautiful terrace, shaded from the fierce August sun and enjoying glasses of chilled white wine. She felt guilty that she now felt more at home here with Luigi than she did in her father's café.

'You think I'm right to follow Paolo's plans?' she asked him as he topped up her glass.

'Oh yes. Going abroad and singing the big roles sounds very glamorous, but Paolo is wise to give you the time you need.'

'Sometimes I feel as though I've been practising forever,' sighed Rosanna. 'It's nearly ten years since I began my lessons with you.'

'And you will continue practising, Rosanna, until the day you die,' reiterated Luigi. 'That's part of your job and how you will continue to improve. Look at it this way: it would be much more profitable for Paolo to immediately put you into a leading role at La Scala. He knows what a big star you'll be and the attention you'll command. But instead, he and Riccardo Beroli wish to nurture you, give you as much time as you need to build up your confidence and your repertoire.

*

You think other sopranos get this kind of special treatment from the artistic director of one of the greatest opera houses in the world?'

Rosanna could see the twinkle of amusement in his eyes. 'No. I'm sorry. I'm being impatient and selfish.'

'All part of the artistic temperament, which will flourish along with your voice,' Luigi chuckled. 'You're exactly where you should be, Rosanna. Trust me, and trust Paolo and Riccardo. We're all on your side.'

Half an hour later, Luigi saw her to the front door. 'You must send my best wishes to your brother. I hope all goes well for him in his chosen path.'

'I will,' Rosanna nodded. She reached up and kissed Luigi affectionately on both cheeks. 'Thank you, Luigi. Maybe I will see you in Milan on my first opening night?'

'I wouldn't miss it for the world.' He returned the kisses. '*Ciao*, Rosanna. Keep practising.'

'I will.' She smiled and waved as she made her way down the drive.

Four days after their return to Milan, Rosanna accompanied Luca to the Stazione Centrale, where he would embark on his journey to Bergamo. As her brother boarded the train, Rosanna gave him one last hug.

'I'm so proud of you, Luca.'

'And I of you, *piccolina.* One word before I go – you have a great gift, Rosanna, and as with all blessings, there will be a high price to pay. Trust nobody but yourself,' he entreated her.

'I won't, I promise.'

'Abi will look after you. And you must look after her too.'

'Of course. I think she's more upset about you going than anyone.'

'Yes, we had grown close.' Luca's reply was deliberately light in order to mask his true feelings.

'You will write to both of us, won't you?'

'I'll try, but forgive me if you don't hear from me for a while. They have strict rules for novices. *Ciao, bella.*' Luca kissed her on both cheeks. 'And may God bless you and protect you while I'm gone.'

'*Ciao*, Luca.'

Rosanna waited until the train had disappeared from view before she stopped waving. As she walked slowly back along the platform and out onto the busy Milan streets, Rosanna felt bereft. Luca had always been there. Now he was gone and she had to face her future alone.

15

Roberto was woken by the telephone. Cursing, he reached for the receiver.

'*Pronto*.'

'*Caro*, it's Donatella.'

'Why do you call me at this time? You know I arrived back late last night,' he replied irritably.

'My apologies, but you've been away for six weeks. I wanted to hear your voice and make sure you were home safely. Don't be angry with me, *caro*,' she pleaded.

Roberto relented. 'Of course I'm not angry. I'm tired, that's all.'

'How was London?'

'It rained all the time. And in August too. I caught a bad cold.'

'Poor thing,' she soothed. 'But never mind. I read the reviews for *Turandot*. They were simply stunning.'

'They were quite good, yes,' he conceded modestly.

'Shall I come and see you this afternoon? We have some catching up to do.'

'No, this afternoon isn't possible. I have a meeting with Paolo de Vito about the forthcoming season.'

'Tomorrow then?'

'Okay. Tomorrow.'

'I can't wait. I'll be with you at three. *Ciao*.'

'*Ciao*.' Roberto put the receiver down and lay back with a sigh, his relief at returning to Milan after the greyness of London ebbing away.

In the past three years, Donatella had changed. In the beginning, the relationship had been based on a strong mutual attraction, and the looming presence of Donatella's husband had stopped things being taken to a more serious level. But slowly, as Roberto's fame had increased, so had Donatella's possessiveness. It had been so gradual that he'd hardly noticed, but in the past year, words of love had begun to creep into her vocabulary. She'd become angry if she saw newspaper reports or magazine photographs of Roberto with other women. She constantly accused him of having affairs, and on occasion she had been correct. But while Donatella was still rich and influential, she was not his keeper. He may have been nothing when he met her, but now he was an international star and nobody, *nobody*, could tell him what to do.

But then, no other woman excited him sexually quite the way she did. The physical spark that had first ignited the relationship was still there and he found her maddeningly hard to resist.

Roberto pondered his dilemma as he got out of bed and made his way to the bathroom. He turned on the shower and stepped under the jet. He wondered whether Donatella had seen the newspaper photographs of him and Rosalind Shannon, a young soprano at Covent Garden. London's dreary weather had been considerably brightened by her warming his bed on more than one occasion. Of course she'd been upset when he'd left London yesterday, but he'd promised the usual things and that had seemed to pacify her. Roberto doubted he'd bother contacting her again. It had been fun while it lasted, but . . .

He towelled himself dry and slipped into a pair of casual Armani trousers and a silk shirt. He went to the kitchen to make his special honey-based drink, which soothed and protected the vocal cords. While he waited for the kettle to boil, he couldn't help smiling as he surveyed what his success had brought him. Others might claim material possessions were unimportant, an addendum to their fame. Roberto disagreed. He loved being rich.

His new apartment was just off the Via Manzoni, a mere stone's throw from La Scala, and it suited his needs well. It was small enough to be manageable. He didn't like the thought of an army of maids stumbling upon him *in flagrante*. But it was smart enough to reinforce his status as one of the world's greatest living tenors.

He'd come a long way, and he liked to think he'd done it all by himself.

If Donatella wanted part of him, then she'd have to learn to play by the rules. Otherwise, it would be goodbye.

The following afternoon, Donatella slipped into her new Ferrari. She checked her make-up in the mirror, then started the engine and roared out of the palazzo drive, eager to be in Roberto's arms once more. She could hardly believe how much she'd missed him.

She'd grown weary of their part-time relationship, of being forced to keep their affair secret when she wanted to shout to the world that *she* was the woman in the great Roberto Rossini's life.

She'd spent most of the summer with her husband in a villa in Cap Ferrat. As she'd lain by the pool soaking up the sun, she'd studied her husband: short, balding, coarse-featured and with a paunch that grew larger in proportion to the years. She could hardly bear for him to touch her anymore. Previously, the sacrifice had been worth it. His wealth, power and position had given her the things she'd always craved.

But since then, a man had come into her life who made her feel young again, who was just as successful as her husband, but, more importantly, who was a man she loved and desired. As Donatella had swum slowly up and down the villa's spectacular pool overlooking the Mediterranean, she'd convinced herself that the only reason Roberto had never said he loved her was because he knew it was hopeless. After all, she reasoned, she was a married woman who had no intention of leaving her husband and she'd made that clear from the beginning.

But . . . what if she was single?

By the time Donatella had arrived home from France, she'd made up her mind. She would divorce Giovanni and, after an appropriately seemly interval, marry Roberto. In the meantime, having announced the separation from Giovanni, she'd be free to travel the world with her younger lover. No longer could she stomach reading about his dalliances in newspapers. She wanted him all to herself.

After all, his success was due to her.

*

'*Caro*, oh, how I have missed you.'

Roberto groaned as her snakelike tongue worked its way down his belly. She flicked her tongue backwards and forwards on the most sensitive part of him.

'Say you love me,' she demanded, as the sensation suddenly stopped.

'I adore you,' he whispered, lost in the moment and his own needs.

As Donatella's mouth encircled him, she smiled inwardly.

It was all she needed to hear.

Rosanna and Abi took their places on the stage of La Scala with the rest of the company. After three weeks in the rehearsal room, it was the first run-through in the theatre itself.

'It's huge,' whispered Rosanna nervously, gazing up from the stage into the vast space of the empty auditorium.

'I feel like a speck,' replied Abi, equally nervously.

Rosanna was staring at the great chandelier, suspended 550 feet above them, daydreaming of one day making her debut below it, when Riccardo Beroli clapped his hands and brought her back down to earth.

'So, we will run through Act One.'

As the chorus took their opening places on the complicated set, Rosanna watched Anna Dupré enter from the wings, deep in conversation with Paolo de Vito. She was playing Adina in Donizetti's *L'Elisir d'Amore*, the opera that would open the season. Rosanna had been given the role of Giannetta and had one short aria with the ladies' chorus. She'd waited day after day for Roberto Rossini, who was playing Nemorino, to appear. Even though they'd been rehearsing for the past month, he was yet to attend.

'Okay, we sing!' Riccardo signalled for the pianist to begin.

Six gruelling hours later, Abi and Rosanna left the theatre.

'God! I for one need a drink,' Abi announced as the two of them linked arms and headed off in the direction of a café just off the Piazza della Scala.

They sat at a table by the window. Abi ordered a glass of wine and Rosanna a mineral water.

'That was exhausting,' exhaled Rosanna. 'It's all the hanging around while they get the lighting right.'

'Yes, and you didn't notice the stars having to do that, did you? Anna Dupré was only here for an hour this morning, and, of course, the great Signor Rossini didn't bother to appear at all,' sniffed Abi.

'I heard Paolo tell Anna that Roberto was in Barcelona for a concert last night.'

'Someone told me he's had a couple of private rehearsals and will apparently only appear for the dress runs. He obviously doesn't wish to associate with us mere mortals.'

'Don't be so judgemental, Abi, you don't even know him.' Rosanna sprang immediately to Roberto's defence.

'No, I don't, but even you know the stories of his bad behaviour are legend at La Scala. Apparently, he actually had one of the chorus in between "*The Toreador Song*" and "*The Smugglers' Chorus*" during last season's *Carmen*. And still had enough breath to sing the finale!'

'You are terrible, Abi.' Rosanna had to chuckle. 'I'm sure it's all exaggerated.'

'Probably, but a night of Roberto Rossini, however much

of a Lothario he is, might be worth it. I've heard he's brilliant in the sack.' Abi sipped her wine and rather enjoyed Rosanna's shocked expression. 'Besides, I really am going to have to give up all hope of Luca reciprocating my feelings now he's in a seminary, so surely I deserve some comfort for me and my broken heart?'

'I'm sorry, I really didn't realise you were serious about him.'

'Oh, I was.' Abi was solemn for a moment. 'I lost and God won,' she murmured. 'Anyway, no use crying over spilt milk, as we say in England. By the way, did you see the tenor sitting next to me on the steps?'

'You mean, the one who looked a little like Luca?'

'I suppose he did a bit,' Abi acknowledged with a blush. 'I think he'll be my first target. Cheers.' She raised her glass and drained the remnants of her wine.

A week later, in their heavy costumes, Rosanna and Abi made their way towards the wings for the dress rehearsal. Rosanna could hear the discordant sound of the orchestra tuning up and saw that there were still a couple of carpenters banging nails into a flat on the vast stage.

Paolo gathered the chorus and cast together on the stage.

'Okay, ladies and gentlemen, I hope to run straight through with no pauses. We'll get through as much as we can. Right, opening positions, everyone.' Paolo nodded to Riccardo, who went to take his position in the orchestra pit.

The chorus had sung only a couple of words before 'Stop!' was shouted from the stalls. A wait of twenty minutes followed while something unseen was adjusted to Paolo's satisfaction. Finally they began again.

Four hours later, Rosanna and Abi were sitting in the stalls drinking coffee out of plastic cups and waiting for Paolo to continue with the rest of Act One.

'Well, well, well, look who's decided to grace us with his presence.' Abi nudged her.

Rosanna looked up and caught her breath as she saw Roberto Rossini speaking to Paolo on the stage.

'God, he really is attractive, isn't he? Whoops, I've got to go. The chorus are on again.'

Rosanna watched as Abi made her way back to the stage. The chorus sang the last two bars before departing into the wings, then the lights dimmed and Roberto made his entrance.

He stood bathed in the white glow of the spotlight. As he began to sing '*Una furtiva lagrima*', Rosanna sat transfixed.

Two days later, Rosanna stood in the wings, ready to walk on stage and sing her own solo in front of the expectant first-night audience. Although she knew it backwards, and it was not vocally demanding, adrenaline was rushing through her system. She swallowed and concentrated on her breathing to try and calm her nerves. A huge surge of applause came from the audience as Roberto finished singing and strolled off stage towards her. She thought he was going to walk straight past her, but instead he stopped in front of her. He was breathing heavily and she could see the beads of sweat on his forehead.

'*In bocca al lupo*, Miss Menici,' he whispered.

'*Crepi il lupo*,' she returned shyly.

He leant towards her and kissed her gently on the forehead. 'You will make a perfect debut. Now go.'

Rosanna heard her cue and, with no more time for thought, stepped out onto the stage.

Ten minutes later, she was back in the dressing room she shared with another soloist. Her nerves had left her the minute she'd begun to sing, the years of training allowing her to enjoy the atmosphere of her very first opening night. The applause had been warm and she knew she had sung well. And what was more, Roberto had noticed her. She put her fingers to her forehead, tracing the spot where he had kissed her.

An hour later, the company were assembled on stage taking the thunderous applause of the audience. Roberto and Anna took five curtain calls. Eventually, they made their way back to their dressing rooms. Smiling at her reflection in the mirror as she marked to memory this very special moment, Rosanna changed into a dress and went along the corridor to see Abi in the dressing room she shared with other members of the chorus.

'Rosanna, *bravissima*!' Abi kissed her on both cheeks. 'You sang beautifully. All the chorus thought so. There, you've made your first appearance on the stage at La Scala. You might get a review in the paper tomorrow.'

'Do you think so?'

'Who knows? But honestly, darling, I still can't believe you haven't bought anything new to wear to the party!' exclaimed Abi. 'That old black dress of yours is ready for the bin,' she said, taking her own new red cocktail dress off its hanger.

Rosanna ignored Abi's comment. She had little interest in clothes. She pulled her dress straight as Abi wriggled into hers, then brushed her blonde hair and expertly touched up her make-up. 'You look lovely, Abi,' she said admiringly.

'Thank you, my darling. Come on, Cinders, let's go before we miss all the fun.'

They made their way up to the foyer of the opera house. It was already packed with members of the cast and invited members of the audience.

'Champagne, Rosanna?' Abi took two glasses from a passing waitress.

'Thank you.'

'May this be the first of many first nights!' Abi smiled. 'Look, there's the man himself, surrounded by his adoring public.'

Rosanna turned and saw the top of Roberto's head just visible above the throng.

'He's talking to my aunt. The perfect opportunity. Come on, let's go over and introduce ourselves.' Abi took hold of Rosanna's hand.

'No, not tonight. I mean, there are so many people, he's too busy,' protested Rosanna, suddenly overwhelmed by shyness.

'Yes, but we *are* members of the same company, even if Signor Rossini acts as if he's on a superior planet.'

Abi pushed determinedly through the sea of people with Rosanna following meekly behind. Just before they reached the crowd around Roberto, a familiar figure appeared at Rosanna's side.

'*Ciao*, Paolo.' She smiled with relief.

'*Ciao*, Rosanna. I was hoping you would come and join us.'

Much to Abi's annoyance, Paolo took Rosanna's arm and steered her firmly away. Abi shrugged and continued to make her way towards her aunt and Roberto.

'So, how was your first night as a soloist with the company?' Paolo asked as they walked across the foyer.

'It was wonderful,' she breathed.

'Good, good. You sang beautifully, Rosanna. It was a perfect debut. Now, tell me honestly, did you wish you were in Anna Dupré's shoes tonight?'

'Of course,' Rosanna admitted reluctantly.

'Well, from your performance tonight, I'm sure it won't be long. And Riccardo says you are making great progress in your study together. Cover rehearsals start on Thursday. Work hard, Rosanna. They're an excellent chance to perfect the roles you will one day sing.'

'I will, Paolo,' she promised.

'Now, Rosanna' – Paolo lowered his voice – 'there's a gentleman over there who I'm afraid is desperate to meet you. He's a major benefactor of the school and as you are after all last year's star pupil, I think it would be prudent if I introduced you. Would you be so kind as to follow me?'

Rosanna nodded her acquiescence and allowed Paolo to lead her to him.

Abi tapped her Aunt Sonia on the shoulder. Sonia turned, and, on seeing her niece, kissed her warmly on both cheeks.

'Darling, congratulations. I thought you looked beautiful in your costume.' She smiled. 'I'm sure you must have met Roberto Rossini?'

'No,' Abi said, boldly meeting Roberto's eyes. 'Even though we're in the same company, we've not been formally introduced.'

'Well, Roberto,' said Sonia, 'this is Abigail Holmes, my niece. I just know she's going to be a big star one day.'

'It is a pleasure to meet you, signorina, although I have seen you before,' he responded. 'Did you not sing at the benefit for La Chiesa Della Beata Vergine Maria?'

'*What* a good memory you have, Roberto,' simpered Sonia.

'I never forget a pretty face.' He grinned wolfishly. 'You were sitting next to Rosanna Menici.'

'Yes, I was.'

'She sang her aria exquisitely tonight. Is she here at the party?'

'Yes, she's over there somewhere with Paolo.' Abi was somewhat put out by his apparent interest in Rosanna's whereabouts.

Noticing her expression, Roberto continued: 'I've known her since she was a little girl, you see. In fact, you could say that I discovered her. She has the most beautiful voice, but then again, I'm sure you do too, Signorina Holmes.'

The way Roberto pronounced her surname sent a tingle up Abi's spine. But before she could say anything else, she felt a hand on her arm.

'You must excuse me, my dear, but I need to circulate,' interrupted Sonia. 'Take care of her for me, Roberto.'

'Of course.' He bowed gallantly as Sonia departed, then looked up at her niece. 'A glass of champagne, Signorina Holmes?'

'Yes, I'd love one. And please, call me Abi.'

Roberto retrieved a glass from a nearby waiter and handed it to her. 'Now, Abi, you must tell me all about yourself.'

*

An hour later, Rosanna managed to extricate herself from what was becoming a difficult situation. The patron, an older man with a goatish gleam in his eye, had begun to slide his arm up and down her back as they talked. He'd actually had the temerity at one point to rest a hand on her bottom. Having finally escaped on the pretext of visiting the powder room – the only place she could think of where he wouldn't have an excuse to follow her – she searched the dwindling crowd for Abi. She spotted Sonia and walked over to her.

'Hello, Signora Moretti. Have you seen Abi anywhere?'

'No, not for the past half an hour. She was talking to Roberto, but' – Sonia scanned the room – 'she seems to have vanished. Maybe she's already gone back to your little apartment, my dear.'

'Oh no, she would have told me if she was leaving.'

'Maybe she was tired. You go home, and I'm sure Abi will be there.' Sonia smiled at her, then turned away to speak to another guest.

When Rosanna arrived home, the apartment was in darkness. As she sank into bed, she thought how unlike Abi it was not to tell her she was leaving.

Abi lay staring at the silhouette of the man beside her. After he had made love to her, with surprising gentleness, Roberto had promptly fallen asleep. Now she wasn't sure whether she should stay or go home.

She'd put up no resistance when he'd asked her to accompany him back to the Via Manzoni. The kissing had started in his limousine and when they'd arrived at his apartment, they'd only just made it to the bed. Abi sighed to herself in the darkness. The fleeting pain of losing her virginity had soon been outweighed by pleasure, and, she reflected, by the exhilaration of his having chosen *her* tonight. Her thoughts strayed briefly to Rosanna. She chewed her lip as she imagined her friend's disappointment at her actions, but eventually fell into a deep and dreamless sleep.

16

'I'm sorry, what did you say?'

'I just told you. I'm leaving you.' Donatella continued to calmly eat her tiramisu at the other end of the table.

'Are you out of your mind?' Giovanni exploded. 'We sit down to dinner as we normally do, you wait for the dessert, then announce this as though you're asking me for a new dress!'

'I didn't want to spoil your appetite, *caro*,' she replied.

Giovanni slammed his spoon down on the table. 'Don't treat me like a child!' he shouted. 'Who is he?'

'I don't understand what you mean.'

'I assume that the only reason you have for wanting to leave me is that you've been screwing another man.'

'Please, Giovanni, don't use such language at the dinner table.' Donatella's tone was mocking, which served to incense her husband further.

'I'll use whatever language I want! It's my table and I can swear at it if I so wish. Just as I can forbid you to leave me if I so wish.' Giovanni's face had turned puce and a throbbing vein stood out on his left temple.

'Please, try to keep calm, *caro*,' she soothed. 'I apologise if my announcement is a surprise. I thought you might have already known.'

'Donatella, I've been aware for many years that you've had lovers. I've turned a blind eye to them, as you have done for me. That is the marriage we have and it has worked well. Therefore, I can only assume that the reason you wish to have a permanent separation is because you want to be with another man full-time.'

'How very perceptive you are, Giovanni,' said Donatella with heavy sarcasm. 'And after the appropriate length of time, we can divorce.'

'*What?*' Giovanni stared at her. 'Under no circumstances will I divorce you. You are . . . you are my wife! It's completely out of the question. Our social position in Milan, my reputation . . .'

'Don't be so old-fashioned, *caro*. Yes, I accept that a few years ago divorce was not an option, but now, well' – she turned her palms upwards with a nonchalant shrug – 'we have many friends who have done it. It's not a big deal anymore.'

'It is to me.' Giovanni had finally realised she was serious. 'But why, Donatella? Why would you put us both through this? You know how messy these things can be, how the media will latch on to it. We are very well-known figures here in Milan. Surely we can carry on as before? You can have as much freedom as you wish.'

'Really? Even the freedom to live publicly with another man?' she asked quietly, examining her long red fingernails.

Giovanni slumped back in his chair and studied his wife in silence. Then he sighed heavily. 'So, finally I see. You've fallen in love with this new man.'

'Yes.'

'Who is he?'

'That's not important.'

Determined to reassert his authority, Giovanni stood up, wiped his mouth on the linen napkin, and glared at his wife. 'I warn you, Donatella, I will not allow you to humiliate me in front of the whole of Milan. The matter is closed. You will stay here and forget all about this ridiculous idea.'

'Oh, I think you will grant my wish.' Donatella knew she held the winning card and now was the time to play it. 'After all, I'm sure you wouldn't wish the Italian authorities to hear of the exquisite drawing that is hanging at this very moment in the New York penthouse of a wealthy Texan, and of the several million dollars that sits in your Swiss bank account because of it.'

Giovanni's eyes narrowed as he surveyed his wife. 'May I remind you who it was that brought the drawing to me? Who it was that lied to that naive priest about it being virtually worthless? And who had a present of a million dollars as a result of the sale?' Giovanni laughed bitterly and shook his head. 'Oh no, Donatella, you will not go to the authorities, you would implicate yourself as well.'

'Ah yes, *caro*, but remember I'm not only a *very* good actress, but I'm much prettier than you are. I think I'd look wonderful in the newspapers as the used wife of such a terrible criminal and national traitor.' She laid the back of her hand against her forehead and raised her eyes to heaven in a parody of the swooning victim.

Giovanni was silent, his mouth half open in disbelief.

Donatella stood up briskly. '*Caro*, there's no rush. You go away tomorrow for a month. You must think it through and when you come back, we'll talk. I won't be greedy. Of course

I'll want this house and a good allowance, but I'm happy if you wish it to be known that I'm divorcing you on the grounds of *your* adultery. I understand male pride. Goodnight, *caro*. Have a successful trip to New York.'

Donatella swept from the room, leaving only a whisper of the Joy perfume she always wore behind her. Giovanni had never liked it, even if it cost a fortune. Now the smell made him want to vomit.

She had him over a barrel and she knew it. If she went to the authorities, his reputation, his business, his *life* would be in ruins.

Donatella had gambled correctly that he would not take the risk. And, what was more, if she was prepared to go through with a messy, public divorce that would taint the both of them, she must have either taken leave of her senses, or, as she had admitted, fallen in love.

Giovanni went to his study. Standing behind the enormous mahogany desk, too agitated to sit down, he checked a telephone number in his rolodex then picked up the receiver. The first step was to find out who her lover was. Donatella thought she was clever, but he would show her that she'd underestimated him. He was a powerful man, with powerful friends. And now he would use them.

Rosanna had settled into her new life as a member of La Scala with surprising ease. She enjoyed the performances and relished the opportunity to study and learn from the principal singers she worked with. When she was not performing or rehearsing, she had singing lessons or worked alone to learn a new role. Her sessions each week with Riccardo Beroli were proving invaluable. The slight, grey-haired conductor was volatile and irascible at times, but also a musical genius, able to teach her little tricks, such as phrasing the words of a particularly difficult coloratura section in a way that would make the notes sound longer and fuller than they really were.

Every Thursday afternoon, Rosanna attended cover rehearsals, which gave her a chance to sing and practise the moves of the principal roles on the stage itself. As the season progressed and more operas joined the repertoire, Rosanna realised that Paolo had been right in his plans for her. Standing on the large stage in a pair of jeans and a sweatshirt with a piano rattling out the accompaniment might not be as glamorous as performing in costume with a full orchestra in front of two thousand people, but it allowed her to make mistakes. Singing one aria for two or three minutes was one thing, but learning to sustain a taxing role for up to three hours was another.

Rosanna sometimes felt as though she was trying to pat her head and rub her stomach at the same time. Not only did she have to remember the words and the notes and her stage moves, but she was also learning how to bring a character to life. As Riccardo never ceased to remind her, the great sopranos not only possessed wondrous voices, they were consummate actresses with the ability to move an audience emotionally.

Occasionally, Rosanna managed to get it absolutely right, when all the ingredients came together, and, as Paolo was so fond of saying, the 'magic' happened. Rosanna lived for those moments, but she knew she had a way to go before she could make it happen all the time.

It was mid-May and Rosanna was standing on stage singing the difficult duet '*Vogliateme bene*', from the end of Act One of *Madama Butterfly*. Unseen, Paolo had joined Riccardo in the stalls. The two men sat in silence as Rosanna's voice soared to a pure high C.

'She's improving, is she not?' said Riccardo.

'She's gaining experience, stagecraft and, most importantly of all, maturity. The way she's progressing, my plans for *La Bohème* next December are looking very good indeed,' answered Paolo.

'She's the big one, isn't she?' mused Riccardo. 'Our very own home-grown discovery.'

'Yes, although of course we mustn't forget Roberto Rossini.'

'Did somebody mention my name?'

Paolo stood up. 'Roberto, *ciao*.'

Roberto looked irritated. 'We were meant to be meeting in your office at three. Your secretary said you were in the theatre so I came to find you. I have to leave for Copenhagen in two hours.'

'My apologies, Roberto. I forgot the time.'

But Roberto was now staring at the stage. 'That's Rosanna Menici.'

'Yes. She's covering the female leads this season.'

'So I heard. And what a voice she has. But the tenor singing Pinkerton is dreadful. Let me sing it with her, show her how it should sound.'

Before either Riccardo or Paolo could protest, Roberto was striding down the aisle towards the stage.

'Stop playing,' he ordered the pianist.

Rosanna and Fabrizio Barsetti, the young man singing Pinkerton, paused in surprise and peered over the lights as Roberto climbed the steps onto the stage.

'Forgive me, but Signorina Menici and I are old friends. Would you mind if I took your place to sing the love duet?'

The young tenor agreed helplessly and walked away from them towards the wings.

'Pianist, we will begin with the last two bars of "*Viene la sera*".' He turned to Rosanna and smiled, taking her hands in his. 'Don't be frightened. Sing as you have always sung and I shall fit around you,' he whispered. 'Okay,' he ordered the pianist. 'Begin.'

Roberto started to sing, and, when the moment came, Rosanna joined him.

Riccardo and Paolo sank back into their seats, enchanted by what they heard. The two voices, one so experienced and powerful, the other fresh and youthful, combined in the most exquisite way. They also looked perfect together, she so delicate and he so masculine, standing side by side on the empty stage.

'Magic,' whispered Paolo contentedly. He'd always been confident that Rosanna's voice was the find of his life, but now, listening to the way she was responding to Roberto, unabashed by his fame, he knew she was gathering the confidence she needed to soar to the stars.

As the final notes of the love duet hovered around the empty auditorium, Rosanna and Roberto stood looking at each other, seemingly oblivious to their surroundings.

Riccardo grabbed Paolo's arm. 'We must premiere her with him. They are wonderful together.'

'Strangely enough, I'd intended to talk to Roberto this afternoon about *La Bohème*,' agreed Paolo.

'You are learning, my little one,' Roberto said to a flushed, exhilarated Rosanna. 'Maybe a little more vibrato on the last note, but apart from that, well . . . you are a true professional. Forgive me, I must go, Paolo is waiting for me.' He smiled and, kissing Rosanna's hand, left the stage and walked back up the aisle.

'Okay, so we talk,' Roberto said, signalling to Paolo. '*Ciao*, Riccardo.'

The two men made their way out of the auditorium.

'I presume you're grooming Signorina Menici for stardom?' Roberto asked as they began to climb the stairs to Paolo's office.

'Let us say that I think she has enormous potential.'

Roberto stopped on the stairs. 'Promise me that, when you premiere her in her first leading role, I will sing opposite her.'

Paolo could have kissed him. 'As a matter of fact, I've already been talking about this with your agent, Roberto. I want you and Rosanna to open the next season as Rodolfo and Mimi.'

'Perfect! I think we will bring out the best in each other, yes?'

Paolo frowned slightly as he saw the spark of excitement in Roberto's eyes. 'Of course,' he said, as they began to ascend the stairs once more.

After the performance that evening, Rosanna and Abi made their way home. Rosanna was still buzzing with adrenaline from singing with Roberto earlier, but Abi seemed unusually quiet.

'Coffee?' asked Rosanna as they entered their apartment.

'No, thank you. I think I'll have an early night,' replied Abi.

'Please, Abi, tell me why you look so miserable. It is Roberto?'

'No . . . I . . . oh yes, yes, it is . . .' Abi burst into tears and sat down abruptly on the sofa.

Rosanna sat down beside her and put a tentative arm round her shoulder. After Abi had finally confessed the liaison to her, Rosanna had been devastated. But somehow she'd managed to quash her own deep feelings for Roberto for the sake of her friendship with Abi, by convincing herself that her only interest in him was a professional one. And that the cavalier way he treated women must mean he wasn't worth wasting her feelings on. Yet however hard she tried, she still found it difficult and unsettling to talk about the affair.

'I thought he made you happy, Abi,' she managed. 'What's happened?'

'Nothing. That's the whole point. It was fine at first. You know how when he was in Milan, he used to find me at the theatre after the performance and we'd go back to his apartment? But ever since Easter he's ignored me completely.' Abi wiped her streaming eyes.

'But you knew what he was like, Abi. You told me yourself that you wouldn't care if it ended, you were just going to enjoy it while it lasted.'

'Yes, yes, I know. I'm stupid, completely stupid. I promised myself I wouldn't be like the others and fall for him, but I have. Oh Rosanna, do you think he's found someone else?'

'I don't know, Abi,' Rosanna replied honestly, wanting to comfort her friend, but thinking her supposition was probably true. 'Please, try not to worry. You'll forget about him soon anyway. There'll be someone else for you.'

'Excuse me for saying this, Rosanna, but you've never even had a crush, have you? You don't know how it feels.'

'No, you're right. But all I can say is that he might be a

miracle on the stage, but in matters of the heart I think he is a . . . bastard!'

A ghost of a smile hovered round Abi's lips. 'You swore, Rosanna!'

'Yes, well, I think that this once God will forgive me. Abi, I know I'm no expert when it comes to relationships, but you will get over Roberto. After all, you told me you loved my brother Luca a few months ago. You seem to have got over him,' Rosanna reminded her gently.

'Have I?' For a moment, Luca's face hovered in Abi's mind, but she shook her head to dispel the vision. 'Anyway, it's just my luck to meet someone else who's out of my reach,' Abi pouted. Then, noticing Rosanna's concerned expression, she added, 'Oh, you're probably right. I'm sure I'll get over Roberto soon enough. And whatever you may think, I don't feel the same for Roberto as I did for your brother. I feel used, and my pride's hurt, that's all. But nothing's permanent with Roberto, is it? God, he really is a shit and yet, when you're with him, it's like you're the only woman in the world. He just makes you feel so . . . special.'

'Well, you *are* special anyway, without needing Roberto. Now, I'll make some coffee and we'll talk some more, okay?'

'Okay. Thanks, Rosanna.'

'Don't thank me. You're my friend,' she replied.

Later, instead of lying in bed and dreaming of Roberto and how she'd felt when they had sung together that afternoon, Rosanna brutally forced herself to think of arpeggios instead.

The following Thursday, she arrived for cover rehearsals to find Roberto standing on the stage.

'Signor Rossini thinks it would help you if you had one of the principals to work with you on *Butterfly*.' Riccardo immediately saw Rosanna's uncertainty. 'This is a problem for you?'

'Oh, no, of course not. It's very kind of Signor Rossini to offer to help me,' she said stiffly.

'Okay, we begin!'

Two hours later, Rosanna was putting her music away in her case.

'Are you going out?' asked Roberto.

'Yes. I want something to eat before tonight's performance.'

'May I accompany you?'

'No. I'm meeting someone. Excuse me.'

Roberto watched Rosanna hurry off the stage. It had been a long time since a woman had refused him. He frowned in puzzlement, trying to work out why Rosanna Menici fascinated him so much. She had great self-containment and didn't seem at all intimidated by him. In fact, she had just been positively rude to him.

'Are you leaving, Signor Rossini? The cleaners wish to come into the auditorium,' said the theatre manager.

'Yes, I'm leaving.' Roberto walked backstage and made his way towards his dressing room. He opened the door and his heart sank when he found Donatella sitting on the sofa.

'*Caro*.' She stood up, wound her arms around his neck and planted a full-blooded kiss on his lips.

'Why are you here?' Roberto asked irritably.

'Do I need an excuse?' A hand travelled stealthily to the button of his trousers.

He tried to brush it away. 'I have things to do, Donatella. Tonight I perform and I . . .'

The hand undid his zip and found its way inside.

'They can wait,' she whispered.

He groaned and, hating himself for his weakness, resisted no more.

Donatella left the theatre by the stage door. The camera clicked five times. Two minutes later, Roberto Rossini also left by the stage door. The camera clicked again. The photographer smiled. This was the final proof. He also had photographs of her leaving Rossini's apartment last week. He opened the door of his car, started the engine and headed off to develop the film.

The envelope flopped onto the doormat of the apartment in New York a few days later.

Five minutes later, Giovanni Bianchi was studying the contents with interest. So, it was Roberto Rossini that his wife had fallen for.

This surprised him. Every woman in Italy was in love with Rossini and he couldn't imagine the man favouring exclusivity.

Maybe Donatella was merely infatuated, or maybe it was the menopause clouding her judgement. Roberto Rossini was years younger than she. She was obviously deluding herself.

Whichever, it was time to put Rossini out of harm's way.

17

One bright July morning, Paolo was waiting for Roberto to arrive to discuss the forthcoming season. There was a brief knock at the door.

'Come,' he said.

'Sorry I'm late. I overslept.' Roberto nodded at Paolo as he swept into the office and took a seat. 'Any chance of coffee?'

'Of course.' Paolo hid his irritation and rang through to his secretary to order one. 'We need to talk through the schedule for the next six months, Roberto. I know you go to London in August for *La Traviata*, and take your usual month's sabbatical in September. Then you have another three weeks at Covent Garden, as well as recording *Ernani* for EMI.'

Roberto nodded.

'So, you'll be back here by the middle of November to rehearse for *La Bohème*?'

Roberto nodded again. 'Yes. And then after Paris in February, I'm back here to do Il Duca in *Rigoletto*, is that right?'

'Yes. We'll need you to be here for a couple of preliminary rehearsals. There's a whole new set being built and you need to be familiar with it.'

'With many steps?' Roberto rolled his eyes.

'Yes, many steps,' confirmed Paolo.

'After that, I believe I'm off to New York and the Met to do *Tosca* and then there's a concert in Central Park, but you'll need to confirm the dates with my agent.'

'Of course. We've got a phone call booked tomorrow morning.'

The telephone on Paolo's desk rang. 'Excuse me,' he said as he picked up the receiver. 'What is it? I told you I didn't want to be disturbed . . . I see. Then I suppose you must put her through . . . Anna, good morning.' He smiled apologetically at Roberto. The next second the smile was wiped abruptly from his face. 'You have *what*? Are you absolutely sure? No, of course you mustn't. We'll just have to reorganise things. Take care of yourself and I'll ring you tomorrow morning. Yes, of course I understand. *Ciao, cara*.' Paolo put the receiver down and grimaced.

'What's the problem?' asked Roberto.

'The problem is that our Madama Butterfly has got scarlet fever.'

'Scarlet fever?'

'Yes, scarlet fever. Her baby daughter had it two weeks ago. Of course that means she won't be here tonight or for the rest of the week, unless we want the entire company infected. Excuse me, Roberto, but I must call Riccardo. He's downstairs with the orchestra and he's not going to be happy.' Paolo dialled backstage and ten minutes later Riccardo came huffing up the stairs. Once he was seated, Riccardo looked at Roberto, clearly expecting him to leave the room.

'I want to hear who you'll choose. I'm singing opposite her tonight, remember,' said Roberto, staying put.

'Of course, as you wish. I think that Cecilia Dutton must take Anna's place,' said Riccardo.

'She has a recital in Paris tonight,' Paolo reminded him.

'Ivana Cassall then, or Maria Forenzi?' suggested Riccardo.

'Forenzi is a possibility but—'

'No, she is wrong. She's far too old. She has problems remembering her words. I refuse to perform with her,' stated Roberto flatly.

For five minutes, Paolo and Riccardo suggested various names that in turn Roberto vetoed. Finally, when they had run out of suggestions, they sat in a dejected silence. It was broken by Roberto.

'Gentlemen, I have the answer for you.'

They stared blankly at him.

'You do?' they chorused.

'Of course. It's obvious, surely? You must let Rosanna Menici sing Butterfly tonight. She is the cover after all, and that's what covers are for, is it not? She's been rehearsing for weeks with me, so she knows the role well. And I'll be there to help her through it.'

'Absolutely not,' said Paolo curtly, holding up his hand in protest. 'We haven't nurtured her all this time to see her pushed into a role like this before she's ready. Butterfly is for a mature singer with experience. It could be a disaster.'

'Butterfly is meant to be a fifteen-year-old girl,' Roberto reminded them. 'If she pulls it off, as I know she will, it is in some ways better than making her debut in *La Bohème*. Think of the publicity she'd receive.'

'Think of the critics,' groaned Paolo. 'Riccardo, what's your opinion?'

Riccardo took a deep breath. 'I think we have no alternative. It's too late to fly someone in. It's either Rosanna Menici or we cancel. My instinct is that she won't let us down. Maybe it's fate,' he shrugged.

'Do I sense a conspiracy here?' Paolo's eyes darted shrewdly between the two men, assessing the situation. He rubbed his chin in contemplation for a moment. 'Let me make a telephone call and try to trace Cecilia, see if she has already left for Paris. If she has, then I'll tell Rosanna she's to go on tonight.'

'Wonderful! You won't regret this.' Roberto jumped up eagerly. 'Tell Rosanna I'll be available this afternoon to run through anything she's worried about.' He nodded briefly and left the office.

Paolo stared searchingly at Riccardo. 'Is he right?'

'I think he is.'

Paolo tapped his pencil on the table. 'All this interest from Roberto in Rosanna. Is it purely professional?'

'It seems to be. When he works with her, he's the perfect gentleman.'

'He always is before he pounces,' murmured Paolo.

'But more importantly, Rosanna doesn't seem in the least interested in him,' added Riccardo.

'Well, I hope it stays that way, for her sake, because if Roberto Rossini so much as touches a hair on her head, I'll—'

'Paolo, I understand how special Rosanna is to you, but it's really none of our business what singers do in their private lives.'

'I'm aware of that, Riccardo,' Paolo replied tersely. 'Now, let me make some calls.'

*

At noon, Abi answered the ringing telephone.

'Hello, Abi speaking.'

'Abigail, it's Paolo. Is Rosanna at home?'

'Yes, but she's in the shower. Can I take a message?'

'No. I think you'd better tell her to come to the telephone.'

'Okay.'

Two minutes later, a dripping Rosanna picked up the receiver. 'What is it, Paolo?'

Abi watched her visibly pale as she listened to what Paolo had to tell her.

'Okay, so I'll see you at two at the theatre, yes? *Ciao*.' Rosanna replaced the receiver and sank into a chair.

'What on earth is it? Has someone died?' asked Abi.

'No.'

'Then what? You look terrible.'

Rosanna inhaled deeply, then looked at her friend. 'Tonight I am to sing the role of Madama Butterfly at La Scala.'

Rosanna sat in front of the mirror as the make-up artist transformed her into the young Japanese girl, Cio-Cio-San. She was dazed, her thoughts unclear. She didn't feel nervous or excited – in fact, she felt very little at all. She glanced at the large bouquet of red roses on the table in front of her.

Rosanna,
I will be with you,
Roberto
P.S. I have paid the claque on your behalf.

Rosanna couldn't help but smile. Roberto had been wonderful at the afternoon's rehearsal: calm, concerned and eager to help. If it wasn't for the fact that she knew how he'd behaved towards Abi, she might have given way to her feelings for him completely. But, whatever happened tonight on stage, she swore that Roberto Rossini would not win her heart.

'Does the wig feel comfortable?'

'I'm sorry?'

'I said, is the wig comfortable?'

Rosanna dragged herself back from her thoughts to answer the dresser.

'It feels fine.'

'It's slightly too big, but I've stuck so many hairpins in it that it wouldn't move during a tornado,' the dresser laughed. 'Right, I'll leave you to prepare. Good luck, Signorina Menici.'

'Thank you.'

A minute later there was a knock on the door. 'It's Paolo.'

'Come in, please.'

'How are you?' he asked as he opened the door.

'Fine, I think.'

'Good. You look calm. I've come to take you up to the wings. Riccardo wants to see you before beginners.'

Rosanna stood up, took one last glance at herself in the mirror and followed Paolo along the corridor and into the vast wings where Riccardo was waiting for her. He kissed her on both cheeks.

'Rosanna, I'll be in the orchestra pit watching you. If you need guidance, look at me. Are you nervous?'

'No. It's strange, but I don't feel nervous at all.'

'It's good you're calm. You know the role very well. You will do La Scala proud, *cara*.'

'I'll do my best, Riccardo, I promise.'

'I'm off now to greet a very special friend of yours,' said Paolo.

'Who?'

Paolo tapped his nose. 'Wait and see.'

Ten minutes later, the overture began. People were buzzing around Rosanna, making last-minute adjustments to her costume and make-up, checking props, but she hardly responded. Tonight was the night she'd dreamt of and yet she felt distant, as though it wasn't really happening to her.

The familiar music that signalled her entrance began. She sent up a prayer, crossed herself and stepped out onto the stage of La Scala.

Luigi Vincenzi sat in Paolo's box looking down at the slim figure, so tiny and demure. The effortlessness of her singing, combined with her youth and vulnerability, made her the most perfect Butterfly he'd ever seen. And she had such presence, such magnetism. It was rare for the audience at La Scala to be completely silent, but now, as he looked around, he saw that every eye was fixed on Rosanna, the hush palpable, as if two thousand people were holding their collective breath. Yes, there were a few technical imperfections, but those could be worked on easily enough. Luigi felt the tears trickle down his cheeks. His Rosanna, whom he'd discovered and nurtured, was making the most perfect debut. Luigi knew he was witnessing history.

As the bouquets fell at Rosanna's feet, Paolo let out a sigh of relief. The cries of 'Bravo!' echoed round the auditorium. The audience were on their feet, applauding the birth of a new star. It was not the way he'd ever foreseen Rosanna's debut, but Paolo knew he couldn't have asked for more. She had been magnificent. He turned to Luigi, who was foraging for a handkerchief to wipe his eyes. Without speaking, the two of them clasped each other in an embrace.

Rosanna stood in front of the curtain watching the deluge of flowers rain in from the audience, and drank in the wildly enthusiastic cheers. She couldn't remember whether she'd managed to sing a note, let alone in the right key. Robot-like, she let Roberto lead her forward time and again as they took bow after bow.

Then it was over. The company congratulated her, crowding round her from all sides to tell her she had been incredible. Rosanna made her way in a daze back to her dressing room, opened the door and gasped as she saw who was waiting for her.

'Luigi!' She fell into his arms and began to sob loudly.

'Oh Rosanna, is it really that bad to see me?' Luigi laughed as he patted her heaving shoulders.

'No . . . of course not. I'm so glad you came. I . . . don't know why I'm crying, really.'

'It's the release of tension.' Paolo had followed Luigi into the dressing room. 'She was so calm before she went on, Luigi – I feared almost too calm. But I needn't have worried.'

Rosanna lifted her head from Luigi's chest and saw in the mirror that her heavy make-up had started to run down her face. She picked up a tissue and attempted to repair it as best she could. There was another knock on the door and Roberto entered the dressing room.

Ignoring the other two men, he walked straight over to Rosanna, taking in her tear-stained face. 'Why, what is wrong, Rosanna?'

'Nothing, I . . . I'm okay.' And suddenly, she was. The world came into sharp focus again as she turned to smile at him.

'Just a natural reaction, I think. She is now a true emotional artiste, Roberto,' said Luigi, beaming at the pair of them.

'And you have helped her become one, Luigi. It's good to see you again.' Roberto embraced his former teacher.

'And you too sang magnificently tonight. I do believe you're improving with age.'

'I'll take that as a compliment, Luigi,' Roberto replied wryly.

'Was I terrible?' Rosanna looked anxiously at the three men now gathered around her. 'I can't remember anything about it.'

'Rosanna.' Luigi clasped her hands in his. 'No, you were not terrible – anything but. You should be happy. Tonight you made the perfect debut.'

'Really?'

Luigi nodded. 'Really. I'm very proud of you and so are Paolo and Riccardo.'

'And so am I, my little Butterfly. I have rarely seen an audience so enraptured.' Roberto took Rosanna's hands and drew her towards him. The look that passed between them in that moment was akin to a chemical reaction. 'I just came to congratulate you,' he said softly. Then, suddenly aware that two other pairs of eyes were staring at them, he added, 'And to say that I've booked a table at Il Savini. After I've signed autographs, I'll take us all out to dinner to celebrate.'

'That sounds like an excellent idea,' agreed Luigi.

Rosanna looked at Roberto, and though every fibre of her body was reacting to his presence, an instinct of self-preservation held her back. 'That's most generous of you, but I think I should go home. I'm very tired.'

'As you wish,' Roberto said in surprise. He glanced at Paolo. 'She conquers La Scala and now our Butterfly wishes to go home to bed.'

'Rosanna has had a long day. Come now, Roberto, let us leave Rosanna and Luigi to talk quietly.'

Roberto kissed her hand, his lips lingering on her skin just a fraction too long for mere politeness. 'Goodnight, little one. Sweet dreams.' He made for the door with Paolo following in his wake. 'I'll see you in my dressing room, Luigi. We three will toast the absent star.'

Luigi nodded. As the door closed, leaving the two of them alone, Rosanna sank into a chair and yawned. 'I hope he didn't think I was rude. I'm seriously too exhausted to move,' she added.

'Of course. It's perfectly understandable.' Luigi privately thought that it was a very good thing that Rosanna was going home early. Like Paolo, he had not missed the extraordinary chemistry between Roberto and his leading lady. It made him strangely uneasy.

'Luigi, tell me truthfully, was I all right tonight?' Rosanna's anxious voice broke his reverie.

'I'm beginning to think you are fishing for compliments,' he smiled. 'Yes, you were much more than all right. Of course, there were small things you could improve on, tricks that will take time and experience to learn, but if I tell you that you upstaged the great Signor Rossini himself, you'll understand just how good you were.'

'Did I really?'

'Yes, and he still wants to take you out to dinner!'

'He's been very kind.'

'It's a quality which is most unusual in the man. I think maybe he has a soft spot for you, eh?'

'I don't know.' Rosanna yawned again.

'And now, I will leave you. I'm in Milan until tomorrow. Maybe we could have lunch and I shall give you some proper notes on your performance tonight, yes?' Luigi's eyes twinkled.

'Of course.'

'Good. I shall see you tomorrow at Biffi Scala at twelve.'

Luigi left the room and Rosanna was finally alone.

She sat back in the chair, staring into space and trying to recall the performance.

All she could remember were Roberto's eyes gazing at her as he sang his words of love.

18

Paolo put down the receiver and stared moodily out of the window.

All the care he'd taken, the hours of discussion with Riccardo, and now, owing to an attack of scarlet fever, his plans for Rosanna's future had gone up in smoke.

He knew that some would say what had happened was better: Rosanna's unexpected debut in such a difficult role had produced a flood of superb reviews. The critics had been unanimous about her voice – it was startling – and they were predicting great things for her future.

This was all positive, he knew, but Paolo had hoped Rosanna would slip quietly back into solo roles for the rest of the season, then open the new season with *La Bohème* as planned. However, this had proved impossible. Rosanna was the new young soprano all of Milan wanted to see. News of her sensational debut had spread like wildfire. La Scala's box office had been deluged with people wanting tickets for her next performance. The situation had been compounded by the fact that Anna Dupré's scarlet fever had left her very debilitated and her specialist had prescribed rest for the next few months. That meant there was a vacancy for a leading soprano and Paolo had been convinced by those around him that Rosanna was the obvious choice to fill it. So Paolo had gritted his teeth and given his audience what they wanted: his new young star, Rosanna Menici.

She had tackled the roles quite brilliantly, he had to admit. And she was now the somewhat unwilling toast of the town.

Other opera companies had begun sniffing around in earnest. Paolo had reluctantly advised Rosanna that she needed an agent. Chris Hughes, Roberto's American agent, had been more than happy to take her on.

Paolo knew his fledgling had finally spread her wings and begun to fly.

Rosanna and Chris Hughes were sitting at one of the best tables in Il Savini. Chris had ordered a bottle of champagne and insisted Rosanna have a glass.

'Here's to you, my newest client. I think we'll make a good team, Rosanna.'

She nodded at the handsome blond man opposite her. Chris reminded her of every clean-cut American she'd seen in Hollywood films. 'I hope so, Chris.'

'Now, I thought, before I go through the bookings I've made, that I should just explain again exactly how I work, okay?'

'Yes.'

'I'll take care of your schedule for you, and, for the time being, arrange all your PR. It might come to the point where you're so successful you'll need someone to handle your PR full-time, like Roberto has.'

Rosanna nodded.

'I have offices in London and New York with a secretary in each. They'll deal with all your travel arrangements, book your flights and hotels, and so forth. If there's ever a problem, you can reach the London office in the day, and New York up to midnight. I'll also give you my home numbers. We've already discussed my commission and I think you're happy with it?'

'Yes, Chris.'

'Good. Now all I really need to know is where you want your money deposited. All your fees will be paid to me and it's much easier if you give me a bank account number so I can put the cheques straight in without having to bother you.'

'I don't have a bank account,' said Rosanna, her head spinning from all Chris was telling her.

'Really? Well then, I think you'd better open one, honey.' Chris smiled. 'There's every chance you're going to become a wealthy young lady in the next few years. I'm always paid in dollars by the opera companies. It makes it simpler for everyone, but I can change it into whichever currency you choose. Now, that's the financial stuff out of the way. Let's order and we can move on to the interesting bit and discuss your schedule.' Chris studied his menu for a few minutes, then signalled for the waiter. 'What would you like, Rosanna?'

'The *vitello tonnato* and a salad, please.'

'Good choice. I'll have the same.'

'Thank you, sir.' The waiter scribbled the order on his notepad then glided away.

Chris poured some more champagne into Rosanna's glass. 'Right, back to the schedule. It's all good news, Rosanna. The world sure is your oyster at the moment. The Garden have offered you Violetta opposite Roberto's Alfredo. They're desperate for you as their star soprano's just announced she's pregnant and is taking a sabbatical. You'll rehearse for four days, then there'll be eight performances during August.'

Rosanna paled. 'Four days' rehearsal? But it's a role I've never sung!'

'I'm sure Paolo and Roberto will help you before you go. After Covent Garden, you have a month off, then it's back to London for a charity concert at the Albert Hall. There's a possibility I may have got you your first recording deal with Deutsche Grammophon. They're interested in recording *Butterfly* with Roberto, who's already under contract to them, but the details aren't firmed up yet. They obviously want to meet you and I'll let you know the date of that. Anyway, if the deal does come off, there's a window to record in London during October. Also, the Palais Garnier in Paris wants you for a gala concert at the end of that month, then you fly back to Milan to rehearse for *La Bohème*.'

Rosanna took a nervous gulp of her champagne. 'How long have I got to rehearse for that? An hour?'

'A week actually.'

Rosanna shook her head. 'No, Chris, I need longer. Playing Mimi at La Scala has been my dream. I want to make sure I have enough time to prepare, and also give my voice a chance to recover.'

'Well, we can probably manage ten days.' Chris barely looked up from his diary before continuing. 'Then you fly to Vienna to sing Butterfly for a couple of weeks in March, which Paolo has okayed, before you return to Milan for Gilda opposite Roberto's Duca. Then you have two months in New York to prepare for your debut at the Met in *Roméo et Juliette*.'

The waiter arrived with their order.

'This looks great. Tuck in, Rosanna,' Chris encouraged, picking up his knife and fork.

Rosanna did her best, but her appetite had deserted her.

Chris checked his watch. 'Okay, fifteen minutes for coffee. You have an interview with *Le Figaro* in forty-five minutes. Anything you want to ask me?'

'Yes, but I feel exhausted just listening to you, Chris,' she replied honestly.

'I apologise, Rosanna. Paolo's warned me not to push you and I'll do my best. I promise I'll try and give you some breathing space, but, sweetheart, when you're hot, you're hot.' He held out his hands in a 'What did you expect?' gesture.

'It's happened so quickly, that's all.' Rosanna bit her lip and averted her gaze, afraid she might burst into tears.

Chris, realising how overwhelmed she was, reached over to squeeze her hand reassuringly. 'I understand. Look, Rosanna, if at any point you feel you're pushing yourself too hard, just say the word. I'm on your side, remember?'

'Then can you give me more time to prepare for *La Bohème*?' she pleaded.

'It would mean cancelling the Palais Garnier . . .' He ran a finger down the list of engagements. 'But yes, if you feel that strongly about it.'

'I do.'

'Okay,' he sighed, 'consider it done.'

After her interview with *Le Figaro* in the foyer of La Scala, Rosanna walked up the stairs to Paolo's office. Everything was moving so fast and her head was spinning. Chris's plans sounded exciting, but was she taking on too much? She needed to talk to Paolo, see what he thought.

Rosanna knocked on his door and Paolo opened it.

'Come in, Rosanna. How are you? You look a little pale.'

She sat down in a chair. 'I feel pale. I've just had lunch with Chris and he was like a steamroller! He has things arranged for the next eighteen months. He went through the schedule so fast I couldn't keep up with him.'

'Chris is very dynamic,' agreed Paolo, 'but I suppose that's what makes him successful as an agent.'

'I'm just worried I'm running before I can walk. I still have so much to learn, Paolo.'

'Then you *must* tell Chris what you feel.'

'I did.'

'That's good. Remember, he works for you, not the other way round. He's a decent man, Rosanna, a lot better than others I could mention. They'd have you flying halfway across the world for one concert if the money was big enough.'

'I know, and I realise how lucky I am that all these people want me. But I've told Chris that my priority is La Scala. The other companies are important, but here is what really matters to me.' Rosanna paused and stared out of the window. 'I had no idea it would be like this.'

'It's early days, you're bound to find it strange. I'm sure you'll cope well once you get used to it,' Paolo reassured her with an outward show of confidence he didn't entirely feel in his heart. 'So, tell me how you feel about going to London with Roberto?'

'I think we sing well together.' Rosanna was guarded.

'You do. Everyone thinks your pairing is inspired.' Against his better judgement, he couldn't resist adding: 'I know this is none of my business, but Roberto can be . . . most charming when he wishes and—'

Rosanna cut him short. 'It's all right. I understand what you're trying to say and I promise I can take care of myself.'

'I'm glad to hear it.'

Paolo accompanied her down to the foyer and kissed her on both cheeks. 'Just remember, any time you need advice, or just to talk things over, you know where I am. I'm proud of you, Rosanna. *Ciao*.'

'*Ciao*, Paolo. I can never thank you enough.'

He watched her leave the foyer, then climbed the stairs to his office, picked up the telephone and dialled the number of Roberto's apartment. There was no reply. He replaced the receiver and tried to concentrate on some paperwork.

19

Roberto heard the telephone ringing, but ignored it. He reached his climax with a roar and collapsed on top of Donatella.

'*Caro*, that was wonderful,' she gasped.

Roberto rolled over and lay next to her, his eyes closed, his hands over his face.

'Darling, I have some news, some very good news.' She gently stroked his shoulder.

'Oh yes?'

'I'll be able to travel to London with you in August. In fact, from now on, anywhere you go, I can go too.'

Unaware that he'd ever expressed a wish for her to join him when he was singing abroad, Roberto uncovered his face slowly and turned to look at her. 'What do you mean?'

'I'm leaving Giovanni. I've told him and it's settled. I can move in here whenever you wish. From now on, we can be together always.'

Roberto stared at her in disbelief.

'Don't look so concerned, *caro*. It was not a hard decision to make. I'm very happy. It's what I wanted.'

Roberto managed to find his voice. 'Let me get this straight: you've told Giovanni you're leaving him?'

'Yes.'

'But why would you do that?'

'Do you really need to ask? Because it's you that I love, because any relationship I had with my husband ended a long time ago, because—'

Roberto cut her off. 'And he's agreed to all this, just like that?'

'He can't stop me. He has no choice.'

'Does he . . .' Roberto cleared his throat nervously. 'Does he know about me?'

'No, not yet, but of course he will.' Donatella saw the concern flash across Roberto's face. She tipped his chin towards her. '*Caro*, you mustn't worry. I've made sure he can't touch either of us. I've money of my own, a lot of money. We'll want for nothing for the rest of our lives.'

The reality of the situation was beginning to dawn on Roberto. He jumped out of the bed like a scalded cat and grabbed his robe from the back of a chair.

'Where on earth are you going?'

'To shower. I just remembered I have to be at the theatre early tonight.'

'But we must talk. I'll come to meet you later after your performance and drive you back here.'

'NO! I have other plans.' He paused at the bathroom door and turned to look at her, lying so seductively on the bed, but at this moment she repulsed him. 'Donatella, you cannot organise my life without me having some say in it too! I can't believe you went ahead with this without asking me!'

'But your wishes are always foremost in my mind. This is why I'm leaving Giovanni, so we can be together and one day be married and—'

'Please, Donatella, enough. I wish you to leave!'

Roberto watched her face crumple as she turned away to bury it in the pillow. Overcome with remorse, he sat down heavily in a chair, raking his hands through his hair and inhaling deeply. 'Okay, I'm sorry I shouted. This has been . . . well, it's been a shock. Think of the scandal, Donatella. Your husband is a powerful man in Milan. I can't believe he'll just let his wife walk away from him without a fight.'

'He will. He has to. I'm sorry, Roberto. I should have told you of my plans sooner. I'll do as you wish and leave.' With a visible effort, she climbed out of the bed and started to dress.

Roberto watched her. '*Cara*, I just need some time to think, that's all.' He followed her to the front door. She turned away as he tried to kiss her. 'I'll call you tonight, okay?'

She didn't look back as she walked down the corridor towards the lift.

Roberto shut the door, his mind racing. For weeks now, he'd been steeling himself to tell Donatella it was over, that the fun they'd had for the past few years had drawn to its natural conclusion. Yet she'd just informed him she'd already told her husband she was divorcing him so the two of them could be together.

It was so ridiculous that Roberto wanted to laugh. To think Donatella really believed that he would marry her. She was nearly fifty years old, for God's sake, hardly prime child-bearing age.

The telephone rang once more. Roberto automatically went to answer it.

'*Pronto?*'

'Paolo here.'

'What do you want?' Roberto asked rudely, his thoughts still swimming with Donatella's news.

'Only to tell you that Covent Garden have asked Rosanna Menici to accompany you to London,' replied Paolo crisply.

'Yes, Chris told me yesterday.' Roberto regained control of himself with an effort. He must think of his career. 'I'm delighted, of course. We're good together, yes?'

'Yes, Roberto, you know you are. But just promise me one thing.'

'What's that?'

'Rosanna has never travelled abroad before. She's going to a strange country and is nervous at the prospect. I want you to take very good care of her for me.'

'You don't even need to ask, Paolo. You know how fond I am of Rosanna. I'll protect her from all harm, I promise you.'

'Good. Would you be willing to rehearse *La Traviata* with her before you leave? She needs as much practice as she can get.'

'Of course.'

'Thank you. And Roberto?'

'Yes?'

'Just remember I have my spies in London. *Ciao*.'

Roberto slammed the receiver into its cradle. Why did everyone treat him like a naughty little boy who had to be told how to behave? He was fed up with Paolo, fed up with Donatella, and fed up with Milan. He was glad he had some months away. After London, he'd visit the villa he'd bought a couple of years ago on Corsica. He was exhausted. He needed a rest.

The one bright light on the horizon was that Rosanna would be with him in London. Roberto was amazed at just how fond of her he'd become, and had mused that she might be one of the reasons why Donatella's charms had paled so dramatically of late. Rosanna didn't demand, didn't take from him as everyone else did. She was serene, balanced and a joy to sing with. Then, of course, there was that heavenly face and body. He found himself thinking about her incessantly and had dreamt of her on several occasions.

A strange thought entered Roberto's head, and he wondered if he might be just a little bit in love with her. He pushed the thought from his mind as quickly as it had entered. It was almost certainly the fact that she seemed immune to his charms that made him want her more.

As for Donatella, she would have to be told she'd got it wrong. Roberto stood up and headed for the shower, grimly trying to convince himself that she'd understand.

Later that evening, Roberto arrived home, drained by a particularly difficult performance of *Don Giovanni*. The audience had been raucous, distracting the performers. The patrons at the after-party had seemed even more vacuous and demanding than usual. He'd left for his apartment at the earliest opportunity, longing for peace and some sleep.

He turned the key in the lock and discovered the door was already open. Chastising himself for his carelessness, Roberto wandered down the hall and opened the door to the sitting room.

'Signor Rossini.' The man stood up from the sofa and smiled at him with a chilling lack of warmth.

'How . . . how did you get in here?' Roberto stuttered.

'It was very simple. I made a copy of my wife's key. I'm Giovanni Bianchi. I believe we've met on a number of occasions at La Scala. I hope you don't mind, but I poured myself a brandy while I waited. Shall I get you one too?'

Roberto nodded, too shocked to object. He sat down as he watched Giovanni pour the brandy into a glass. He mentally searched for an object to defend himself with and wondered whether, if he called out, the neighbours would come and investigate. With a sinking heart, Roberto realised his neighbours were used to regularly hearing him air his vocal cords at strange hours of the day and night.

This was it. Giovanni Bianchi had come to kill him for screwing his wife. He probably had a gun in his inside pocket that he would pull out at any moment. Roberto took the brandy and lifted it to his lips, his hand shaking.

Giovanni sat down in a chair opposite him.

'So, my wife Donatella wishes to leave me to come and live with you. Well' – Giovanni glanced around the room – 'this apartment is certainly a little smaller than she is used to.' Giovanni placed his brandy glass on the table in front of him and leant forward. 'Signor Rossini, or may I call you Roberto?'

He nodded uneasily.

'Roberto, let me be honest with you. I find myself in a strange and difficult position. My lovely wife of many years suddenly announces she wishes to leave me. This is bad enough, but then I discover the source of her *amore* is one of the most famous tenors in the world, certainly in Italy. I then think of the media, the way they would take such pleasure in dragging all three of us and our reputations through the mud.'

Giovanni paused to take a sip of his brandy. 'Roberto, I am a man with a certain position in Milan. You might well understand that my pride would not allow me to be publicly humiliated by you and my wife. Besides that, I have to tell you there has never been a divorce in the Bianchi family. My mamma would turn in her grave. No, I think to myself, the situation is completely unacceptable. So what should I do? Arrange for Roberto to be disposed of?' Giovanni looked at Roberto's pale face, smiled, then shook his head. 'No, even though he has committed adultery with my wife, I am a peaceful man. I decide that the best plan would be to discuss this with Roberto in a civilised fashion. Do you not agree?'

'Yes.'

'So, here I am. Tell me, have you asked my wife to move in with you?'

'No, I haven't. Ever.' Roberto was surprised by the vehemence of his own voice. 'And then, this afternoon, she tells me she's leaving you. I was horrified, Signor Bianchi, believe me.'

'Giovanni, please, Roberto. Do you love my wife?'

'I . . . she is very beautiful and I am very fond of her but—'

'You have had a pleasant arrangement that Donatella is now trying to make into something more permanent.' Giovanni finished the sentence for him. 'This is not something you want, I take it?'

Roberto shook his head nervously, not wishing to insult Giovanni's wife, but wanting to clarify his position.

Giovanni nodded thoughtfully. 'I imagined this might be the case. Donatella is at a . . . difficult age. She is losing her youth, her hormones may be playing tricks on her and she believes she's in love with you. So, Roberto, what can we do to stop her making this bad decision?'

'I'll tell her tomorrow it's all over between us. In a way, it will be a relief to end it,' replied Roberto candidly.

'And you think that will stop her pursuing you?'

'Of course. I shall refuse to take her calls, avoid her completely.'

Giovanni shook his head. 'It's not so easy to avoid a determined woman. Especially a woman like my wife. There'll be many occasions in the future when you are bound to meet. You see, Roberto, my wife and I have always had an understanding between us. We have each turned a blind eye and used discretion. I'm a tolerant man, but I would be so unhappy if a whisper of your affair with my wife appeared in any newspapers.'

'But it won't. We were always careful.'

'Perhaps, but that was before Donatella fell in love with you. While she is so unstable, she may not wish to be careful any longer. I gather she would like the whole world to know of your affair. No.' Giovanni shook his head again. 'Merely telling her it's over is not the answer.'

'So . . . what do you suggest?'

'I believe I've thought of the best plan, Roberto. Distance is the key. If you are not here, she cannot see you.'

'I'm to go away to London in a few weeks. I'll be out of the country for three months. That should be long enough for the dust to settle.'

'It's a good start, certainly, Roberto, but I think it will take longer than that for Donatella's obsession to leave her. I would suggest you stay away from Milan . . . no, let us say from Italy, for at least five years. Maybe forever, if necessary.'

Roberto looked at him as if he were mad. 'But I have professional commitments, performances at La Scala that are already booked for the next year.'

'Then I suggest you cancel them.' The smile was still in place, but Giovanni's eyes were hard and cold. 'As I've said, I'm a reasonable man. If you agree, we can solve this conundrum very simply. If you don't agree, then things become . . . a little more complicated.'

'You're threatening me, Giovanni.'

'No, I'm suggesting a solution.'

'And what if I refuse?'

Giovanni picked up his brandy glass and drained it. 'Life is sadly full of unseen perils and freak accidents, Roberto. I would hate to think of you falling prey to such things.' He stood up. 'I think we understand each other. You are a sensible man. You will make a sensible decision. To help you, I've provided two gentlemen who will watch your every move. Until you leave Italy they will be with you. And remember, there will not be a pleasant welcome here if you ever decide to return.'

'But Donatella will call me. She might even arrive here unannounced if I don't speak to her.'

'No. Tomorrow Donatella leaves with me for New York. She has agreed to come on the premise of discussing a separation agreement. We will be away for three weeks. By the time we arrive back in Milan, you will have gone. Don't think you can come back to any part of Italy unnoticed. I have . . .

friends who will inform me of your arrival. Do we have a deal, Roberto?'

'Yes,' he murmured miserably, knowing he had no choice but to agree.

'Good. Then it's settled. I'm glad. I do loathe violence of any kind. Goodbye, Roberto. I shall miss you at La Scala.'

Roberto watched Giovanni leave the room and heard the front door close behind him. After a few seconds, he stood up and walked over to the window. Down below, he could see a car parked on the opposite side of the street. Two men were leaning against it, staring up at his apartment. He moved away from the window.

An hour later, after three more large brandies, Roberto checked again. The car and his minders were still there.

Should he call the police and tell them what had happened? No, it would do no good. Giovanni was too powerful, almost certainly with Mafia connections, and even if they did manage to bring charges of threatening behaviour, Roberto would fear for his life every time he set foot on Italian soil.

Roberto tried to think about how all this would affect his future. Apart from *La Bohème* and *Rigoletto* at La Scala, he had no other Italian engagements planned. Paolo would be furious when he heard the news, but given the circumstances that couldn't be helped. Roberto went to bed a little calmer. After all, it could have been worse. He could be dead.

And at least Donatella was no longer his problem.

20

As the plane began to taxi along the runway, Roberto breathed a sigh of relief and relaxed back into the cushioned leather of his first-class seat. The longest three weeks of his life were finally over. He'd hardly slept since Giovanni's visit. He'd watched the car containing the two henchmen tail his own limousine everywhere he went. They'd even followed him as far as the check-in desk at Linate Airport.

After much thought, Roberto had decided to make London his base for the next few years. His Milan apartment would be sold fully furnished, and the proceeds from the sale, along with the contents of his Milan bank accounts, would be transferred to London. While he was at Covent Garden, he would look around for a suitable house to live in. Chris Hughes, his agent, had no idea that his leaving Milan was permanent. Roberto would tell him of his plans in the fullness of time.

He turned and studied his companion's pale face as she stared out of the window. He noticed that she was twisting her hands round in her lap. He stretched out his own hand and covered hers with it.

'Don't panic, *principessa*. Soon we'll be in the air, high above the clouds.'

The engines began to roar as they sped down the runway. Roberto said a silent goodbye to Italy, then watched as Rosanna closed her eyes and crossed herself as the nose of the plane lifted and the wheels left the ground. He chuckled softly.

'If you're to be an international star of the opera world, you'll have to get used to flying, little one.'

'Are we in the air yet?' Rosanna asked, her eyes still tightly closed.

'Yes. We are up. You can look now.'

Rosanna opened her eyes, peeked out of the window and gasped with a mixture of fear and exhilaration. 'Look! There are clouds below us!' she breathed in awe.

'Yes. Although if it was a clear day, you would see the spire of the great Duomo beneath us.'

'Champagne, sir?' An attractive stewardess offered two glasses and a bottle.

'Thank you.' Roberto turned to Rosanna. 'Have one – a little champagne may calm you down. Normally I don't drink on a flight as it dehydrates you. But today I feel like celebrating.'

The stewardess poured champagne into two glasses and smiled at Roberto shyly. 'I saw your Nemorino at La Scala. We sat in the upper gallery, so we didn't have the best view, but I thought you were wonderful.'

Roberto smiled back. 'Thank you, Signorina . . . ?' he prompted.

'Call me Sophie,' the stewardess said, blushing. 'Are you staying in London for long?'

'A month. I'm singing *La Traviata* at Covent Garden.'

'Oh, how lovely. Maybe I'll be able to get tickets.'

'Give me a call at the Savoy and I'm sure we can arrange some for you.'

'Oh, thank you, Mr Rossini, I'll definitely do that.' Her heavily mascaraed eyelashes fluttered coquettishly.

Roberto's eyes followed the stewardess's shapely legs as she moved forward to serve the passengers in the seats in front of them.

'Well, *principessa, salute*!' Roberto took a gulp of his champagne. Rosanna, who had quietly observed the flirtatious exchange, was staring at him in disgust.

'What is it? What have I done?' he protested.

Rosanna sighed and shook her head. 'Nothing,' she replied.

'No, please tell me why you look at me with such disdain.'

'No, it's none of my business.'

'I want to know why you're cross with me,' he persisted.

'Okay, if you insist, but don't blame me if you don't like what I have to say,' Rosanna warned. She hesitated for a second before blurting out, 'I think you're terrible with women.'

Roberto threw back his head and laughed.

'I don't think it's funny, actually, especially when you treat them so badly. Like you did my friend Abi Holmes.'

Roberto's face immediately became serious. 'Ah, now I understand. You hate me because I had an affair with your friend.'

'No, I don't know you well enough to hate you. It's just that, well . . .' Rosanna struggled to find the words, then gave up and shook her head. 'It doesn't matter.'

'Yes it does. For some reason I value your opinion.'

'Well, I think you never take women's feelings into

account. You promise them things and then you drop them when it suits you.'

'And you have that on good authority, do you?'

Rosanna flushed. 'The whole world knows what you're like.'

'Rosanna, I know of my reputation. And I have to take most of the responsibility for it. Yes, I enjoy female company and in my position I'm given plenty of opportunities, which I frequently take advantage of. I don't deny it. But don't you see that it's because I love women? I worship them. I think they're one of the only things on this planet of ours that make life worth living. And I never make promises I can't keep. They know what Roberto Rossini is like. If they cannot accept that, then they shouldn't become involved with me. It's simple,' he shrugged.

'Have you ever told a woman you loved her?'

'Not of my own free will, no.'

'They force you to say it, do they?'

'There are moments when, in the height of passion, a woman asks you and you respond. But I've never been in love.' Roberto sipped his champagne contemplatively. 'You know, Rosanna, you must understand the other side of the story too before you judge me. I am easy prey for women. They like to be seen with me because it's good for their egos, and often for their publicity campaigns too. Many times they are using me more than I am using them.'

Rosanna rolled her eyes in disbelief at his defence.

'You see? Nobody understands poor Roberto. They always think badly of him. One day, when you too are a big star, you'll see for yourself how lonely it can be.'

Rosanna finally gave in and chuckled at his blatant

attempt to garner sympathy, shaking her head at the same time. 'I can't feel sorry for you, Roberto.'

He looked at her squarely. 'You don't like me, do you, Rosanna?'

'Of course I do.'

'Really?'

'Yes, really. Now, I wish to study the *La Traviata* score.' Flustered, Rosanna pulled her music case onto her lap, retrieved the score and turned away from him.

Roberto closed his eyes and wondered yet again why he was so keen to have Rosanna Menici's approval.

A sleek limousine was waiting for them outside Terminal 3 at Heathrow and they were driven into the centre of London. Conversation was limited to pleasantries, since Rosanna spent most of the journey gazing out at the unfamiliar landscape, from the grey suburbs to the increasingly grand buildings that flanked the road as they made their way through Kensington and Knightsbridge. The car finally came to a halt beneath the imposing art deco canopy of the Savoy hotel, where the manager was waiting in the lobby for them. Roberto was ushered to a suite and Rosanna to what she considered to be a delightful room. She was beginning to unpack when there was a knock on the door. She opened it and Roberto swept in. He looked around, then shook his head.

'No, no, no. It will not do.' He went to the telephone and dialled reception. 'This is Roberto Rossini. Tell the manager that Signorina Menici requires a suite. He is to come and meet us both in mine immediately.'

'Roberto, please, this room is more than fine,' Rosanna protested as Roberto flung clothes back into her case.

'Rosanna, you are coming to this country as a guest artiste of the Royal Opera House and you are entitled to all that I have. Now, you will come to my suite until they find you one of your own.'

Rosanna followed Roberto down the corridor, realising it was pointless to argue with him.

'You see, you have to establish these things from the beginning, otherwise people will walk all over you. Just remember it's *you* doing *them* a favour, not the other way round. Ah, here is my friend the manager.'

They reached the door to Roberto's suite, where the manager was already waiting for them. Roberto put an arm round his shoulder. 'Only a small problem. We wish Signorina Menici to have a suite in your beautiful hotel.'

'Of course, madam. I'm so sorry for the mistake. Come this way.'

'Wait, I need to get my suitcase.' Rosanna was about to turn back but Roberto put a hand on her arm to stop her.

'No, little one. The bellboy will deliver it to your new room. Remember who you are. I will collect you from your suite at eight. Then we shall dine together in the restaurant.' Roberto winked at her, unlocked his door and disappeared inside.

Two hours later, Rosanna was luxuriating in the large bathtub, scented bubbles caressing her skin. She felt disorientated, but not unhappy. The silence in the enormous suite was deafening and she realised this trip to London would be the first time she'd ever had more than a few hours alone. At home, there'd always been Mamma, Papa, Carlotta and Luca. When she'd moved to Milan, there had been Luca and then Abi. Now, for the next month, she would have to learn to stand on her own two feet, with only Roberto to give her advice.

Rosanna soaped herself with a flannel. Her feelings for Roberto were confused. On the one hand, she found him insufferably arrogant, but on the other . . . she could not help but be drawn to him.

Just like hundreds of women before me, she scolded herself as she stepped out of the bath and towelled herself dry.

Rosanna dressed, then sat in front of the gilt-edged dressing table and applied a little mascara and lipstick. After fiddling with her hair for a few more minutes, she stood up and smoothed down one of the elegant new dresses Abi had insisted she buy before she left Milan. She sighed as she stared at her reflection in the mirror. For a girl who had not an iota of interest in her appearance, she wondered why she had just spent almost an hour getting ready for dinner tonight.

Roberto knocked on the door of the suite. When Rosanna opened it, he drew in his breath. The short black dress clung lightly to her slender figure, accentuating her long, slim legs, and her freshly washed hair shone under the light. She looked so young, so fresh, so beautiful. Roberto was surprised by the deep impression she made on him, for she had none of the assets he normally found attractive in a woman – no deep cleavage or shapely hips. It was almost as if her body was still suspended somewhere between childhood and adulthood.

'Rosanna, may I say that you look stunning.'

'Thank you.' She smiled shyly.

He offered an elbow and she tucked her arm in his. 'It will be my honour to escort you to dinner.'

They walked off down the corridor towards the lift.

The following morning, even though the Royal Opera House was only a five-minute walk away, a car was waiting to drive them to rehearsals. They were dropped at the stage door rather than at the colonnaded main entrance, but Rosanna still felt overwhelmed as she entered the building. The artistic director took them onto the stage and showed them the set that was being constructed.

After lunch, rehearsals began. The chorus filed onto the stage behind Roberto as he stood studying his score.

'No, no, no!' he shouted, gesturing impatiently for them to leave. 'During this part I sing alone on stage.'

Jonathan Davis, the artistic director, smiled patiently at Roberto.

'I know it's different, but because of the set-change going on at the back, we have to bring the chorus forward. There's no time to get them off stage then on again. The audience won't see them, though.'

'But I will *feel* them behind me, that's what matters.' Roberto yawned and looked at his watch. 'It's past four and I'm tired. I will go back to my hotel for a rest. Signorina Menici will leave too. She's also tired from our travels.'

'I'm fine,' Rosanna clarified defensively.

'But, Mr Rossini, we need to go through the . . .'

Jonathan's words were lost as Roberto walked off towards the wings.

Rosanna remained on stage. 'I don't want to go yet. Is there anything we can run through without Mr Rossini?'

'Of course. We can work on "*Sempre libera*".' Jonathan smiled tiredly at her.

'I'm sorry for Roberto leaving like that.' For some reason Rosanna felt moved to apologise for his behaviour.

'Miss Menici, we are all used to the . . . shall we say, eccentricities of the stars. Now, we will continue.'

Rosanna returned to her suite two hours later feeling drained and fractious. She couldn't bear to think that in four days' time she would be opening in her debut at Covent Garden in the taxing role of Violetta. She felt completely unprepared.

The telephone rang almost immediately.

'*Pronto*, I mean, hello?'

'It's Roberto. Where have you been?'

'Where do you think I've been? I've been rehearsing, as best as I could, without you.'

'Attch! You'll be fine. I'm taking you out to Le Caprice for dinner tonight. It's a very good restaurant.'

'No, Roberto,' she said firmly. 'I, unlike you, haven't had a rest this afternoon. I'm going to send for room service, study my score, then get some sleep. Goodnight!'

The telephone rang again a few seconds after she'd replaced the receiver, but Rosanna ignored it. When it stopped, she dialled room service and ordered a salad. Then she told reception to block her line and settled down to study her score.

The next morning Rosanna was up early. She arrived at Covent Garden before most of the cast and spent an hour with Jonathan Davis going through the sections she was still unsure of.

Rehearsals began officially at ten o'clock. At eleven, Roberto had still not arrived.

'Don't worry, Miss Menici. He's always like this during rehearsals. Then he turns in a superb performance when it matters.' Jonathan seemed perfectly calm.

Rosanna kept her thoughts about her co-star to herself, and tried to concentrate on her singing. Eventually, at midday, just as they were about to break for lunch, Roberto appeared.

'I'm so sorry. I forgot to order my wake-up call last night,' he announced blithely.

'Okay, everyone, we'll continue for another hour as Mr Rossini is now with us,' called Jonathan patiently to the rest of the cast.

An hour later, Roberto announced he had a sore throat and was going back to the Savoy to nurse it in bed.

'It's this climate – it is so damp.' Roberto waved his arms dramatically as he left. 'I'll see you at the hotel, Rosanna.'

Rosanna turned her back on him.

Later that evening, Rosanna was in the bath when she heard a knock on the door. She ignored it. The way she felt at the moment, she couldn't trust herself to control her temper. Getting out of the bath, she dried herself and pulled on a thick towelling robe. She walked into the sitting room and was startled to find Roberto lounging on the sofa watching television.

'What on earth do you think you're doing here?' She pulled the lapels of her robe more tightly together.

'The door was not locked.' He smiled disarmingly. 'You should be more careful. You never know who might walk in. I've come to take you out to dinner.'

Rosanna sank into a chair, her senses on high alert. 'I thought you had a sore throat.'

'I did, but it has gone. Come, get dressed and we'll go.'

'No. I don't want to.'

Roberto looked surprised. 'Why not?'

'Because I'm exhausted and . . . besides, I don't wish to have dinner with you.'

'Rosanna, I think you're angry with me. What have I done?'

'What have you done? *Mamma mia!*' Rosanna thumped a cushion in frustration with her fist.

'Tell me, please,' he urged.

She could control herself no longer. 'All right, Signor Rossini, I *will* tell you. I've come here to make my debut at Covent Garden. I'm nervous, frightened, I feel under-rehearsed. And in the few days that I do have to get the role right, I find that my co-star isn't willing to give more than a couple of hours' rehearsal time, so the company and I have to carry on without him when there's little more than two days left before we open! And . . .'

Rosanna stopped talking as she saw the corners of Roberto's mouth twitch. He began to laugh.

'Why are you laughing? I don't think it's at all funny!'

'Ah, it is, only because I see that at last Rosanna Menici has some fire in her belly – the temperament of a true artiste.'

'Me? Temperamental?' Rosanna walked menacingly towards Roberto. 'Let me tell you something about temperament, Signor Rossini. I've heard all the stories about you being difficult, but because you helped me in Milan, I decided others were jealous of your success and I chose to ignore the rumours. But, after the last two days, I see I was wrong. You're completely selfish. You treat me and everyone else in the company as though we're not worthy to stand on the same stage with you. When you do come to rehearsals, you behave like a petulant child if something is not completely to your liking. I don't know why anyone should put up with you. If I was Jonathan Davis, I would have sacked you that first day.'

Rosanna stood over Roberto, her body taut with anger.

Roberto looked up at her.

'Do you know that you're at your most beautiful when you're cross?'

Before she knew what was happening, Roberto had grasped her hands and pulled her down onto his knees. As if in a trance, she watched as his mouth moved towards hers. But just as their lips were about to make contact, Rosanna came to her senses and wrenched one of her hands from his grip. She raised it and slapped Roberto hard across his face.

Both of them sat in shock for a few seconds. Then Rosanna stood up and turned away from him, shaking with emotion.

'I want you to leave now.'

She didn't turn round, but listened as Roberto stood up and walked towards the door. It slammed shut behind him.

She sank to the floor and burst into tears.

21

Rosanna was awoken by a knock on the door. Still half asleep, she searched for the light. Turning it on, she looked at the clock by her bed and saw it was almost eight a.m. Finding her robe, she headed towards the door.

'Who is it?' she asked nervously.

'I have a delivery for you, madam.'

Rosanna opened the door and found a bellboy submerged under a lavish bouquet of orchids and lilies.

'Where shall I put them?' The bellboy carried the flowers into the sitting room. 'On the table over there?'

'Yes, that'll be fine, thank you.' Rosanna waited until the bellboy had shut the door behind him, then went across to the bouquet. A small white envelope was tucked among the blooms. She pulled it out and opened it.

You were right. I am a shit. My deepest apologies. See you at the Opera House (on time). R.

Rosanna tore the note into small pieces and dropped them disdainfully into the wastepaper basket. Then she went to get dressed.

*

'You are exactly one minute and twenty-five seconds late.'

Roberto was already standing on stage, a woollen scarf wrapped round his neck.

Rosanna ignored him and walked across the stage to talk to Jonathan Davis.

Over the next two days, Roberto behaved like an angel. He was helpful and polite, and didn't argue when Jonathan asked him to do something different. He even offered to stay late to work with Rosanna on their complicated duets. Rosanna was grateful, but still maintained her distance.

Each evening after they arrived back at the Savoy, she half expected to hear a knock at the door, but it didn't come. He didn't telephone her suite either.

Rosanna hated herself for feeling disappointed.

There were two lovely bouquets of flowers in her dressing room when she arrived for the first night. Hurrying to open the cards, she was crestfallen when she saw that one was from Paolo and the other from Chris Hughes. Roberto had clearly been offended by her lack of appreciation for his last floral offering. She tried to push thoughts of him to one side as her dresser helped her into the extravagant silk gown that she would wear to play the beautiful but doomed Violetta. She began to mentally prepare herself, but she felt freezing and saw that her hands were shaking. Two minutes later, her temperature had soared and her palms became sweaty. Her heart was beating fast and she felt sick every time she thought about walking onto the stage. She tried opening her mouth to practise some arpeggios, but nothing more than a squeak came out.

Rosanna, she told herself firmly, *it's stage fright. Luigi told you this could happen. Concentrate on your breathing.* She studied her reflection in the mirror and tried to calm herself.

By the time she was made up and dressed she was so shaky she could hardly stand. She wanted to cry and wished desperately that Paolo or Luigi was there to hold her hand and tell her everything was going to be all right.

'Beginners, please!' The call of the assistant stage manager roused her as he passed outside her dressing room door, summoning the opening performers to take their positions. Somehow, she made her way unsteadily to the wings. The orchestra was warming up and Rosanna could hear the expectant hum of the audience behind the famous red curtains.

As she stood shivering like a willow tree in the wind, a hand was placed on her shoulder.

'Good luck, Rosanna. We will triumph together tonight.' Roberto looked gloriously masculine in his costume of top hat and tails.

'I feel so sick, Roberto,' she whispered desperately.

He took her cold hands in his and rubbed them. 'Good. You're playing a consumptive, so your acting will be supreme tonight.'

Rosanna was too nervous to even register the joke. 'But I have no voice,' she added.

'Rarely before a performance do I have one either. Think of it like this: you are standing in the music room at Luigi's villa. The piano is playing and you are singing for yourself because you love it. Nobody is listening – you are all alone.' Roberto smiled down at her and placed a kiss on each of her cheeks. 'We will be superb tonight. I know it.'

He left her to take up his position and Rosanna stood alone in the wings listening to the first strains of the overture. She closed her eyes and thought of the calmness of Luigi's music room and the happiness she'd felt when she'd sung there. Then she stepped out onto the stage and her voice began to soar.

Many hours later, Rosanna arrived back in her suite at the Savoy. She was still on a high, every nerve ending in her body tingling.

The applause at the end of the performance had seemed to go on forever. Jonathan had told her she and Roberto had taken twenty-two curtain calls. At the after-party, she'd been surrounded by strangers offering superlatives and claiming her Violetta to be the best since Callas.

Rosanna sat down in a chair. Without doubt, it had been the most wonderful three hours of her life. For the first time on stage, she had really felt the power she'd had over the audience. Her confidence had soared and she'd begun to enjoy herself, portraying her tragic heroine as a woman of feverish excitement, temptations and fears. Her Violetta had come alive tonight.

And Roberto . . . Roberto had helped her. In his role as Alfredo, he'd supported her generously, never upstaging her, and had handled their duets with a calmness that had transmitted itself to her too. It was almost as if he had stepped back and allowed her to fly. And there had been moments when she'd looked up into his eyes during '*Parigi, o cara*' and felt all the force of her character's doomed love. Rosanna sighed. Whatever Roberto was, however selfishly he behaved, she knew there was part of her that had loved him since she was a little girl. And after tonight, despite her best efforts to convince herself otherwise, she knew she still did.

Tonight, she'd meant to make her peace with him, to thank him for his words before the performance, for all his help. But at the party, she'd been surrounded by so many people that she hadn't had a chance to talk to him. When she'd eventually looked for him, he'd disappeared.

Rosanna paced around her sitting room wondering what she should do. Eventually, she opened the door and walked along the corridor to his suite.

There was no response to her light tap on his door. She listened but could hear nothing. She knocked again. Then she thought she heard a muffled sobbing. Puzzled, she checked she had the right suite. Finding she did, she listened again. There was no mistake. Someone inside was crying.

'Roberto,' she called softly through the door. 'It's Rosanna.'

The sound did not abate. Rosanna turned the handle and found the door was unlocked, so she opened it and stepped tentatively inside. The sitting room seemed to be deserted, but the sobs guided her behind the sofa. Roberto, still in full evening dress, was slumped on the floor, his head in his hands. He was weeping so hard he hadn't heard her enter the room, so when she put a hand to his shoulder, he jumped in shock.

'It's only me,' she whispered as she knelt down next to him. 'Roberto, what is it? What has happened?'

He looked at her with such anguish in his eyes that she could only respond by putting her arms round his shoulders and hugging him awkwardly.

'I had a message, tonight during the party. My mamma . . . she . . . is dead.'

'Maria? Oh Roberto, I'm so sorry.'

'My father came home to find her in bed as usual, but he couldn't wake her, she wouldn't stir, and then he realised she wasn't breathing. The doctors think it was a stroke. I kept promising to go home and see them, but I did not and now . . . now it's too late. My mamma is dead. I will never see her again. She is gone.' This statement precipitated another sobbing attack.

'Roberto, would you prefer me to leave? Perhaps you want to be alone.'

'No. Please . . . please stay. You knew her, Rosanna, you understand.'

'Would you like a drink?'

Roberto nodded. 'There's some brandy in the cabinet over there.'

Rosanna found the bottle. She poured a large measure and handed it to him.

'Thank you.' He swallowed it in one go.

'Do you want me to ring reception and see if they can arrange for you to fly to Naples as soon as possible?'

Roberto looked at her and his eyes filled with tears once more. 'No, Rosanna. I can't go to Naples. I've been so bad, so selfish, that now I cannot even attend my own mamma's funeral.' Roberto's shoulders heaved.

'Roberto, everyone will understand if you have to cancel a performance. Your mother is dead and you have to return home.'

'You don't understand. I cannot go and that is the end of it!'

'Come, Roberto, why don't you sit down on the sofa?' she said gently.

He allowed her to help him up from the floor and guide him to the sofa, where he sat down heavily. Rosanna settled next to him, reaching out her hand to clasp his as he stared into space.

'You know, I think I've loved only one person in the whole of my life: my mamma. And I've let her down, as I let everyone down. I'm such a shit that now I cannot even say goodbye to her.'

'I'm sure she didn't think you'd let her down. You're one of the most famous tenors in the world. I know how proud she was of you. She talked of nothing else whenever she visited our café,' Rosanna comforted him, understanding he was hysterical, overcome with shock. Nothing he was saying was making sense.

'Yes, but I didn't make time for her when I became famous. I've seen her twice in the past six years, and that was only when she made the journey to Milan to see me.' He turned to look at her mournfully. 'You were right when you said I was completely selfish. I am a bastard, Rosanna. I hate myself.' Roberto put his head in his hands and began to cry again as Rosanna sat silently next to him, understanding there was nothing she could say that would help. Eventually, he stopped sobbing and wiped his eyes. 'I've never cried like this before. I feel so guilty.'

'It's natural to feel guilty, Roberto. When my mamma died, I felt terrible that I'd ever thought bad things about her. I'm sure Maria understood that you were busy. Mothers understand and forgive better than anyone, especially when it comes to their children.'

'You think she'd forgive her son for not being at her funeral?' he asked her quietly.

'I'm sure if there's a good reason she would, yes.'

Roberto sighed and blew his nose hard on the handkerchief. 'I'm so sorry for ruining the end of your evening. You were a triumph tonight, Rosanna. You should be celebrating, not sitting here comforting a grieving old man.'

'Now you *are* being self-indulgent,' she chided him gently.

'Middle-aged then. Why did you come to see me?' he asked suddenly. 'It's very late.'

'Because I wanted to say sorry.'

'No, it is I who should apologise. I'm a shit. It is true.'

Rosanna took his hand once more. 'And I wanted to say thank you for tonight. Without you there, I couldn't have done it.'

'Do you mean that?'

'Yes,' she said softly.

'Then even though my mamma is dead, at least I can tell myself that I did something tonight – for once – that was not selfish.'

'You did. And I will never forget it. Thank you.' Rosanna kissed him on his cheek. 'Now, I think you should try to get some sleep.'

Roberto looked at her as she moved to get up. 'Rosanna, please, I don't think I could bear to be alone. Would you stay with me?'

'Roberto, I . . .'

'No, Rosanna, I'm not asking what you think. You and I go back many years. I would just like you to be here, that's all. Nothing else. I swear.'

'Okay,' she agreed reluctantly.

'Come and sit next to me.' Roberto held his arms out towards her.

She sat back down and folded herself into them, and was amazed by how natural it felt.

'It must be fate that sent you up here tonight.' He kissed the top of her head tenderly. 'You know, I still remember so clearly hearing you for the first time. I watched Mamma weeping as you sang. I knew then that you would become a big star.'

'Did you?' Rosanna was glad to be able to help him think of happier times.

'Yes. Your voice had such clarity, such emotion.'

'I remember you singing too. I wrote in my diary that night that I would marry you when I was older.' She smiled at the memory.

'And would you? Now that you know what I am really like?' he said harshly.

There was a pause before Rosanna answered. 'I don't think you're made for marriage, Roberto.'

'I wouldn't be a good husband?'

'No. I'm sorry.'

'You're right, of course,' he agreed finally. 'Tonight when I heard the news of my mother's death, I saw myself for what I am. I don't like it. So, I must change. Maybe I need the right woman to help me.' Roberto looked down at the girl in his arms, so sweet, so pure, so untainted by life's disappointments. 'Rosanna, I have something to tell you.'

'You do?'

'Yes.'

'Well?'

'Do you remember I told you that I have never been in love?'

'Yes.'

'I was lying to you. I am in love.'

'Who with?'

'You.'

Rosanna sat up and looked him squarely in the face. 'I will not sleep with you, Roberto. You can't use me just to blot out the pain you're feeling.'

He chuckled despite himself.

'Oh *principessa*, at least you have made me smile. Of course I wish to make love to you, because you are so very beautiful. But it's something more than that. It's a very strange experience for a man who has not had these feelings before. Truthfully, I want to please you, I want your happiness, I care what you think of me. I was so very shocked when you slapped me, not from anger, but because I couldn't bear to think of you hating me, that your opinion of me was so low. I've tried my best to mend my ways in the last few days. And after tonight, I will try even harder. Tomorrow I must go to Mass, light a candle for Mamma and have confession. Then I will start afresh. I will become a better person. Rosanna,' he entreated her, 'please say you'll give the new Roberto a chance.'

Rosanna studied him watchfully, but remained silent.

'You don't believe I love you, do you?' he said, slumping back on the sofa.

'I believe that you're simply overcome with emotion this evening.'

'Do you . . . feel anything for me?'

'I have nothing to compare my feelings with,' she answered cautiously.

'So you do admit you feel something?' Roberto encouraged.

'I know of your reputation, so I haven't dared to think how I feel.'

'Rosanna, I'm telling you the truth. I'm in love with you. I know it. Here.' He touched his chest. 'It's terrible! It hurts when you are not with me. I long to see you, I dream about you at night, I—'

'I'm going to leave now, Roberto. It's very late and we're both exhausted.' Rosanna stood up. 'And you must have some time to come to terms with the loss you've suffered tonight,' she added gently.

'Please, Rosanna, stay with me,' he begged her.

'No.' She kissed him lightly on his forehead. 'We'll talk in the morning. Goodnight, Roberto,' she whispered as she left the room.

Roberto stayed where he was. 'I love her,' he practised. 'I love her,' he said louder, enjoying the sound of his words and the relief he felt as he said them.

He knew it was wrong to suddenly feel so euphoric when his poor mamma lay dead hundreds of miles away, but he couldn't help it. It was a wonderful, frightening feeling. He would change, he *could* change. Rosanna made him a better person. Tonight was a catharsis. He knelt on the floor and asked his mamma to forgive him.

Eventually, Roberto made his way slowly towards the bedroom.

Perhaps, he thought, on the night his mother had died, he'd been born again.

The telephone woke Rosanna from a heavy sleep.

'Yes?'

'Chris here, Rosanna. Have you seen the papers?'

'No. I'm still asleep . . . I mean, in bed.'

'Well, I suggest you call down to reception and ask them to bring you copies of *The Times*, the *Telegraph* and the *Guardian*. Apart from some great photographs, there are also normally sober-suited reviewers waxing lyrical on your performance last night. I've already had calls from the BBC and a couple of Sunday papers who want to interview you as soon as possible.'

'Oh,' said Rosanna.

'You don't sound too pleased. Maybe you don't understand the importance of reviews like these. They're calling you the new Callas. You're a sensation, honey!'

'I'm glad, Chris, really, but . . . did you hear about Roberto's mother?'

'Yes. It's awful news for him, but life goes on, I'm afraid. Would you call me back when you're properly awake and let me know when you could see these journalists? They're really keen. I'll be at the apartment for the next half-hour. Congratulations, Rosanna. Bye for now.'

Rosanna fell back onto her pillows with a sigh. She felt completely drained and wondered how Roberto was feeling. Last night he'd said he was in love for the first time in his life, in love with *her* . . .

No. Rosanna stopped herself. He'd been distraught over the death of his mother, not thinking straight. He'd probably apologise today for being overemotional and their relationship would continue as it had before.

So she picked up the receiver and asked reception to send up the newspapers, then she called Chris back and arranged interviews for the afternoon.

An hour later, she was sitting eating breakfast when there was a knock on the door.

'Who is it?' she called.

'Roberto.'

Rosanna stood up and went to open the door.

'*Cara!*' He took her gently by the shoulders and kissed her tenderly on both cheeks.

'Come in.'

'Thank you.'

She closed the door and he followed her over to the breakfast table. He looked tired and pensive, but oddly at peace considering the events of last night. 'I have, as I said I would, attended Mass this morning. I've confessed my sins and prayed for forgiveness. I feel cleansed. And what is more, I'm determined to prove to Mamma in heaven that I can be a better person.'

'Well, that's good, Roberto.'

Rosanna watched as he determinedly blinked back tears, then picked up a newspaper that was lying on the table.

'I've read the reviews. I think you've arrived in London, little one. Congratulations,' he said with a warm smile.

'They're good for you too,' she said generously.

'Yes, yes.' He waved his hand dismissively. 'They're all the same. "Roberto Rossini, as always, brings great personality and his remarkable voice to the role of Alfredo." I am old news, *cara*. You're what they're interested in now. May I give you a little advice?'

'Of course.'

'Enjoy this moment. Enjoy every second of it. The first time these things happen it's miraculous, wonderful. And even though you may perform again at Covent Garden, and your reviews may be even more ecstatic, you will have had them before, so it won't give you quite the same pleasure as today.' He studied her face carefully. 'You are happy, aren't you?'

'Yes, of course I am. I mean, I've dreamt of this moment many times before. Now it's here, I almost feel guilty,' she sighed. 'It's happened so easily for me, when so many others never receive the acclaim they deserve.'

'Rosanna, there'll be thousands who will read the reviews of your performance, see the photographs of the beautiful young opera star and wish they were you. But they don't see the price you must pay – the years of hard work, the isolation, the jealousy, the pressure of living in the public eye. It's a lot to cope with, especially for one as young as yourself.'

'I've nothing to be sad about, yet I feel so low today.' Rosanna swallowed hard to quell the sudden lump that had risen in her throat.

'Little one, last night you opened triumphantly at Covent Garden in a role you have never before performed. Today it's over and the adrenaline has left you. No wonder you feel emotional. You're completely drained. Come here. It's my turn to comfort you.' Roberto patted the space on the sofa beside him.

Rosanna stood up, walked around the table and sat down next to him.

'You understand,' she whispered.

'Of course I do. And I'm here to take care of you.' He leant towards her and pushed a stray strand of hair back from her face. 'Everything I said to you last night is true. And yes, it happened on a night of high emotion, but I know I love you, Rosanna Menici. I don't know why or how, but it *is* true. Do you believe me?'

'I don't know,' she answered truthfully.

'Well, if you'll allow me, I'm going to try to convince you. But you must tell me one thing. Do I have a chance?'

She studied his anxious expression and shrugged. 'I haven't liked you much recently, but I know in my heart that I've always loved you, Roberto.'

'Then I will kiss you.'

He tipped her chin up to his, pausing just before their lips met.

'You know this will change both of our lives. There's no going back after this, Rosanna.'

'I don't want to go back.' Then she shut her eyes and surrendered completely as he kissed her.

The Metropolitan Opera House, New York

So, Nico, that was how Roberto and I began our love affair. When I told him I hadn't always liked him, I was being truthful. I couldn't condone the way he behaved towards others with no regard for their feelings. I loved him, had always loved him. I wasn't so stupid to think he wouldn't cause me pain in the future, but I also knew the pain would be greater without him.

From that first kiss, we knew we'd sealed our fate, that it was our destiny to be together whatever the cost. I can't tell you how beautiful those days in London were, both of us discovering together for the first time what it was to be in love.

It has been said that our pairing in La Traviata *that August was one of the greatest ever. Both of us sang with the asset of real passion and I believe this took each of us to new heights. There is a copy of the recording we made for Deutsche Grammophon somewhere at home. I'm so sad to think you can never truly hear it.*

Of course we were so wrapped up in each other, we paid little heed to what others would think. And, to be honest, at the time I don't think either of us cared. Roberto knew the interest our relationship would create in the media and warned me that I must be prepared to deal with it. In retrospect, the fact that neither of us was given the chance to explain our love to those who mattered before the whole world knew of it was to cause much pain.

And, of course, there were still many things about Roberto that I didn't yet know . . .

22

Rosanna awoke in Roberto's arms a week after their first kiss. She carefully moved his restraining arm from around her waist, then climbed out of bed, put on her robe and tiptoed into the sitting room. She drew the curtains, unlocked the French windows and opened them wide. Although it was early morning, the sun was already warm on her face and the clear blue sky boded well for the rest of the day. The noise of the Embankment and the River Thames beyond it rose up from beneath her. People were going about their everyday business, wrapped up in their own lives. She wanted to shout down, to tell them what had happened to her: that suddenly her life had become an exhilarating roller coaster of happiness.

Rosanna turned inside and wandered through to the bathroom. She studied her face in the mirror. Her features looked exactly the same, but it was as if she'd been illuminated from within. Even though she was exhausted from last night's performance, her eyes sparkled and her hair shone.

She was in love, in love with Roberto Rossini, and he was in love with her.

They'd spent the past week barely leaving each other's

side. Although they'd shared a bed, for the first two days Roberto had refused to make love to her, concerned she might presume that was all he wanted.

Eventually, it had been Rosanna who had begged him to make love to her. Yesterday, for the first time, they'd actually left their suite and enjoyed a leisurely lunch at Le Caprice.

Last night, Rosanna felt sure she had sung Violetta better than ever, her inner feelings mirroring the words she sang. Their performance had earned them both an extraordinary standing ovation.

'*Cara*.' An arm snaked round her waist and she saw the frown on Roberto's face reflected in the mirror. 'I woke and you weren't there.'

'I'm sorry. I left you to sleep.'

He turned her round. 'Don't ever leave me without telling me where you're going. I want to know everything you do, everything you think.'

'Everything?' she teased.

'Of course.'

'Well, at this moment I am thinking I would like you to leave the bathroom so I can use it in private.'

'Okay, okay.' Roberto began to retreat. 'Don't be too long.'

'I won't, and please order some breakfast. I'm starving.'

'Never did I see a woman who eats so much!' he laughed as the bathroom door closed. He crossed the sitting room, telephoned room service and ordered a full English breakfast for them both. Then he padded to the door of the suite, opened it and retrieved the pile of newspapers lying outside. He sat on the sofa and flicked through a tabloid.

OPERA STARS ENJOY A LOVE SONG OF THEIR OWN

A photograph showed him and Rosanna walking out of Le Caprice hand in hand. She was looking up at him with undisguised love. Roberto read the passage underneath.

> Handsome opera star Roberto Rossini was caught outside one of London's finest restaurants yesterday holding hands with his co-star, the beautiful young Italian soprano Rosanna Menici. The two of them are singing *La Traviata* to packed houses at Covent Garden.
>
> Mr Rossini is well known for his amorous pursuits and, from this photograph, it looks as though he's caught another exquisite butterfly in his net . . .

Roberto closed the newspaper quickly and hid it under the sofa. Until this moment, he'd been so wrapped up in his newfound pleasure that he'd rarely thought beyond the next hour. Even though this was an English paper, he knew the media. A titbit of gossip about him in London would very soon be front-page news in Milan. Their secret was out. By tonight, the story would be sweeping Covent Garden and, by tomorrow, La Scala and Paolo . . .

'Damn!' he cursed. He hated the gossip columnist for belittling what he felt for Rosanna. The presumption that she should be compared to his former lovers made his blood boil. But then, the reaction was only to be expected. There was no reason for anyone to think his affair with Rosanna was any different to those that preceded it.

But it *was* different. *She* was different. Roberto knew

without any doubt in his mind that he'd found what he'd been searching for. Rosanna had filled the empty spaces, made him whole. When he was with her, he liked himself. She brought out the best in him. The thought of her ever leaving him, of him going back to the way he'd lived until only a few days ago, produced a shiver of horror.

But, he mused, she was still so young. There was an age gap of seventeen years between them. He knew he was her first love. What if she used him the way *he'd* used others and moved on?

Roberto sat back on the sofa and sighed. He knew there would be many, many people who would try to dissuade Rosanna from continuing their affair once they knew of it. Paolo de Vito in particular would be mortified. Rosanna was his protégée. He behaved like a possessive father towards her and the thought that Roberto might have taken advantage of her would fill him with anger.

'God, please, help me keep her,' he whispered.

And then it came to him: the way to convince Rosanna that this was forever, as well as silence his detractors.

He was going to marry her.

Later that morning, Roberto and Rosanna took a taxi to Mayfair.

'Please, where are we going?' Rosanna asked. She sounded like a child, full of eagerness and excitement, and in her simple pink cotton dress, Roberto thought she looked little older than one.

'Have patience, *principessa*.'

'I'm trying, but—'

'We're here,' announced Roberto as the taxi drew to a halt in New Bond Street.

'Where?' she asked as he paid the driver.

'Cartier, one of the finest jewellers in the world. I'm going to buy you a present,' Roberto replied as he ushered her out of the taxi and into the shop.

Rosanna stood on the threshold and stared apprehensively at the banks of glass cabinets that housed a glittering array of spectacular jewels. A dark-suited, elderly gentleman appeared beside them.

'Sir, madam, may I be of assistance?'

'Yes. We're looking for a special piece of jewellery for my lovely lady.' Roberto nodded gallantly in Rosanna's direction.

'I see. Is there anything you particularly had in mind?'

'Could we see a selection of rings, necklaces and earrings?'

'Of course, sir.'

He unlocked the back of several cabinets and placed velvet-lined trays displaying four necklaces and a selection of rings and earrings on the table.

'Point if you see anything you like, *principessa*,' said Roberto, as he picked out an elaborate gold necklace encrusted with sapphires and diamonds.

'But, Roberto, I don't need a—'

'Hush.' Roberto put a finger to her lips. 'It's impolite to complain when a man wishes to buy you a token of his affection.'

The necklace was fastened around Rosanna's neck. She glanced at herself in the mirror. 'It feels so heavy,' she said, twisting her head uncomfortably.

'May I suggest this? It's more delicate and therefore

perhaps more suited to madam.' The sales assistant was holding another gold necklace, its feather-light chain supporting a single beautifully set diamond.

Rosanna tried it on.

'Oh!' she breathed, turning her shoulders from side to side as she studied the way the diamond sat snugly between her collarbones.

'That looks quite exquisite, if I may say so, madam. May I also show you these?' The manager held forward a tiny pair of matching earrings and a beautiful solitaire diamond ring.

Rosanna turned to Roberto questioningly. 'Yes, try the earrings.'

She did so.

'Perfect,' Roberto smiled. Then he slid the diamond ring onto the third finger of her left hand. It was far too big.

'A pity, it is much too large,' sighed Roberto. 'It matches so well. Do you like it?'

Rosanna held her hand out in front of her and admired how the stone sparkled under the lights. 'It's beautiful, as are the necklace and the earrings. But Roberto . . .'

'I told you before, to complain is impolite.' He turned to address the manager. 'We'll take the earrings and the necklace.'

'Very good, sir,' he said. 'Allow me to help you remove the jewellery, then I shall have it packed for you.'

'Rosanna, why don't you visit the shoe shop next door while I pay for these? You said you needed some new ones.'

'Okay. I'll see you there. Thank you, Roberto.' She kissed him on the cheek and left the shop.

Roberto emerged from Cartier ten minutes later and twenty thousand pounds poorer, but feeling happy that he'd managed to accomplish his aim without arousing Rosanna's suspicions. The ring was to be properly sized and all the jewellery delivered to the Savoy later that day.

As he pushed open the door of the neighbouring shop, Rosanna was trying on a pair of elegant high-heeled evening shoes. She stood up and wobbled across the thick carpet to meet him.

'What do you think?'

'I think they make your legs even longer. You look almost grown-up,' he teased. 'We'll take those,' he instructed the assistant.

They left the shop arm in arm. 'Oh Roberto, I've never had such presents before. Thank you so much!' She threw her arms round him and showered him with kisses.

'Now, you need some new clothes. We'll go to Harrods.' Roberto hailed a taxi and they climbed in. 'Your wardrobe is a disgrace and I can't be seen with a tramp. It's not good for my image,' he teased her as he hailed a taxi.

'You think I dress badly?'

'No, I don't think you dress badly, I merely think that you don't care *how* you dress. It is a different thing all together. At the risk of you becoming vain, you must learn. You have a public image now and must live up to it.'

'But I'm not interested in clothes,' said Rosanna defensively.

'*Principessa*, you are a very beautiful girl. You have lovely long legs' – Roberto ran his hand along her thigh – 'a slim waist' – his hands circled her middle – 'and wonderful high breasts . . .'

'Stop it,' giggled Rosanna.

'. . . and an oh-so-beautiful face.' He kissed her on the

lips. 'You must learn to do your assets justice, for yourself and for the man who loves you. Ah, we are here.'

Roberto paid the driver and guided Rosanna inside the store.

For the following hour Rosanna paraded in front of Roberto in a variety of day and evening clothes, as he sat on a gilt chair and pronounced on each outfit.

'No,' he said, shaking his head, 'it makes you look like my beloved nonna, my sainted grandmama.'

Rosanna lifted a hat off a display and put it on her head. It was so big that it covered her face down to her chin.

'Aha, it is the headless woman,' laughed Roberto as she stretched out her hands and walked towards him. 'Go away, you silly girl, and find something that is as lovely as you are.' He pulled the hat off her head and kissed her playfully.

Eventually, Rosanna found five outfits that met with Roberto's approval. He paid for them and then took her into the lingerie department.

'Having witnessed the state of your undergarments, I believe I must truly love you to still find you attractive,' he teased. 'So now we'll buy you lingerie that befits your delectable body.' His hand caressed the slender curve of her hip as they moved together along the racks, picking out delicate strips of silk for her to try on.

Finally, laden with bags and boxes, they made their way down from the upper floors. On the ground floor, Roberto stopped to admire a paisley silk scarf. 'So very English,' he mused.

'Do you like it?' asked Rosanna.

'Yes, I do.'

'Then I shall buy it for you.'

She hurried towards a till before he could stop her.

'There,' she said as she returned and triumphantly tied the scarf round his neck.

He fingered it gently. 'It's the best present I have ever had. Thank you, *cara*.'

After a long lunch in the Grill Room at the Savoy, they spent the afternoon lazing on a grassy slope in Victoria Embankment Gardens overlooking the Thames, arms entwined just like the other couples around them.

'Will you wait here for five minutes?' Roberto asked. 'I have to return to my suite to make a telephone call.'

Rosanna nodded, closing her eyes against the bright sun. 'Yes, of course, it's so beautiful here.'

'Don't move,' he ordered before dashing off in the direction of the Savoy.

Rosanna lay back, enjoying the feeling of the sun on her skin and the texture of newly mown grass beneath her fingers. She wished it was possible to hold this moment, encapsulate it forever. Whatever happened in the future, Rosanna knew she would always remember lying here in the sunshine, waiting for Roberto to return to her.

A few minutes later, she felt his fingers brush her cheek, smelt his familiar aftershave.

'Rosanna, please don't open your eyes. I have something to say to you and I don't want you to see anything else while I say it. I love you, Rosanna Menici. I don't understand what has happened to both of us since we arrived here in London. All I know is that I've changed. I'm like a different person. I am not just happy, I'm ecstatic. I never want you to leave me.' Roberto paused, drinking in her beautiful face, the long lashes of her closed eyes fanned out across the top of her cheekbones. '*Cara*, I want you to be my wife.'

Rosanna felt him take her third finger and slip a ring onto it.

'If you refuse me, I shall go back to my suite and drown myself in the bath,' he announced. 'Now, you can open your eyes.'

Rosanna looked first at Roberto, then at the diamond on her finger. She let out a small gasp.

'But how . . . ?'

'The kind gentleman at Cartier altered it to fit your finger. Rosanna, please, forget the ring – I am a man in turmoil. Do you say yes?'

She studied the ring silently, watching the way the sun glinted off the diamond. Conflicting emotions ran round her head. On the one hand, she felt euphoric at his proposal. On the other, would she be mad to accept, given his chequered past?

Roberto read her thoughts. '*Cara*, believe me, I have never felt like this,' he persisted. 'To know deep in your soul that something is right, that it must happen. I've realised that spending our lives together is our best chance for happiness. And asking you to be my wife is my way of showing you and the world that this love we have for each other is permanent.'

Rosanna did not look at him and continued to study the ring. 'You think that, Roberto? You don't believe you will change your mind? As you have with all your other women?'

'I understand that you must ask these questions because of my wicked past, but love has changed me. *You* have changed me. Will you have me beg you, Rosanna?'

'I told you I once wrote in my diary that I would marry

you,' she whispered, finally meeting his eyes. 'I must be a clever girl. It's my prophecy coming true.'

'Does that mean you are accepting my proposal?'

'Yes, I'll be your wife, but only if you swear to me now there will never be any other women.'

'No, never, never, please believe me.'

'Roberto' – Rosanna's eyes glittered with sudden pain – 'I warn you, if there are, *ever*, I will leave you and never return.'

'*Cara*, you must not doubt me. No one but you, ever. Please, don't look so sad. Surely it's a happy thing we are talking about? I have never asked a woman to marry me before.'

'I know. And it frightens me. Perhaps we should wait a while—'

'No! I'm sure.' Roberto put his arms around her. '*Amore mio*, I will love you and protect you always. You will not regret this, I promise.'

As he kissed her tenderly, then held her against him so tightly that she could scarcely breathe, Rosanna knew there was nothing, even if she wished it so, that she could do.

Roberto Rossini had always been her destiny.

23

'*Bastardo, bastardo!*'

Paolo's secretary hurried into his office.

'Signor de Vito, what is it?'

'I'm sorry, Francesca, I am angry at something I have read in the newspaper.'

Francesca nodded nervously and left the room.

Paolo ran a hand through his hair as he studied the photograph of Rosanna and Roberto emerging from Le Caprice.

'Why, Rosanna, why?' he groaned.

He picked up the receiver and dialled the number of the Savoy in London.

'Could you kindly put me through to Signorina Menici's room?' he asked the receptionist.

'Thank you, sir.'

A few minutes later the receptionist informed Paolo that there was no reply from Miss Menici's suite.

'I see.' Paolo looked at his watch. It was only eight thirty in the morning in England. He guessed where Rosanna must be and pondered whether he should ask the receptionist to put him through to Roberto's suite instead.

'Could you ask Signorina Menici to call Paolo de Vito when she's available?'

'Of course. Goodbye, sir.'

Paolo put down the receiver and tried to concentrate on details of the proposed set of *Rigoletto*, which sat on the desk in front of him.

Donatella, too, had seen the photograph in the newspaper. She burst into tears, then, wiping her eyes, paced up and down the sitting room, simmering with all the rage of a woman scorned.

Three weeks Roberto had been in London. And many times she'd tried to contact him at the Savoy. She had good news to tell him. While they'd been in New York, Giovanni had agreed to her request for a separation. He'd even offered to consider a divorce in the future. He'd seemed remarkably calm about it and there'd been little argument.

When she'd returned to Milan, Donatella had raced to Roberto's apartment, convinced that, finally, they could be together, but had been amazed to find an estate agent measuring up the rooms. The agent had told her that the apartment was to be sold fully furnished, but had no idea where Roberto was planning to live in the future.

Donatella had driven back to Como fuming. Why had Roberto not told her of his proposed move? Why was he not answering her telephone calls?

That evening, Giovanni had been peculiarly amiable. He'd greeted her with a smile and presented her with a beautiful pearl necklace. She'd managed to hide her distress and had pretended her plans for moving out were still imminent. But that was all before this morning, when she'd finally seen the evidence of what she'd dreaded all along. Roberto had taken a new lover.

In an attempt to alleviate her anger, Donatella threw an expensive jade statuette across the room. It landed unharmed on the thick Aubusson rug.

She tried to console herself with the thought that this affair with Rosanna Menici was probably a last fling, that he would return to her, tail firmly between his muscular legs, asking forgiveness and promising never to stray again. After all, it was not as though Roberto had married the girl.

'Don't do this to me, Roberto, please, I love you,' she moaned as she knelt down to pick up the jade.

There was little more she could do until Roberto returned to Milan. She'd been prepared to give up a lot for Signor Rossini. And she was damned if she was going to let him go without a fight.

'Carlotta, Carlotta, look! Here!' Marco Menici spread the newspaper on one of the tables in the café. 'See, it's Rosanna with Roberto Rossini.'

Carlotta stopped cleaning the café floor, propped the mop against the wall and looked over her father's shoulder at the photograph. As she read the words underneath, Carlotta held on to the back of a chair for support.

'Who would have believed it? They make a handsome couple, do they not? Just think, Carlotta, if Rosanna was to marry the son of our best friends!'

'Yes, Papa, it would be remarkable indeed. But I must get on. It's getting late and I have still to go shopping.' Carlotta moved away and grabbed her mop as Marco walked off to the kitchen.

As soon as he left the room, Carlotta groaned with inner pain. Roberto and Rosanna . . . 'No! It cannot happen!' she whimpered.

Later that day, Carlotta walked to the local church. She went inside, lit a candle for Mamma and knelt down to pray.

Afterwards, she walked back towards the café, feeling a little calmer. There were always photographs in the newspapers of Roberto Rossini with different women; surely Rosanna was just another and the relationship would come to nothing?

Luca . . . she wished she could talk to Luca. In his cloistered world at the seminary in Bergamo, he would not have seen the photograph. She must write to him, ask his advice. He'd tell her it would be all right.

Carlotta went up to her bedroom, drew out a sheet of notepaper and a pen, and began to write.

Two weeks later, the subjects of so much high emotion were on their way in a taxi to Marylebone Register Office. Roberto clasped his bride's hand tightly in his.

The taxi stopped in front of the steps and Roberto climbed out. Having told no one but Chris of the engagement, he had arranged the marriage ceremony for nine thirty in the morning, thinking it less likely they would be spotted. Their final performance at Covent Garden had been last night. In three hours the two of them would be on a plane heading for Paris and after that . . . he would whisk his new wife away for three whole weeks to a secret place where they could remain undiscovered by the paparazzi. He was not ready to share her with the world yet.

'The coast is clear.' Roberto helped Rosanna out of the taxi and they hurried up the steps.

Chris Hughes was waiting inside. He smiled at them.

'Rosanna, you look beautiful.' He kissed her on both cheeks, then shook Roberto warmly by the hand. 'I've brought my secretary, Liza, to be your other witness. She's just gone to the ladies' room.'

'Good, good,' Roberto nodded. 'You understand, we just want a few weeks' peace before the newspapers hear of our marriage.'

'Sure. Ah, here she comes.' Chris indicated a thin young woman who was walking down the steps towards them.

'Thank you for coming, Liza.' Roberto shook the girl's hand. 'You're sworn to secrecy, of course.'

'Of course.' Liza nodded tremulously. 'I think it's very romantic.'

'Right, let's get on with it. You've got a plane to catch and so do I,' said Chris briskly.

'Good morning. Would you like to come through?' The registrar appeared from the office.

The four of them followed him into an adjacent room that contained a desk at one end with three rows of chairs in front of it. The registrar indicated that the witnesses should sit down, then beckoned the bride and groom forward.

As Rosanna stood in front of the desk next to Roberto, she felt sad that none of her family and friends were here to share this special moment with her. But Roberto had been insistent about marrying before they left London.

'There's no reason why we shouldn't have a proper ceremony later, *cara*, and invite all our friends and family, but I don't want to give you the opportunity to change your mind. Or for others to change it for you,' he had added darkly.

Luca, Papa, Carlotta, Abi, Paolo, Luigi . . . Rosanna thought of them all as she listened to the words that would legally tie her to Roberto for the rest of her life. She knew they'd all be terribly hurt that she hadn't told them, but it couldn't be helped.

Rosanna repeated her vows after the registrar, while Roberto smiled encouragement at her.

Then he slipped the wedding ring onto her finger.

'And that concludes the ceremony,' beamed the registrar. 'You are now Mr and Mrs Roberto Rossini. May I be the first to congratulate you.'

'Thank you.' Roberto shook the registrar's hand. 'I trust I can count on your discretion?'

'Of course. If I had a pound for every clandestine marriage I've conducted, I'd be a rich man. My lips are sealed. Now, at the risk of sounding like a stickler for tradition, I do think you should kiss the bride,' the registrar encouraged.

'Of course. How could I forget.' Roberto leant across to Rosanna and kissed her tenderly on the lips.

'If you and your witnesses would like to sign the register, that will be everything,' said the registrar.

Ten minutes later, Roberto and Rosanna climbed into a taxi that Chris had hailed for them.

'Have a great honeymoon, guys,' he said, closing the door.

'We will, Chris. You know where we'll be, but only contact us if it's really urgent,' called Roberto through the open window.

'Sure. But you'd better let me know how, when and where you want the world to discover your happy news. Prepare yourselves for a storm of media interest, especially from the direction of Milan.' Chris raised a knowing eyebrow. 'See you when you get back to London.'

He waved as the taxi drew away.

'Well, Signora Rossini, we've done it.' Roberto smiled at his new wife.

'Yes, I've married an old man.' Her fingers twined themselves round his.

'Well, I'm going to show you just how young you make me feel when we reach Paris.' He kissed her gently on the forehead.

'Will it be the first time you've made love to a married woman?' asked Rosanna, enjoying his caresses.

'Of course,' murmured Roberto. 'Of course.'

When they arrived in Paris, a limousine drove them to the Ritz hotel.

'Welcome, welcome, *monsieur et madame*. Please follow me. Your suite has been prepared.' The manager ushered them swiftly into the lift.

Rosanna drew in her breath as she followed the manager into the suite. The sitting room was elegant and ornately furnished, with heavy gold damask curtains framing the floor-length windows which looked out over the Place Vendôme.

'This is the beginning of the most wonderful honeymoon, Signora Rossini,' Roberto said as he took a bottle of champagne from the ice bucket and popped the cork.

Rosanna accepted the glass he handed to her.

'*Principessa*, I want to tell you that you have made me the happiest man in the world. To us.'

'To us.' Their glasses touched and, leading her into the bedroom then cupping her face in his hands, he began to kiss her. '*Ti amo*, I love you, *cara*.'

His hands began to undo the buttons of her blouse. He slid it from her shoulders and let his fingertips glide across the smooth contours of her breasts, barely touching the skin. They fell back onto the bed, locked in an embrace.

Later as they lay naked, their legs entwined on the rumpled sheets, Roberto gently brushed a lock of Rosanna's hair out of her eye. She propped herself up on her elbows and looked down at him.

'I'm hungry,' she announced.

'Then I shall call down and ask them to deliver us our wedding feast. Maybe some *foie gras* and some tender *filets mignon*, yes?'

'I think I would like pasta,' Rosanna shrugged.

Roberto rolled his eyes. 'Pasta! You are in the Ritz in Paris, the culinary capital of the world, and you want pasta?'

'Yes. A big plate of pasta and a salad. And you, you should watch your waistline.' Rosanna put her arms around Roberto's torso. 'I don't want a husband with middle-age spread,' she teased.

Roberto pulled in his stomach, a wounded expression on his face. 'You think I am fat?'

'No, but like any man of your age, I think you must be careful.'

'I am married for only a few hours and already my wife puts me on a diet! Well, tonight we feast; tomorrow – maybe – I fast.' Roberto went over to the telephone and dialled room service while Rosanna slipped into the bathroom to shower.

After they'd eaten, they climbed between the soft linen sheets and lay together, staring at the beautiful mural on the ceiling. Roberto's hand lazily caressed her naked body.

'*Cara*, I know I say it often, but you have reformed me. Before you and I first made love, I used to think sex and love were two different things. I finally understand now why it's possible to be monogamous. Once you've experienced what we have, then you need never seek pleasure from another.'

'I thank God you feel that way,' Rosanna murmured, 'and I pray that you always will.'

'*Principessa*, you do understand that many people will tell you what you have done is stupid?'

'Yes, I know, Roberto.'

'That they will say a leopard can never change his spots? That it cannot last?'

'Yes.'

'Please, Rosanna, whatever you might hear in the future about me, please, I ask this of you: remember this moment, remember me looking down at you and telling you how much I love you, how much I need you. You have lodged in my heart and will be there until the day I die. Tell me you will not let anything break us apart.'

'As long as you can look me in the eye as you are doing now and never lie to me, then we'll be together always.' Rosanna settled herself for sleep in his arms. '*Caro*, when we come back from our honeymoon, can we visit Naples before we go back to London?' she asked drowsily. 'I feel very bad not telling my family about our marriage. Maybe if we went to visit them together, they might forgive us. We could go to Milan too, and see Paolo.'

'I . . . yes, if we have time.'

'Can we see a little of Paris tomorrow?' she whispered. 'I've never been here before.'

'Yes, if we can take care to disguise ourselves from the scum of the paparazzi.' His face hardened for a moment, before adding gently, 'Then I will whisk you away to a place where no one can find us. Sleep well, *amore mio*.'

Roberto leant across the bed and switched off the light. He was tired, but sleep would not come. Eventually, hearing Rosanna's steady breathing, he got out of bed and went to the window. He opened it and let the cool night air into the muggy room. Paris was still wide awake, even at two in the morning.

As long as you never lie to me . . .

Roberto felt unsettled, uncertain. Every time Rosanna talked about returning to Italy, his heart rate tripled.

And there was another thought nagging at the back of his head, something else he knew he should tell her lest she discover it for herself. One hot summer evening, long ago in Naples . . . Roberto shook his head. She'd hate him for that, much more than she'd hated him for what he had done to Abi.

Roberto could only pray that his previous stupidity would not ruin his future with the woman he loved.

The following afternoon, as the two of them strolled hand in hand in the Tuileries Garden, an eagle-eyed young photographer spotted Roberto, despite his hat and dark glasses. Standing behind a bush, he adjusted the powerful telephoto lens of his camera and zoomed in, just as Rosanna threw her arms around Roberto's shoulders and kissed him. The shutter clicked twelve times before their lips parted. The photographer followed them at a safe distance as they walked, darting behind the greenery after each shot. Neither of them noticed a thing, despite Roberto's warning to Rosanna the previous night.

Later, as he watched the pictures developing at the lab in the offices of his newspaper, the young photographer couldn't believe his luck when he spotted the two rings on the third finger of Rosanna Menici's left hand. Hurriedly checking the picture library, he saw that three weeks ago in London Rosanna's finger had been bare. He ran down the corridor with the barely dry photographs and knocked frantically on the news editor's door.

Twenty minutes later, a journalist was despatched to London to discover the truth.

24

Donatella stared at the headline in utter disbelief.

'No! No!' she moaned.

She reread the article and then howled in anger. She examined Rosanna's face, trying to find fault with it. Her rage heightened when she could not. Rosanna was beautiful, and by all accounts hugely talented. More to the point, she was so young. Donatella hated her for it.

The affair must have started before the two of them left Milan. That explained the sale of the apartment and his refusal to take her telephone calls. Oh yes, while Donatella was telling him of her plans to move in with him, Roberto had been organising his future with Rosanna.

Torn between fury and devastation, Donatella spent the day getting slowly drunk. By the time Giovanni arrived home, she'd fallen asleep on the sofa.

He picked up the newspaper lying on the floor beside his wife, stared at the photograph and read the passage underneath.

Roberto Rossini was indeed a very sensible man.

*

On arrival at the seminary, Carlotta was ushered into a small room, the whitewashed walls bare apart from a crucifix. The one small window had bars across it, like a prison cell. Even though the day was warm outside, the room was chilly and smelt of damp. Carlotta shivered and sat down on one of the spartan wooden chairs. Five minutes later, the door opened.

'Luca, oh Luca!' Carlotta stood up and fell into her brother's arms, weeping.

He stroked her hair. 'Come now, don't cry. Whatever is it?'

Carlotta pulled away and tried to gather herself together. She smiled weakly and wiped her eyes. 'I'm sorry for coming here to the seminary, but I didn't know what else to do.'

'You told Don Giuseppe it was an emergency,' Luca said tensely. 'Carlotta, we don't have long. Tell me, please, what is it?'

'You received my letter?'

'Yes. And I wrote back to tell you not to worry. Roberto is not the marrying kind. It's bad luck for Rosanna that she's allowed herself to become involved with him, but . . .' Luca stopped in mid-sentence as he stared at the newspaper that Carlotta thrust in front of his face.

'You were wrong, Luca.' She sat down abruptly. 'What am I to do? I should have told Roberto about Ella long ago, then this terrible situation would not be happening. Oh, *mamma mia*, what have I done, what have I done?' She began to sob.

'Carlotta, you did what you thought was best for your child and your family. You could not have foreseen that this was going to happen.' Luca, usually so sure about what God would wish, found at this moment that he didn't know. He tried to think rationally. 'If you tell Rosanna, it may destroy her marriage before it has begun. If you don't, then we both must keep the secret for the rest of our lives.'

'But can we do that? She's our sister. Oh, it's impossible!' Carlotta hung her head. 'Haven't I been punished enough for my mistake? And now this?'

'Carlotta, Carlotta.' Luca went to comfort her. 'Please try to believe that God has a reason for everything.'

'I try, Luca, I try every day as I work in the café. The only thing I live for is Ella, but when I think that all she might have in the future is the same existence as mine, I sometimes wonder whether it's worth going on. The guilt is so heavy in my heart. I've deceived Ella, Papa and now Rosanna.'

There was a tap on the door. 'I'll be out in a few minutes,' Luca called. He clasped his sister's hands in his. 'Carlotta, I have to go. I think maybe it isn't as bad as it seems. After all, we are the only two who know of this. There's no other way Rosanna can find out. Sometimes it's best to keep the secrets of the past. And our sister will have enough to cope with: she has married a . . . very difficult man. God forgive me, but the marriage may not even last. Remember, if Rosanna knows, then Roberto, Papa and, most importantly, Ella must know too.'

'You're saying I should do or say nothing?'

'Yes, I think that's for the best. But in the end, it's for you to decide.'

There was another tap on the door.

'I must go.' Luca kissed Carlotta warmly on both cheeks. 'Try not to fret. Send my love to Papa and Ella. How are they?'

'Both well.' Carlotta nodded. 'We all miss you – and Rosanna.'

'I know. And you must take care of yourself. You look very thin – too thin. May God go with you, Carlotta. *Ciao, cara*.'

Luca watched from a window as Carlotta was let out of the front gates of the seminary. Her shoulders were hunched, her despair obvious. He'd been so sure when they were younger that it would be Rosanna who would always need his protection. It seemed now it was Carlotta.

After twenty-four hours in Paris, Rosanna and Roberto boarded a plane headed for Corsica. When the flight touched down at Ajaccio airport, Roberto hired a car. As they drove out of the town, they met little traffic, apart from the odd farmer driving a donkey with his children perilously balanced on the cart behind. The late afternoon sun was beginning its descent towards the sea and Rosanna rolled down the car window as they drove along the winding coast road. Around each rocky headland, a new view of the Mediterranean emerged below them, with secret coves and beaches nestling beneath the cliffs. As they climbed higher, olive trees clung to the hillside and clumps of rosemary and wild mint by the roadside filled the warm air with their heady fragrance.

'It's beautiful here, Roberto,' she enthused. 'The sea is a wonderful blue.'

'Yes, it's like the coast of Italy used to be before the tourists arrived. Completely unspoilt. That is why I love it. I come here when I need some peace and quiet.'

'Where are we headed for?' asked Rosanna.

'Wait and see,' he smiled. 'I want to surprise you.'

Two hours later, Roberto drove through a cluster of whitewashed houses set high on a hillside. He turned right down a steep road lined with pine trees. They travelled along the road for a few minutes, before turning down a steeper, narrower track. At the end of it was a pretty stone villa with a terracotta roof and trumpet vines, laden with vibrant orange flowers, clambering up the walls.

'We have arrived, *principessa*. This is Villa Rodolpho, without doubt my favourite place in the world.'

Roberto jumped out of the car as an old lady emerged from the villa. She waddled over to Roberto, arms outstretched, and held him in a tight bear hug, showering him with endearments.

'Nana, this is my new wife, Rosanna.'

'I am very pleased to meet you, Signora Rossini,' said the woman, a smile lighting up her wrinkled, nut-brown face.

'Nana looks after the villa while I am away and after *me* when I'm here. She lives down there with her good husband, Jacques.' Roberto pointed to a white cottage some distance away. He put his arm around Rosanna's shoulder. 'You see the path going down the hill?'

'Yes.'

'It takes us to our own private beach. Come.' Roberto led her towards the villa. 'Do you like it?'

Rosanna stopped as they approached the entrance and watched the sun dip beneath the skyline. She took a deep breath, smelling the pine resin and the salty, iodine tang of the sea. 'I think it's the most beautiful place I've ever seen.'

'You must look inside before you say that. It's homely, but not luxurious.' He ushered her through the front door into a spacious tiled entrance hall and flicked a switch to illuminate their surroundings.

'See, here is the bedroom,' said Roberto, indicating a

whitewashed room to their right, where Rosanna caught a glimpse of a large bed made up with a cheerful patchwork counterpane. 'And this is the kitchen.' He led her across the hall and held open the door while Rosanna peered in for just long enough to note the cosy wood-burning stove and the long scrubbed table with its mismatched chairs. Then they climbed a set of narrow wooden stairs to the upper floor. 'And this is the sitting room. The view from here is magnificent.'

Rosanna stood at the top of the stairs. The pine floor was strewn with brightly coloured kilims. There was a battered leather sofa covered with cushions and a bookcase full of novels. In one corner stood an old piano and glass doors led onto a terrace that overlooked the rugged coastline. Roberto threw them open and drew her to his side as they stepped out into the balmy evening air. The view was, as he had promised, quite magical. The last apricot rays of the sunset were reflected in the sea and the first stars were emerging on the fast-darkening horizon.

'Who owns this villa?' she asked.

'I do. I bought it three years ago. We can come here and live in complete seclusion. No one will ever find us. Jacques and Nana fetch anything I need from the village at the top of the hill.'

'It's wonderful, Roberto.' Rosanna sank with a sigh into the comfortable sofa.

'Ah, *principessa*, you must be exhausted. I shall bring you a glass of wine, then you can shower. We'll eat by candlelight on the terrace.'

Later that night Rosanna lay in bed, her head reeling from the events of the past week. She glanced at Roberto and pondered how strange it was that, having spent so many years chasing the limelight, the minute one became famous, one spent one's life searching for privacy.

Rosanna and Roberto enjoyed three perfect weeks at Villa Rodolpho. They woke late, swam, read and made love. They ate fresh fish on the gorgeous terrace overlooking the sea and drank the tart local wine.

'I hope I shall lose this tan in time for the opening of *La Bohème* in a few weeks' time. I'm meant to be dying of consumption,' commented Rosanna one night as they stood on the terrace after dinner, admiring the moonlit landscape below them.

Roberto took a deep breath. '*Cara*, we must talk about the future.'

'Oh Roberto, do we have to? Can't we just stay here and—'

'No, you know we can't.'

'But what is there to talk about? On Sunday we fly to Naples to see Papa and announce our news. Then we go to London.'

'I think everyone will know by now.'

'Do you?'

'Rosanna, listen. I didn't want to tell you this before, but . . . I cannot go to Naples with you and I won't be going to Milan to play Rodolpho.'

Rosanna stared at him. 'What? I don't understand. I . . .'

'You have asked me never to lie and I won't. But I'm warning you, the truth will be difficult for you to hear.'

'But . . .' Fear grew in her eyes.

'Sit down and I will tell you, *cara*. I beg you not to despise me when you have heard.'

Rosanna took a seat as he asked, her eyes full of trepidation. Roberto sat down opposite her.

'Six years ago, when I was an unimportant soloist at La Scala, I began an affair with a very rich married woman. The affair continued whenever I was in Milan. Then, this summer, the lady announced she wished to live with me. She'd not asked my opinion on this, but had decided she was in love with me and was going to divorce her husband. I was shocked and horrified. Believe me, Rosanna, I never loved her. Three weeks before we left for London, I had a visit from her husband. He's a very rich and powerful man in Milan. I thought he was going to kill me there and then, but instead he advised me it would be in my best interests to stay away from Italy for a long time. He indicated that there would be very unpleasant consequences for me if I decided to return. And that, *cara*, is why I cannot return with you to Italy.' Roberto put his head in his hands. 'I'm so ashamed, Rosanna, so ashamed.'

They sat in silence for a long time. Eventually, she spoke. 'So that is why you were unable to attend your mamma's funeral?'

'Yes. Because of my stupid behaviour, I could not. And now the dream we have both shared, to sing Rodolpho and Mimi at La Scala, cannot be. I would give anything to make it different. I know I should be punished, but you should not.'

'And you've known you wouldn't be returning to Milan ever since we arrived in London?' Rosanna spoke in a quiet, strangled voice.

'Yes. *Cara*, I wanted to tell you, but I knew how much it would upset you.'

'You should have told me sooner, Roberto. You promised you would never lie. This . . . woman, what was her name?'

'Rosanna, please! She is not important.'

'Tell me. I must know,' Rosanna urged.

'Donatella. Donatella Bianchi. You will not know her.'

'On the contrary. As you and I know perfectly well, she and her husband are great patrons of La Scala. They gave a large donation to the Beata Vergine Maria church. I know exactly who Donatella Bianchi is,' she imparted coldly.

'Please believe me,' he begged her, 'it's all in the past.'

'It began six years ago, you said. We've not been together six weeks, and already you have kept a secret from me.'

'Rosanna, it's over. It's finished. It was nothing. Now, please tell me how you feel about returning to Milan alone?'

'I cannot . . .' Rosanna's voice trembled. 'I cannot even begin to think about it.' She stood up and leant over the railings of the terrace. 'Why don't you go to the police? Tell them you've been threatened by this man?'

'It will do no good. You know how things are in Italy. Corruption is everywhere, and you can bet Giovanni is part of it. I wouldn't stand a chance against him and his connections.'

'You think Signor Bianchi will carry out his threat?'

'I'm in absolutely no doubt.'

'What about Paolo? What will you say to him?'

'Well, I cannot tell him the truth. I will ask Chris to say I need a rest, that my voice is tired, anything. I don't much care about that, but the thought of you returning to Milan without me, of us being apart . . . I can hardly bear it. Of course, I cannot stop you going. In fact, you *must* go.'

Rosanna turned to him, tears glistening in her eyes. 'And

how will it look if I return to Italy alone? All the things you said people would think will be reinforced by your absence. I can't tell them the real reason, so they'll think the marriage has already gone wrong. I'm wondering if they are right.'

'No!' Roberto jumped up and went to her side. 'Please, Rosanna, don't say that.'

'What am I meant to say? That I'm glad you had an affair with a married woman whose husband has threatened to have you killed? That I'm happy I must go back to Milan alone for weeks on end without my new husband? And, worst of all, that you have deceived me from the beginning? I cannot believe it! I . . .' Rosanna, too shocked to find any further words, fled from the terrace and into the villa. Roberto heard the bedroom door bang shut.

He exhaled slowly and filled his glass from the half-full bottle of wine. Her reaction had been no worse than he'd expected. And no better than he deserved.

Rosanna lay on the bed, holding a pillow over her head in a useless attempt to block out the pain of Roberto's confession. The exquisite, dreamlike feeling she'd had for the past five weeks had vanished in an instant.

Her new husband had not only told her of some sordid affair, but had also announced that, because of it, he could not return to Italy. There would be no triumphant return to Naples together to visit their families, either now or in the future. She realised that Roberto had known from the start that it had never been a possibility.

And La Scala . . . *La Bohème*. How many times had she imagined the two of them taking the applause of an ecstatic first-night audience? She was booked to sing at La Scala on and off until the following September. And now, each time she went, it would be without Roberto.

Of course, she didn't have to go back to Italy. There were other houses that would welcome her debut as Mimi – Chris had told her of the offers that had flooded in since London. So far she had refused them all outright.

But to let Paolo down after all he had done for her . . . How could she?

Yet, if she allowed Chris to alter her schedule, she could sing with Roberto at houses around the world. Everyone wanted them together and, after the news of their marriage, Rosanna knew that the interest in their pairing would grow even more intense.

She also knew, deep down, that she was frightened of leaving him alone. She believed Roberto loved her, but a tiny part of her still wondered whether, if she was hundreds of miles away, he would be able to resist temptation.

Rosanna was sure the only chance she had of their marriage working was to be at his side. It would mean making the greatest sacrifice and hurting Paolo, but what was more important to her?

She already knew the answer.

Emitting a muffled scream of frustration, she pulled the pillow even more tightly over her head.

Much later, Rosanna walked back out onto the terrace, looking composed but ashen beneath her suntan.

Roberto jumped up. 'How are you? Will you divorce me?'

'Roberto, I have made a decision. But before I tell you, I must ask you one thing. Is there anything else I should know about you? Any other secrets you are hiding from me?'

Roberto wavered for a second, then shook his head. 'No, *cara*. I've told you everything.'

'Then I'll tell you what I've decided. I cannot go back to Milan without you. When you telephone Chris Hughes to tell him you won't be returning to La Scala, you speak for both of us. There are other houses, other places we can sing *La Bohème*.' She managed a wan smile.

Roberto was stunned. 'Do you mean it?'

'Yes. I'm your wife. I must be by your side. There is no other choice because . . . I love you,' she said miserably.

'*Cara, mia cara*, that you would make this sacrifice for me, I . . .' Roberto held out his arms to her. 'I'll make it up to you, I promise. You're an angel, an angel of forgiveness. And yes, we must be together always. You have made the right decision, I am sure of it.'

As Rosanna melted into his embrace, she could think of many people who would not share Roberto's opinion.

'He's *what*?' The voice at the other end of the phone was like a gunshot.

Chris Hughes repeated his last statement. There was silence from the receiver.

'I'm sorry, Paolo, and Roberto is devastated, but he feels that his voice isn't up to it.'

'But we're talking about an entire season here, Chris, not just one performance! Has he cancelled his other bookings too?'

'Umm . . . no, he hasn't.'

'So he's making up this ridiculous excuse about his voice. Chris, at the very least, you owe it to me to tell me the truth.

Why doesn't he want to appear at La Scala? His new wife will be here often enough.'

'Ah, yes, well, that's what I was coming to. Rosanna is cancelling too.'

Paolo was silent for a moment, then he said, 'I don't believe I'm hearing this, Chris.'

'It's true, I'm afraid. Apparently she's written to you to explain. She's desperately sorry and hopes that you'll understand, but she feels she has to be with her husband.'

'No! NO!' Paolo groaned in rising despair. 'Singing *La Bohème* at La Scala was her dream. I know Rosanna would not cancel that for anything.'

'She just has done, Paolo. What can I say?'

'*Mamma mia!* I simply can't believe it. I must speak to her, Chris. Where is she?'

'Look, Paolo, Rosanna doesn't want to talk to you right now. She and Roberto—'

'Rosanna doesn't want to talk to *me*? She and her shit of a husband have just completely wrecked my season, which I might remind you begins in less than two months' time. Quite apart from the fact I have personally guided her development for the past five years!' Chris was very glad he was not in the same room as Paolo at that moment. Sometimes he hated his job.

'Look, I understand how you feel. I'm there too. I've accepted a year of bookings on Rosanna's behalf and this morning she tells me she wants them altered to fit in with Roberto's schedule.'

'She's going to destroy her career before she's even begun,' thundered Paolo. 'All that talent and—'

'I know, I know. But look at it this way, Paolo: if you

come down heavy on Rosanna now, you may lose her for good. On the other hand, if you stay cool, allow her to play happy families with Roberto for a while, she might just begin to see the light.'

'So what you're telling me is that she's blinded by love?'

'That seems to be about the size of it. I told her that even if Roberto is refusing to sing at La Scala this year, she must. She wouldn't hear of it. If you want my opinion, there's a hidden agenda in this somewhere, but I'm damned if I know what it is.'

'I could sue Roberto for breach of contract, although I can't touch Rosanna, as you well know. Her contract's sitting here on my desk ready for her to sign on her return. I could never have foreseen this . . . Well, I obviously didn't know her as I thought I did,' finished Paolo crisply.

'Sure, you could sue Roberto and with good reason. But, as we both know, Rosanna is becoming a big star. If you sue her husband, you'll have no chance of persuading either of them back to La Scala.'

Paolo sighed. 'I just don't understand. This has got to be Roberto's doing. It sounds as though Rosanna has lost her mind.'

'Well, at the very least I'd agree that her mind's completely made up on being with her husband every second of every day.'

'Does he love her, do you think?' asked Paolo, feeling sick at the finality of the situation and the loss of his home-grown star.

'He's certainly very protective of her. I'd say that yes, he does.'

'Well, in my experience, Roberto Rossini loves no one but himself,' growled Paolo.

'Who knows? Only time will tell. Anyway, I apologise again for being the bearer of such bad tidings. Let me know if there's any way I can help you find replacements for them.'

'We'll be in touch.' Paulo dropped the receiver into the cradle and put his head in his hands.

The following morning, a letter addressed to him arrived from London.

Dear Paolo,

I'm sure that by now Chris Hughes has told you I will not be coming to Milan to sing Mimi. I'm so very sorry to let you, Riccardo and La Scala down, especially after all the help you have given me. Paolo, I cannot go into detail, but it is impossible for either of us to come to Milan. Roberto is my husband and that is where my loyalties must now lie. I have to be with him wherever he is. As you know, singing Mimi at La Scala was my dream, but please believe me, I have no choice.

I understand how angry you must be and I'm truly sorry. It's the wrong moment to thank you for all you have done for me, but I say it anyway.

I wish with all my heart things could have been different.

With love,

Rosanna

Paolo reread the letter twice. He knew for certain now that this wasn't Rosanna's doing. It was Roberto's.

The Metropolitan Opera House, New York

So, Nico, you can already see that our marriage started out in stormy waters. And yet, I count the two years that followed our wedding among the happiest of my life.

And, Nico, if there is one thing I wish for your future, it's to find the joy that Roberto and I found during that time. We went everywhere together. Not only were we inseparable as husband and wife, but our names became entwined on stage too. We sang Puccini in London, Verdi in New York and Mozart in Vienna, and became the toast of the opera world. We were fêted everywhere we went. Our private passion only enhanced our performances and every opera house in the world begged us to sing on their stages. We were booked three years in advance.

The sadness I felt that the only country we did not sing in was that of our birth never left me. But it was the price I had to pay for the happiness Roberto and I shared.

And what of Roberto? Well, Nico, if only you could have seen him then. I could not have asked for a more devoted or loving husband. He protected me and nurtured me and loved me in a way that others who had known him before found difficult to believe.

Admittedly, he made most of our important career decisions and I rarely questioned his judgement. I was simply happy to be with him and sing wherever he wished me to. It seemed then that the Roberto of old had well and truly disappeared. Love – my *love – had changed him, I believed, forever.*

Soon after we married, we bought a lovely house in Kensington in London. We used it as our base and returned to it as often as we could. In April 1980, we arrived back there from New York. We were to sing (at last) La Bohème *at Covent Garden, our favourite opera house outside of Italy, and all seemed perfect . . .*

25

London, April 1980

Rosanna awoke to the sound of a car backfiring in the street. She lifted her head in the gloom and looked at the radio alarm clock beside the bed. It was six o'clock. She lay back with a sigh, knowing she'd spend the rest of the day feeling exhausted. The plane from New York had touched down late last night and she struggled terribly with jet lag.

Knowing she wouldn't be able to go back to sleep, she delicately removed Roberto's hand, which was resting on her stomach, and slipped out of bed. She put on her robe and tiptoed quietly out of the bedroom.

Downstairs in the kitchen she made herself some coffee, then sat at the table to watch the birds as they chirruped in the tree in the small courtyard garden. Rosanna smiled contentedly, glad to be back. She loved this house. It was the one place that felt like home, after the endless impersonal hotel suites they stayed in when they were travelling. The house was arranged on four floors, with a large kitchen and laundry room in the basement, a sitting room, dining room and music room on the ground floor and the bedrooms and bathrooms on the two upper floors.

They had three weeks before they started rehearsals for *La Bohème* at Covent Garden. Roberto had suggested they escape to Corsica, but for once Rosanna had put her foot down. She wanted to be in *her* house, in *her* bed, with *her* things around her. The past two years had been unremitting and Rosanna felt drained.

When she'd mentioned her exhaustion to Roberto he'd looked concerned and suggested all she needed was a good rest. He'd promised there would be no concerts, no interviews and no parties during their break. She heard the rattle of the letterbox, and walked up the stairs to collect the post from the hall. There was one letter on the mat and she recognised the writing at once. Rosanna sat on the bottom stair and tore the envelope open.

San Borromeo Seminary
Bergamo
12th April

My dear Rosanna,

How are things with you? I try to keep up to date with your movements but it's difficult now you're such an international star! I hope that you will receive this letter in good time.

Rosanna, it's four years since I have seen you. For reasons I and others do not understand, you and Roberto have not been back to Italy. Maybe you're simply both too busy. So I think I must try to visit you. I have a little money saved, and if you're in London soon I would very much like to fly over and see you. The beginning of May would suit me, as I have a few days' break from the seminary. Could you let me know what dates are suitable and then I can book my ticket? I've told Papa of my plan and suggested he come with me, but he refuses to set foot on a plane. He plays all the records you've sent him, but I do hope one day you'll return to La Scala so he can come and hear you sing live.

From her letters, Carlotta seems fine and Ella is growing fast. She'll soon be thirteen. I doubt you'll recognise her when you next see her. The café has just been renovated, with a brand-new fitted kitchen, a proper bar and new tables and chairs. Papa has spent a fortune, but hopes to recoup it by putting up the prices this summer.

I can hardly believe it's almost four years since I entered the seminary. And still another three years until I am ordained. I have to admit that sometimes I find I miss the outside world and look forward to the short recesses in the summer, but I'm still confident I made the right decision.

How is Abi? Do you ever hear from her? If you do, send her my love and best wishes.

I must end now for I have a class. Please let me know if May would be convenient for you.

Are you happy, Rosanna? I hope so.

All my love, piccolina.

Luca x

Rosanna sighed as she folded up the letter and slotted it back into the envelope. The past two years had been wonderful, but her one regret was that she had been unable to see her family, although she had begged her father and Carlotta to come to London to see her. She also felt guilty that not only had she failed to inform Abi of her marriage at the time, she'd subsequently neglected to keep in regular touch with her. The simple truth was that her own life revolved around Roberto and their love.

She went into the sitting room and checked the calendar on the desk. There was a weekend at the beginning of May, just after they began rehearsals for *La Bohème*, when Roberto was booked to give two concerts in Geneva. Usually she would accompany him, but she could just as easily remain in London and have Luca to stay then. She wanted to give her brother her full attention and, with Roberto around, Rosanna knew that would be difficult. She sat down at the desk, pulled paper and an envelope out of the drawer and began to write to Luca.

'*Principessa*.' She jumped as warm hands encircled her shoulders and Roberto leant down to kiss the top of her head. 'Where did you go? I woke up and you were not there.'

'I didn't want to disturb you, darling.' She smiled as he massaged her shoulders. 'And I've had a letter from my brother. He's going to fly to London to see me. I'm going to suggest he comes when you go to Geneva.'

'We will be apart for three days?'

'Yes, but it's such a long time since I saw any of my family. I miss them, Roberto. Surely you won't begrudge me this time with my brother?'

'Of course not,' he sighed guiltily. 'We both know this is

my fault. I'll pine for you every moment I am away. Let me look at you.' Roberto tilted her face up towards him and shook his head. 'Still pale,' he remarked. 'I think you should come back to bed. It's too early to be up.'

'But will you let me sleep?' she laughed, as a hand snaked inside her robe.

'Later, *cara*, later.' With that, Roberto picked her up from the chair and carried her back up the stairs towards the bedroom.

Even though Rosanna rested for the next seven days, she found she felt no better. She couldn't shake off the exhaustion and often felt dizzy and faint. By the end of the week, when it was obvious that rest alone was not the answer, Roberto made her an appointment with his doctor and insisted on accompanying her to Harley Street.

'Shall I come in with you?' he asked as Rosanna was called into the consulting room.

Rosanna shook her head firmly. 'Wait for me here.'

'As you wish, but make sure you tell Dr Hardy exactly how you feel.'

'I will,' she promised as she followed the nurse down the corridor.

Dr Hardy gave Rosanna a full physical check-up.

'I have nothing bad wrong with me, do I?' she asked nervously, once Dr Hardy had finished his examination.

'Not at all. Quite the opposite, in fact. You're in excellent health. And, from what I can tell, so is your baby.'

'I . . .' Rosanna was stunned. The thought had not even crossed her mind. 'Are you sure?'

'Ninety-nine per cent sure, yes. We'll obviously double-check by sending your sample to the lab. You had no idea that the symptoms you're experiencing could be the result of early pregnancy?'

'No. My cycle has never been regular and' – Rosanna blushed – 'Roberto and I, we . . . we've always been careful.'

'Well, these things do happen, Mrs Rossini. The little darlings sometimes arrive without being expected or planned.'

'How pregnant am I?' she asked.

'I'd say you're in your third month, perhaps a little more than that.' He studied her pale face. 'Once you've accepted the idea, I'm sure it'll be one of which you'll approve.'

'Yes.' Rosanna stood up. 'Thank you, Dr Hardy.'

'Give me a call tomorrow, Mrs Rossini. We must organise a scan and decide which hospital you want to give birth in.'

Dazed, Rosanna walked down the corridor towards the waiting room. Immediately, Roberto saw her anxious expression and stood up, but she walked straight towards the door and he followed her out onto the street.

'*Amore mio*, please, tell me. What did the doctor say? Was it bad news?'

'Oh Roberto.' Rosanna crumpled into his arms and burst into tears.

'Whatever it is, we can solve it. I'll get the best doctors or surgeons, whatever you need. Please don't cry, my darling, Roberto is here.'

'You'll be angry with me. This is my fault. I—'

'Rosanna! Please! Just tell me what is wrong with you?' Roberto entreated in frustration.

Her shoulders sagged and she stared down at her feet. 'I'm going to have a baby.'

Roberto looked blankly at her. 'A baby? You mean, my baby?'

'Of course!'

'But . . . but this is the most wonderful news I've ever heard! I, Roberto Rossini, am going to be a papa!' He let out a yelp of joy, then picked Rosanna up in his arms and twirled her round, covering her face with kisses. 'Oh my clever girl, my clever mamma! When is our baby due?'

'The doctor said he thought mid-November, but I need a scan to make sure of the date. You're not angry with me?' she asked as he set her down.

'Angry?' Roberto rolled his eyes in mock despair. 'Rosanna, what do you take me for? When I'm told that the woman I love is to have my child and make me a papa for the first time, you think I might be angry? You silly girl! I'm overjoyed, over the moon and probably over the hill to be starting a family, but you have once again made me the happiest man in the world. Come.' He took her hand. 'We will go and celebrate.'

Rosanna watched Roberto as he sat down opposite her in Le Caprice and ordered a bottle of vintage champagne, apologising profusely when she reminded him gently that she was not supposed to drink alcohol.

'I'm sorry, *cara*,' he said, summoning the waiter back and ordering an orange juice for her. 'I just cannot believe it. I want to celebrate with the whole world,' he laughed. 'Just imagine how talented the child will be. With our voices, he or she will be blessed with a superlative gift. We must think of names and which bedroom will make the most suitable nursery. Should we buy a bigger house, do you think? Perhaps our child should grow up in the country, where the air is fresher . . .'

Rosanna listened to Roberto's excited chatter, unable to catch his enthusiasm. Eventually, she said, 'But, Roberto, what about my career?'

'Well, of course there should be no problem with you singing *La Bohème* in July. I shall be there to make sure you rest and take care of yourself. Then, once that is finished, you must remain in London and nest until the baby is born.'

'But we're due in New York in October. What happens then?'

Roberto shrugged. 'The Met will understand. Women have babies all the time. I'll have to go alone.'

'And leave me behind in London for a month? Couldn't I come with you?' Rosanna felt the tears welling.

'Rosanna, the airline will not carry a heavily pregnant woman – even a star such as you. Besides, it's only for a month.'

'Perhaps I could take a boat?'

'And what if you went into early labour? You'd be putting yourself and our child at risk at so late a stage in your pregnancy. I'm sure Dr Hardy will agree that you should be relaxing at home in the last few weeks.'

'Couldn't you cancel the Met?'

Roberto shook his head. 'No, Rosanna, you know I could not.'

'I cancelled for you when it was necessary,' she shot back.

He eyed her across the table. 'That's unfair, Rosanna. It's the premiere of a new opera and these chances don't come along often. I shall be back by your side when you have the baby and I have only occasional concerts until after Christmas. Then, well, we shall see. Please, *cara*, don't think about the bad things. Let us enjoy this wonderful news, this gift from God. You do want this baby, don't you?'

She looked at him and nodded. 'Of course I do.'

Over the following few days, it was impossible not to let Roberto's euphoria affect her and Rosanna began to get used to the idea that she was to be a mother. The nagging doubts about having a baby and the way it would complicate her perfect existence began to lessen. Her career would have to go on hold for a few months, but there was no reason for her not to return to singing after the birth. Babies travelled abroad all the time these days. She'd hire a good nanny and the problem would be solved.

Roberto wanted to tell everybody he knew of the impending arrival, but Rosanna swore him to secrecy.

'Let me tell my family first,' she'd said. 'I'll break the news to Luca when I see him in two weeks' time and then write to Papa.'

26

'Ladies and gentlemen, please return to your seats. We are now commencing the descent to Heathrow.'

Forty-five minutes later, Luca pushed his trolley out of customs and into the arrivals hall. He spotted Rosanna leaning anxiously over the barrier. The sight of her made Luca catch his breath. Last time he had seen his sister, she'd still been a young girl. Now she looked like a woman. Her hair had been cut to just above her shoulders and hung in shiny waves around her face. Her features had matured and the light make-up she was wearing enhanced her natural beauty.

'Luca!' Rosanna saw him and ran towards him, opening her arms and hugging him to her. 'I can't believe you're here. Oh, it's so wonderful to see you!'

'For me too, *piccolina*.'

'Come, there's a car waiting outside to take us home.'

At the Kensington house, Rosanna led Luca downstairs to the kitchen. As she busied herself making coffee, he wandered round the kitchen, admiring the space and examining the photographs on the dresser. They settled down at the table nursing a mug each.

'This is a beautiful home, Rosanna. A little more comfortable than our apartment in Naples, wouldn't you say?'

'Yes. Roberto and I love it.'

Luca leant across the table and took her hands in his. 'So here we are, brother and sister reunited after far too long. You look radiant, Rosanna. You have the same face, the same body, but you are so . . . sophisticated now.'

'Am I?'

Luca saw that this seemed to please her. 'Yes. I still remember when you were a shy little girl. And now, your clothes, your hair . . . your perfect English.' He smiled. 'You're a cosmopolitan woman.'

'It's not a bad change, is it?'

'Of course not. Everyone grows up.'

'Well, I'm still that same little girl inside. I can't believe it's almost four years since I last saw you. You look thinner, Luca. Do they feed you in the seminary?'

'Of course they do,' he chuckled.

There was a pause, then both of them spoke at once.

'Have you—'

'Are you—'

They laughed. Rosanna shook her head. 'There's so much to tell, I really don't know where to start. And I want to hear all about Papa and Carlotta and Ella. But we have three days, so maybe we should start with you. Are you happy, Luca? Was it the right decision?'

'I think that after all those years of searching, I have found my calling, yes.' He took another sip of coffee. 'Of course, it's impossible to be happy all the time, and sometimes I feel that what I must learn in the seminary has less to do with God and more to do with human tradition. There are so many rules and regulations, some of which I feel might restrict the work that I wish to do in the future.' He shrugged. 'But I'm fine, really, maybe just too eager to get out there and begin to help.'

'I understand what you're saying. After all, I had ten years of training before I made my debut,' Rosanna mused. 'It can be frustrating, but it's worth all the hard work in the end, I think.'

'Well, it certainly seems to have paid off with you. You look so happy, *piccolina*.'

'I am. I too feel I have found my destiny.'

'With your career?'

'Of course. But more importantly, with Roberto.'

Luca steeled himself to make no comment. If Rosanna was happy – and she seemed to be – then so was he. *Whatever* he felt about Roberto.

'Ever since that first night when Roberto sang in our café, I knew deep down I loved him. It's odd, because I remember he only had eyes for Carlotta then. I felt very jealous, even though I was only eleven. You know, that night I wrote in my diary that I would one day marry him.'

Luca swallowed hard, digging his nails into the palm of his hand to stop himself from reacting.

'Speaking of Carlotta, how is she?' Rosanna asked.

'She is . . . okay.'

'I've written her a letter. I have something I want to tell her.'

'What is that?'

'Some news I heard recently. She's the only one who will truly know how I feel.'

'How do you feel?'

'Well, at first I was very shocked. It was such a surprise. I mean . . . I had no idea, but now I've got used to it, I know that it was meant to happen.'

'*What* was?'

Rosanna saw the confusion on his face and smiled delightedly. 'Oh Luca, I'm going to be a mamma. My baby is due in November and that's why I've written to Carlotta, to tell her she's going to be an aunt and to get some advice on being pregnant. I was thinking she might be able to come to London for a holiday. Roberto has to go to New York for a month and I'll be alone. There, what do you think? You will be an uncle. And I would like you to be godfather too,' she added.

As Luca paused just a second too long, she frowned.

'You are happy for me, aren't you?'

'Of course I am. It's wonderful news.'

'Are you sure you're pleased? You don't look it.'

'I'm sorry.' Luca managed a small smile. 'It's just the thought of my little sister being a mamma, that's all. It's a big thing.'

'I'm twenty-four, Luca. Old enough, I think.'

'And Roberto? Is he pleased?'

'I've never seen him happier. I thought he might be angry because the baby wasn't planned, but no – he was more excited than I was. He cannot believe he'll become a papa for the first time at forty-one.'

'And does Roberto make you a good husband?'

'Luca, I could not have asked for anyone to love me better. I know everyone disapproved when we married, but he's a changed man. I thank God each day that I've found him. And now the baby too. We're blessed, Luca, so blessed.'

'But you say he has to go to New York in the last month of your pregnancy?'

'Yes. It's sad but it can't be helped. That's why I was thinking Carlotta could come and be with me. I haven't seen her for so long. She would know what to do if the baby comes.'

Luca chose his words carefully. 'I cannot speak for Carlotta, but I think it would be difficult for her. She has Ella and Papa to care for, and the café to run.'

'Of course, but she should have a break sometimes. Is she happy, do you think?'

'I believe she has accepted her lot.'

Rosanna stared into the distance. 'When I was young, she was so vibrant, so beautiful. And then, when she married Giulio and Ella was born, she changed. I hope that it won't be the same for me.'

'Sometimes, things happen that change us in ways we least expect, *piccolina*. Look at you meeting Roberto.'

'You think he's changed me?'

'Well, your *life* has certainly changed. You haven't been back to Italy for a long time. Is there any reason for that?'

'I . . . yes . . . it's just that Roberto cannot . . .' Rosanna shook her head. 'It's a long story. I had to be with Roberto, wherever he was. That's why I didn't return to La Scala to sing Mimi in *La Bohème*. I still feel terrible about letting Paolo down but I didn't feel as though I had a choice.'

'Then I'm right. Marrying Roberto *has* changed you. It's maybe not my place to say so, but be careful you don't cut everyone else out of your life, Rosanna. Your family still love you and I know Papa is hurt that you and Roberto haven't visited him since you married. He's not getting any younger, you know.'

'I know, Luca,' Rosanna sighed. 'I miss the family too, but apart from anything else, our schedule has been so tight. There are so many people I'm always meaning to write to or try to visit. But when *La Bohème* finishes at the end of July, I'll at last have time to catch up. And maybe when the baby is born, I'll fly over and visit Papa and Carlotta. Now, you must be hungry.'

Anxious to change the subject, Rosanna stood up and went over to the fridge. She retrieved some cold meats, pâté and a salad she'd prepared earlier. Luca watched her as she set the table and deftly sliced a loaf of bread. He knew his sister too well to try to press her any further on the topic of Roberto.

'Do you ever hear from Abi?' he asked as she sat down again opposite him.

'It's funny you should ask, as I got a postcard from her this morning,' she replied, offering him the salad bowl. 'Apparently she's travelling in Australia at the moment, then intends to visit the Far East. But she said she'll be in London in the autumn. To be truthful, I've not tried as hard as I could have to keep in touch. Abi had a brief affair with Roberto, you see. It was hard for me and I think we both needed time for the dust to settle. Maybe we can see each other when she's back in London.'

Luca hid a stab of pain at the thought that Abi too had apparently succumbed to Roberto Rossini's charms. 'That would be good for you. It's nice to keep in touch with old friends. You and Abi were very close.' He spread some pâté on his bread.

'Do *you* ever hear from her, Luca?'

Luca's eyes softened as he shook his head. 'No. I cared for her, very much.'

'But you cared for God more?'

'He's my priority, Rosanna, just as now Roberto is yours.'

'Do you ever get lonely in the seminary?'

'What do you mean?' he asked her.

'Well, you're unable to share your life with anyone.'

'Rosanna, I have God, and He is all I need. There are many different types of love, you know. And as yours is for Roberto, so mine is for Him. Now, tell me of all the places you have visited since you began your travels.'

The following day, Rosanna took Luca sightseeing in London and in the evening they went to the Royal Opera House to see a production of *Aida*.

'If only it was you on that stage, Rosanna. It's so sad that I have never seen you sing since you were at school in Milan,' Luca lamented as they took a taxi back to Kensington.

'In a few weeks' time, it *will* be me. But I enjoyed watching the performance and then picking that poor soprano to pieces afterwards,' Rosanna giggled.

On Sunday they attended Mass at Westminster Cathedral, then Rosanna cooked roast beef. They took a walk in Kensington Gardens and returned home, tired but relaxed.

'Are you okay, *piccolina*?' asked Luca as he came into the sitting room later that evening and saw the sadness on her face.

'I just don't want you to leave tomorrow, that's all.'

'I know. It's been wonderful to see you. It has reminded me of all the old times in Milan. We had a lot of fun in between the hard work.'

'We did,' Rosanna nodded, before yawning. 'Oh dear. I

seem to get sleepy so early in the evening these days. Is that normal, do you think?'

'Of course it is, and you must go to bed. Promise me you'll take care of yourself when you start *La Bohème*. You have another tiny soul to think of now.'

'I will.' Rosanna agreed. 'It's such a shame that you didn't see Roberto, but at least we've had time to ourselves to catch up.'

'Yes.' Luca privately thought that the less his and Roberto's paths crossed, the better for everyone concerned.

Rosanna stood up and threw her arms around her brother. 'You don't know how much I've enjoyed seeing you again. Please can we try and see each other more often?'

'We can try, but you know it's difficult.'

'I know. There's always a price to pay for everything, isn't there?'

Luca kissed her on both cheeks. 'Remember, Rosanna, if I'm not here in person, I'm always thinking of you.'

'Come and see your new godchild when he or she is born, won't you?' she said, making her way to the door.

'Nothing could stop me doing that. Goodnight, *piccolina*. Sleep well.'

Luca sat downstairs for another hour before making his way up to bed. He leafed through a scrapbook full of newspaper and magazine cuttings that Rosanna had given him. In every photograph, Rosanna was looking up at Roberto with love shining out of her eyes.

It was obvious that the man made his sister very happy. And for that reason alone, he'd ask God to help him find forgiveness for all that Roberto had done before.

*

Rosanna arrived back from saying goodbye to her brother at Heathrow feeling very low. In the past four years, she'd forgotten how close she and Luca had been. Now he'd gone and she had no idea when she'd see him again.

Slowly, she climbed the steps to the front door. Then, as she searched for her key, the door was opened and she was enveloped in Roberto's arms.

'My darling girl,' he said. 'Where have you been? I was getting worried, *cara*. I arrived from Gatwick and you were gone.'

'I went with Luca to Heathrow.'

Roberto led Rosanna inside and took her coat from her shoulders, hanging it over the banister.

'How was your brother?'

'Very well.'

'Good. Come here.' Roberto pulled her towards him and kissed her hard. 'You don't know how I missed you, *cara*.'

Rosanna smiled up at him, her heart lifting. This was home and Roberto was all that mattered.

27

London, October 1980

Rosanna awoke and saw it was only half past six. She crept out of bed, went to the bathroom, then made her way downstairs to the kitchen. A heavy autumnal mist was hanging outside. The leaves on the tree in the garden were turning brown and dropping one by one to the ground, a signal that summer was well and truly over. She made a cup of tea, then manoeuvred herself into a chair and laid her head down on the cool surface of the table.

At eleven o'clock, Roberto would leave for New York.

Eight weeks ago, the final night of *La Bohème* had been all the more poignant as it was the last time they would sing together for many months. Since then, they had tried to remain cheerful and enjoy the time they had together, but their imminent separation had hung over them both like a pall.

The baby gave a kick under her ribs. She sat upright and tried to rally her spirits. She would not cry when he left. She didn't want Roberto's last memory of her to be a bloated wreck with red, puffy eyes. Rosanna drained her teacup and waddled upstairs to shower.

An hour later Roberto arrived in the kitchen. With a sigh, he sat down at the table.

'There's coffee in the pot and I've cooked you some sausages – I know you like sau . . . sausages.' Rosanna's voice faltered but she managed a smile as she turned to look at him.

'Thank you, *cara*.'

She dished out the sausages, together with some fried mushrooms and tomatoes, onto two plates and took them over to the table.

'This looks delicious.'

'Well, I wanted you to have a treat as airline food is always terrible. But promise me you'll watch your weight when you get to New York. Dr Hardy said you should lose at least twelve kilos.'

'Yes, of course.' Roberto began to eat. 'Now, you know that I'm staying at Chris's apartment, so you'll be able to reach me there. And if there's an important message you can always call me at the Met. I'll warn them they must find me urgently.'

'Don't worry, *caro*. I have told this bump it can't make an appearance before its papa's back home. I still have six weeks to go. Six more weeks of this,' she sighed. 'Am I having a baby or an elephant? Imagine how huge I'll be when you get home. I might have exploded by then,' she said seriously.

'Any problems, Rosanna, call Dr Hardy immediately.'

'Of course.'

'I'm sure you won't be lonely, *cara*. Lots of people from Covent Garden will pop in.'

'I'm sure I'll be fine.'

Neither of them finished their breakfast. In the end, Rosanna stood up and began to clear the table.

'I'd better go and shower,' said Roberto.

She looked at the clock as he left the kitchen. In less than an hour, he would leave her.

'The car is here.' Roberto shrugged on his overcoat.

Rosanna watched him as he did so, willing herself not to let the tears pour down her cheeks.

'*Amore mio*.' Roberto's arms encircled her. 'How I love you, how I miss you already. I'll count the days until I'm back with you again.'

'Take care of yourself, Roberto. *Ti amo, caro*.'

He nodded as he left her arms and hurried down the steps to the waiting car. He turned, blew Rosanna a kiss before climbing inside, and waved as the car pulled away from the pavement.

Then he was gone.

The first week without Roberto seemed endless, although Rosanna had a stream of visitors appearing on her doorstep. Sometimes, they provided a blessed relief from boredom. At other times, she felt so tired and low and fragile that she wished they would leave almost as soon as they'd arrived. Roberto called her three times a day, whispering words of love down the telephone line, telling her how much he missed her. For those few minutes, Rosanna was happy. Then she'd put down the receiver and weep.

The way she missed him . . . it was a physical pain. Having to do alone the things they had always done together, even simple everyday chores, actually *hurt*.

And the nights . . . the nights stretched before her like a yawning abyss. Without him there beside her, she found it almost impossible to sleep. And when she did drop off, the baby would kick her awake.

On her first Saturday night alone, Roberto didn't ring at his usual time. When he did call an hour later, she burst into tears and sobbed down the telephone, begging him to come home. Roberto was apologetic: rehearsals had run over and there had been nothing he could do. She replied mournfully that she was sorry for being such an idiot, and put the receiver down.

She went to the bathroom, and, as she washed her hands, she stared at her reflection in the mirror.

You look dreadful, she told herself. *You have to pull yourself together*.

Rosanna showered, donned her accommodating towelling robe, then made her way downstairs to make some supper. As she sat in the kitchen forcing the food down her throat, she realised how her love for Roberto controlled her.

What if one day he left her? Rosanna gulped as her heartbeat increased. She was being stupid. She couldn't – *mustn't* – contemplate it. Stress was bad for the baby and she'd given it a literal bellyful in the past two weeks.

Rosanna stood up and put on a cassette tape of the two of them singing '*Dolce notte! Quante stelle!*' from *Madama Butterfly*.

The voices soothed her and she smiled.

In three weeks' time he'd be back home and she could forget this nightmare. One thing was certain: she would never let him leave her behind again.

*

Roberto felt drained and a little drunk. He glanced around at the animated crowd gathered on the stage of the Metropolitan Opera House, chatting and drinking champagne. Yet he felt lonely and bereft. Although he'd been aware of the deep feelings he had for his wife, it was only after two weeks alone that the truth had begun to sink in.

Tonight's opening of the new opera, *Dante*, had been a huge success. New York was at his feet. He was at the pinnacle. And as miserable as hell.

Without Rosanna, it all meant nothing.

He yawned, then checked his watch. He would leave in five minutes. He'd promised Rosanna he'd call her the minute he got home.

'Don't you agree, Mr Rossini?'

'Forgive me, signora, I didn't catch what you said.'

The wealthy New York matron repeated her theory about funding for the arts.

'Of course I agree completely. Governments must provide more money for the opera if they wish to see it last into the next century. Now, if you'll excuse me, I must go home and telephone my wife.'

He nodded to Chris Hughes. 'I'm off. I'll see you tomorrow morning.'

His limousine was waiting for him by the stage door.

'Home, sir?'

'Yes, please.'

The limousine pulled away from the pavement and headed for Chris's apartment on the Upper West Side of Manhattan.

'Here we are, sir.' The chauffeur opened Roberto's door and he stepped out under the awning of the smart apartment block.

'Goodnight.'

'Goodnight, sir.'

Roberto took the elevator to the twenty-eighth floor. As he opened the front door, he could hear the telephone ringing from within. He ran into the sitting room and picked up the receiver.

'Hello?'

'It's me. I've just woken up and I thought I'd call you. How did it go?'

'It was a sensation, *principessa*. Apart from the fact you weren't there beside me.'

'How was Francesca Romanos?'

'The audience liked her.'

There was a pause before Rosanna answered. 'Oh.'

'Would you prefer me to tell you she was dreadful?' Roberto chuckled.

'Of course I would.'

'Francesca is not and never will be you. You are the greatest soprano in the world. You know that.'

'I'm being silly, but you can imagine how I've felt, knowing another singer was taking my place opposite you, while I've been lying here like a great fat dumpling.'

'Well, my little dumpling, I think you are the most beautiful creature in the world.'

'Are you still missing me?' she asked plaintively.

'Of course I am, Rosanna. See? I even left the party early so I could telephone you. It was still in full swing.'

'Who was there?' Rosanna's voice sounded strained.

'Oh, the usual crowd. Everyone sends their love and their best wishes.'

'That's nice. No beautiful women trying to steal you from me?'

'A few . . .' Roberto heard Rosanna catch her breath. 'I'm only teasing you, *cara*. You mustn't be so sensitive.'

'I know, I'm sorry. But you don't know how lonely it is without you. I sleep with your sweater next to me.' She sighed wistfully.

'Well, not for much longer. I'll be there before you know it,' Roberto reassured her gently.

'At least Abi's coming to see me tomorrow. We might go out for lunch, so don't worry if I'm not here if you call.'

'Okay. But please don't listen to anything she says about me. You know what happened between us,' Roberto said uncomfortably.

'I know, but that's all in the past now. She was my best friend and it's high time we saw each other again. Will you call me tomorrow when you wake up?'

'Of course.'

'Then I'd better let you go. You must be exhausted.'

'I am a little tired. Now, you try and get some more sleep. It's good for you and the baby.'

'I will try but it's impossible. *Ti amo*, Roberto.'

'I love you too.'

'Sleep tight.'

Roberto put down the receiver and paced restlessly around the sitting room, unable to settle. His libido always rose with his adrenaline when he performed and this was the first night in over two years Rosanna hadn't been there to calm him with her beautiful body.

There was nothing for it but a cold shower.

*

At one o'clock the following day, the telephone rang and Rosanna hurried to answer it.

'*Principessa*, it's me. I love you, I miss you, I long for your body, I want to drown in you . . .'

Rosanna giggled. 'Good morning, Roberto.'

'Oh *cara*. Without you, the days seem endless,' he groaned.

'Roberto, I know, but they'll pass quickly and soon we'll be together. That's what you're always telling me.'

'What is this? You're not missing me anymore? You sound far too happy!'

'You've been chiding me for sounding miserable for the past two weeks.'

'You've found someone else, that is it. Who is he? I shall kill him with my bare hands.'

'No one would want me like this, I promise you.'

'*I* would, Rosanna. I ache for you. Be prepared for a week in bed when I return.'

'I long for it too,' she smiled, experiencing a frisson of anticipation.

'So, you still haven't told me why you sound so happy?' Roberto continued.

The doorbell rang.

'I . . . Roberto, Abi has arrived. I must go.'

'Okay, okay, I understand. You don't wish to speak to me now you've another woman to gossip with,' he laughed, happy to hear her sounding so positive, even if he was nervous of Abi's attitude towards him. '*Ti amo*, Rosanna. And remember not to listen to any bad things she might say about your husband.'

'I won't. *Ti amo, caro*.' She put down the telephone and hurried to the front door.

*

'Rosanna! Oh my God! You're huge!' Abi exclaimed as she kissed her friend, then hugged her warmly.

'And you are even more beautiful than ever, and very thin!' Rosanna laughed ruefully. 'Please, come in.'

As Abi followed Rosanna inside the house, she let out a whistle. 'Wow! This is rather grand. Lucky old you.'

'I love it here, but we're looking to buy something out of London once the baby comes. Here, let me take your coat.'

'God, it's cold out there today,' said Abi as Rosanna led her downstairs into the kitchen.

'I know,' Rosanna agreed. 'I spend my time in London looking like an advertisement for wool. I can't believe my baby is to be born into a climate like this. In Naples, I doubt I wore any clothes at all until I was three. Would you like something to drink?'

'A glass of wine would be lovely,' said Abi. 'I'll get it. You stay there.'

'Thank you. There's a bottle in the fridge and I'll have a Perrier.'

'Sure.' Abi walked across the room to organise the drinks. 'There.' She returned to the table and handed Rosanna the glass of fizzing water. 'To us – together again.'

'Would you mind if we stayed here for lunch?' Rosanna queried. 'I'm feeling so tired at the moment. I have some soup and fresh bread.'

'Sounds good to me,' said Abi. 'You really are large, Rosanna. How much longer do you have?'

'About a month.'

'Can I ask you what's it like? I mean, being pregnant?'

'Strange, very strange,' mused Rosanna. 'It's like you're

taken over by an alien. You're not in control of your own body any longer. Or your emotions, for that matter.'

Abi studied her. 'It's hard to take in that you're going to be a mother in a few weeks' time.'

'And it's already changed me. You know how I used to hate cleaning, but yesterday I had to hoover and dust and iron, even though we have a housekeeper who comes in four mornings a week.'

'I think that's called the nesting instinct. Apparently, a lot of women get it just before the baby arrives. It could mean he or she might put in an appearance sooner than you think.'

'No!' Rosanna looked horrified. 'It can't . . . it mustn't, not until Roberto is home.'

'It's difficult enough to imagine you being a mummy, but the thought of Roberto being a daddy, well . . .' Abi rolled her eyes.

'But, Abi, he's different now, believe me. So many people have noticed. You would too if you met him again. He's a changed man.'

'I hope you're right, Rosanna,' Abi said seriously.

'I'm sure of it, truly . . .' Rosanna stopped suddenly and looked at her friend. 'Abi, before I say anything else, I want to apologise for not telling you I was marrying Roberto. We decided it was best to say nothing until afterwards. We didn't want to be hounded so soon by the media. Even my family didn't know.'

'Well, I admit to being hurt that I had to read the news in the papers. Were you worried I'd try to talk you out of it?' Abi asked her bluntly.

'No, because I knew whatever you said, or anyone else said for that matter, I would marry Roberto.'

'You always had a strange connection with him, didn't you?'

'Yes. I did. We both believe it was destiny.'

Abi sipped her wine. 'Did it upset you terribly when I had an affair with him? You didn't show it at the time.'

'Of course it did, Abi. Although after you told me about him dumping you, I did my best to dislike him. When we went to London together, I didn't let Roberto near me at first. I was scared that if I did, he'd hurt me the way he hurt you and I would never have got over him the way you did. You don't still care for him, do you?'

'God, no. It was a quick fling, that was all. I was hurt, but now I understand – as I remember you saying at the time – that he was only a Luca substitute. I transferred all that unrequited passion onto Roberto, at least briefly. Hindsight's a wonderful thing. How is Luca, by the way?'

'He's very well. He was here in May. He asked how you were.'

'Did he?' Abi smiled, but her eyes were filled with sadness. 'That's nice. Anyway, let's not dwell too much on what's passed. We've so many other things to talk about.'

'Yes.' Rosanna too was happy to move the conversation on. 'I want to know everything you've been doing.'

'Well, after you left Milan, I stayed at La Scala for another year. Then I had a long talk with Paolo and he told me what I already knew: that it was doubtful I'd ever graduate beyond the chorus. So I decided to quit and take a year out to travel. And I've had a wonderful time, Rosanna. I went to the Far East and, as you know, spent six months in Australia. Two weeks ago, I came home to London and now I'm staying with my parents in Fulham, trying to decide what I'm going to do with the rest of my life.'

'Have you any ideas?'

'No, not really. The trouble is, once you've become involved in the arts, any kind of nine-to-five routine seems impossibly dull.' Abi sighed. 'I really don't know, although I have thought about writing, as a matter of fact.'

'Oh, what sort of writing?'

'Again, I'm not sure. Maybe some journalism; even a novel perhaps. I've always had a vivid imagination,' she grinned, looking more like the Abi of old.

'That sounds interesting, although I'm sorry to hear you're no longer singing. I think you had a lovely voice.'

'Yes, but not lovely enough, apparently. Anyway, it's kind of you to say so and Milan was such fun that I don't regret one second of it.'

'Tell me' – Rosanna took a sip of her Perrier – 'was Paolo furious when I didn't return to La Scala?'

'Well, you know Paolo. If he was, then he didn't show it to the company. All I can say is that I never heard your name mentioned again. Just out of interest, why didn't you go back? I thought playing Mimi there was your dream.'

'It was to do with Roberto. Please believe me when I say I had no choice,' Rosanna answered abruptly. She didn't want the conversation turning back to *that* painful subject.

'I just wish you'd let me know what was happening. For weeks I had no idea where you were. And the press door-stepped our apartment when the news finally broke. Still' – Abi shrugged good-naturedly – 'it's water under the bridge now, I suppose.'

'Abi, forgive me,' Rosanna said guiltily. 'I know I was

selfish, but . . . well, it was as if Roberto and I were living on another planet. I only had thoughts for him.'

Abi studied her friend. 'It really is a grand passion between the two of you, isn't it?'

'Yes, it is,' Rosanna replied simply.

'I'm glad for you, Rosanna, really, but do try and take care.'

'What do you mean?'

'Well, I think that sometimes – and please don't take this the wrong way, darling – an overpowering depth of feeling can make one a little selfish.'

'I agree, Abi, and, as I said, I'm sorry,' replied Rosanna ruefully.

'Well, I think I know how it feels.' Abi sighed. 'I know we agreed that we shouldn't look back, but if I'm completely honest with myself . . . I know I'm still in love with Luca. It sounds stupid, because it can never come to anything, but I just can't seem to forget him.'

'Oh Abi.' Rosanna looked at her friend with surprise and sympathy. 'It must be so hard knowing you can never be together. Although I know Luca was always very fond of you.'

'Don't get me wrong, there've been plenty of other men, but unless something changes drastically, it will always be Luca in my heart.'

'I feel for you, Abi, really. Do you have a boyfriend at the moment?'

'Of course I do,' she replied, glad for the chance to steer their talk in another direction. 'You must meet him. He's awfully sweet. He's called Henry and I met him at a party a couple of weeks ago. He's very keen and I only wish I could fall in love with him as he'd suit me down to the ground.'

'You must give it time, Abi. You've only known him two weeks.'

'Rosanna, you of all people must understand about love, the intuition that tells you this is something special. Well, with Henry, it isn't. I just know it.'

'Yes. I've never felt so miserable as I have for the last two weeks. Roberto and I have rarely spent an hour apart, let alone a month.'

'Well, in some ways, a month being miserable is a small price to pay for all you have: the man you love, a baby on the way, wealth and a stellar career. I wouldn't mind being you.' Abi smiled. 'Now, where's that soup?'

After lunch, they sat at the table drinking coffee.

'So, what are you doing next Saturday night?' Abi asked Rosanna.

'Nothing, absolutely nothing.'

'Well then, you can join Henry and me for dinner. Henry has a friend who went green with envy when I said I was seeing you today. Stephen is one of your biggest fans and he's absolutely desperate to meet you. Come along and have your ego massaged for an hour or two.'

'Thank you for the offer, but I don't feel like going anywhere at the moment.'

'Oh, come on, show you can be humble and dine with the rest of us mortals.'

Rosanna flushed. 'You know it's nothing to do with that, Abi. I'm just not feeling very social.'

'Well, an evening out might do you good. Besides, you owe me for leaving me in the lurch in Milan,' pressured Abi.

'Okay. You win,' Rosanna conceded.

'Good. I'll collect you at eightish on Saturday evening.' Abi looked at her watch, then stood up. 'I'm afraid I've got to go. Don't get up, I can let myself out.' She kissed Rosanna warmly on both cheeks. 'Goodbye, darling. Look after yourself. It really is good to see you again.'

'And you, Abi.'

'Anything you need,' she said as she walked towards the door, 'you have my number.'

Rosanna realised she was nervous about going out alone on Saturday night. In the past two years, Roberto had always accompanied her. She spent most of the afternoon fretfully trying on clothes that would fit over her bulge, then washed her hair and put on some make-up. By the time Abi rang the doorbell, she was ready.

'You look lovely,' Abi said approvingly.

'Thank you.'

'Right, let's go. We're supposed to be meeting the boys in fifteen minutes.'

'We are going somewhere discreet, aren't we? I don't want to sound like a diva, but I'd hate Roberto to see a photograph in the papers of me with another man,' Rosanna said, embarrassed to admit it.

'Of course. In honour of you, we're going to an Italian restaurant.' Abi unlocked the door of her Renault 5. 'It's not what I'd call the smartest place, but the pasta's wonderful. Get in.'

Abi negotiated the heavy traffic in Earl's Court Road then turned left onto the Fulham Road. 'That's lucky,' she said as she deftly manoeuvred the car into a space outside a small restaurant.

Inside, the restaurant was packed with diners sitting at rough wooden tables, tucking into pasta and drinking carafes of wine.

'It reminds me of Papa's café,' said Rosanna wistfully as Abi waved at two men sitting at a table in a corner. One of the men was stout, losing his hair prematurely, and wore a pair of horn-rimmed glasses. Rosanna presumed this was Stephen, her fan. The other man was extremely handsome, with dark hair and merry blue eyes.

'Henry, darling.' Abi kissed the balding man on both cheeks then turned to the other. 'Stephen, didn't I promise to deliver her?' She smiled at Rosanna. 'He didn't believe you would show tonight. Rosanna, may I present your greatest fan.'

'Stephen Peatôt. I'm honoured to meet you, Mrs Rossini.' He smiled shyly as they shook hands.

'Right, make way for the baby elephant,' said Abi, pulling the chair next to Stephen as far out from the table as she could.

Rosanna blushed as she struggled to fit into the gap between table and chair.

Stephen thoughtfully poured drinks for the two women: red wine for Abi and mineral water for Rosanna. They then perused the menu and ordered while they listened to Henry, a stockbroker, regale them with details of an enormous and lucrative deal his firm had completed yesterday.

'Are you also in the City?' Rosanna asked Stephen, who was sitting next to her.

'No, nothing as grown-up as that, I'm afraid. I'm an art dealer. I started off at Sotheby's in the Renaissance department and now I work at a contemporary gallery in Cork

Street. I'm trying to learn as much as possible before I set up on my own.'

'I see. I'm afraid I know nothing about art.'

'Interestingly, when I've seen you singing, I've had that gut reaction I only feel when I'm studying a very rare painting. You stir the emotions, you see. Like artists, there are few opera singers who can achieve that.'

Rosanna was used to flattery, but the warmth with which Stephen spoke made his words seem much more genuine. 'Which is your favourite opera?' she asked him.

'That's a difficult one. I'm a Puccini fan and I love all his works. I think, if I was pushed, I'd have to say *Madama Butterfly*. I saw you sing it in New York last year. I thought you were perfect.'

'Thank you,' she answered, 'though some would say I'm still too young to give the role the proper emotional and vocal depth.'

'I say that's rubbish. Butterfly is meant to be fifteen years old. Directors don't think of the audience,' Stephen countered. 'Forgive me for sounding rude about some of your female colleagues, but it's hard to believe in, say, a consumptively beautiful Violetta from *La Traviata* when she's over fifty and weighs a hundred kilos!'

'You mean, looking a bit like I do now?' Rosanna chuckled. 'I sang Mimi at Covent Garden when I was six months' pregnant.'

'Well, I saw you and I would never have known,' said Stephen gallantly.

'It was a clever costume,' conceded Rosanna.

A waiter momentarily stopped the conversation as he delivered the heavily loaded plates of food to the table.

'So, when's the baby due, Rosanna?' asked Henry when the waiter had left.

'In about three weeks' time.'

'Your husband will be home by then, presumably?'

'Yes. How do you and Stephen know each other?' she asked, wishing to change the subject.

'We were at boarding school together. Stephen, being the kind of clever chap he is, won a scholarship to Cambridge while I had to make do with law at Birmingham,' Henry explained good-naturedly and raised a glass in Stephen's direction.

Rosanna began to relax a little. It was good to be out with people whose sole topic of conversation was not opera. But as they were drinking espressos, Rosanna began to shift uncomfortably in her seat. Stephen noticed immediately.

'Are you all right?'

'Yes, thank you. It's just a little difficult to sit in one position for too long at the moment.'

'Of course. Would you like to go home?'

'I think I should, yes.'

'Oh spoilsport. I was hoping we might go on somewhere,' admonished Henry playfully.

'Well, why don't you and Abi do that and I'll drive Rosanna home?' Stephen suggested. 'I need my beauty sleep too. I'm flying to Paris tomorrow to authenticate a painting.'

'Oh no, Stephen, please don't worry. I can get a taxi,' said Rosanna.

'Nonsense. Abi says you live in Kensington. I do too. It couldn't be less trouble.'

'All right then. It's very kind of you.'

'My pleasure.'

Rosanna took a credit card out of her bag. 'I must pay for this.'

'Absolutely not. Henry and I will get the bill,' said Stephen, signalling for the waiter.

Once the bill was paid, Rosanna stood up and let Stephen help her into her wrap, then they all left the restaurant.

Abi unlocked the car door and Henry climbed into the passenger seat. 'Bye, darling. I'll call you tomorrow.'

'Bye, Abi.' Rosanna waved as the car drove off.

'This way. It's not far.' Rosanna walked with Stephen up a side street. 'I'm afraid the mode of transport might not be quite what you're used to.' Stephen indicated a rusty Volkswagen Beetle and unlocked the passenger door. 'She isn't pretty, but she's never let me down yet.'

They both climbed in and Stephen started the engine. As he did so, the sound of Rosanna's voice singing an aria from *Madama Butterfly* filled the car.

'I'm so sorry, that was tacky. I was playing it on the way here.' Stephen hurriedly removed the cassette tape as they drove off.

'Which recording of *Madama Butterfly* was that?' asked Rosanna.

'I think it was your first, actually.'

'But that's not the best version. Roberto and I made a new one last year and I much prefer it.'

'I'll be off to buy it then,' he grinned.

'Oh no, I have lots of copies at home. You must have one.'

'Really? That's awfully kind of you.'

'Not at all. Consider it my way of saying thank you for dinner.' Rosanna pointed as they approached the top of her street. 'I live just there, on the left by that tree. I'll give the cassette to Abi next time I see her.'

'Or maybe I could save you the trouble and just drop by to pick it up sometime? I literally live round the corner.'

'Okay,' she agreed as Stephen got out of the car, opened the passenger door and helped her out.

'Thank you, Rosanna, for a lovely evening.'

'I enjoyed it too.'

'Goodnight then.'

'Goodnight.'

Stephen waited until Rosanna was safely up the steps and had closed the front door behind her. As he got back behind the wheel, he stuck the cassette of *Madama Butterfly* back in the tape recorder and, as he turned on his engine, Rosanna's voice flooded the car.

28

Roberto woke up and reached automatically for the smooth, silken body that always lay next to him. It wasn't there. He groaned, and slapped the pillow where his wife's head should rest.

It was Sunday and he'd been invited to a champagne brunch, the thought of which bored him; but he decided it was better than hanging around Chris's apartment all day. So he climbed out of bed and went to shower.

The brunch party was being held in a plush penthouse apartment overlooking Central Park. John St Regent and his wife, Trish, a buxom blonde dressed from head to toe in Gucci, greeted him at the door.

'It's so wonderful you could come to our little gathering, Roberto,' Trish gushed.

'Yeah, good to see you,' John St Regent said as he shook Roberto's hand vigorously.

'And how's that divine little wife of yours?' Trish enquired. 'Such a shame she had to cancel New York. You must be lonesome without her.'

'Yes, I have been,' Roberto agreed.

'Never mind, we've got some company here to keep you amused for a while.' Trish squeezed his shoulder in a show of solidarity. 'Come through and let me introduce you to some of our other guests.'

Roberto was led out of the entrance hall and into a vast sitting room, with floor-to-ceiling windows affording spectacular views over the park and the city beyond.

'Here we go,' said Trish, leading Roberto over to a small group of elegantly dressed women. 'May I present Mr Roberto Rossini. Please take care of him, ladies, he's very precious,' she said with a smile before drifting off to greet another guest.

'Drink, sir?' One of the uniformed maids offered Roberto a glass of champagne.

'Thank you. Good afternoon, ladies.' He smiled at the assembled group.

'Oh Mr Rossini, we've all seen you in *Dante* at the Met. We thought you were truly wonderful, didn't we, girls?' one of the women said.

'Well, thank you, Signora . . . ?'

'Mattheson. Rita Mattheson. And this is Clara Frobisher, Jill Lipman and Tessa Stewart. We're all great fans of yours.'

'I'm honoured,' murmured Roberto as he nodded to each of the women and prepared for fifteen minutes of polite small talk.

Thankfully, just as he reached the limits of his conversational endurance, the butler announced that brunch was served and the assembled company made their way through to the dining room.

Roberto was seated to the left of Trish St Regent, who sat at the head of the long and extravagantly dressed table.

'So, is it straight back home to London when you finish at the Met next week?' she asked.

'Yes, I . . .'

Roberto was suddenly distracted by the familiar smell of Joy perfume. As he involuntarily turned his head to view the late arrival, he saw her sauntering down the room to a chair at the far end of the table.

'Roberto, honey, are you okay?'

'I'm so sorry, Trish. I . . . what were you saying?'

Roberto surreptitiously studied the new arrival throughout the meal, wondering what she was doing here in New York. She was deliberately ignoring him, refusing to make eye contact, even when John St Regent gave the toast in his honour.

Eventually, curiosity got the better of him. He turned to Trish. 'Signora Bianchi, is her husband not with her in New York?'

'Oh my goodness, Roberto, if you know Donatella, I'm surprised you haven't heard. Giovanni died of a heart attack . . . let's see, it must be six months ago now. It was tragic, as John and he have done business together for many years. He really helped us out when we wanted some pictures to brighten our little apartment. Donatella was real devastated, so she decided to make a fresh start and moved over here from Milan three months ago. I'm trying to help her get over her grief.'

A huge surge of relief poured through Roberto as he realised that Donatella's presence was mere coincidence and nothing to do with him. And he didn't feel an ounce of remorse that Giovanni was dead. In fact, he was delighted. It meant he was free to travel to Italy once more.

After lunch, as the guests wandered back into the sitting room, Roberto felt a tap on his shoulder.

'How are you, Roberto?' The low, husky voice hadn't changed and neither had she.

'I . . .' Roberto experienced the same animal reaction he'd had when she'd first approached him that night at La Scala. 'I am well, very well indeed,' he murmured.

'Life is strange, is it not? I expect you were surprised to see me here.'

'I was. Trish says you live in New York now.'

'I do, yes. How is your wife? I hear she's pregnant.'

Roberto looked at her warily. 'She is fine, thank you.'

'You don't need to be embarrassed. Yes, of course I was furious when I realised you'd dumped me to marry Rosanna, but then I discovered what my husband had done to you, to us both. He confessed on his deathbed, the old fool. Besides' – she shrugged elegantly – 'it's all behind us now. Maybe it was for the best. I'm happy here in New York and you have your Rosanna.'

'So, you know now what happened, that I had to leave Italy. It wasn't easy and I've paid a heavy price. I had to cancel all my Italian engagements and I couldn't even attend my mamma's funeral. It devastated me.'

'I apologise on Giovanni's behalf, Roberto. You know Italian men. They have such pride when it comes to their women.' Donatella smiled bewitchingly.

'Would he have carried through his threat? I've often wondered,' mused Roberto.

'That's something only Giovanni could have answered. He was a powerful man and he certainly knew many people who could have done so. You were wise to stay away.'

'I'm glad I've seen you, if only because it means that now Rosanna and I can go and visit our families in Naples.' Roberto knew he was deliberately goading her with his wife's existence, but she was not to be deflected.

'I hope,' said Donatella softly, 'that you have other reasons for being glad to see me.' She reached over and briefly touched his hand.

There it was again, that unbidden attraction surging through him. This was dangerous. He had to leave. Right now.

'How long are you in town for?' she asked.

'I fly to London next Sunday.'

'Would you like to have dinner? For old times' sake?' Donatella pulled a card out of her sleek clutch-bag.

'No, I . . . unfortunately I won't have time.'

'Well, just in case you change your mind, my number's on the card.'

'I . . . I have to leave now. I have another engagement to attend.'

'Of course.' Donatella smiled knowingly. '*Ciao, caro*, if you get lonely, call me.'

Roberto watched as she turned away and sauntered across the room. She looked fantastic, even better than he'd remembered her, but he refused to listen to the traitorous stirrings of his body. The woman was nothing but trouble. He excused himself, said his goodbyes to the St Regents, then left.

That evening, Roberto sat in the silent apartment alone, studying the empty bottle of wine and contemplating whether to open another. He reached unsteadily for the telephone and dialled Rosanna.

'It's me. Did I wake you, my darling?'

'No. I was lying here reading a book. How are you?'

'Lonely. Chris is away in Europe and the silence is driving me mad.'

'I'm sorry, darling, but it won't be long now.'

'How are you? You sound happy. Why?' Roberto asked.

'Oh, no reason really. I went to dinner last night with Abi and two of her friends. Maybe it did me good to get out,' Rosanna replied.

'Female friends, I hope?'

'No, male actually. I had a nice time.'

'I see. So, you're gallivanting around London with strange men while I sit, lonely and sad, in this horrible apartment by myself?'

'Roberto, really, Chris's apartment is beautiful!'

'I cannot bear to think of you having dinner with other men.'

'Roberto, don't be silly.'

'In fact, I absolutely forbid you to go out again,' he growled.

'What? You're being ridiculous. It was nice to go out for a change, that's all.'

'And what exactly were they like, these men?'

'They were both charming, if you must know.'

'Good-looking, I suppose?'

'Roberto, stop this, please. There's absolutely nothing for you to worry about, I assure you.'

'And how can I be sure of that? One of them could be in my bed now for all I know, some eager young stud just panting to sleep with the famous opera star,' he added, the wine and loneliness making him ridiculously irrational and grumpy.

'Roberto! Don't speak to me like that,' Rosanna said, the quiver in her voice betraying how upset she was. 'I want you to apologise – now.'

There was an agonising pause as Roberto struggled against his alcohol-fuelled jealousy, and lost. 'Well, I won't apologise,' he said petulantly. 'This situation is your doing, not mine. Goodbye.'

He slammed down the receiver, knowing that he was being supremely childish but unable to help himself. Minutes later the telephone rang, but Roberto ignored it. He went to the kitchen and opened the other bottle of wine, tossed back a glass, then went to take a shower. When he emerged, he looked at the clock. It was only eight p.m. He sloshed more wine into his empty glass, and roamed the apartment like a wounded animal.

He loved Rosanna, he loved her with all his heart.

He didn't love Donatella.

But Rosanna was thousands of miles away and apparently perfectly happy to spend an evening out with 'charming' men. More than that, she seemed oblivious to the hurt it had caused him.

Donatella was just five blocks away, probably waiting for his call.

He just needed some company, he told himself, that was all. The company of an old friend, someone who would understand his isolation. Roberto groaned, the temptation driving him mad.

An hour and an empty bottle of wine later, his hand reached for the receiver and dialled the number on her card.

29

Rosanna was in a state of high tension and exhaustion. She'd hardly slept in the past week.

Roberto would be home in twenty-four hours. He'd called her twice since their argument, but the conversations had been brief and Roberto had sounded distant.

She'd decided to keep as busy as she could, trying to convince herself she was overreacting. Roberto was tired and missing her, that was all. Tomorrow he would be home and everything would be all right.

Rosanna struggled back from Kensington High Street carrying several bags. She'd been tempted to buy herself a new dress for his arrival, but she felt so fat and frumpy that she'd decided to buy a teddy bear for the baby instead.

She hummed along to *La Traviata* as she arranged fresh flowers in a vase and bustled around the house, making sure all was immaculate for his homecoming.

That afternoon, Rosanna lay down, exhausted from her frenetic burst of activity. She felt achy and unwell. She dozed off and, when she woke up some hours later, she went down to the kitchen to make herself some supper. At ten, she glanced at the telephone. She calculated that Roberto would be getting ready to leave for his last performance at the Met. He had said he would call before he left, but the telephone remained silent. At half past ten, in an agony of frustration, she dialled the number of Chris's apartment.

'Hello.'

'Hello, Chris, is Roberto there?'

'No, honey, he isn't.'

'Where is he then?'

'He left early for the theatre tonight.'

'Well, could you ask him to call me when he gets back after the performance? It doesn't matter what time.'

'If I see him, I will.'

'Surely you'll see him later?'

'Yes, of course. Are you feeling okay, Rosanna?'

'Yes, but I'll be much better when Roberto's home. He's still catching the morning flight from Kennedy Airport tomorrow, isn't he?'

'I believe so.' Chris sounded vague.

'Well, tell him I'm planning to meet him at Heathrow.'

'Sure will. Bye, Rosanna. Take care of yourself.'

'Bye.'

Rosanna replaced the receiver, her heart beating unsteadily. The sooner he was home, the quicker she could calm down and silence the demons that were asking questions at the back of her mind. She went to bed an hour later and drifted into a troubled sleep.

The following morning, Rosanna woke at eight o'clock. She climbed out of bed and felt a sharp pain shoot across her stomach. Wincing, she sat down and waited until it had passed before walking gingerly to the shower. While she was towelling herself dry, she felt another pain.

Surely, she couldn't be . . . No, she told herself firmly. She had another two weeks to go and, besides, she had read all about the phantom contractions you could have. It was her body practising, that was all.

Two hours later, Rosanna was beginning to realise there was every chance the pains were not merely a practice. She had begun to time the contractions and they were starting to come every eight or nine minutes. Dr Hardy had told her that there was no need to go to the hospital until they were coming every five or six minutes. Still, she'd better be ready to go when the time came.

Slowly and painfully, she climbed upstairs to the bedroom. She retrieved the small case she'd already packed for the hospital and carried it back downstairs, having to stop halfway as another contraction ripped through her. She checked her watch. That one was more like seven minutes and much stronger than the last. She made it to the hall and placed the case by the front door, pausing to catch her breath before shuffling into the sitting room to find her address book.

She was just about to dial Dr Hardy's number when the doorbell rang.

Rosanna made her way laboriously back into the hall.

'Who is it?'

'Stephen, Stephen Peatôt.'

Rosanna hesitated, thinking a visitor was the last thing she needed at this moment. But he knew she was at home and she couldn't very well just leave him standing there. She unlocked the door and opened it.

'Hi,' he said. 'I hope it's not inconvenient. I was passing and I wondered whether you'd managed to dig out that copy of *Madama Butterfly* for me.'

'Yes, I . . .' Rosanna gasped and bent over.

'Hey, are you all right? What on earth's the matter?' Stephen put his arm round her, helped her inside and closed the door behind them.

'I . . . I think I'm in labour. The pain will pass in a minute,' she gasped. It did so and she stood up and smiled. 'I'm sorry, Stephen.'

'Don't be so silly. Are you on your own?'

She nodded.

'Is there anything I can do?' He followed her into the sitting room and watched her sink onto the sofa.

'Yes, if you wouldn't mind. Could you pass my address book so I can call my doctor? I think I need to go to the hospital soon. The contractions seem to be speeding up quite fast.'

Stephen picked up the address book and passed it to her. Rosanna dialled the number and asked to speak to Dr Hardy.

'Yes, hello, Doctor? This is Rosanna Rossini. I think I'm in labour and . . . no, my waters haven't broken. Contractions? About every seven minutes, and getting closer all the time.'

Rosanna listened then said, 'Okay. Thank you, Dr Hardy, goodbye.' She replaced the receiver.

'What did he say?' asked Stephen.

'That if my waters hadn't broken, it's doubtful the birth is imminent, so I'm not to panic. He wants me to go to the Chelsea and Westminster hospital anyway and he'll meet me there. I'll call a taxi.'

'No need to do that, I'll drive you there. It'll only take ten minutes on a Sunday.'

'Are you sure? It's not the kind of weekend outing you'd probably planned.' She managed a weak smile between puffs.

'Of course I'm sure. As long as you promise not to give birth in my Beetle,' he joked. 'Now, where's your coat?'

'In the hall . . . oh, I must call Roberto and let him know what's happening. He's coming back from New York today and is expecting me to meet him at Heathrow,' she explained.

'Are you sure you don't want me to make the call?' asked Stephen, concerned that her breath was now coming in shallow pants.

'No, no. I must speak to him myself,' she gasped.

'Of course. I'll put your case in the car while you call him.'

'Thank you.' Rosanna dialled Chris's apartment, gritting her teeth at another contraction as the line rang and rang.

'Wake up, wake up,' she groaned.

Stephen came back into the room. 'No answer?'

'No. He's probably asleep and hasn't heard the telephone. It's about five in the morning in New York.'

'Well, I really think we should get going. You can try and call when we get to the hospital.'

Rosanna reluctantly replaced the receiver. 'I'll leave a note here telling Roberto what's happening, just in case I don't manage to get him before he boards the plane.'

She scribbled a note on a piece of paper, left it on the hall table, then followed Stephen out to the car.

Dr Hardy was waiting in the hospital reception area, where he immediately helped Rosanna into a wheelchair.

'Have you contacted your husband?' he asked.

'I've tried but I haven't managed to get hold of him. He's flying back to England today, but his plane doesn't arrive at Heathrow until tonight. I was going to meet him.'

'I see. Well, the chances are he'll arrive to a new son or daughter.'

Rosanna winced as another pain ripped through her.

'Let's get you upstairs to the maternity unit. Those contractions are coming fast and furious, my dear. Hang on just one moment while I fetch a nurse. Stay with her,' he added to Stephen, who was hovering uncertainly close by.

'Listen,' Stephen said, coming over to her side, 'give me the number and I'll try calling Roberto again.'

Rosanna nodded weakly and fumbled in her handbag for her address book. 'It's in there, under "Chris Hughes".' She handed him the book.

'Fine. Don't worry, I'm sure I'll manage to get a message to him somehow.'

A nurse bustled over and began to wheel Rosanna towards the lift, closely followed by Dr Hardy.

'Take the lift up to the fourth floor and meet us there,' he instructed Stephen.

'Oh, but . . . I mean, I hardly know Mrs Rossini. It's just coincidence that I arrived at her house when I did.'

Dr Hardy frowned. 'I see. Well, is there anyone else who could come to the hospital and be with her? A relation or a friend, perhaps? I'm sure she'd be happier to have someone she knows with her.'

Stephen immediately thought of Abi. 'Yes, there is.'

'Good. You can use the telephone by reception. Excuse me.' Dr Hardy jumped into the lift with Rosanna as the doors began to close.

Stephen picked up the receiver on the reception desk and dialled the New York number. The line rang and rang.

'Come on, come on,' he murmured. Finally, to his relief, it was answered.

'Yeah?' The voice was sleepy and disgruntled.

'Hello, is this Mr Rossini?'

'No, it's Chris Hughes, his agent. Are you the jerk that called half an hour ago? I just made it to the phone as you rang off!'

'No, that was Mrs Rossini actually, and I do apologise for disturbing your sleep. Is Mr Rossini there?'

'No, he isn't. Who are you?'

'Stephen Peatôt. I'm a friend of Mrs Rossini. I'm calling you from the Chelsea and Westminster Hospital in London. Mrs Rossini has gone into labour and she asked me to let her husband know.'

'Oh Christ! I thought she wasn't due for another couple of weeks?'

'Well, it seems the baby's decided to make its entrance a little ahead of schedule. Can you pass the message on to him? I'm sure Mr Rossini will want to come straight to the hospital when he lands in London.'

'Yeah, of course, leave it with me. I'll let him know.'

'Great, thanks,' said Stephen.

'Look, send my best to Rosanna and tell her Roberto's on his way.'

'I will.' Stephen replaced the receiver, leafed through Rosanna's address book and dialled Abi's number. Abi's mother answered the telephone and told him that she and Henry had gone off for a long weekend in Scotland and she had no idea where they were staying. Stephen thanked her, and asked her to tell Abi the news as soon as she arrived home.

With all other avenues now closed, Stephen realised it was down to him.

Five minutes later, he was ushered by Dr Hardy into Rosanna's room. She was sitting up on the bed looking anxious.

'Did you manage to get in contact with Roberto?'

'Yes. He's coming straight here.'

'Thank goodness.' Rosanna sank back onto her pillows.

'How are you feeling?' Stephen went to the bed.

'I'm okay in between the pains. Dr Hardy has examined me and says I still have quite some time to go, but everything's fine with the baby.'

'Good.' Stephen twiddled his thumbs. 'I tried to call Abi but her mother said she and Henry have gone away for the weekend.'

'Never mind,' said Rosanna. 'Thank you so much for your help. You can leave me now. I'll be fine.'

'Are you sure?'

'Yes. I have a very nice midwife who—' Rosanna's face contorted.

Stephen moved to her and instinctively grasped her small hand.

Her grip tightened on his knuckle until she breathed out and gave a small smile. 'Ouch,' she said, the mistress of understatement.

'Maybe I'll stay a little longer,' Stephen said wryly.

'Thank you,' Rosanna replied gratefully.

The midwife appeared in the room.

'Okay, Mrs Rossini?'

'I think so, yes.'

'Shall I leave?' asked Stephen.

'No, no need, unless you want to,' said the nurse, placing a strap round Rosanna's waist and turning on the monitoring machine. 'It's nice for Mrs Rossini to have someone with her. It can get quite boring having a baby, you know. Especially as it's her first – she could be here for some hours yet.' She searched across Rosanna's stomach with a round silver monitor until a small thumping sound was heard.

'There's baby's heartbeat. It sounds fine. That green line there shows your contractions, Mrs Rossini. I think there's one on its way. Now, er . . . ?'

'Stephen,' he replied.

'Stephen, come and squeeze Mrs Rossini's hand like you were doing before. Give her something to concentrate on.'

Stephen moved next to Rosanna and took her hand. He had a feeling it was going to be a very long day.

The telephone rang, breaking the silence in the apartment. Roberto awoke and the shape next to him stirred and moaned, then lay still. The ringing did not abate. Finally, she cursed, reached for the light switch and picked up the receiver.

'Yes?'

She turned towards Roberto. 'It's for you.'

Roberto's heart missed a beat.

'Who is it?'

'Chris Hughes.'

'What the hell is he doing calling me here at five thirty in the morning?' Roberto snatched the receiver from her hand. 'It's me. What do you want?'

She watched as his face drained of colour.

'*What?* Oh, *mamma mia*! When?' Roberto looked at the clock by the bed. 'Okay, I'm on my way. Can you check and see if there's a seat on the ten o'clock flight to London? I'll stop by and collect my case and you can order me a car to take me to the airport. *Ciao*.'

Roberto handed Donatella the receiver and leapt out of bed.

'Where are you going? What's happened?' she asked as Roberto struggled to put on his clothes.

'It's Rosanna. She's gone into labour. She is having our baby while I . . .'

The agonised look on his face told Donatella all she needed to know. Her heart sank.

'I see.' She watched him silently as he hurriedly finished dressing and then made for the front door.

'Don't I even get a goodbye kiss?'

He turned and shook his head.

'I . . . I'm sorry, I should not have been here, I . . .' He shrugged despairingly. 'Goodbye.'

The door slammed and he was gone.

Donatella sank back onto her pillows and burst into tears.

On arrival at Chris's apartment, Roberto frenziedly packed an overnight bag, then said goodbye to his manager. 'See you in London. And I'm sure you don't need me to remind you that if I ever hear a whisper of my whereabouts this morning, I'll know where it came from and you and I will be finished.'

Chris nodded. He who paid the piper called the tune, after all. 'Sure, Roberto. Now, the car's waiting downstairs. Go and take care of your wife and child.'

Roberto sat and stared into space for most of the flight, refusing everything except endless cups of coffee. He wore his sunglasses to hide the tears of remorse that kept trickling out of his eyes.

Again and again, a picture of Rosanna alone and in pain kept entering his head. His wife had needed him while he was making love to Donatella on the other side of the Atlantic. How *could* he have done this to her?

Roberto made his way to the small bathroom, took off his sunglasses and wiped his eyes. If Rosanna ever discovered the truth, she would leave him. He'd been so stupid, so selfish, and, what was more, unbelievably careless. He knew there were a number of people at the Met who'd suspected what was going on during his last days in New York. He'd even bumped into Francesca Romanos, his leading lady, when he and Donatella were having dinner one night at The Four Seasons.

'Oh God . . . I am a complete shit, a dirty, rotten cheat . . .' Roberto put his head in his hands.

A few minutes later he returned to his seat. As the number of miles between him and New York grew larger, Roberto saw starkly just what he'd been putting at risk.

Surely it wasn't too late? If he stopped now and never saw Donatella again, there was no reason why Rosanna should ever know. And he'd make it up to her in any way he could. He would never leave her side again. The two . . . the *three* of them would be together. He would buy her the house in the country that she'd talked about, cancel his commitments for the next six months and help Rosanna with their baby. Yes, yes, that was it.

Roberto began to feel calmer as he planned his penance.

He would just have to bear the burden of guilt alone – and make damn sure that Rosanna was never exposed to the terrible pain of discovering his secret.

'Come on, Rosanna, a few more pushes and the baby will be here,' said Dr Hardy. 'I can see its head.'

She looked up at Stephen and groaned. 'I can't, I can't.'

'You can,' said Stephen, understanding she was almost at her limit after hours of labour, and so was he. 'Come on now, here we go.'

Stephen gripped Rosanna's hand as she pushed and let out a groan of pain.

'Good, good, two more and baby will be in your arms,' encouraged Dr Hardy.

Stephen winced as Rosanna's nails cut into his hands. 'That's it, Rosanna, that's it,' he said, smiling down at her as she drew in her breath and prepared for another huge effort.

'Good, good, Rosanna, that's it. Baby's coming, keep pushing,' Dr Hardy urged as she gave a final howl and he lifted a small red body with a crown of jet-black hair into his arms. The tiny figure immediately let out a high-pitched cry.

An exhausted but jubilant Rosanna propped herself up on her elbows to take her first look at her newborn baby.

'You have a little boy, Rosanna. Congratulations,' Dr Hardy said, as he swiftly cut the cord then swaddled the wriggling baby in a white blanket before handing him to his mother.

'He's so beautiful,' she whispered. She put her finger inside the tiny hand and felt her baby grip it. 'He looks just like his father, doesn't he?'

Stephen looked down at the tiny, wrinkled face. 'I suppose he does.'

'Okay, Rosanna, now we have a little bit of tidying up to do,' said Dr Hardy. He turned to Stephen. 'Why don't you go and get yourself a cup of coffee? There's a machine just along the corridor and a lounge where you can relax.'

'Does the machine sell cigars?' Stephen grinned. 'I feel as though I should smoke one. I'll pop back in a little while,' he added to Rosanna as he left the room.

Half an hour later, Stephen found Rosanna sitting up in bed, her hair brushed, wearing a fresh nightgown, the baby sound asleep against her chest. Rosanna's eyes were sparkling with happiness and Stephen didn't think he'd ever seen a woman look more beautiful. He sat down in the chair by her bed.

'How are you?'

'Wonderful,' she smiled. 'Stephen, how can I ever thank you?'

'There's no need, really. Any chap would have done the same.'

'Well, I don't know how I can ever repay you, but would you like to hold him?'

'If you're sure you don't mind.'

'Of course not. You're one of the first people he ever saw. He might think you're his papa,' she chuckled as she handed the bundle carefully to him.

Stephen took the baby and held him in his arms. He looked down as two bright, dark eyes opened and gazed, unfocussed, up at him.

'He's very alert.'

'Yes.' She reached over and stroked the baby's cheek, then rested her hand on Stephen's. 'You were so very kind.'

The two of them looked up as the door burst open and Roberto entered the room.

'Roberto! Oh Roberto, you're here, you're here at last. We have a boy, a beautiful boy!' Rosanna stretched out her arms as tears began to plummet down her cheeks.

'My darling.' He walked swiftly to the bed and held her tight in his arms. 'I am so proud of you. How can I forgive myself for not being here with you?'

'It doesn't matter. Stephen was wonderful, Roberto. You must thank him,' she urged.

Roberto glanced at Stephen, a man he'd never before met but who was holding his baby. 'Of course I will, but first may I hold my son?' he asked brusquely.

'It goes without saying,' Stephen replied, feeling horribly uncomfortable as he held out the small bundle to its father.

Roberto gathered the child up in his arms, then turned his back on Stephen to face Rosanna.

'He's beautiful,' he murmured, 'just like his mamma.' Gently, he lowered the baby into Rosanna's arms, then encircled them both in a tender embrace. '*Amore mio*, I'm so proud of you. I love you.'

'And I love you.'

Stephen stood up and edged towards the door, realising his presence was no longer needed. 'I'd better be . . .' He started to speak, but, seeing they were oblivious to him, he walked quietly out of the room.

The Metropolitan Opera House, New York

So, Nico, that is how you came into the world. Some might say that that is when the rot set in for me and Roberto; after all, it was another man who saw you born. Your father, for reasons I only became aware of later, missed your birth. Perhaps it was an omen.

But at the time, I was the happiest woman alive. I had my perfect baby and my beloved husband back by my side.

Soon after we had returned home, your father drove us up to the picturesque village of Lower Slaughter in the Cotswolds. When we reached the outskirts of the village, he turned off the road into a long gravelled drive bordered by huge lime trees. As we rounded a bend, I could see up ahead one of the most beautiful houses I'd ever laid eyes on. Roberto told me it was named The Manor House. It had been built during the seventeenth century and was surrounded by sweeping lawns. Even in the middle of a rainy November afternoon, the house looked welcoming, with its honey-coloured stone exterior and mullioned windows. Roberto had a key and we looked round inside. Every room was cosy and inviting, with beamed ceilings, exposed stone walls and open fireplaces smelling of wood smoke. Roberto asked me whether I liked the house and I replied that I loved it. He said he was glad as he'd bought it for me as a present. His plan was that we'd keep the London house, but this was to be our new home. He wanted us to move in as soon as possible.

I shall never forget the moment when Roberto took me in his arms in the hall, kissed me and told me that he was cancelling all his commitments for the next six months so that the three of us could be together. He told me nothing else mattered but his wife and his child, that he could live without singing but not without us.

So, a month later we moved in. Nico, you should have seen your father then. How he worshipped you! Many was the night you would wake up crying and Roberto would nurse you back to sleep by singing to you. He was the perfect papa. He bathed you, fed you, read you stories and even changed your nappies occasionally! It was the most wonderful sight, to see him hold you as you slept happily in his arms. I have never seen him so content before or since.

Those were halcyon days. Just the three of us, in our beautiful home. There was no one to disturb us and we lived a simple, comfortable existence. For some it would have been dull but for me it was heaven. I had even lost my urge to sing and rarely joined Roberto when he practised in the mornings.

But of course things had to change, as they always do . . .

30

Gloucestershire, April 1981

Roberto put the phone down and looked out of the open study window. The sun was shining brightly and the day was warm. He watched Rosanna as she played with Nico on the daisy-studded lawn. He heard the baby laugh as Rosanna lifted him high into the air and back down onto her lap. Then she noticed Roberto looking at her and waved. He smiled and blew her a kiss.

Roberto rubbed his forehead. The telephone call had been from Chris Hughes, who'd taken him through his schedule for the next two months. Roberto was to finally resume his engagements in two weeks' time. To ease him in gently, there was first a concert at the Royal Albert Hall, then Covent Garden for a four-week run. After that he was back on the hamster wheel of concerts, recordings and performances on stages all over the world.

Until six months ago, Roberto had never even considered the possibility of there being a different way of life that he might enjoy. But the time since Nico's birth had proved a revelation. The tranquillity of The Manor House was enticing. Previously, he'd always pitied the man who wound his life round his wife and child, the ordinary man in the street who worked only as a means to an end, to provide a roof and food for his family. But at this moment he almost envied others their steady, unchanging work pattern, as the years before him currently seemed filled with intolerable pressures and separations from his wife and son.

At least while he was singing at Covent Garden it was possible for him to have the best of both worlds. He'd decided he would commute, staying at the house in Kensington only when absolutely necessary. And even then, it would be possible for Rosanna and Nico to be there with him.

After that . . . Roberto swept a hand through his hair. He would have to talk to Rosanna, see how she felt. One thing Roberto was sure of: it was dangerous for him to be alone. He was not going to give his weakness when it came to women a chance to rule him again.

Later that evening, after Nico had been tucked up in his cot, the two of them sat down to supper in the large, comfortable kitchen.

'I can't be sure, but I think Nico said "Papa" today,' smiled Rosanna.

'Did he? But he is only six months old!'

'It sounded like it. Remind me tomorrow to buy some more vests. He's growing out of the ones he's got,' she said as she forked a piece of tender lamb into her mouth.

'Rosanna' – Roberto took a deep breath – 'Chris Hughes called me today.'

She frowned. 'Did he? What did he want?'

'To go over my schedule for the next year.'

'Oh.'

'I know you don't like to think about it. Neither do I, but we must discuss the future.'

'Roberto, couldn't we just stay like this? We've been so happy. We have enough money, don't we?'

'Not to live for the next twenty or thirty years as we do now. Think of Nico. Surely we want him to have the privileges we never had as children – to attend the best schools? To travel? The bottom line is, I have to go back to work sooner or later.'

'I suppose so.'

Roberto watched his wife as she chewed a piece of lamb far more times than was necessary. 'What about you?' he asked tentatively.

'What about me?'

'Have you retired permanently from your career?'

'Maybe, maybe not.'

'Rosanna,' he chided, 'you must have thought about whether or not you wish to continue singing.'

'No, I haven't. For once, I haven't worried about anything, except whether Nico's nappy rash is clearing up or if he'll sleep through the night. It's been so perfect here, I haven't missed singing at all.'

'*Principessa*, you know that if you stay here with Nico, we'll be forced into long separations.'

'I know,' Rosanna said. 'So what you're really saying is that I might as well resume my career because I shall be following you around the world anyway.'

'My darling, neither of us wishes us to be apart from the other. What I was thinking is that we compromise. Covent Garden is now the house in which I feel most comfortable. So

I could ask Chris to make sure that a lot of my work is based in England. Maybe six months of the year we can live here.'

'And the other six months we will spend in hotels in all corners of the globe.' Rosanna looked at Roberto. 'Do you really think that can be good for Nico?'

'Other children do it. He's only a baby, *cara*. He won't know where he is. And if his mamma is with him, he won't care. We can even rent apartments instead of hotel suites when I have a long run somewhere.' Roberto was pleading now.

'But if I went back to singing too, then not only will Nico be in strange places, but he would have a stranger looking after him.'

'We can find a very good nanny, I'm sure. Maybe even a private tutor as well when he's a little older. And after that, there are scores of excellent boarding schools he could go to. Please, Rosanna, we're not good when we are apart, you know that.'

She picked up a piece of broccoli and chewed the end of it thoughtfully. Finally she said: 'Roberto, I will try and explain to you how I feel. When I discovered I was pregnant, I was very confused, unhappy almost. My career was going well, I had you – I thought life was perfect. I wanted nothing to spoil it. And then along came Nico and, with him, a new way of life and a new priority.'

'Then you're saying you love Nico more than you love me?' he countered.

'Don't be childish, Roberto. You know the love I feel for you is stronger than ever. But I have a different kind of love for Nico – a mother's love. And a child needs routine. I don't think it's right for us to drag him around the world.'

Roberto sighed. 'Well, we have two months before I have to go abroad. *Cara*, I understand how you feel about Nico, but surely your career is important too? What will happen when Nico grows up? When he goes away to school? You will have sacrificed everything for him and will have nothing left for yourself.'

'Roberto, please can we talk about something else?' she begged. 'Tonight I can't cope with this conversation.'

Roberto saw the anguish on his wife's lovely face and nodded. 'I'm sorry. I hate talking of it too. But please, *cara*, think of what I have said. We must make some decisions soon.'

That night, Rosanna couldn't sleep. She tossed and turned and eventually she climbed out of bed, put on her robe and went down the corridor to Nico's nursery. In the dim glow of the night light she saw he was sleeping peacefully.

Rosanna sank into the nursing chair, pulled back the curtain and stared out of the window into the blackness. Why was life so complicated? All she wanted, all she loved, was under this roof. But very soon the components that made her so happy were going to be dispersed.

The choice was almost impossible to make. She knew it came down to either her son or her husband. If she bowed out of her career and stayed here, which was what she was convinced would be best for Nico, then she would rarely see Roberto. However, if she decided to continue singing and travelled with Roberto, it would mean Nico would be deprived of his mother's full attention.

She knew she was lucky that she had the choice to stay at home with Nico if she wanted. Many women did not. But then . . . Rosanna remembered that dreadful month Roberto had been away in New York and how miserable she'd been.

It was hopeless.

Slowly, Rosanna made her way back down the corridor to her bedroom. Roberto's arms encircled her as she slid under the duvet.

'Are you okay?'

'Yes. I can't sleep, that's all.'

'Try not to worry. We'll work it out.' He kissed her gently on the cheek.

Rosanna nodded in the darkness. 'Whichever way, it seems I will lose,' she murmured.

31

Four weeks later, Rosanna had still made no decisions about her future. Roberto, heavily involved in preparations for *Tosca* at Covent Garden, was as sympathetic and supportive as he could be.

'I think you should come to the first night,' Roberto remarked as they sat having breakfast, Nico gurgling happily in his baby bouncer at their feet. 'If you come and see Francesca Romanos sing Tosca in your place, it might help you make up your mind,' he teased.

'You hope I'll be so jealous that I will return immediately.'

'*Principessa*, I miss you,' Roberto entreated. 'Francesca is technically very good, but she has none of the empathy that you and I share. You cannot blame me for trying to persuade you.' He glanced at his watch and sighed. 'Sadly, I must be leaving for rehearsals.' Roberto stood up, then reached down and picked Nico out of the bouncer. 'You be a good boy for your mamma and I shall see you later.' He kissed his son, then relinquished him into his mother's arms as they walked outside.

'What time will you be home?' asked Rosanna as Roberto slid inside his Jaguar and wound down the window.

'Early enough to bath Nico,' he said, smiling as he started the engine. 'Please, *cara*, think about the opening night. It would be good for you to have a little time away.'

'What about Nico?'

'Rosanna, I'm sure there are plenty of young girls in the village who would babysit. Go and ask, or put an advertisement in the post office. *Ciao*.'

Rosanna watched the car roar off up the drive. She carried Nico inside, put him back in his bouncer and cleared up the breakfast things.

A little while later, she tucked Nico up in his pram and set off in the direction of the post office.

When Roberto arrived home that evening, Rosanna handed him a glass of wine.

'I've found a very nice girl to babysit Nico. The lady in the post office has four children of her own and said her daughter would be happy to look after him. So, I met her and I'm going to come to the first night.'

'Wonderful! I know I'll sing especially well if you are watching.' Roberto stretched out his hand towards her. 'Thank you, *cara*.'

It felt strange to wear high-heeled shoes after months of flat ones, and even more peculiar to wear make-up, Rosanna thought as she surveyed her reflection in the mirror. The evening dress was one she had bought just before she became pregnant and she had been unable to wear it as her stomach had grown larger. Now it fitted her perfectly and she felt proud that her figure had returned so soon.

She left the bedroom and went into Nico's nursery. He

was lying on the floor chuckling as Eileen, the babysitter, knelt beside him and tickled him.

'Are you sure you'll be all right?' Rosanna asked anxiously, for the umpteenth time.

'Of course, we'll be fine, won't we, Nico? You go and have a lovely evening, Mrs Rossini.'

'I won't be later than midnight. His bottles are in the fridge and there's a clean romper suit in his drawer. If there's a problem—'

'Ring the number on the pad by the telephone. I know,' said Eileen patiently.

Rosanna kissed Nico and went downstairs as the car Roberto had organised to take her to London swept up the drive.

'I'm off,' Rosanna called up the stairs.

'Bye, have fun,' came the reply.

Two hours later, the car pulled up outside the Royal Opera House. Rosanna stepped out and made her way inside and up the grand staircase to the Crush Room bar, where she had arranged to meet Chris Hughes.

'You look lovely, Rosanna.' Chris kissed her on both cheeks and ushered her towards a table. 'Here, have a glass of champagne to toast Roberto's success and your return to the scene of some of your greatest triumphs.'

'Thank you.' Rosanna took the glass. 'It seems ages since I've been to London.'

'Do you miss it?'

'No, never,' she answered honestly.

'I'm sure it's much healthier for Nico to live in the

country. He's a good kid, isn't he? You've been real lucky with him so far, Rosanna.'

'I know. They say an easy birth makes an easy baby and the hospital staff were so good. And Stephen too, of course,' she added.

'Stephen?'

'My stand-in husband. He took me to the hospital.'

'Oh, sure, I think I spoke to him.'

'Did you? When?' Rosanna shot him a surprised look.

Realising what he'd said, Chris chose his words carefully. 'When he called the apartment to say you'd gone into labour early. I heard the telephone ring first and went to answer it.'

'Oh, I see.'

He swiftly changed the subject. 'Anyway, are you looking forward to tonight?'

'I think so, but it'll be hard to watch someone else singing with Roberto.'

'That's what I'm hoping,' Chris grinned. 'You know, there's no reason why you couldn't come back gradually. Say, the odd concert at first, then a few days in Paris, for example. The offers are still coming in, Rosanna, but they won't for much longer.'

'I know, I know,' she sighed. 'But Nico's still so small. I need a little more time, Chris, please.'

'I understand.'

The two-minute bell rang. 'Right, we'd better make a move.'

Rosanna sat in the box beside Chris, drinking in the smell of the old theatre. She leant over the plush velvet rail and stared up at the saucer-shaped dome of the magnificent pale blue and gilt ceiling. A smile curved her lips as she reflected that in normal circumstances she would be waiting nervously on the other side of the red curtain, not admiring the architecture. A shiver of excitement ran though her as the lights went down and the orchestra launched into the overture.

She watched as Roberto sang with Francesca Romanos, not even pausing for breath on the hard semi-tone lift during the Act One love duet. As he sang '*Vittoria! Vittoria!*' during Act Two, Rosanna felt a tremor of emotion run round the audience. And after '*E lucevan le stelle*', the audience rose to their feet, stamping and clapping for several minutes until the conductor raised his baton to begin again.

It was then that Rosanna knew how hard it would be to stay away. All those years of dedication and training . . . how could she leave this world? It was hers as much as Roberto's and part of their magic was being together on stage.

Tears welled up in her eyes as she watched Roberto and Francesca take a five-minute standing ovation. She had listened to Francesca carefully, trying to spot faults. There were few. She was very, very good. She was also young and extremely pretty.

'How are you feeling?' asked Chris as they made their way out of the box.

'Depressed,' sighed Rosanna. 'I was hoping it wouldn't touch me, but of course, it has.'

'That's good news.' Chris led her into the Crush Room where a crowd was gathering for a champagne reception.

There was a round of applause as Roberto and Francesca entered the bar. Roberto spotted Rosanna and made straight for her.

'*Principessa*, did you enjoy it?'

'I don't think "enjoy" is the right word,' grimaced Rosanna, 'but you were superb, *caro*.'

'Excuse me,' said Chris, switching into full-on agent mode. 'Can I borrow Roberto for two minutes? There's someone over there I want him to meet.'

Rosanna was left by herself as the two men made their way across the room.

'Hello, Rosanna.'

Rosanna turned to find Francesca Romanos smiling at her. As a performer, Rosanna respected Francesca, but she'd always found her somewhat frivolous as a person. Still, she knew when to give credit where it was due. 'Congratulations, Francesca. I thought you were very, very good,' she said.

'Thank you. You don't know what that means to me. I've always been a huge admirer of yours. And Roberto, as always, was brilliant. I think we sing well together.'

'You do.' Rosanna tried not to let her feelings show.

'So, how is your baby?'

'Oh, he's fine. Thriving, in fact.'

'And have you decided when you're coming back?'

'No.'

'I see. Is there a chance you might not?'

'I really don't know,' said Rosanna, growing more uncomfortable by the second.

'It'll be hard if you don't,' Francesca chattered on regardless. 'I mean, letting Roberto go off by himself all the time. He's such a charmer. He had a string of beautiful admirers queuing up in New York.'

'Did he? Well, that's nothing new. My husband is indeed a charismatic man,' Rosanna said, trying to sound unconcerned, but already dying inside.

'I'm sure you're used to it, but the way some women throw themselves at famous men like Roberto would drive me mad. I mean, there was one in particular – Donatella, I think she was called – who just wouldn't stop pestering him. I told Roberto he ought to be more careful. He should know better than anyone what gossip can be like, even though *we* all know it was innocent,' she added cosily, winking at Rosanna as though they were sharing some private joke.

'Of course. I'm sure it was. Now, if you'll excuse me, I must find my husband.' Rosanna knew she was being rude, but she couldn't bear another moment.

'Oh. Yes, of course. Goodbye, Rosanna . . . maybe I'll see you later.' Francesca looked petulant as the conversation came to an abrupt end.

Rosanna didn't care. She walked swiftly in the direction of the ladies' powder room.

'Donatella,' she moaned as she locked herself in a cubicle and leant heavily against the door. 'Why, Roberto, why?'

'I want to go home. I promised the babysitter we'd be back by twelve.'

Roberto looked down at his wife. Her face was pale, her eyes tinged with red.

'But, *cara*, I have people I must see before I leave.'

'Then I will ask Chris to drive me home,' she responded tartly.

'Rosanna, please, I . . .' But she walked away before he could finish. Immediately, a conductor accosted him.

'So, I hear you're coming to Glyndebourne next year, Mr Rossini?'

Ten minutes later, Roberto extricated himself to look for Rosanna.

'Have you seen my wife?' he asked Francesca.

'Yes, she left a few minutes ago with Chris Hughes. I think she was tired.'

A waiter appeared at his side. 'Champagne, sir?'

'Why not?' sighed Roberto, grimly taking a glass from the waiter's tray.

Rosanna remained silent as Chris drove out of London.

'You're very quiet,' he commented. 'Did it hurt badly, watching Francesca?'

Rosanna didn't reply.

'You know that she isn't a patch on you, honey. All the opera houses want you back with Roberto. Just say the word and I can start to book you again.'

'I have Nico. He's all I need,' she replied robotically.

'And Roberto.'

'I think I must get used to being without him.'

'So, you're not going to return.'

'No. Tonight has made up my mind. I am not.'

'But can you and Roberto really stand all the separations?' persisted Chris. He was, after all, her agent and no matter how much he sympathised with Rosanna's predicament, it was his job to bring her back into the fold. 'I mean, Roberto's a very gregarious man. When he has you beside him, it's all he needs. He turns up to rehearsals, has few temper tantrums and generally behaves impeccably. He's altered completely since you married him and the change has all been for the good. Having you has allowed him to build on his fame. But it worries me to think of you at home while he's away. Sorry if I'm speaking out of turn, but you must know he has this . . . this impulsive streak that he finds difficult to control when you're not together . . .'

'Like in New York, you mean? With Donatella Bianchi?' spat Rosanna.

Chris was silent. Eventually, he said, 'I didn't know you knew.'

'I didn't, until Francesca took it into her head to update me tonight. And thanks for confirming it, Chris.'

'Shit! That stupid bitch!' Chris banged the steering wheel hard with the palm of his hand.

'Were they having an affair?'

'Oh Christ, Rosanna, I don't know,' Chris groaned.

'But you were there with Roberto in the apartment. You must have seen his comings and goings.'

'No, really, I didn't. I was away a lot.'

'So, what about the morning Stephen called you? Did you answer the telephone because Roberto wasn't there? Wasn't there at five thirty in the morning as his wife was in labour?' Tears pricked her eyes.

'No, okay, he wasn't there, but he could easily have been in a club. They stay open very late in New York and it was his last night in town.' Chris steered the car off the motorway and headed into the darkness of a country road.

'But Roberto knew I was having the baby early. He came straight to the hospital. Someone must have contacted him, known exactly where he was before he got on his flight. Was it you?'

Chris fell silent again. In that silence, Rosanna found her answer.

'Look, Rosanna, it really doesn't matter. Whatever

happened in New York is in the past. I know how much Roberto loves you, how he's put his career on hold for the past six months to be with you and the baby. I've never seen him so happy.'

'Please, Chris, don't patronise me. I don't wish to discuss it anymore. It's between me and Roberto.'

'But Rosanna—'

'*Please!*'

Chris drove on in embarrassed silence, finally turning the car into the drive and pulling up in front of The Manor House. He turned off the engine and looked at Rosanna. Her face was impassive.

'Shall I come in with you? We can talk this through. It really isn't as bad as it seems.'

'No, Chris. If you don't mind, I wish to be by myself. Thank you for bringing me home.' Rosanna opened the car door and got out. She shut the door behind her and walked across the gravel.

Chris watched the front door close behind her, swore until the air around him was blue, then started the engine and pulled out of the drive.

Rosanna sat on the window seat in the nursery staring up at the full moon. Nico was fast asleep, the odd gentle snore floating from the cot to reassure her.

She was past caring. Her first thought had been to run away, to take her baby and disappear. But she knew the pain would only follow her and, besides, this was *her* life right here. Roberto could take his and go and live it somewhere else.

He had *sworn* to her it would never happen. He had broken his promise and, although it might kill her to do it, Rosanna was going to keep hers.

She stood up and moved towards the bedroom she had shared with her husband. She had a lot to do before he arrived home.

It was gone two when the Jaguar purred up the drive. Rosanna stood waiting by the front door.

She knew as soon as she saw him that he'd been drinking. He could have killed himself on the way home . . . Rosanna brushed the thought from her mind. It didn't – *couldn't* – matter anymore.

'*Cara*, you are still awake.' Roberto came towards her, arms outstretched.

'There is enough in there for the present,' she said, pointing to the two suitcases standing by the door. 'I'll have everything else packed and sent on to the London house.'

Roberto looked bemused. 'I'm sorry, *cara*, I thought we had agreed I would commute for the next few weeks, and anyway to pack at this time of night . . .'

'You're leaving, Roberto. Now.' Rosanna's voice was icy cold.

'But why? Has someone died?'

'No, nothing has died, except my love for you.'

'What is it? What have I done?'

'You made me a promise, Roberto. And you have betrayed me. I never want to see you again.'

'I . . .' Roberto shook his head in bewilderment. 'What promise? How have I betrayed you?'

'If you cannot remember the night you spent in Donatella

Bianchi's warm bed as your wife was in labour, then it's not for me to remind you. I hate you. Please leave.'

He looked at her, horrified. If Rosanna hadn't totally believed what Francesca had told her, she did now. The guilt was written across his face.

'But I . . . how?' Roberto sank to his knees in the doorway.

'It doesn't matter how I know. Only that I do.'

He burst into tears.

'*Mamma mia*, if only you knew how I have punished myself, Rosanna. Donatella and I . . . it was nothing – *nothing* – can't you see?'

'And how many married men do you think have tried that excuse on their wives? No, I can't see anything at all. I told you when you asked me to marry you that I would leave you if you were unfaithful. You had an affair, but it's not me who is leaving, it's you.'

'Please, please, Rosanna, let me tell you, talk to you about how it was. I can explain, *please*, I beg you. I love you, *amore mio*, I love you.' Roberto covered his face with his hands.

'No. I thought you did, but you do not. You sleep with another woman, you lie to me. How can you call that *love*? You aren't fit to be a father to your child!' Rosanna was shaking. 'Roberto, I wish you to leave immediately.'

He looked up at his wife, her pale face bathed in moonlight. She looked like some ghostly child-spirit and Roberto knew that the expression on her face would haunt him as long as he lived. He also knew she meant what she said. He hauled himself to his feet.

'Rosanna, whatever you think of me, whatever bad things

I have done, I love you, I love you. There is no one else for me; there never will be.'

'I wish you to leave,' she repeated again.

He looked at her, self-pity beginning to replace his shock and remorse. 'Rosanna, if you make me go without giving me a chance to explain, I will never come back again.'

'Then I'm glad you understand what I want.' She motioned towards the two suitcases. 'Goodbye, Roberto.'

Slowly he bent down and picked up the cases. 'You will regret this, Rosanna. It is simple. We cannot live without each other.' Then he turned and walked away.

Rosanna watched as he unlocked the car, threw his suitcases into the boot and slammed it shut. He climbed into the driver's seat and started the engine. The car hummed, reversed and then disappeared down the drive.

Rosanna closed the front door, turned and walked up the stairs to the one thing she still had left that was worth living for.

The Metropolitan Opera House, New York

So, darling, that is how you came to spend your early childhood without your father in our house. But that night I also made a vow that I would never try to prejudice you against him. He had been nothing but a loving, caring papa to you during the first months of your life. I felt guilty about depriving you of his company, so I decided that if he called and said he wished to see you then I would allow him to do so.

The month after he left was the hardest. Even though my resolve was strong, every time the telephone rang I would rush to it, part of me desperate to hear his voice yet dreading the sound at the same time. The disappointment when it was not him was matched by relief, and then disbelief that he could carry out his threat and cut himself off from us so completely.

The only communication I had from him was a generous monthly cheque sent via Chris Hughes to cover our living expenses. There was never a letter attached.

Roberto's time at Covent Garden ended and he left for New York and the Met. I knew of his movements through both Chris and the newspapers. Six months later, I saw a photograph of him with

Donatella Bianchi. They were at a party in New York. I knew then that it was finally over, that any dreams I'd been harbouring of a reconciliation were futile; our marriage had been a sham. How could it have been otherwise? I tried hard not to hate him, but the hurt I felt for his making no effort to see you, his son, ate away at me.

I spent almost all my time alone that year, with only you for company. I could have turned to my family, or my friends, but my pride prevented me.

And yet I would hate you to think I was unhappy. I was not. I had you and the house and the solitude to lick my wounds. I didn't think of the future, or my career. I took each day as it came, my capacity for expressing emotion limited only to you.

It was almost a year to the day on which Roberto and I had parted that things began to change once more . . .

32

Gloucestershire, June 1982

Rosanna awoke to the nearby sounds of a contented toddler playing in his cot, subtly signalling that he was awake and ready for attention. She lay watching the bright sunshine eager to throw its rays of light beyond the curtains and into the bedroom. Rarely did she linger when she first woke, knowing the thoughts that would assail her senses, but this morning she felt unusually peaceful.

Soon, a year would have passed. A year in which she had breathed, slept, eaten . . . *lived* without him. That had to mean something, surely. It was a milestone and she felt proud. And – she brightened at the thought – her dear friend Abi was coming to stay soon. She knew it was high time she started connecting with the world outside The Manor House again.

Finally, Rosanna climbed out of bed. As she walked down the corridor to the nursery, she planned the day. Breakfast, a little housework, then a leisurely walk with Nico down to the village shop. After lunch, while Nico slept, an hour's sun in the garden. She came from a place where warmth was taken for granted, but here in England it was a precious commodity to be relished. Tea with honey sandwiches – Nico's current favourite – then later some pasta and salad for herself with a glass of cold Frascati. But then, as the dusk descended and Nico slept, the night would close in and the loneliness would begin . . .

But first she had the day to enjoy and, Rosanna thought as she opened the door to Nico's room, there were worse ways of living her life.

'Mamma, Mamma!' Nico bounced up and down excitedly, his small hands gripping the rail of his cot. 'Milk! Milk!'

'Then we shall go to the kitchen and make you a bottle, darling.'

Rosanna always spoke to her son in English. If this was to be their home and where Nico would be educated, then she believed his first language should be that of the country in which he'd been born.

Rosanna swept him up in her arms and carried him downstairs to the kitchen. Once she had placed him in his high chair, she filled a bottle with milk and handed it to him. While he was sucking happily, she turned on the radio and set about making breakfast.

'There you go, darling,' Rosanna said as she put an egg and slices of toast onto Nico's tray, then sat herself down next to him. 'Now, today I thought we'd go for a walk and then—' Rosanna broke off as the first notes of '*Addio fiorito asil*' from *Madama Butterfly* echoed from the radio. The memory was so acute, so painful. She glanced down and saw that her hands were shaking. Swiftly, she walked across to the radio and turned her husband's voice off.

*

After lunch, while Nico was resting, Rosanna settled herself in the comfortable deckchair on the terrace. The peaceful state of mind she'd woken to had been destroyed by the sound of Roberto's voice. It seemed she was only deluding herself when she imagined she was getting over him. Every day she ached for him, still longing to feel his strong arms closing around her shoulders, his mouth on hers, the gentleness of his touch as he made love to her.

'Oh God . . .' she moaned, leaning forwards and putting her head in her hands. She rocked herself backwards and forwards, wondering how on earth she was going to get through the rest of her life without him.

That evening, Rosanna let Nico stay up later than usual, putting off the moment when she would once again be alone. But at half past six, halfway through a Winnie the Pooh story, his head sagged against her shoulder, so she gently carried him up to his cot.

Once downstairs, she retrieved a bottle of Frascati from the fridge, took it out onto the terrace and filled her glass. The sun was beginning its descent towards the horizon. In New York, it was just after half past one and the sun would still be high in the sky. Maybe he was looking up at it, thinking of her, missing her . . . Rosanna stopped herself. She'd been down that path too many times before. It was over, *over*, and she had to learn to live in the present.

She began to ponder again whether she and Nico should continue to live here at The Manor House, a place with so many memories. Maybe they'd be better in Milan or Naples. Then Rosanna thought of all the people who would nod their heads self-righteously at the separation, recalling their predictions of disaster and whispering how she'd been misguided to believe that Roberto could ever be tamed.

Maybe, later in the year, she'd take Nico to Naples for a visit. It was such a long time since she'd been back to see her family, but the thought didn't really appeal to her. It would mean making an effort, pretending she was over Roberto when she really wasn't at all . . .

Rosanna heard the crunch of gravel as a car made its way up the drive. Could it be . . . ? Her heart began to beat faster and she leapt up, hurrying round the side of the house in time to see a Jaguar coming to a halt in front of it. She stood, holding her breath, and watched as the driver got out.

'Hello there.' A man was walking towards her, but it wasn't Roberto. 'I'm sorry to just drop in like this but Abi told me you lived here and I was just passing and I wondered how that little chap I watched come into the world was faring and . . .' Stephen tumbled over his words in embarrassment. 'It's probably terribly inconvenient and—'

'No, not at all. How nice to see you, Stephen. What happened to the Beetle?' She gestured towards the parked Jaguar in an attempt to hide her initial stab of disappointment.

Stephen laughed. 'The old girl finally gave up the ghost last month, so I treated myself to a slightly younger model.'

'Please, Stephen, won't you come in and have a glass of wine? I was sitting watching the sunset.' The least she could do was to be polite after all Stephen had done for her and Nico.

'If you're sure I'm not disturbing you.'

'Really, you're not. I promise.'

He followed her round the house and onto the terrace and she gestured to a chair.

'Sit down and I'll go and get a wine glass for you.'

Stephen watched as she disappeared through the door leading to the kitchen. In a T-shirt and a pair of shorts, wearing no make-up and with her lovely dark hair tied back in a ponytail, she looked even younger and more vulnerable than he remembered her. He'd heard of course, from Abi, what had happened.

'So,' Rosanna said as she emerged and handed him a glass. 'Help yourself to wine and then tell me why you came to be passing my house.' She was surprised to find that, despite his not being Roberto, she was genuinely happy to see him.

'I've opened an art gallery in Cheltenham, and I was delivering a painting to a client in Lower Slaughter. Abi told me you lived in The Manor House on the edge of the village, so I thought I'd look you up.'

'Well, I'm glad you did.'

'The view from here is so beautiful,' he breathed as he took a sip of his wine, 'so quintessentially English. And this house is one I've always noticed. I was brought up in a neighbouring village, you see.'

'Well, I love it here.'

'You don't get lonely then, being by yourself?'

'No. I have the baby, and besides, I'm used to it,' she answered a little defensively.

'Of course. I was . . . sorry to hear about your separation.'

Rosanna nodded but didn't venture a response. Stephen took the hint. 'So, how is Nico?'

'Oh, beautiful, and he's such a very good boy. He's walking, or should I say running everywhere and is just beginning to put sentences together. He's starting to be good company.

It's a shame you didn't arrive half an hour ago. He was still up then.'

'Well, maybe some other time,' Stephen suggested. 'By the way, wasn't it good news about Abi's first novel finding a publisher?'

'Yes, wonderful. I haven't seen enough of her in the last year, though we keep in touch by telephone. Anyway, she's coming to stay with me in two weeks' time. She says she needs some peace and seclusion away from London so she can concentrate on writing the next book.'

'I'm sure she'll find it here. And it'll be good company for you, too.'

'Yes, it will. I haven't had any house guests for a while.'

There was a sudden uncomfortable lull in the conversation.

'I really am sorry for gatecrashing like this,' Stephen said as he made to stand up. 'I'll leave you in peace. Thanks very much for the wine.'

'Not at all. It's been lovely to see you, Stephen.' Rosanna realised as she watched him pick up his keys that she had a strong urge for him to stay, for a few hours of company. 'Are you hungry? I haven't had supper yet. It'll only be pasta and salad, but you're welcome to some.'

Stephen turned to her. 'Are you only being polite, Rosanna? Please be honest.'

'No, I'd like you to stay, really. I haven't had any proper adult conversation for ages.'

'Then I'd be delighted,' he said as he followed Rosanna into the kitchen and watched her as she put the kettle on. 'Can I help you?'

'There's a bowl of salad on the top shelf of the fridge. Could you get it out for me?'

'Of course.' He did as she'd asked and set the bowl on the countertop as she hunted in a cupboard for a packet of pasta.

'Thank you.' While she waited for the kettle to boil, she put a pan of sauce on the hob and began to stir it. 'I'm sorry if I was a little rude when you arrived. In the last year I've become very antisocial.'

'I completely understand,' Stephen said with feeling. 'I broke up with my girlfriend about a year ago. She didn't want to move to the Cotswolds when I decided to open my gallery here. We tried a long-distance relationship, but it didn't work,' he said sadly.

'I'm sorry,' Rosanna empathised. 'When I'm feeling sorry for myself, I try to remember that at least I have a lovely home to be miserable in. Now, shall we eat outside? I can take some candles and it's still quite warm.'

'That sounds perfect.'

Twenty minutes later, they were sitting on the terrace eating tagliatelle and salad. Rosanna listened with interest as Stephen told her of his new business.

'Of course, it's only a small place and not at all like working at the Cork Street gallery. But it's all mine. To be honest, my heart lies with the Old Masters, but at least I'm my own boss and if I choose my artists well, there's no reason why I shouldn't do okay.'

'So, you can tell a good painting when you see one, can you?' asked Rosanna.

'I like to think so, yes. My expertise is definitely based around the Renaissance, but I'd like to establish a stable of modern artists too. There's a lot of talent around here, you know. I've already signed two local artists to my gallery.'

'I don't like modern paintings.' Rosanna wrinkled her nose. 'Maybe I'm stupid, but I don't understand how squiggles and blobs of paint can be art.'

'Come now,' Stephen chided her gently, 'not every modern artist produces squiggles and blobs, as you so delicately put it. I have a wonderfully talented landscape painter who works in watercolours. She's reminiscent of Turner. I think she'll do very well. I've a feeling you'd like her work if you saw it.'

'So, do you live up here now too?'

'There's a small flat above the gallery which I'm camping in for the present, until I find something more permanent. To be honest, I've poured all my money into setting up the gallery. I can only hope it works.'

'It must be wonderful to have something that you can watch grow, something you've done all alone, however much hard work it takes,' mused Rosanna.

'It is,' Stephen nodded. 'I suppose it's a bit like watching your voice mature and improve. No plans to return to singing then?'

'No.'

'Never again, or just for now?'

'I don't know. I'd hate to leave Nico, and besides, returning would be difficult with Roberto and I . . .' her voice trailed off.

'Rosanna, I'm not trying to bully you in any way, but surely you owe it to yourself to use your talent?'

'That's exactly what Roberto said,' she replied quietly.

'Well, I know nothing about what happened between the two of you, but on that point, I'm afraid I agree with him.'

The wine had loosened Rosanna's tongue, and she was suddenly overcome with the need to share her thoughts. 'Stephen, as a man, do you believe it's possible to sleep with one woman while still loving another?'

'Well, that's one way to change the subject,' Stephen laughed, half choking on his wine at her bluntness. 'Let's think . . . well, maybe for some men, yes. But also for some women. For example, my girlfriend had an affair whilst still living – *and* sleeping, I might add – with me.'

'Could you do that?' she asked.

'Have an affair, you mean?'

'Yes.'

'Call me old-fashioned, but I believe love and fidelity go hand in hand.' He shrugged. 'Although I don't think one should ever judge others, I'd like to believe that deception isn't part of my nature.'

Rosanna digested this. 'Well, it must be people like us who are different then. Roberto was only away for a few weeks before he became involved with someone else. Men seem to have affairs all the time and wives always seem to be forgiving their husbands, especially if they're rich, handsome and famous. Me, I couldn't excuse it.'

'Has Roberto tried to change your mind?'

'No. I haven't heard a word from him since I threw him out. Sometimes, I wish I *had* forgiven him.' Rosanna sighed, knowing she was on the verge of tears. 'Excuse me, it's almost a year since he left and . . .'

'Don't mind me. All I can say, from bitter experience, is that it does get better eventually.'

'No.' Rosanna shook her head wearily. 'It won't get better.'

'Trust me, it will. Love is a kind of addiction. You have to wean yourself off it and not punish yourself if sometimes you feel you'll never recover.'

'I wish I was like Abi. She has lots of boyfriends but never loses her heart,' Rosanna remarked.

'Don't you think that might be because she hasn't found the right man?'

'Maybe you're right. Abi was in love with my brother when she was younger. And since then it seems she can't settle with anyone.'

'What happened?'

'He entered a seminary!' Rosanna managed a wry chuckle.

'I see.' Stephen also smiled. 'Well, nobody has it easy.'

'No, they don't,' she agreed.

He looked at his watch. 'Is that the time? I really must be going,' he said reluctantly. 'It's getting late and I'm sure you're up early in the morning.'

'Yes. Nico is at his most lively at about six.'

Stephen stood up. 'Rosanna, thank you so much for a lovely evening.'

'Next time you must come when Nico is awake,' she found herself saying as they walked towards his car.

'I'd love to.' Stephen hesitated for a moment. 'Are you busy this weekend?'

'No.' Rosanna almost laughed out loud at the thought of her untouched diary gathering dust on the desk in the study.

'Well, why don't I come over on Sunday and take you and Nico into Cheltenham? You could see the gallery, and we could have a picnic in Montpellier Gardens if the weather's nice.'

'I . . .'

'Please, Rosanna. It might be fun and I'm sure Nico would enjoy it.'

'Okay,' she agreed as she followed him to the front door.

'I'll pick you up at eleven thirty.'

'Fine.'

'If you organise the food, I'll sort out the drink. Now, go inside, it's getting chilly. Goodnight, Rosanna.'

She watched the car drive off before she made her way towards the terrace and began to clear the table.

A little later, she crept into Nico's room to check he was sleeping peacefully. Brushing her hand across his forehead, a habit she'd acquired to check his temperature, she left the nursery and sent up a prayer of gratitude for sending Stephen to her tonight.

33

'*Caro*, you are so stubborn! Why not?' Donatella drained her coffee cup and began to put on her underwear.

'Because I like my freedom, I like my independence.'

'You mean, you like to have a place to screw other women behind my back,' she retorted, reaching for her dress.

Roberto turned around. 'Don't be silly, Donatella.'

'Then why can I not give up my apartment and move in with you here? I hate having some of my clothes here, some there. It's most inconvenient,' she whined.

'No. Not yet.'

'When then?'

'I don't know.'

'Still pining after that little wife of yours?' Donatella said bitchily.

'No!'

'Then why not divorce her?'

'We've only been apart a year. It's too soon. I've told you, Donatella, I have a child to consider.'

'But *caro,* if you did, then you could marry me.'

'She may not give me a divorce, especially if she knew you

had moved in here.' Roberto omitted the fact that marrying Donatella had never seriously crossed his mind.

She reached for her handbag, walked over to him and put her arms around his waist as he stared morosely over the New York skyline.

'Why are you so unhappy, Roberto? We have everything here. Everything. Your wonderful career, friends, each other. Yet it seems as if it's still not enough for you.'

Roberto did not reply.

Donatella sighed. 'I must go. I have a lunch with Trish St Regent. Call me from Paris, won't you?'

'Of course.'

'I love you. *Ciao*.'

Roberto felt her peck the back of his neck, listened to her footsteps as she walked across the room, and then heard the front door close behind her.

He opened his lungs and let an air-splitting high C reverberate around the room. The note contained all the angst and unhappiness he was currently feeling.

Roberto turned away from the window and walked into the sitting room. Maybe it wasn't too late. Maybe, if he picked up the receiver, dialled Rosanna's number, then told her how he still loved her, pined for her, *needed* her as he needed the air he breathed, she would forgive him, and the desperation and misery he'd felt since he left her would finally be gone.

He picked up the handset and punched in the first few numbers. Then he replaced it as his pride yet again overwhelmed him. He collapsed into a chair and let out a long, tortured moan. His heart was pounding and he felt dizzy, nauseous, something that had been happening a lot recently. Perhaps he wasn't well, should see a doctor . . .

Or perhaps it was simply despair.

After he'd left that night a year ago, a self-righteous anger had beset him. So, he had made a mistake, a bad mistake, but surely not an unforgivable one? He was after all Roberto Rossini, the maestro. Other wives of opera stars turned a blind eye to their husbands' antics, understanding that their artistic temperament needed a physical outlet. Was it his fault women desired him and that he had weakened in the face of temptation? Rosanna would realise her mistake and call him, beg him to return. He'd waited in London for her to contact him. Finally, he'd realised she would not.

Then the pain set in, the deep ache that never left him. He'd moved to New York six months ago, convincing himself that distance would be the answer. Donatella was there – convenient, willing and surprisingly loving. Occasionally in her arms he'd forget for a few seconds. But most of the time, he closed his eyes and imagined it was Rosanna beneath him.

And his child, his Nico, who would be walking and saying his first words, without his papa there to see it.

Pick up the telephone, Roberto. Do it, he ordered himself.

He dialled The Manor House once more, his hands shaking. In a few seconds he would hear her voice and his torment would surely be over.

The telephone rang. And rang. If she was out in the garden, it would take her a while to reach the house, especially with a toddling child. Roberto let the line ring for a further few seconds before he crashed the receiver down.

As he stood up, the telephone rang. He picked it up in a flash.

'Roberto? Chris here. Just checking you're ready. I'll be outside in thirty minutes.'

He replaced the receiver and put his head in his hands.

'I think I can hear the telephone ringing,' said Rosanna as she helped Nico out of Stephen's car. 'Can you keep an eye on him while I run inside?'

Rosanna unlocked the front door and ran into the sitting room. As she neared the telephone, it stopped.

'Were you expecting a call?' Stephen asked as he entered the room moments later, with Nico clutching his hand.

'Not particularly. Well, if it's important they'll ring again, won't they?'

'Yes, of course they will.' Stephen was now preoccupied with chasing a waddling, giggling Nico around the coffee table.

Rosanna flopped into an armchair. 'I don't know where you find the energy. I'm exhausted!' She smiled fondly as she watched the two of them. 'Will you stay for tea or coffee?'

'Normally I'd love to, but I'm afraid I'm going to have to get back. I have a pile of admin to do before the VAT man visits on Wednesday.' As he spoke, Stephen scooped up her helplessly laughing son and handed him to her. With the child riding happily on her hip, Rosanna followed Stephen out of the front door and walked with him towards his car.

'Thank you for a lovely day,' she said as he climbed into the driver's seat.

'You really enjoyed it?' he asked.

'Yes, I really did.'

'Good. Then we must do it again sometime.'

'Yes, I think I'd like that. It does both of us good to get

out. Wave goodbye to Stephen, Nico,' Rosanna said as Stephen put the car into reverse. The little boy's beaming smile turned into a scowl. His mouth drooped and he let out a howl of indignation as his erstwhile playmate disappeared down the drive.

'Oh *angeletto*, don't fret, he'll be back soon,' Rosanna reassured him as they walked back into the house.

'Soon,' the child mimicked.

'Yes. Soon.' Rosanna kissed her son's head as she carried him upstairs towards the bathroom.

The telephone rang just as Rosanna had settled herself on the sofa to watch the news. She went into the study and picked up the receiver. 'Hello?'

'Rosanna?'

She smiled at the sound of the familiar voice. 'Luca! How are you?'

'I'm well, very well.'

'Good.'

'I tried to ring you earlier, but there was no reply.'

'I was out with Nico and a friend. The telephone was ringing as we arrived home but I just missed it.'

'Well, I'm glad I've caught you now. How is my nephew?'

'Beautiful, lively, exhausting,' said Rosanna. 'It's about time you came to visit him. He'll be taking his First Communion if you don't hurry.'

'That is why I'm ringing, Rosanna. I was wondering whether you would mind if I flew over and came to stay with you for a while?'

'Mind? I would love it, Luca! When were you thinking of coming?'

'The last week in July.'

'I see.'

'Is there a problem?'

'No, not at all. It's just that Abi will be here too then. Will you mind?'

'Of course I won't. It'll be wonderful to see her after all these years.'

'I'll have to tell her, but I'm sure she'll be pleased to see you too.'

'I hope so. Milan was a long time ago. We are all adults now, yes?'

'Well, we all like to think so,' Rosanna said gently.

'Then I shall arrange my flights and let you know what date and time I'll be arriving.'

'Oh Luca, it will be so good to see you. I have missed you. I . . .'

'Are you okay?'

'Yes, I'm fine, really. I spoke to Papa and Carlotta last week and Carlotta sounded very subdued. Is she all right?'

'I visited a few days ago, and, no,' Luca sighed, 'she has some problems, but I'll tell you more when I see you. Papa is on good form, though. He's found himself a girlfriend.'

'Really?' said Rosanna. 'He didn't mention it to me.'

'No. I think he's embarrassed,' Luca laughed, 'but it's doing him good.'

'He needs a companion. I know what it's like to be alone,' she said with feeling.

'It must be hard for you, *piccolina*. I'm proud of you. So, I'll call you soon to let you know when I'm coming. *Ciao*.'

'*Ciao*, Luca.'

34

Abi arrived at The Manor House on a blazing hot July day.

'Darling!' She squeezed herself out of her smart little red Mazda sports car and ran to clasp Rosanna in a hug. 'My God, you're brown as a berry! Have you been away to the Caribbean without telling me?'

'No, it's the English sun,' said Rosanna, returning the hug.

'And Nico has his first suntan, too.' Abi surveyed the little boy, who was collecting stones from the gravel drive. 'Come to Auntie Abi, your very own fairy godmother.' She swept Nico into her arms and kissed him, and he proudly offered her one of his stones. 'Thank you, my darling. Goodness, Rosanna, he's a big boy for eighteen months and very handsome. He's going to be a heartbreaker when he gets older. Now, Nico, Auntie Abi has presents for you in her car, but before I unload, what about a nice cool drink before I die of dehydration?'

Twenty minutes later, Rosanna and Abi were sitting on a picnic rug on the lawn drinking lemonade and watching Nico trying to stand on his head.

'Oh, it's so beautiful here,' said Abi. 'I love your house, Rosanna. It's so spacious, yet so very comfortable and cosy.

And Nico really is adorable. Some children of his age are revolting.'

'He still has time,' Rosanna said wryly.

'Well, I'm amazed at the way you've slipped with such ease into your maternal role. I take my hat off to you. I could never be a full-time single mum. It would drive me mad.'

'It seems I have little choice – about the single part, at least. Anyway, I love being a mother. You wait until you have your own, Abi, then you'll change your tune, I'm sure.'

'I don't think I will, as a matter of fact. Babies are not in the plan so far, even if I could find someone to help me make one,' sighed Abi ruefully.

'Is Henry off the agenda?'

'God, yes, I binned him months ago. So I'm young, free and single yet again.'

'You must have endless men desperate to replace him, Abi,' Rosanna chided her.

'Well, maybe *I* can't find anyone to fall in love *with* then. I do try, Rosanna, honestly. But anyway, I've decided from now on that it's my career all the way. I've been given a wonderful chance with this book contract and I intend to give it my best shot.'

'Well, you're on the attic floor, where you can't hear any noise from downstairs. It's a lovely, light room and I've put a table in there so you can write.'

'It sounds perfect. You'll hardly notice I'm here, Rosanna. I reckon if I work non-stop for the next four weeks, I should finish the first draft. Can you stand me for that long?'

'Of course I can. It will be lovely to have some company, even if only at breakfast and suppertime. I want you to treat this as your own home while you're here.'

'When did you say Luca arrives?' Abi asked casually.

'Next Sunday.'

'Oh. Right, shall we go and get my bags in from the car and dig out the hundredweight of toys I've brought for your son?'

Later, after Nico had gone to bed, Rosanna opened the bottle of champagne Abi had brought with her and the two of them sat on the terrace as dusk fell, reminiscing and talking of the future.

'To you, Rosanna, for allowing me to come and stay in your beautiful house,' Abi said, raising her glass.

'Anytime, Abi, anytime.' As Rosanna spoke, they heard a car draw up at the front of the house.

'Who's that, d'you think?' asked Abi.

'I don't know,' Rosanna said, embarrassed suddenly.

Stephen appeared round the corner of the house. 'Hello, Rosanna. And Abi, long time, no see. How are you?'

'Very well, thank you.'

Stephen kissed both women warmly. 'Rosanna said your arrival was imminent, but I wasn't sure when.'

'Ah, well, you see, I like to surprise people.' Abi pulled out a chair for their guest and Rosanna went to get another glass from the kitchen. 'Pop in often, do you?' She smiled mischievously at Stephen.

'Fairly often, yes. Usually a little earlier than this, for my twenty-minute workout with Nico before he goes to sleep, but tonight I was delayed by a customer.' Rosanna reappeared glass in hand. 'I sold a painting today,' said Stephen, smiling up at her.

'Wonderful! Did you get the price you wanted?' she asked him.

'Almost. They were Americans and they paid cash, so I gave them a ten per cent discount.'

'Then that definitely calls for champagne,' Rosanna said as she filled the glass and passed it to Stephen. 'Congratulations. I'm thrilled for you.'

Abi raised her glass too. 'Yes, well done. So, tell me all about your gallery.'

'Well, rather than me boring you with details now, Abi, why don't you come and see it for yourself? I'm having an exhibition for a local artist in a couple of weeks. Perhaps you can persuade Rosanna to accompany you. I've asked her and she says she can't because she doesn't have a babysitter.'

'The girl from the post office has gone away to university,' said Rosanna defensively. 'And besides, Luca, my brother, will have just arrived from Italy.'

'Well, he's welcome too, of course. I'll leave it with you, shall I?' suggested Stephen.

He left an hour later and Abi followed Rosanna to the kitchen and helped her prepare a salad to go with the fish for supper.

'Come on then, spill the beans,' Abi teased.

'What "beans"?'

'I mean, tell me all about you and Stephen. How long has your affair been going on?'

Rosanna turned towards her, a horrified look on her face. 'Oh no, Abi, you're completely wrong. Stephen and I are just good friends, that's all.'

'My novels may be full of clichés, but even *I* wouldn't lower myself to use that one.' Abi raised an eyebrow.

'But it's true, really. Stephen sometimes comes to see me and Nico and we've all had a couple of day trips out for a picnic, but it's nothing more, believe me.'

'You swear?'

'Yes, I swear. I like Stephen very much, but not like that. I . . . I couldn't,' Rosanna said, looking away.

'Don't tell me your thoughts are still with that husband of yours?'

Rosanna forced herself to concentrate on draining the lettuce, her back towards Abi. 'It's simple, I shall never love anyone else again,' she said quietly.

'Oh God,' groaned Abi, 'that really is the kind of thing people say in my books.'

'Don't make fun of me, please. It's seriously how I feel.'

'But how can you still continue to love someone who's done what Roberto has?' she probed.

'I don't think love has anything to do with logic, do you, Abi?'

'Maybe not. But just say Roberto arrived on your doorstep tomorrow, would you welcome him back into your home?'

'I've thought about that often and I don't really know the answer. Some days I think yes, if it meant taking the pain away, other days I think no, I could never take him back. Okay, supper is ready. Shall we eat?'

Abi saw the distress in Rosanna's eyes and nodded.

'Yes, of course.'

In the days that followed, Rosanna and Abi settled into a simple routine. They would chat for twenty minutes or so over breakfast, after which Abi would pile a large tray with a jug of mineral water and several chocolate bars and disappear up to the attic for the rest of the day as Rosanna and Nico got on with their usual activities. At six o'clock, Abi would emerge, her hair awry, her eyes glazed, and make herself a stiff gin and tonic. She'd then read to Nico while Rosanna prepared supper, and once he was asleep, the two of them would retire to the kitchen or the terrace to eat.

'I'm beginning to see the reason why you live like a hermit here,' said Abi one night after supper. 'It's so tranquil and calm, one day just falling into the next. There's a sense of security about it. I shall have to watch that my reputation as a party girl doesn't get too badly tarnished while I'm here. For the first time in my life, I'm happy to stay in.' She smiled.

'You're working very hard, Abi. You must be tired.'

'I am. I've had a birth, a divorce and a murder since nine o'clock this morning,' she said, laughing.

'Is the book going well?'

'Very well. Another three weeks and I'll be there. In London it's impossible. The telephone rings, people pop round and, worst of all, there are those incredibly tempting shops and restaurants and parties. I think I shall always have to come and lock myself away in your house to write.'

'You know you're always welcome. And when Luca arrives, we'll all do our best to be quiet,' said Rosanna.

'Oh, don't worry. I'm so high up, the only noise I hear is the birds nesting in the eaves. What time is he arriving on Sunday?'

'His flight lands at eleven o'clock. He'll be here after lunch. I offered to pay for a taxi, but he refused and insisted he catch the train here.'

'That's ridiculous. Why didn't you say? I'll go and collect him. You and Nico could come too, but there are only two seats in my car.'

'Abi, you don't have to, really.'

'Don't be silly. It's settled.'

Rosanna stood up as she heard the telephone ring. 'Won't be a moment.' She ran inside to the kitchen and picked up the receiver.

'Hello?'

'It's me, Stephen. How are you?'

'Fine. And you?'

'Great. I just rang to find out whether you and Abi were going to come to the opening of the exhibition next week?'

'I don't think I can, unless I find a babysitter, Stephen.'

'Try, Rosanna, please. It would mean a lot to me to have you there.'

'All right, I will.'

'Great. Let me know. Excuse me for rushing off now, but I've still got a lot to do. Bye for now.'

Rosanna made some coffee and took the pot and two cups out to the terrace.

'Who was that?'

'Stephen. He wanted to know whether we're going to the opening of his exhibition on Wednesday.'

'I definitely think you should go,' Abi announced as she took a sip of her coffee.

'I'd have to try and find a babysitter. I just so hate leaving Nico with strangers. And Luca will be here too,' prevaricated Rosanna.

'Well, that one's easily sorted. You go and I'll stay and babysit Nico, and Luca, if he needs it. It would do you good to get out, and Stephen's been so kind to you, Rosanna, you ought to support him.'

'Yes, you're right. Don't you want to come too?'

'No. The writing is going so well and I'd like to keep up the momentum. We'll have to bring one of your nice dresses out of mothballs. Even you must draw the line at wearing shorts and a T-shirt to an art exhibition. Now, shut up and drink your coffee. You're going and I don't want to hear another word about it.'

Abi stood by the arrivals gate at Heathrow. She pushed through the sea of people awaiting loved ones behind the barrier, trying to get a better view.

As she scanned the faces emerging from behind the automatic doors, she wondered whether Luca would be in full church regalia, with a little hat with a pom-pom on top of his head . . . or was it only cardinals who wore those?

Her heart skipped a beat as she spotted him. He was dressed not in the uniform of the clergy, but casually, in a pair of rumpled linen trousers and an open-necked light blue shirt. He seemed thinner and more angular than she remembered, his high cheekbones casting elegant shadows on his pale face. There were a few flecks of grey in his black hair, adding a maturity that only served to make him – in her eyes – all the more attractive.

Realising he was not expecting anyone to meet him, she pushed forward and reached out to tap him on the shoulder before he could disappear into the crowd.

Luca turned round, startled.

'Abi?' Warmth spread into his dark eyes. He dropped his

holdall, took her by the shoulders and kissed her on both cheeks. 'It's so good to see you.'

'And it's good to see you too. You look well, Luca.'

'Thank you. And you . . . you look just the same.'

'Come on, let's get the car. Your sister and nephew are on tenterhooks. Rosanna doesn't trust my driving,' she explained with a grin as they walked towards the car park.

'It's most kind of you to collect me.'

'No problem, really.' Abi fed some money into a machine and it printed out a ticket. 'This way.'

Luca stared admiringly at the red sports car, as she pressed a button to wind down the roof. 'You must be doing very well, Abi. This car is expensive, yes?' he remarked as he got in.

'It was. I blew all my publishing advance on it,' she replied as she started the engine. 'You'll understand now why Rosanna and Nico didn't come with me. This car's better than contraception. Every time I feel broody, I remember that I'd have to swap my two-seater for something sensible and I go right off the idea!'

Luca didn't reply as Abi stuck her ticket into the machine and the barrier rose.

'Hold on to your hat, Luca. I aim to be home in two hours. I just love speed, don't you?' she shouted, her golden hair streaming behind her as they hit the motorway at eighty.

'I . . .' Luca's voice was drowned by the wind rushing past and they spoke no more.

Finally, after an hour and a half, they left the motorway and Abi slowed down.

'There, I'm not a bad driver, am I?' Abi asked.

Luca unclenched his hand from the leather armrest as

they approached a roundabout at considerable speed. 'No, not at all, Abi,' he grimaced.

'You haven't seen Rosanna's house, have you? It's beautiful.'

'No. I'm looking forward to seeing it, and Nico.'

'He looks like you,' Abi commented, casting a covert glance in Luca's direction. 'Same slim build, straight dark hair, and your huge brown eyes.'

'Really? He must be very handsome!' laughed Luca.

'Oh, he is, Luca, he is.'

Rosanna was pacing up and down in front of the house, not noticing her son, who was taking the opportunity to dig with his hands into the soft earth of a nearby flower bed and then eat it. She heard the distinctive roar of Abi's car while it was still a hundred yards from the house.

'They're here, they're here! Oh Nico, what have you done?' She picked him up and hurriedly tried to wipe the grime from his little fingers and face, but he squirmed out of her arms as the Mazda pulled to a halt on the drive.

Luca leapt out of the car and ran towards Rosanna and Nico. Abi switched off the engine and sat quietly where she was, not wishing to interrupt the reunion.

'It's so good to see you, Luca,' Rosanna whispered, tears pinching her eyes as she stroked her brother's cheek.

'And you, *piccolina*,' Luca replied, equally moved. 'You look well and healthy. And now, will you introduce me to my nephew?' He knelt down beside his sister so that he was at Nico's level and smiled at the little boy.

'Of course. Nico, this is your Uncle Luca, who has come all the way from Italy to see us.'

Nico allowed himself to be drawn into Luca's outstretched arms and Rosanna was moved at the sight of them. 'Come, bring your nephew inside and we'll have a cold drink. You must be tired, especially after Abi's driving.' Rosanna led him towards the front door, then turned round. 'Are you coming in, Abi?' she called.

'Yes, I'll just pop the roof up. It looks like rain.'

'Okay.'

Abi watched them go inside the house together. She slammed her fists onto the wheel of her precious car in frustration.

He was unobtainable. Completely. And yet she knew she still loved him.

It was nine o'clock and Rosanna and Luca were sitting in the kitchen, the remnants of their supper still on the table. Nico had finally subsided at eight and Abi had disappeared upstairs as soon as she'd arrived back from the airport, saying she wanted to catch up on her writing. They hadn't seen her since.

'So, how is Papa's lady friend? Would I know her?' enquired Rosanna.

'Do you remember Signora Barezi, the hairdresser?'

'Of course. Two thousand lire for a bad trim,' she grinned.

'Well, they are very friendly. She was made a widow last year and they keep each other company.'

'I'm glad. He's been alone for too long. And Carlotta? You said you would tell me about her.'

Luca's expression changed. He'd been dreading this question since he arrived and he drew in his breath before speaking. 'Rosanna, I am so sorry to tell you this. But Carlotta . . . is not well.'

'Oh God.' Rosanna's heart sank to her stomach. She could read from Luca's expression how serious it was. 'What is wrong?'

'Cancer, of the breast. It was removed two weeks ago, which is why I went to Naples, and she's having treatment for cells affected in her lymph glands. They hope they have caught it in time, but . . .' Luca shrugged. 'It's a waiting game and all we can do is pray.'

Rosanna bit her trembling lip. 'Luca, this is such terrible news. How is Papa taking it? And Ella?'

'Papa's devastated, of course, and Ella knows her mamma is ill, but not how bad it is.'

'Poor little thing, or should I say young woman. She must be fifteen by now.' Rosanna shook her head sadly, guilty that she hadn't seen her sister or her niece for so long.

'She is, and very beautiful too. Quite coincidentally, she has a lovely voice, just like her aunt.' A sad smile touched Luca's lips.

'I'd love to hear it one day.'

'I'm sure you will, Rosanna. Carlotta has all sorts of plans for Ella's future. She's obviously worried that if she dies, Papa will expect Ella to take her place and run the café.'

'But, Luca, if she has a talent for singing, then that talent must be nurtured, surely?'

'That is what Carlotta wishes, yes.'

'I should go to Naples and see her. I could leave immediately with Nico.'

'Don't go yet, Rosanna. Leave Carlotta to have her treatment. It might make her feel she has very little time left if you suddenly appeared after so long.'

'You make me feel so guilty, Luca,' she murmured. 'I would have loved to have seen more of Carlotta and Papa. I've missed them and Naples so much. But when I was with Roberto, returning to Italy was so . . . difficult.'

'It's sad he removed you from your family,' Luca agreed.

'Well, Carlotta and Papa could have come to visit me in England and they didn't. Several times I offered to pay their fares,' replied Rosanna, as usual defensive at the criticism of Roberto, even though she had left herself open to it.

'You know Papa refuses to set foot on an aeroplane, and Carlotta . . . well, she too had her reasons for staying in Naples. Let us see how she responds to her treatment and then you can make plans.'

'Surely, Luca, she's too young to die?'

'Yes, of course she is. And we must have faith that she doesn't.'

Rosanna was silent for a few seconds. Then she said, 'Luca, was Carlotta's life ruined by my leaving for Milan? If I hadn't left, she would never have had to stay at home to run the café and care for Papa.'

'I came with you to Milan, remember? I, too, left Carlotta behind.' Luca shook his head. 'What can I say? It was bad timing as much as anything. Carlotta made a mistake, which meant she had to pay a high price.'

'What mistake? Marrying Giulio?' Rosanna persisted.

'Yes, marrying Giulio.' Luca decided it was time he changed the subject. 'Now, Rosanna, I have something to ask you. Would you mind if I stayed on here a little longer than two weeks?'

'Of course not. I'd love it.'

'Thank you. I don't have to return to the seminary until September. I need to do some thinking, and I believe this would be the perfect place.'

Rosanna surveyed her brother. 'Is everything okay, Luca?'

'Of course, *piccolina*.' Luca rallied himself, not yet able to voice the thoughts that lay inside him until he'd had a chance to ruminate on them himself. 'I'm a little tired from the journey, that's all. I'm so very happy to be here and to see your beautiful son. Abi thinks he looks like me.'

'Yes. Now I look at you, I think he does.' Rosanna stifled a yawn. 'I, too, am tired. Let's leave the clearing up until the morning. Unfortunately Nico will be awake in six hours.'

They walked up the stairs hand in hand. At Rosanna's bedroom door, Luca kissed her on both cheeks. 'I always knew you were the most wonderful singer. Now, I see you are also the most wonderful mamma. You should be very proud of yourself. Goodnight, *piccolina*.'

'Goodnight, Luca.'

35

Abi sat on the edge of Rosanna's bed as her friend stepped into a short black cocktail dress. Following Luca's revelation about Carlotta, it had taken all her powers of persuasion to convince Rosanna to still go out for the evening.

'Could you do me up?'

'Sure.' Abi pulled up the zip.

'Do I need tights?'

'No, not with legs as brown as those.'

'Good. Now, are you sure you'll be okay? I've left the number of Stephen's gallery on the pad by the kitchen telephone. If you're worried about Nico, just ring and I can be home in twenty minutes.'

'Rosanna, even I can stick a bottle in a child's mouth and put him in his cot. Will you please stop fussing!'

'Sorry.' Rosanna sat down at her dressing table and began to add mascara to her eyes. 'There's food in the fridge for you and Luca and a bottle of wine—'

'Shut up, Rosanna, and stop treating me as if I'm the same age as your son.'

'Sorry,' she repeated as she put on lipstick and brushed her hair.

'I'll probably just have a sandwich upstairs in my room as I work . . .' Abi saw Rosanna's watchful eyes. 'And yes, I *will* take the baby monitor with me.'

'Where's my other shoe?' Rosanna was now on her knees, peering under the bed. She retrieved the black sandal with a look of triumph and removed a toy car from inside it. 'Right, I'm ready. I'll go downstairs and say goodbye to Luca and Nico.'

'Fine.'

Rosanna walked into the sitting room, where Nico was happily ensconced with Luca, looking at a picture book on his lap. 'You don't mind me going out, do you?' she asked.

'Not at all. It's good that you're going to support your friend. Nico and I will have a lovely time. We've got lots of books to read.'

'Is she still at it? Dear God, anyone would think she was leaving Nico for a year.' Abi rolled her eyes as she entered the sitting room. 'The taxi's just pulled up. Go, go, go!' She shooed Rosanna out of the sitting room to the front door.

'Bye, Luca. Bye, Nico. Bye—'

Abi closed the front door and went back into the sitting room. She stood by the door, gazing at the two dark heads on the sofa. 'Someone has got to tell Rosanna she's far too over-protective of that child.'

Luca glanced at her. 'She has to be both mamma and papa to Nico, that's why.'

'Yes, I suppose so,' Abi sighed. 'Now, would you mind if I went up and did a little more work? I'll come down in half an hour and make Nico's bottle and put him to bed and—'

'You go and write. I'll put Nico to bed. I used to look after Rosanna all the time when she was small.'

'If you're sure . . .'

'I am.'

An hour later Abi looked into the nursery. Nico was tucked up in his cot sleeping soundly. She made her way downstairs to the kitchen.

'Abi, just in time.' Luca was standing by the hob stirring the contents of a frying pan. An appetising aroma filled the air.

'Oh, I . . . well, I was just going to grab a sandwich and go back upstairs,' she said uncertainly.

Luca's face fell. 'But I've cooked you one of my specialities. Risotto, just as we used to eat in Milan.'

'I . . .'

'Please, Abi. Surely a couple of hours away from work will not harm? I've hardly seen you since I arrived. It would be nice to talk. Here.' He handed her a glass of wine.

Abi's resolve shattered. 'Okay then,' she said, accepting the glass. 'As you've already cooked.'

'I've also set the table on the terrace. Go sit down and relax. I shall serve the risotto and join you.'

A few minutes later, Luca put a steaming plate in front of her and sat down at the table opposite her.

'This looks delicious,' Abi commented.

'It's not often I get to cook these days. Please, begin. So,' he said as he picked up his fork, 'how is your new novel coming along?'

'When I'm at this stage, I always think it's rubbish. But it'll turn out okay in the end, I'm sure.'

'What is it about?'

'Unrequited love.' Despite herself, Abi blushed to the roots of her long blonde hair.

'That's an interesting topic,' said Luca, throwing a searching glance in her direction.

'Yes.'

'And when is your first novel published?'

'This September.'

'I see. And writing is something that makes you happy?'

'Very. Although it's a terribly self-indulgent occupation, you know. You just put all your worst fears and your wildest fantasies together, stir them up and hope other people will find them interesting.'

'I'm sure it is not that simple, but it sounds like fun. I must read your novel when it's published.'

'I don't think it's a book you'd like, to be honest, Luca,' she said guardedly.

'Why is that?'

'Well, parts of it are a bit . . . fruity.'

Luca looked confused. 'What is "fruity"?'

'I mean, there's quite a lot of sex in it.' Abi blushed again.

Luca chuckled. 'And you feel that wouldn't be suitable reading for someone training to become a priest?'

'No, not really.'

'Don't think, Abi, that because I want to be a priest that I'm not human. As a man, I have feelings just as any other. And don't think I haven't thought about you over the past few years. I have, often.' He smiled, taking a forkful of risotto before continuing. 'And now is the moment to ask if you'll forgive me. I was weak and selfish that time in Milan. I let the feelings I had for you run away with me, when I knew deep down that nothing could come of it.'

Abi's heart sank. Just for a second she had glimpsed some hope.

'You shouldn't be so hard on yourself, Luca. I should apologise too for trying to force your hand, when I ought to have respected that your life was destined for a different course. The amount of time you used to spend in that old church should have been a clue for starters.' She tried to sound cheerful and hoped he couldn't read her inner feelings on her face. 'Do you mind if I smoke?' She fumbled in her pocket for her cigarettes and a light.

'No, not at all.' Luca put his knife and fork neatly together on his plate.

'So, how's life at the seminary?'

Luca stared at her. 'Can you keep a secret?'

'Of course.'

'You mustn't tell Rosanna of this. I don't wish anyone in my family to know.'

'About what?'

'I'm on a sabbatical. I'm taking time out to think about my future.'

'You mean, you're thinking of leaving the seminary?' Abi's blue eyes were wide with surprise.

'No, I didn't say that, but I'm having a spiritual crisis – or that's what my bishop calls it, at least. Apparently, it happens to many young men in their last stage of training. After the euphoria of a decision and then the years of study, well, then comes the uncertainty.'

'I see.' Abi was listening intently.

'I believe I was put on this earth to do God's work. I wish to give comfort to those in trouble, those who are poor or suffering, and also to spread the word of God to people who haven't heard it.'

'But surely that's what you *will* be doing when you become a priest?'

'Yes, but . . .' Luca sighed. 'The church is like a club and the priests are the members. And, as in any club, there are rules that are laid down, rules that sometimes prevent you from doing things you know would be a good idea. Also, as in any organisation, even God's, there are power struggles, people who see the church as a career and will stop at nothing to reach the top. And, of course, there is corruption.' Luca paused then said, 'May I have one of your cigarettes?'

'I didn't think you smoked anymore.'

'Only very occasionally. I suppose seeing you reminds me of the old days,' he said, smiling, as he took one from the packet and Abi lit it for him.

'Well, I'm amazed by what you say. I thought the priesthood was your calling, all you wanted.'

'It was, it *is*, in an ideal world. But this world is not ideal, because it's made up of human beings. Like the Lord himself, we're not perfect. Anyway, that's why I've been given a little time to think, before I take the ultimate step and am ordained. You see, Abi, unlike others, I'm not interested in rising through the ranks. It would only move me further away from what I want to do. I don't want to be fifty and sitting behind a desk in the Vatican. I want to be out in the world helping people. I'm sorry, I'm boring you.'

'No, not at all. It's fascinating,' said Abi honestly.

'Well, thank you for listening. I needed very much to talk and you've always had a sympathetic ear.'

'Anytime, Luca. You know that.'

'And what of you, Abi?' said Luca, pouring himself another glass of wine. 'Are you happy?'

'I always try to make the best of things, even when they're not perfect. The eternal optimist, that's me,' she shrugged.

'And have you found someone to fall in love with?'

'Well, I've had a few boyfriends and a lot of fun. But I've decided recently I'm not the marrying type, that love brings too much pain. Unlike you, I'm totally selfish, you see.'

'I don't think so at all. You've been a very good friend to both me and my sister.' He leant towards her. 'How is Rosanna, really?'

'Very brave, very strong, a very good mother and . . .' Abi sighed, 'a very talented actress. Underneath it all, I'm sad to say, she's still completely in love with that feckless husband of hers.'

'Yes, I can believe that. I watched my sister fall in love with Roberto when she was eleven years old.'

'There's a fine line between love and hate. Maybe, one day,' Abi said hopefully, 'Rosanna will hate him.'

'And maybe that will be as bad as loving him.' Luca shook his head wearily. 'Fate is a strange thing. I believe very strongly that certain things are preordained by God before we take our first breath. I knew from the outset that Roberto Rossini would be trouble for Rosanna. If there was one man in the world who I prayed many times would never come near her, it was him. I know of things he's done, have seen things that . . .' Luca's voice had become fierce with emotion. 'I'm sorry, Abi. I find it hard, loving my sister, knowing she loves Roberto and being unable to protect her from the pain of it. But that, as I said, is fate, is it not?'

'Yes. And anyway, they haven't spoken for over a year. Plus, you may be pleased to hear she has an admirer: Stephen, that chap she's out with tonight. He absolutely worships Rosanna, although I'm not sure how she feels about him.'

'That at least is good,' agreed Luca. 'Does she ever talk about returning to opera?'

'Not so far, no.'

He shook his head. 'Roberto even managed to take that from her, to separate her from her gift. A talent such as hers is so very rare and yet she no longer seems to recognise or value it.'

'I know, I know. But one day when Nico is older, she may return. She's still very young. And Stephen would encourage her if the two of them ever got together. He's her biggest fan.'

'This Stephen sounds almost too perfect,' smiled Luca.

'I agree. There must be something wrong with him,' giggled Abi.

'Maybe it's simply that Rosanna will never fully appreciate his qualities,' Luca shrugged.

'Probably. Anyway, shall I make some coffee?'

'Yes, that would be nice.'

Abi stood and began to clear the table. As she reached for Luca's plate, he touched her gently on her arm.

'Thank you again for listening, Abi. You are a very good friend with a very good heart.'

Abi carried the plates into the kitchen. She filled the jug with water, poured it into the coffee machine and switched it on, mulling over what he'd told her and how it had altered her situation. If he really was uncertain about the priesthood, then surely . . .

'Oh, what the hell,' she said under her breath as she

watched the coffee drip into the jug. 'It might be the end of you, Abi, but you only live once.'

As the last guest left the gallery, Stephen locked the door behind him and breathed a sigh of relief.

Rosanna was smiling at him. 'That was a great success, wasn't it?'

'Yes. Twelve paintings reserved out of fifteen. I'm going to have to get the artists to paint some more – fast.'

'You were brilliant.' She sat down in a chair. 'You were so nice to everyone, even when they argued about the price.'

'Customer relations is a big part of my job. More wine?' Stephen took a bottle standing on his desk and filled Rosanna's glass.

'Thank you. To you, Stephen, and the gallery.'

'Yes, to me. And to you for coming and being so supportive.'

'It was the least I could do. I enjoyed it.'

'Did you?'

'Yes. It was nice to go out, although I did find it quite stressful at first,' she admitted. 'I'm not used to making small talk these days.'

'Rosanna, everyone thought you were delightful. You know, someone even asked me if you were my wife.' Stephen glanced at her sideways.

'Did they? I . . .' She abruptly put down her glass and stood up. 'I ought to be getting back now. Abi and Luca will be wondering where I am.'

'Of course. I'll take you home.'

'No, I can call a taxi.'

'Don't be silly, Rosanna. Come on.'

They left the gallery and walked along the narrow streets towards his car.

Rosanna was silent on the journey home, feeling guilty for her knee-jerk reaction to his innocent comment. As Stephen pulled the car into the drive, she turned towards him.

'Would you like to come to lunch on Sunday and meet my brother?'

'I'd love to,' he replied.

'Good. About one then?'

'Yes.'

'Thank you for a lovely evening. Goodnight, Stephen.' Rosanna pecked him on the cheek and got out of the car.

36

'Stephen,' said Rosanna, 'this is my brother, Luca.'

'How do you do?' Stephen smiled warmly as the two men shook hands.

'Drinks, everyone.' Abi brought a tray with a jug of Pimms and glasses out onto the terrace. She put the tray down and poured out four glasses. 'Cheers,' she said, taking a sip.

'So, Stephen, Rosanna tells me you run an art gallery nearby,' said Luca.

'Yes, in Cheltenham. I decided to go it alone a few months ago. And so far, the gamble's paying off. And I much prefer working here to the grime of London. It's also an interesting challenge finding modern artists. I used to work at Sotheby's, helping the team there authenticate and value Renaissance works.'

'That sounds very interesting, Stephen. I'd love to learn more about the art world,' Luca encouraged, but at that moment they were interrupted by Abi, who was brandishing a pair of tongs.

'Right, I'd better get on with the barbeque. I'm warning you, I'm useless and I burn everything,' she laughed as she made her way along the terrace. 'Luca, can you bring out the meat? I'll be ready to blacken everything in a few seconds.'

'Of course.'

'And I'd better go and fetch Nico from his cot,' said Rosanna as she followed her brother into the house.

Ten minutes later, Rosanna appeared on the terrace with Nico, who was crying. 'I'm afraid he's always a little grumpy after his rest, aren't you, darling?'

'Hello, little chap,' said Stephen.

Nico immediately stopped crying and stretched out his arms to him.

'I see,' nodded Abi, waving the tongs in the air. 'We all know who's flavour of the month, don't we?' She winked pointedly at Luca as Stephen and Nico set off hand in hand towards a playhouse Rosanna had bought him.

'Babies are always the best judges of character,' said Luca, winking back.

'Would you mind helping me out here?' asked Abi, her face flushed from the heat of the barbeque. Luca did so and the two of them watched surreptitiously as Rosanna joined Stephen and her son.

'They do go well together, don't they?' said Abi.

'Stephen seems a nice man, but let's not push too hard. I know Rosanna of old and so do you. For all her sweetness, she's also stubborn as a mule. It might be better if we disapproved,' Luca replied as he forked the cooked sausages onto a plate.

'Lunch is ready,' called Abi and a few minutes later they all sat down to eat.

Afterwards, Stephen and Rosanna took Nico off for a

walk to see the ducks on the village pond and Luca and Abi were left lying side by side on the picnic rug.

'God, if only life could always be as lovely as today,' she sighed. She rolled onto her front, picked a piece of grass and chewed it thoughtfully, staring across at Luca. 'Are you asleep?'

'No.'

'I feel high on Pimms, sun and happiness,' she remarked. 'Oh, I do love you, Luca.' She leant across and kissed him lightly on the lips. He didn't respond, but he didn't stop her either.

'Did you hear me?' she asked gently. 'I love you. I'm a little drunk so I don't actually care that I've said it.'

Luca's eyes opened. Abi bent to kiss him again and felt his arm travel tentatively up her back. Then a small tornado hurtled towards them and threw itself on top of them.

'Nico, you little monster!' Luca rolled away from Abi and began to tickle his nephew, who giggled delightedly.

Abi sat up abruptly and saw that, thankfully, Rosanna and Stephen were still some distance away on the terrace.

'Dinner sometime next week?' Stephen asked Rosanna as they made their way slowly across the lawn towards the pile of bodies on the rug.

'If Abi and Luca will babysit.'

'I'm sure they'd be glad to. They seem very fond of each other.'

'They are, and it's lovely to see them enjoying each other's company and renewing their friendship.'

'Of course,' Stephen nodded, deciding not to comment

further on what he had seen happen between them a few minutes earlier.

Rosanna went upstairs to her bedroom early that night. She wanted to think about Stephen and what he meant to her. There was no point pretending anymore. In his gentle way, Stephen had made it perfectly clear to her that he wanted more from her than a friendship. Asking her out for dinner was a different thing altogether from passing a few pleasant daytime hours with Nico in tow.

She lay in bed trying to imagine what it would be like to have his hands touch her, make love to her . . . and rolled over in frustration. She knew she could never love Stephen in the way she had loved Roberto, but then, maybe she couldn't feel for anyone that way. She didn't want to hurt him, to make him believe she could feel something she couldn't, but neither did she want to lose him: she and Nico would miss him terribly. Maybe she needed more time, maybe the love would grow . . .

Rosanna's eyes were heavy. She couldn't think of it any longer tonight. She turned off the light and prepared for sleep.

Downstairs in the kitchen Abi was washing the dishes and handing them to Luca to dry.

Luca yawned. 'Sorry, it's too much alcohol. I'm not used to drinking these days. I think I must go to bed.'

'No! Luca, please, stay for a while. We have to talk.' She sank down forlornly at the kitchen table and lit a cigarette.

His arms went immediately around her shoulders. 'Abi, please, I don't wish to upset you. I—'

'Did you hear what I said this afternoon, Luca? I said I loved you. I know you think it was just the Pimms talking, but it's true. I've loved you ever since those days in Milan. And I've done my best to keep away from you while you've been here. It was all going fine until you cooked supper for me the other night and told me about your disillusionment with the Church. And then . . . and then I kept thinking, maybe there's a chance for us . . . I can't help it.' She ground her cigarette into the ashtray. 'I can't help wanting you. Oh, for Christ's sake, you're the priest! Comfort me, tell me what to do!' She burst into helpless sobs and put her head in her hands.

'Abi, don't you understand that I loved you too?'

'Did you?'

'Yes.'

'But Luca, do you still love me? That's what I need to know.' Her voice was muffled by her hands.

He looked down at her and exhaled slowly. 'Yes, Abi, I still love you. Like you, I wondered if what I felt all those years ago was gone, but it hasn't. And here I am with you again, at a time when I'm trying to make the most difficult decision of my life. How can I encourage our love when I can't yet promise you anything? That would be selfish and unfair.'

She looked up at him. 'Couldn't you become an Anglican vicar or something? Then you could have me and religion!'

'Abi,' Luca chuckled as he stroked her hair.

She stood up. 'Look, I think I ought to leave. It would be best for both of us. I can't . . . I can't . . .' She shrugged helplessly. 'I can't control what I feel for you.'

'Abi, do you wish me to be honest with you?'

'Yes.'

'Then I will tell you I couldn't bear for you to leave. Besides that, you have your work to finish. Abi' – Luca took her hands in his – 'we could go upstairs now and consummate our love. That is what we both want, yes?'

Abi nodded. 'Yes.'

'But don't you see it would be wrong? I'm too confused about my future. I could make you promises that I may not be able to keep. Then you would hate me and I would hate myself for hurting you and for breaking the vows I took when I went into the seminary.'

'I know all that, Luca,' she sighed. 'That's why it's better I go back to London.'

'Wait a little, *cara*. I've been thinking that God does not say love is wrong. So . . .' Luca paused and took a deep breath. 'Is it not possible to look on the few weeks we have together as a gift? Time to be with each other, to be close again, to talk? And for us to work out whether what we feel is right for both of us?'

'So, what you're saying is that we can be lovers, but without the physical side,' said Abi slowly.

'Yes. In our heads' – Luca pointed – 'in our hearts. Maybe it's too much to ask, but it is all I can offer.'

She stared at him. 'Are you saying there might be a chance for us? In the future?'

'I cannot promise anything, Abi. You must know that now.'

She nodded slowly and stood up. 'Well, that's certainly going to take some thinking about.' She walked towards the door, then turned to look at him. 'If I'm here tomorrow morning, then . . .' She shrugged slightly. 'If not, well . . . goodnight, Luca.' She opened the door and left the kitchen.

The following morning Luca woke, climbed out of bed and went immediately to the window. He opened the curtains, his heart beating hard against his chest, and saw the little red Mazda still parked in the drive.

There was a knock on his door and he went to open it.

'Abi, Abi.' He took her into his arms and held her. 'I was so frightened you might have gone.'

'How could I? I love you. I have to take the chance, however small.'

She kissed him gently on the cheek then pulled away from him. 'But for now, my darling, I must do some work. We'll talk more later.'

The door shut behind her. Luca knelt down and asked God to forgive his weakness.

The Metropolitan Opera House, New York

So, Nico, Abi stayed on, although at the time I had no idea she had been thinking of leaving. And I remember that summer as a time of, if not perfect happiness, then at least of peace, and respite for my broken heart. Stephen visited most days, coming to the house after he'd shut the gallery. He'd play with you for a while before you went to bed, then the four of us would sit down to supper on the terrace, enjoying those glorious English summer evenings. Stephen was not a replacement for your father – no one could ever fill that space in my heart – but at least he brought back a little normality to my life. Sometimes, sitting on the terrace, I'd look round the table and realise how lucky I was to have people I cared for with me.

And I began to slowly come back to life. The numbness that had been there since your father left started to thaw a little. Instead of living just one day at a time, I was able to look to the future, face making plans that did not include Roberto. I started to believe there was a chance that one day the pain would leave, and even if it didn't, that I had enough in my life to be fulfilled. I even began to think about returning to singing. Stephen, Abi and Luca were all encouraging. But I knew it wasn't right just yet, that I needed a little more time.

And your uncle looked happier than I'd seen him for years. There was a quiet contentment about him, and Abi too. I should have seen what was right under my nose, but I was blind to it then, selfishly involved with my own feelings.

Then the days became shorter and the leaves on the trees began to turn lazily from green to gold and red. Abi and Luca talked of leaving, but then made no plans to do so. It was as if the four of us were trying to make time stand still, knowing the summer had to end, but unable to face reality just yet . . .

37

Gloucestershire, September 1982

In the kitchen, Luca was preparing dinner. Abi sat at the table drinking a glass of wine.

'Abi, *cara*, I have something I must tell you. I telephoned Papa today and I must fly to Naples as soon as possible. Carlotta has asked to see me. I'm sorry, but I must leave you.'

'Of course you must go,' she comforted him. 'Don't worry about me, I have to get back to London anyway. My editor's screaming for the new manuscript and the publicity girl's arranged some interviews for me. I . . . How long will you be away?'

Luca sat down in a chair opposite her. 'I can't tell. It depends on Carlotta.'

'I see.'

'I'll telephone you, of course, as soon as I know how long I must stay. Abi' – he took her hands in his and kissed them softly – 'this summer has been the most wonderful time of my life. Whatever happens, I—'

'What do you mean, "whatever happens"?' She snatched her hands away.

'I mean that I will always love you, even if . . .'

'No, you mean that you don't love me enough to offer me a future. Excuse me, I thought I could handle this, but . . .'

Abi stood up abruptly and left the kitchen. Luca called out to her, but she ran up the two flights of stairs to her room and slammed the door behind her. She walked across to the desk where her finished manuscript had lain for the past ten days. Since then, there'd been nothing further she needed to do to keep her from leaving and returning to London. She'd simply been unable to dig up the courage to say goodbye to him. She sat down in her chair and gazed out of the window and across the open countryside. The summer had been so perfect. They'd spent every day together, walking, talking, *loving* each other in every way but one.

Abi laid her head on her manuscript, the joy of the past few weeks replaced by dread. He'd said from the start he could promise her nothing. She could not blame him. And she knew the pain was only just beginning.

By the time Abi was packed and ready to leave the following morning, Rosanna and Nico had already said their goodbyes and had left the house to meet Stephen for lunch in Cheltenham.

As she was cramming her suitcase into the tiny boot space of the Mazda, Luca appeared at the front door.

'Abi.' He walked towards her and took her in his arms.

'I . . . I can't take this. Please try to understand.' She pulled away from him and climbed behind the wheel. She turned the key and the engine hummed.

He leant through the window. 'I love you, Abi. I will write to you from Naples.' She moved the gearstick into reverse, desperate to leave before she cried like a baby in front of him. 'Just promise me one thing, Luca.'

'What is it?'

'That you won't forget the way you felt this summer. I defy even God himself to make you happier. Goodbye.'

Luca watched as Abi reversed the car, turned it round, then roared out of the drive.

She was gone.

He stood, shell-shocked by her abrupt departure. And for the first time, Luca truly understood Rosanna's pain over Roberto.

Twenty-four hours later, Luca also clasped his sister in his arms. '*Ciao, piccolina*.'

'*Ciao*, take care of yourself and send my love to Papa, Carlotta and Ella. And please, let me know if I should come and see Carlotta.'

'I will, I promise. I'll telephone you when I arrive in Naples.' Luca bent down to kiss Nico. 'Take good care of your mamma, *angeletto*.'

Stephen was waiting to take Luca to the airport. 'I should be back by five,' he called to Rosanna as he got into the car and closed the door. Waving as they watched the car crawl down the drive, she picked up Nico and hugged him, shivering a little in the autumnal air.

Summer was over.

When Stephen returned from the airport, they had supper on trays in front of a film.

'The house feels so empty and quiet, doesn't it?' Rosanna commented.

'Well, it will for a while. I must admit, completely selfishly of course, that it's nice to have you to myself for a change. Do you think Luca and Abi will keep in touch with each other?'

'Of course. They have reclaimed their friendship and they became very close over the summer.'

'Do you think that's all it was? Friendship, I mean?' Stephen persisted.

'Of course. My brother will soon be ordained as a priest. Why do you ask?'

'I just happen to think they're still in love with each other, Rosanna.'

'No, they're just very good friends. They enjoy each other's company. I'm sure that's all.'

'If you say so. Anyway' – Stephen stood up – 'I must be going. I'm tired after all that driving and if I stay any longer, I'll fall asleep.' He pulled his discarded sweater over his head. 'Thank you for supper. I'll pop round sometime next week, shall I?'

It hit her like a hard thump on her chest. She wanted him to stay, to feel his arms around her. She didn't want to be alone in this silent, empty house.

'Don't go,' she whispered.

'Sorry?' Stephen turned back from the door.

'I said, please don't go.'

He looked confused. 'I . . . are you saying you want me to stay?'

'Yes.' Rosanna stood up and walked towards him. She stood on tiptoe so she could kiss him on the lips. His arms wound round her shoulders and they kissed properly for the first time.

Rosanna pulled away from him. 'Take me upstairs, Stephen,' she murmured, before she could change her mind.

'I have a proposition to put to you.'

It was a few days after Luca and Abi had left and Stephen had popped in as usual after work. He was pushing Nico on the swing at the bottom of the garden.

'Will I like it?' Rosanna enquired with a smile.

'I don't know. I hope so.'

'Then you'd better ask me.'

'I have to go to New York at the end of this month. There's a very wealthy collector I know from my days at Sotheby's. I sent him a catalogue of my landscape artist who sold so many of her paintings at the show last month and he called me today, expressing interest in buying a couple of her pieces. He's invited me over to discuss it.'

'If he's seen the catalogue, then why must you go over too?' asked Rosanna.

'Because he's outrageously wealthy, so he's worth keeping sweet,' replied Stephen. 'And I thought it would be the perfect excuse to spend a weekend in New York with you,' he added casually. 'Would you come, darling? I'd love it if you did. This man really is a well-known collector. If he buys from me, then other major collectors might have the courage to follow his lead. I need you with me to charm him.'

Rosanna shook her head. 'Thank you very much for asking, but I don't think New York is a good idea.'

'Are you worried about bumping into your husband?'

'Yes.'

'Well, don't be. It just so happens that Roberto is singing in Paris for three weeks at that time. I've already checked. So will you come?' he pleaded. 'We could have a wonderful time.'

'But what about Nico?'

'I've already asked Abi and she says she's happy to take care of him while we're away. It'll only be two nights, Rosanna.'

Rosanna hesitated for a minute then said, 'Okay.'

'You'll really come?'

'Yes, I will.'

'Nico,' he said to the little boy, 'your mother is a star.'

38

Naples, Italy

'Papa!' Luca kissed his father on both cheeks. 'You look well.' He thought that Marco hardly seemed to have aged a day in the past ten years.

'It's wine, food and the love of a good woman that keeps me young,' quipped Marco. 'Come, Luca, have a drink with me.' He poured two glasses of Aperol and handed one to Luca.

'How is she?'

Marco's face became grave. 'I don't know. She'll tell me nothing.'

'Has she said whether the treatment has worked?'

'No, I told you, she tells me little, but, Luca, you only have to look at her to see the truth. And as for Ella' – Marco shrugged – 'she knows nothing except that Carlotta was in the hospital for a while and is now recovering. The poor girl keeps asking me why her mamma is still so pale and sick. But what can I do? I promised Carlotta I would not tell her daughter anything.'

'Well, maybe she's hoping there will be no need.'

'You see your sister and then tell me there is no need,' sighed his father.

'Is she upstairs?'

'Yes, she is resting. She was very happy you were coming. I've sent Ella to a friend's for the night so you can have a talk with Carlotta. Try to get something out of her, Luca.'

'I'll go up now.'

Marco put a hand on Luca's shoulder. 'She's hiding the truth from all of us and it's better we know.'

Luca nodded, then walked up the stairs and along the corridor to Carlotta's room. He knocked softly on her door.

'Come in,' a voice answered weakly.

Luca opened the door and saw Carlotta lying on top of the bed. She was skeletal, her previously curvaceous figure eaten away with disease, her once lovely complexion turned a ghastly grey. He knew then that Carlotta was dying.

She lifted herself up onto her elbows and a smile came fleetingly to her face, sending memories of the old Carlotta flooding back into his mind.

'Luca, come and give your sister a hug.'

He walked towards her, then put his arms around her and held her, steeling himself not to cry.

'I'm so glad you are here.'

He released her from his arms and she lay back on the pillows, her hand chasing his and clasping it.

'I'm sorry I wasn't downstairs to greet you, but I'm afraid I feel a little tired today.'

'Carlotta, it doesn't matter. I'm your brother. You lie there and we'll talk.' He stroked her forehead as her body stiffened. 'Is the pain bad?'

She nodded. 'Yes.' Tears came to her eyes. 'You know, don't you, Luca? You can see?'

'See what?'

'That it will soon be over for me.'

'No, Carlotta, please, you mustn't say that.'

'The doctors have told me. The treatment didn't work. The cancer has spread – it's everywhere. There's nothing more they can do.' She closed her eyes as if unable to look at him any longer.

Luca realised it was pointless offering her platitudes. 'How much time do you have?'

'They don't know. Between three and six months. The way I am today, maybe a few hours.' She winced. 'Can you pass me those tablets?' She pointed to a bottle on the bedside table. 'I'll feel a bit better once I've had one of these. They work for about two hours, but I'm only allowed to take them every *four*.' Luca handed her a tablet and she put it in her mouth, took a sip of water and swallowed. 'There.' She slumped back onto her pillow and exhaled. Then she closed her eyes. 'Give me a little time for the tablet to work.'

'Of course. As long as you need.' Luca sat silently on the edge of the bed holding Carlotta's hand. Slowly, her jagged breathing began to ease and the tension in her body lessened. Luca thought she slept a little, but eventually, she opened her eyes and smiled at him.

'Okay, it is better. My dear brother, I'm so glad you are here. Did you have a good holiday with Rosanna in England?'

'Yes, very good.'

'How are Rosanna and Nico?'

'They're both well.'

'Good. Luca, I need to talk to you.' Carlotta sounded almost normal now the pain was under control. 'But not yet. Tonight we shall go out to eat.'

'Are you sure you're up to it, Carlotta?'

'No, but then I'm not up to anything. As long as I take the painkillers half an hour before we leave, I will manage. We must talk somewhere private, where we can be sure no one will overhear.'

'Carlotta, do you not think you should be in hospital?' Luca entreated.

'Yes,' she agreed, 'it's what the doctors have suggested. But don't you see that I have a choice? I can go to hospital and have my pain controlled and lie there and think about death, or I can try and continue to live and suffer a little more. Which would you do?'

'I . . .' Luca looked at her with admiration. 'You're being very brave, Carlotta.'

'Yes, at this minute I feel brave. Maybe it's because you are here. Sometimes, it's not so easy.'

'Papa says you won't talk to him about what's happening to you. Carlotta, you must tell him the truth. He feels shut out. He, too, must have time to come to terms with it.'

'Yes, I will talk to Papa when I'm ready. But I don't want to risk Ella knowing the truth. What is the point of making her suffer for as long as it takes me to die? It could be many months. She would see me in pain every day while she waited for the inevitable. It would be dreadful for her, cruel.'

'It's your decision, of course, but I wonder whether Ella would be better off knowing the truth? She isn't a child any longer and she may resent you taking the decision for her.'

'Yes, she probably will.' Carlotta's eyes glinted with their old fire. 'But it's one decision in my life that I insist on making. And there are others too, but I'll tell you about those when we go out to eat later. Luca, would you mind if I slept while the pain is easier, then I'll be rested for tonight?'

'Of course.' Luca kissed her on the forehead and left Carlotta's room to go to his own. Shutting the door, he leant against it and took some deep breaths to stem the shock of seeing his dying sister. Wandering over to his bed, he sat down on it heavily, thinking how he should get down on his knees and pray for her, but something was preventing him from doing so.

A year ago, he'd have had absolute confidence in Carlotta's future in heaven, safe in the arms of God. But now, he was struggling to reassure himself, to believe it.

She was his sister and he did not want to lose her, even to God.

'Why? Why her?' he asked Him.

For once, He had no answer.

Later that evening, Carlotta leant on Luca's arm and they walked slowly down to the seafront. The sun was setting over the water and, even though it was September, the restaurants and bars were doing a brisk trade. They chose a small candle-lit restaurant and decided it was warm enough to take a table outside.

Carlotta had put on one of her best dresses. Her face was made up and her hair freshly washed. As he sat down opposite her, Luca thought she could pass for normal again, despite the ravages her illness had inflicted.

They ordered fish, and as they ate they talked of the old times when they'd grown up together in Naples.

'Now, Luca Menici, I want you to answer me one question.' Carlotta had closed her knife and fork on her empty plate. 'Do you love me?'

'That's a stupid question, Carlotta.'

'It is, but I want you to do something for me.'

'Anything, within my capability,' he replied guardedly.

'Well, I have asked God many times recently why He has put me on this earth only to remove me so quickly. I feel my life has been pointless, apart from one thing. I had Ella. And what will become of her when I die has been causing me sleepless nights.'

'Surely Papa will take care of her?'

'No, Luca.' Carlotta shook her head firmly. 'That's the point. Ella will take care of Papa. The moment I die, he'll expect her to step into my shoes. She'll have to run the café, cook his meals and do his washing like the good little granddaughter she is. I want more for her, Luca, so much more than I've had.'

'I understand that, of course, but what other choices does she have?'

'Wait, I haven't finished yet. There is something else. She has a beautiful voice and it needs to be trained.'

'Her aunt's voice,' Luca murmured.

'I think perhaps it's more like her father's,' Carlotta replied without emotion. 'Luca, I have a plan. It may not be one you approve of, but I've made up my mind. If I died and Ella was no longer here in Naples and Papa was all alone, what do you think he would do?'

'I have no idea, Carlotta. Get very drunk every night, I expect,' he sighed.

'Well, I know exactly what he would do: he'd marry

Signora Barezi. Then she would take over the running of the café and look after Papa the way he's been used to. Because Papa has me and Ella, he has had no need to marry again. I've performed most of the functions Mamma provided. And his other needs . . . well, he's had Signora Barezi for those. But he will only marry her if he's forced to by circumstances. I believe it would be best for him, and for Ella, of course. It would mean she was free.'

'But where could she go? She's too young to be alone somewhere,' questioned Luca.

'Of course. She needs a family, who will care for her, nurture and protect her and her beautiful voice.'

Luca shook his head. 'But we have no other family, other than Rosanna and . . .' He stared at his sister aghast, seeing her determined face in the flickering candlelight. 'No, Carlotta. Surely you would not send her to Rosanna?'

'I admit it has major drawbacks,' she replied, 'but it's the best I can do for her. I must give her a chance, Luca. I want her to have a future. Rosanna has money. She's cultured, cosmopolitan. She can teach Ella all the things she will need to know. And once she hears that voice, she'll know where Ella must go to train it.'

Luca looked at his sister in horror. 'But, Carlotta, what about Rosanna? Sending her husband's illegitimate child to live under the same roof? You couldn't do that to her, surely?'

'Luca' – Carlotta smiled suddenly – 'that is the only beauty of knowing you will die. It gives you power. It's a long time since I had any and I will use it because I must. I know Rosanna will be happy to care for Ella, to look after her dead sister's child. If nothing else, she'll feel it's her duty. Besides, it's only for a couple of years. Ella is almost an adult. All I ask is that Rosanna steers her along the right path. And besides, there's no reason why Rosanna should ever know.'

'And what if Roberto and Rosanna reunite? What then, Carlotta?'

'Is it likely? They have been separated for a long time now. You tell me Roberto does not even come to see his own son. It sounds unlikely there will be a reconciliation. And even if there is, I can see no reason for either of them to ever learn the truth.'

'So you will take the secret with you?'

She paused, then nodded. 'Yes. Luca, this is my plan: I want you to take Ella to England as soon as possible. We will tell her she is going on a holiday and I want you to make sure that after I die, she never returns permanently to Naples.'

Luca stared at her in shock. 'You would send your daughter away, knowing you will never see her again, or her you? Is that fair on Ella?'

Carlotta shook her head in frustration. 'No, of course it isn't "fair", but nothing about this situation *is*. It's simply the best I can do. Don't you see? If I die and Ella is here, Papa will cling to her. Ella will never manage to get away, just as I didn't.'

'But she will have to return for your . . .' Luca couldn't say the words.

'No, I don't want her to attend my funeral,' Carlotta said bluntly. 'I have made a will, asking for only you and Papa to be present. Luca, she must *not* come back. Please, I beg you to make sure she doesn't. I don't care how you do it – lie to her if you have to.'

He studied his sister, admiring her courage and determination to make such a decision, but questioning its morality.

'What about Rosanna? She'll have to be told of your intentions.'

'Yes.'

'She wants to come and see you.'

'No.' Carlotta suddenly looked very tired. 'It's best if I don't see her. I wouldn't trust myself. Please, Luca. I know what is right for my child. You will help me, won't you? Allow me that much peace of mind in this dreadful situation.'

If it was her last wish, then he must help to grant it. Finally, he nodded. 'I will do everything I can.'

'Thank you.' Carlotta's features relaxed in relief. 'And once you've taken Ella to Rosanna in England, would you come back and be with me? I have been told of a convent hospital near Pompeii that takes the dying in their final weeks. I think I would like to go there.'

'I must speak to the seminary, but you know I'll be with you for as long as you wish.'

Carlotta stretched her hand across the table and held on to his, her eyes suddenly full of fear.

'Until the end, Luca.'

Much later, as he tucked himself up in the narrow bed he'd slept in as a child, his head spinning with confusion, Luca pondered sadly how many wrong decisions were made out of love.

39

The British Airways jumbo jet taxied down the runway at JFK. Stephen squeezed Rosanna's hand as he saw her frown.

'Okay, darling?'

Rosanna nodded and smiled weakly at him. She was beginning to wish she hadn't agreed to accompany him to New York. Nico had been crying as they'd left home at six thirty that morning and Abi had looked distinctly fraught. And now, as she left the plane and accompanied Stephen into the terminal building, she couldn't help but remember how many times in the past she'd made this walk with her hand in Roberto's.

They waited ages in the queue at immigration; Roberto and she had always been whisked straight through and out to a waiting limousine. Then they stood in another queue for a cab, eventually setting off for Manhattan. Their room at the Plaza was lovely, but it wasn't a suite with the best view. Rosanna chided herself harshly for making the comparison. Those days – *and* Roberto – were gone.

Lying on the bed, she called home as Stephen took a shower. Abi told her that Nico had settled down the minute they'd left and was now tucked up in his cot fast asleep.

Relieved, Rosanna stood up and began to hang her clothes in the wardrobe. It was only just past two New York time, and she felt fractious and exhausted.

Stephen emerged from the shower. 'That feels better. I always feel so grubby when I get off a plane.'

Rosanna nodded and continued to unpack. Stephen surveyed her. 'Is there anything you'd like to do this afternoon, Rosanna? Shopping? Sights?'

'I don't mind, whatever you wish.'

'Are you sorry you've come with me?' he asked her suddenly.

She saw the hurt expression on his face and felt immediately guilty for her churlish thoughts, which Stephen had read well enough to feel. 'No, I'm just very tired from the flight.'

He saw her bottom lip pucker and tears well in her eyes. 'What is it? Is it memories of him?'

'I'm sorry, I can't help it. I thought I was getting better, really. But coming here . . . I can't explain it.' Rosanna brushed her eyes with the back of her hand. Stephen reached for a tissue from the table and gently wiped the tears from her face.

'Don't you see that the very fact you were able to get on the plane and fly here means you *are* getting better? A few weeks ago, you'd never even have considered it. Really, darling, the amount you and Roberto travelled, if you don't face the demons now, there'll be no-go areas for you all across the globe.'

'This one is the worst. We spent so much time here and now he's made New York his home.'

'But Roberto's not here, Rosanna. He's thousands of miles away in Paris.'

'I'm so sorry, Stephen, I'm being selfish and awful. Maybe this was just too soon. Maybe I should go home. I—'

'Please stop apologising, Rosanna. If you can't talk to me about these things, then who *can* you talk to? I'd much prefer you to be open with me. It's the only chance we stand of ever having a proper relationship.'

'You're so kind, really, I don't deserve you. What would I have done without you?' she snuffled into his shoulder.

'Nothing much is the answer to that,' he chuckled. 'Now, what do you say to room service? We'll have a club sandwich and a cup of tea, and then I'm going to tuck you up in bed for a rest while I go out and see some potential clients. I want you to think where you'd like to go for dinner tonight. Does that sound okay?'

'Perfect.' She nodded gratefully.

Stephen left Rosanna in bed an hour later. She fell into a deep sleep and awoke feeling refreshed and much calmer. She showered, then chose a favourite cocktail dress to wear for the evening. She chastised herself for breaking down and being such a misery, when Stephen had been kindness itself. 'If you don't pull yourself together, you'll lose him,' she told her reflection firmly in the mirror as Stephen opened the door to their room.

'Wow, you look gorgeous.' He kissed her on the top of her head. 'Are you sure you want to go out?' he murmured, his hands travelling down the silky back of her dress.

'Of course. I've put this on specially, and besides, I'm starving. We could always eat downstairs in the hotel restaurant, then it won't be far to come back to our room, will it?' she said playfully.

They went downstairs and had a drink in the Oak Bar,

then decided to stay in and eat at the Edwardian Room. Rosanna ignored the surprised stares of several other diners as she took her place at their table.

'See? Your public haven't forgotten you, Rosanna,' said Stephen, winking at her.

At midnight, they finished their liqueurs and took the elevator to their room. As soon as he'd closed the door behind them, Rosanna kissed him hard on the lips. They fell onto the bed, tearing at each other's clothes. In that moment of passion, she felt desperate to finally exorcise the ghosts of the past.

The following day, feeling much calmer, Rosanna and Stephen went shopping. It was a long time since Rosanna had bought any new clothes, and the stores were full of lovely new-season items. Stephen followed her as she made her way through the ladies' department of Saks, appearing from the changing rooms and twirling for his approval. She insisted on buying him Ralph Lauren shirts, ties and a Dior suit in navy blue. She also chose numerous presents to take back home to Nico.

They arrived back at the Plaza laden with carrier bags. Rosanna sank onto the bed and surveyed her purchases. 'I'd forgotten what fun that could be.' She smiled. 'Abi will be proud of me.'

'You used to do this regularly, did you?'

'Oh no. I'm a once-a-year shopper. I used to go with Rob . . . I mean, go and have one day of madness in whatever city I was in. I know I spent a lot today, but those clothes will last me for the next three winters at least.'

'Rosanna, you hardly need to excuse yourself. I've never known you spend any money on yourself before. And talking of clothes, what will you wear to dinner tonight at the St Regents'? I should think it'll be quite formal.'

'Then I shall wear this.' Rosanna knelt down and opened one of the boxes. She held up an exquisite lilac silk shift dress with a matching jacket. 'Okay?'

'Perfect,' Stephen nodded.

An hour later, they were in a cab heading up Fifth Avenue.

'What does your client do?'

'He originally made his money in the oil business in Texas. He's one of the richest men in America. You'll die when you see their penthouse – it's so over the top. Lots of money, but little taste – except in art, that is,' Stephen clarified. 'The man has a collection worth tens of millions. I go there and spend the entire time staring at the walls.'

'What a waste.' Rosanna shook her head.

'What do you mean?'

'Well, surely beautiful paintings should be seen by lots of people, not hoarded like a commodity for only the wealthy to stare at?'

'I agree, but please don't say that to our host. People like him are my living, Rosanna,' Stephen teased her gently.

'Of course. I will behave perfectly,' she said primly.

The cab stopped at the canopied entrance to a prestigious apartment block on Fifth Avenue. A liveried doorman hurried forward and the two of them climbed out.

'Good evening. We're guests of Mr and Mrs St Regent,' said Stephen.

'Then you'll want the top floor, sir,' the doorman said as he led them inside and pressed the button to summon the elevator. 'Have a nice evening.'

When the doors reopened, they stepped out into a thickly carpeted corridor. Stephen rang the bell by the front door and a maid opened it immediately.

'Good evening, sir, madam. May I take your coats?'

As she handed her jacket to the maid, Rosanna saw a comely woman with bouffant blonde hair and far too much make-up hurry into the hall. She wore an obviously expensive garish purple gown, but her smile was broad and welcoming.

'Stephen, honey. I'm so glad you could come tonight. John was so excited by your little catalogue.' She kissed him on both cheeks. 'And this is . . .' The woman stared at her. 'Oh my God! You're Rosanna Rossini! Well, I'll be damned!' Trish St Regent turned and called her husband. 'Hey, Johnny, come and look who's standing in our hall!' She turned her attention back to Stephen. 'Well, sugar, I really had no idea that this little lady was your girlfriend. You dark horse, you,' she giggled girlishly.

A large, ruddy-faced man with a bald, egg-shaped head came towards them.

'So who is this mystery guest, Trish?'

She turned to her husband excitedly. 'None other than Rosanna Rossini. Do you remember us, sweetheart? We used to come to your premieres at the Met. We spoke at a party afterwards once when you were with Roberto, before you parted company. Now he lives in town, he's become a real good friend of ours and—'

Rosanna went white as the woman continued to gush about Roberto.

John St Regent saw her face. 'Trish, you're embarrassing the poor girl.' He brushed past his wife, smiled warmly at

Rosanna and held out his hand. 'John St Regent. Welcome to our home.'

'Hello.' Rosanna managed a smile as John shook hands with her, then Stephen.

'Pleased you could come, buddy. We got a lot to talk about, but later.' John offered Rosanna his arm. 'You come through with me, honey. I'll take care of you.'

Leaving Stephen in the hall with Trish, admiring a new sculpture the couple had recently acquired, Rosanna took John's arm as he led her into the magnificent sitting room.

'Champagne?' he asked her, signalling to a uniformed maid to bring over a tray.

'Thank you.' Rosanna took a glass as John steered her over to the floor-length windows.

'No better sight anywhere in the world,' he said, gesturing at the lamp-lit expanse of Central Park far below them.

'It is a stunning view, yes.'

Leaning closer he said, 'Don't mind my wife. She still sometimes behaves like the cocktail waitress she used to be – always wants to know the customer's gossip.'

As he winked conspiratorially at her, Rosanna warmed to him and relaxed a little.

'There'll be no more talk of your ex. I'll see to that, okay?'

'Thank you,' Rosanna said gratefully.

'Anyway, seems to me you've got yourself a far better guy for company now. I've known Stephen for ten years. He's a good man.'

'Yes, he is,' she responded as Trish and Stephen came into the room.

'Oh, isn't this cosy? Just the four of us. I so love intimate dinners. It means you can really get to know each other,' Trish chirped, as the maid offered Stephen a glass of champagne.

Rosanna gave an inward sigh and knew it was going to be a long night.

After dinner, Stephen and John went off to his study to talk business. Trish moved next to Rosanna on the sofa and took her hands in hers. 'Now, I know my husband asked me to lay off about Roberto, but sometimes it does you good to have a chat.' Trish looked at Rosanna expectantly. When nothing was forthcoming, she prompted: 'We see him all the time, you know. Donatella Bianchi is a friend of mine, and . . . you do know about him and Donatella, don't you?'

'Yes.' Rosanna stared down at her new shoes. She was strongly tempted to make her excuses and leave immediately. Yet there was something strangely disarming about Trish's Texan bluntness and this entire weekend was turning into a test of her mental strength. Maybe, she pondered as she listened to the woman, it could provide a catharsis, too.

'Oh honey, now I'm beginning to understand. You're still holding a candle for him, aren't you? I just thought that now you were with Stephen, that—'

'No. It's over,' Rosanna said, looking Trish straight in the eye. 'In fact, when I get back to England, I'm going to divorce Roberto.'

Rosanna was more surprised than Trish at the words she had just spoken.

'Now, I've upset you,' Trish said. 'Johnny's right, I just can't learn to keep my mouth shut.'

'No, you haven't upset me. In fact, you might have been

right, Trish. It helps to talk about it sometimes,' Rosanna said, determined now not to crack.

'Honestly, honey, you're better off without him. I know for a fact he hasn't been faithful to Donatella, but she doesn't seem to mind. They're suited, those two, whereas a delicate blossom like you needs a good old-fashioned, faithful man to tend to her. Now, more important than Roberto, when are you going to return to the opera? We've all missed you at the Met,' Trish said genuinely.

'I don't know, Trish, I really don't. Maybe when my son is older.'

'Well, as long as it's your baby stopping you and not your soon-to-be-ex-husband. You have a real gift and you can't allow yourself to waste it. One thing I've learnt about life is that it ain't a dress rehearsal. It's harder for us women. You gotta be tougher than men if you want to be happy. Take it from someone who knows.' She smiled kindly, and, for all her lack of subtlety, Rosanna knew she meant well.

'Darling, would you like to come with me and see John's most precious piece?' Stephen came into the sitting room, guessing that Rosanna might need rescuing.

'Yes, I'd love to,' Rosanna answered gratefully.

'Then follow this way.' Stephen led her by the hand through the sitting room and along a corridor virtually collapsing under the weight of stunning works of art. At the end of the corridor was a steel door. John was waiting beside it. He tapped a code into the security keypad on the wall then pushed the door open with his shoulder.

Inside, the room was dark and cramped, with only a dim picture light shining above a small frame mounted on the wall. John steered Rosanna by the shoulders to the chair facing the picture. 'There, take a look at that. Isn't it one of the most beautiful things you ever did see?'

Rosanna gazed at the drawing in front of her. It was of the Madonna. 'Who is it by?'

'Leonardo da Vinci.'

'Oh my goodness!' she breathed and stepped forward to take a closer look.

'It's a bit of a secret, Rosanna, but we trust you not to spill the beans,' said Stephen.

'You see, honey' – John stood behind her and rested his hands on her shoulders as he stared at the painting – 'sometimes you have to be cunning to acquire a special work of art. It's all a case of knowing the right dealers and I sure got lucky with this one.'

'Do you mind me asking what you paid for it?' asked Stephen.

'Several million dollars. I reckon I got it cheap, considering it's priceless. But to be honest, it isn't really the money, nor the artist. I just love that goddamn face. I sit in here for hours staring at it, you know. Trish thinks I'm crazy. Maybe I am.'

'Have you had it authenticated?' asked Stephen.

'The dealer who sold it to me was as solid as a rock and produced the appropriate paperwork. It's the real thing all right.'

Stephen nodded. 'Would you let me take a closer look at it next time I'm over? As a Renaissance expert, it's of incredible interest to me. You know, it would be of huge importance if you were to go public with your find. There are only a handful of undisputed Leonardos in the world. If this *is* one of his, it's priceless indeed.'

'Sure you can look, but I know you'll find it's kosher,' John confirmed. 'What do you think of it, Rosanna?'

'I think it's exquisite. I understand why you love it so much.'

'Got taste, your girlfriend.' John held the door open as Stephen switched off the light and they filed out of the room. Trish was sipping brandy in the sitting room.

'Had your fix, sweetie?' she asked her husband. 'Honestly' – Trish raised her eyebrows at Rosanna – 'some men get off on chasing other women, some on drink and gambling. My husband, he sits in a closet for hours and gets his kicks staring at a drawing of a virgin! Ah well,' she sighed, standing up and throwing her arms around John, 'I love him anyway.'

'I think Rosanna and I ought to be making a move.' Stephen placed a hand on Rosanna's shoulder. 'We're flying home tomorrow morning.'

'Such a shame your stay was so short,' said John.

'Well, you'll have to come back and see us soon, maybe when you decide to make an honest woman of this one. We'll throw a party for you.' Trish's eyes twinkled.

'One day maybe,' smiled Stephen, while Rosanna yet again stood beside him uncomfortably. 'I'll call the airline about shipment tomorrow, John. I reckon you should have the first painting by the end of the month.'

'Great. You see, Rosanna, sometimes you got to get in at the beginning. Spot the artists that'll be big in twenty years' time,' John explained.

'When you're in your grave,' quipped Trish as the four of them walked into the hall.

'Don't listen to her. She just doesn't appreciate art. This

landscape artist Stephen's gotten hold of, I reckon she's going to be one of them.'

'I hope you're right,' said Stephen, kissing his hostess on both cheeks. 'Thanks for a lovely evening.'

'Anytime, Stephen. And you take care of this little lady of yours, you hear?'

'I'll do my best,' he promised.

'Our chauffeur is waiting outside to take you back to the hotel,' called John as Rosanna and Stephen made their way towards the elevator.

'Thanks. Goodnight, John.'

A few minutes later, they were sitting in the back of the stretch limousine as it cruised slowly down Fifth Avenue towards the Plaza.

'What did you think of that drawing?' Stephen asked her.

'I thought it was exquisite, as I said. Is it really by Leonardo?'

'Well, it certainly looks as though it could be, but I'd have to take it through a proper authentication process to be absolutely certain. Truth be told, I'm itching to get my hands on it. If it *is* a Leonardo, it's the find of the century.'

'But what does it matter? No one but John and a few guests will ever get to see it.'

'One day they will. John was telling me of his plans to donate his entire collection to the Metropolitan Museum of Art when he dies. My goodness, I'd like to see the look on a few faces when they see that little drawing.'

Rosanna stifled a yawn. 'Excuse me.'

'You look exhausted, darling.' Stephen turned his attention back to her. 'Have you enjoyed New York? I know it hasn't been easy for you.'

'Oh yes, I really have, thank you.'

'I could have died when Trish started going on about Roberto.'

'It doesn't matter, really. And I know I have to move on. This weekend has really helped me do that.'

'Well, I'm sorry I had to leave you alone with Trish, but it was important. Look at this.' Stephen took his wallet out of his jacket and produced a cheque. 'It's for fifteen thousand dollars. Pocket change to John, but a few months' rent on the gallery for me.'

'I'm so glad for you. You obviously have a gift for spotting new talent.'

'Thank you. I just hope it continues,' he breathed. 'Did Trish quiz you when we left the room?'

'Of course she did.'

'And you coped?'

'Well, I told her I was going to divorce Roberto as soon as I got back to England.' Rosanna turned and stared out of the window.

'I . . . are you?' Stephen looked astonished.

Rosanna nodded. 'Oh yes. I am.'

40

As Stephen drove the Jaguar down the country lane that led to The Manor House, he glanced at Rosanna and saw that she was twisting her hands in her lap. 'You really have to learn to control those nerves of yours. I'm sure everything's fine with Nico,' he said gently. 'Abi would have called if it wasn't.'

'Of course it will be. I'm being silly again, I know.'

They pulled into the drive and Abi opened the front door, with Nico standing beside her.

As Rosanna stepped out of the car, Nico's eyes lit up.

'Mamma! Mamma!' He reached out for her and Rosanna ran to him and swept him into a tight embrace.

'Hello, darling, have you been a good boy for Auntie Abi?'

'Yes, he has, actually. We've had a great time, haven't we, Nico?'

'He certainly looks very well,' said Rosanna, kissing the top of his head.

'See? I managed not to maim, suffocate or electrocute him.' Abi sniffed in mock hurt and turned to Stephen. 'Honestly, you'll have to start controlling this woman of yours. If she refuses to trust me, I may not play nursemaid again.'

'Forgive me, Abi, it's the first time I've left him for more than a few hours.'

'Well, he's been absolutely fine.' The two women walked towards the house with Nico while Stephen unloaded their cases. 'Now, did you have a good time?'

'Yes, I did; we both did. You must see what I brought back with me.'

Abi glanced behind her at Stephen, heaving the bags and cases out of the boot. 'The whole of New York, from the looks of things.'

'Can you bring the bags into the sitting room, Stephen? Then I can give Nico his presents,' Rosanna called.

'I'm at your service, m'lady,' Stephen retorted, tipping his imaginary cap.

Half an hour later, the three of them were drinking tea and watching Nico playing with his new Mickey Mouse stuffed toy and miniature Chevrolet car.

'That child will be ruined if you're not careful, Rosanna,' admonished Abi.

'I like spoiling him sometimes.' Rosanna stroked her son's dark head.

'Have you told Abi of your big decision?' asked Stephen. He needed to hear her say it to someone else, to make it real.

'And what "big decision" is this?' Abi enquired.

'That I am going to divorce Roberto as soon as possible,' Rosanna answered as casually as she could.

'That's wonderful news! You *must* have had a good time in New York,' said Abi meaningfully.

The telephone rang and Rosanna crossed the room to answer it in the study. When she returned ten minutes later, her face was pale.

Stephen was immediately by her side. 'Bad news, darling?'

Rosanna nodded and sat down. 'My sister, Carlotta, is very ill. She's asked whether I would have her daughter, Ella, to stay for a while as she's in no state to look after her.'

'I see. How old is Ella?'

'Fifteen. Luca is flying over with her in two days' time.'

'The poor thing,' Stephen sighed.

'Yes,' said Rosanna, 'and I haven't seen her for years, since she was nine or ten. Now she's almost a woman.'

'Well, it'll be company for you here if nothing else. How long is she staying?' asked Stephen.

'I don't know. Luca didn't say. Would you mind going to the airport to meet them?'

'As I said, I'm at your service.' Stephen tried to lighten the atmosphere with his chauffeur impression, but Rosanna ignored him, too lost in thoughts of her poor sister. Although Luca hadn't elaborated on Carlotta's condition, Rosanna knew the news must be bad.

'Luca and I had hoped Carlotta was recovering, but, oh dear . . .' Tears came to Rosanna's eyes.

'I *am* sorry, Rosanna, truly,' said Abi. 'What awful news to return to. I wish I could stay on and try to help in some way, but sadly, now my child-minding duties are over, I really have to get back to London. Publication is the week after next. You're both invited to the launch party, of course, but I'll understand if you can't make it. Oh, and if Luca is still here, tell him he's invited too,' she added.

While Abi went to collect her holdall, Stephen sat, watching the grave expression on Rosanna's face. He reached out a hand to her. 'I'm sorry, darling. I'm not sure what I can say or do to help.'

'From what Luca said, Carlotta wants Ella away from her so she doesn't have to watch her mamma die. She doesn't wish to see me either,' Rosanna sighed. 'I can't help but feel hurt.'

'Well, I'm sure she has her reasons. And she must trust you, if she's sending her daughter into your care.'

'Yes,' Rosanna agreed, brightening a little, 'I suppose she must.'

A few minutes later, they stood outside saying goodbye to Abi.

'Bye, darling Rosanna. Thank you for everything. And if you need a chat, you know where I am. Oh, and give my love to Luca.' She started the engine and, with a wave, pulled out of the drive.

Two days later, Rosanna spent the morning cleaning her house from top to bottom. It was what she always did when she was tense. Nico followed behind her, wielding a large feather duster.

'Your cousin is coming to see us today, Nico. Her name is Ella. Can you say Ella?'

'Lala,' Nico repeated, as Rosanna plumped the pillows in one of the guest bedrooms, then placed a vase of flowers on the window ledge.

'Ella,' repeated Rosanna.

'Lala,' trilled Nico.

'There, everything is ready. Now, shall we go downstairs and have some lunch?'

Later in the afternoon, while Nico was resting, Stephen's car pulled into the drive. Rosanna watched from the sitting room window as he turned off the engine, then waited as Luca got out and opened the rear passenger door. A young girl emerged from it. She was tall and slim as a willow, with a crown of thick, dark hair. As she walked with Luca towards the house, Rosanna ran to open the front door.

'Luca, Ella . . . it's so lovely to see you both.' She hugged Luca, then kissed her niece on both cheeks. The girl looked at her aunt nervously. Her face was very pale, making her dark eyes seem even larger.

'*Come va*, Aunt Rosanna? I thank you for having me to stay,' Ella said in Italian, as she managed a weak smile.

The smile looked so familiar somehow, yet it wasn't Carlotta she was reminded of. Dismissing the thought, Rosanna put a comforting arm round Ella's shoulders and led her inside. 'How was the journey?'

'Oh, it was exciting. I've never been on a plane before. I like flying very much.'

'You must be hungry. I have some scones and jam to keep you going until supper.'

'Excuse me, but what are scones?' Ella asked as Rosanna led her into the sitting room, Luca and Stephen bringing up the rear.

'They're little English cakes. I think you'll like them. You sit down here with Luca and I'll go and make some coffee and bring it through.'

'Thank you, Aunt Rosanna.'

'Just call me Rosanna. "Aunt" makes me sound very old.' Rosanna smiled and left the room, wondering why the presence of her niece was unsettling her. Stephen followed her into the kitchen.

'Ella seems like a lovely young girl, although she didn't

speak much in the car. I'm not sure how much English she understands. She looks a bit overwhelmed, though,' he commented, taking a scone from the plate and biting into it.

'Of course. She's never been out of Naples, let alone across the sea to a strange country to stay with an aunt she hasn't seen for years. I want to make her feel at home, to help her settle down. It's the least I can do for Carlotta.'

'You know,' said Stephen, contemplatively munching on his scone, 'she reminds me of someone.'

'Who?' Rosanna asked.

'You, silly. She reminds me of you.'

Of course, that was it, that was why the smile seemed familiar, she thought. 'Stephen, please take those scones into the sitting room before you eat them all,' Rosanna scolded him affectionately.

'Then I'll be off. You need to talk to Luca and Ella, darling. I'll keep out of the way.'

'Come over for supper tomorrow then?'

'Lovely.' He kissed her on the tip of her nose and left.

'Hello, Rosanna.' Ella came into the kitchen so quietly that Rosanna didn't hear her.

'Hello, Ella, I'm just bringing in the coffee now.'

'I only came to say that, if you don't mind, I'll go to bed. I'm very tired.'

'Are you not hungry? Would you like to join us for supper later?'

She shook her head. 'No, thank you. *Buona notte*, Rosanna.'

'Goodnight, Ella.'

The girl turned and left the room. There was something

so vulnerable about her, so lonely, that a lump rose in Rosanna's throat.

'I think she knows Carlotta is dying, Luca,' said Rosanna as they sat down later together in the kitchen and ate supper.

'Maybe, but Carlotta has refused to talk to Ella about her illness, or the future.'

'How long has Carlotta got left?'

Luca put down his fork and shook his head. 'I don't know, Rosanna, but not long. Her spirit is breaking. She's in so much pain.'

'Then Ella must go back soon, before it's too late.'

'No, Rosanna. Carlotta does not want her to. She has said goodbye to her daughter.'

'But what about Ella?' She was horrified. 'Has she not the right to choose what she would like to do?'

'Carlotta has made her decision. She believes it to be for the best.'

'And after she dies? What happens then?'

'Rosanna, I have a letter for you from Carlotta. I think it will explain things better than I can. I'll give it to you after supper. Now, please, we should eat with happier thoughts. How was New York?'

'It was very good . . . and very bad.' Rosanna picked at the baked potato on her plate. 'Stephen was lovely, but I met some people who know Roberto and his mistress, Donatella Bianchi.'

Luca raised his eyebrows. 'He's back with her?'

'Yes.'

'They deserve each other, those two. They are made of the same stuff.'

'That's exactly what Trish said, that they suited each other.'

'Trish?'

'Sorry, the wife of Stephen's client in New York. She's friendly with Donatella and Roberto. It was a little awkward at first, but actually I think she's a nice person. Her husband is a billionaire with a wonderful art collection. He took me into a little room where he has an exquisite drawing of the Madonna.' Rosanna gestured with her hands to indicate its size. 'He said the drawing is by Leonardo da Vinci. He paid millions of dollars for it, apparently.'

'Really?' Luca paused, then said, 'This drawing, where did he find it?'

'I don't know. He said it was a secret, so I suppose I shouldn't be telling you. Maybe Stephen will know. You can ask him. Why?'

'Oh,' Luca shrugged, 'no reason.'

Throughout the evening, the suspicion in Luca's mind began to grow. He excused himself early and went to his room, desperate to put together his thoughts: Donatella, a friend of the art collector, a small drawing of the Madonna, reminiscent of Leonardo . . . could it be the same one, or was it merely coincidence?

The next morning, as Ella and Rosanna sat in the kitchen with Nico having breakfast, Luca went into the study. He looked through his sister's address book, found Stephen's number at the gallery and dialled it.

'Stephen, it's Luca Menici here. Excuse me for disturbing you and this may seem a strange question, but last night

Rosanna told me about a drawing of the Madonna that your client in New York has.'

'Did she indeed? She was meant to keep quiet about that one,' said Stephen sternly.

'She wouldn't tell anyone else, Stephen. Don't worry. But why is it supposed to be a secret?'

'Oh, many art collectors prefer to keep their more valuable paintings quiet. Art theft is a major problem nowadays.'

'Do you happen to know where your client purchased this drawing?'

'Yes, but I'd be breaking client confidentiality to tell you, Luca.'

'Stephen, please, it's very important that I know. You have my word I will not tell.'

'Well . . . it was a well-known Italian dealer called Giovanni Bianchi. Luca, why do you ask?'

At the other end of the line, Luca closed his eyes and shook his head in disbelief.

'Luca, are you still there?'

'Yes. Stephen, we must talk. It's a matter of great importance.'

'Well, I'm coming over for supper tonight. If I come earlier, we can chat while Rosanna baths Nico.'

'Okay, but not a word to Rosanna, please.'

'Of course not. Goodbye, Luca.'

Luca replaced the receiver, went back into the kitchen and tried to forget that his beloved church and his country may have been cheated out of a priceless treasure from right under his nose.

41

Later that afternoon, while both Nico and Ella were resting, Rosanna sat at the kitchen table and read the letter Luca had handed her from Carlotta.

Vico Piedigrotta,
Naples

My dear Rosanna,

I thank you from the bottom of my heart for having Ella to stay. It means a lot to me to know that she is with you in England, far away from what is happening to her mamma. Luca will have told you about my illness and that I have very little time left. Forgive me, Rosanna, for not wishing to see you; when death is sudden you are unable to make choices, but the one consolation I have with my slow death is that I'm able to organise it the way I wish. And I wish to see no one. Very soon I am going away to somewhere peaceful. Shortly, Luca will join me and help me through my last days.

If it seems I have made little effort to

communicate with you in the past few years and have ignored your kind offers to come and stay with you in England, I ask you to forgive me. I cannot really explain. Our lives turned out so differently and, if I'm truthful, I might have found it hard comparing yours to mine. There, I have said it. And some day, if fate chooses, you may know the whole truth and then you will understand.

Rosanna, you may wonder why I wish Ella to be away from me. My heart tells me it is right, that she should not watch her mamma suffer anymore. I know you will treat her kindly. She will be very upset for a while, but she is young and I'm sure with the love I know you will show her, she will recover in time.

I have two things I wish you to do for me. When I die, I do not want you or Ella to attend my funeral. I will be buried quietly with only Papa and Luca to lay me to rest. The second thing is – and I hope you do not feel I ask too much – I don't wish Ella to return to Naples after I'm gone. I would like her to stay with you in England. If she returns here, her life will be a repeat of mine. She deserves more. She is a very special child. Ask her to sing for you one day.

So, I'm putting her future into your hands. I have a little money saved and when I die, my lawyer will forward the amount to you to help towards her keep. I thank you now in advance for Ella's care. I know you will do your best for her.

Rosanna, do not mind that I say this, but I'm glad you have left Roberto. He is destructive and, however much you loved him, he could only bring you pain. There are some people in the world who are made like that. Luca tells me you have a good man now who cares for you in the way he should.

Finally, do not let Roberto take away your talent. You were born to sing! You MUST sing.

Goodbye, Rosanna.

Ti amo,

Your sister, Carlotta

Rosanna dropped the letter from her hands and wept.

'Rosanna, Rosanna? I . . .'

She looked up and saw Ella watching her, a worried frown on her face.

'I came to tell you Nico is awake,' Ella continued. 'Are you all right? What is wrong?' She glanced at the letter on the floor.

Rosanna quickly scooped it up. 'I'm sorry, Ella. I—'

'It's a letter from Mamma, telling you she is dying, yes?'

Rosanna saw the pain in her lovely eyes.

'I know it's why I'm here with you in England, so Mamma can die without me watching. I know I have said goodbye to her. I . . .' Ella's shoulders heaved and she began to sob.

'Yes, Ella, and I'm so, so sorry.' Rosanna went to her and held her and they cried together. Eventually, she steered Ella to the sofa, sat her down and smoothed the hair back from her face. 'I know how difficult this must be for you.' She spoke softly in Italian. 'But it's what your mamma wanted.'

'But not what *I* wanted,' said Ella in a choked voice.

'I know, I know, but she's only trying to spare you pain. She doesn't wish to see me either.'

'But she needs me, she is all alone,' Ella moaned.

'No. Luca is flying back tomorrow and he will be with her. They are very close and it's he whom she wanted.'

'But what about me? The future?' Ella shook her head. 'Without Mamma, what will I do?'

'*Cara*, she has made plans for you, so please do not worry. For the moment, you are going to stay here with Nico and me. I know it's strange and difficult for you, but it will get easier, I promise. We'll make our own little family. I'll look after you.'

'But . . . do you want me here? After all, you hardly know me.'

'Now, that's a silly thing to say, *cara*. You are my niece and I love you, Ella. And I get very lonely in this house by myself. You'll be company for me, and I can see Nico already adores you. We're both very happy to have you here, really, and we'll help each other through this, yes?'

Ella nodded. '*Sī*.'

Rosanna gave her a big hug. 'Now, I'd better go upstairs before my son thinks I've abandoned him.' She stood up and offered Ella her hand. 'Come with me?'

Ella smiled and took it gratefully. 'Thank you for being so kind.'

'So you're saying that you discovered what you think is John St Regent's drawing in the crypt of a church in Milan?'

Luca nodded, watching Stephen's unbelieving face.

'I know it's an amazing coincidence, but yes.'

'Okay. Tell me the story again, slowly.'

Luca went through how he had discovered the drawing

and the silver chalice, and how Donatella Bianchi had taken them to her husband to be valued.

'So she told you the silver chalice was worth a lot of money, but the drawing was worth next to nothing?' confirmed Stephen.

'Yes.'

'Why didn't you get a second opinion?'

'The priest and I were in a difficult position. We knew that if we told others of my discovery, the money would be unlikely to come to our church. It would be immediately swallowed up by the Vatican coffers and we needed funds urgently for restorations. So Don Edoardo, the priest at the church, agreed for Giovanni Bianchi to sell the chalice. Then Donatella said she would also buy the drawing of the Madonna as she had grown so fond of it. She gave us three million lire for it and made a large public donation to the restoration fund.' Luca shook his head. 'We trusted her, Stephen, and we needed the money. If I had known the truth, then . . .'

Stephen exhaled loudly. 'Well, if it *is* the same drawing, you've been the victim of the most amazing con. But Luca, if it's any comfort, you're not the first and you won't be the last. There are unscrupulous dealers and collectors the world over. It often works like this: the dealer discovers a painting of value and knows if he tells the authorities they'll claim it as a national treasure. It'll be hung in a public gallery and he'll receive little recompense for his endeavours. However, if he can find a private buyer, then, as you've seen, the rewards can be exceptional. I reckon at least a third of the world's most valuable paintings are hidden in secret vaults around the globe.'

Luca shook his head. 'I cannot believe Don Edoardo and I were so naive.'

'Not at all. You weren't to know this woman was lying. Anyway, before we go any further, we need to discover whether or not it *is* the same drawing.'

'I sincerely hope I am wrong and it's only coincidence. If they stole that drawing, not only from us, but from the church and Italy itself, well . . .' Luca shook his head despairingly.

'Yes, well, first let's see if it's the same drawing and take it from there.'

'Have you any idea how we do that, Stephen?' Luca asked.

'Well, as a matter of fact I did mention to John St Regent last time that I'd like to examine the drawing in greater detail. He trusts me completely.' Stephen sighed. 'So far, he has no reason to do otherwise.'

'Stephen, really, you must not compromise yourself.'

'I won't, I can assure you, but I'm prepared to examine and authenticate the drawing, and, during the process, take a photograph of it for you. But if it *is* the one you found, I'll have to insist from then on that my name is kept out of it. Discretion is the name of the game in my business.'

'Of course. I have no idea what I'd do if it is the drawing, but I must at least know the truth. Thank you, Stephen.'

'Not at all. I'm as eager to discover the truth as you are.'

'When will you go to New York?'

'Not for a couple of months, I'm afraid. I'm snowed under at the gallery. It'll be the beginning of December at the earliest. Anyway, it would be far too suspicious if I was to return to see the drawing so soon. There's another client in

New York who has a painting for me to look at and authenticate. I can kill two birds with one stone. I really suggest you try to put the whole business to the back of your mind for now.'

'I'll try, but—'

Stephen touched a finger to his lips as he saw Rosanna and Ella enter the sitting room.

Rosanna climbed into bed and the warmth of Stephen's arms.

'I'm so tired,' she yawned as she made herself comfortable.

'Ella looked happier this evening,' Stephen commented.

'We had a talk today. She does know about Carlotta – that she's dying and she's said goodbye. Carlotta wrote me a letter and God, Stephen, it's one of the most tragic things I've ever had to read.'

'I'm so sorry, darling.' Stephen pulled her closer. 'And the tragedy is that your sister's so young. There really is no rhyme or reason in life, is there? It's such a lottery.'

'Yes, it is. Carlotta wants Ella to stay here with me.'

'I know.'

'I mean, to live here permanently after she dies.'

'I see. And how do you feel about that?'

'Of course I'm happy to have her, and remember, Ella's almost sixteen. She'll want to be off to college or university in a couple of years. Talking of which, if she is staying here, I must enquire about local schools and find her an English teacher to give her private lessons. She has the basics, but she'll need help if she's to go to school here.'

'Yes.' Stephen stroked her hair gently. 'But tomorrow, darling, worry about it all tomorrow.'

'Oh, one other thing,' said Rosanna as she settled down for sleep and turned off the light, 'do you have the name of a good solicitor?'

'Yes, I do, as a matter of fact.'

'Then you must give it to me. I want to begin divorce proceedings.'

'Now, that *is* good news.' Stephen kissed the top of her head. 'Darling?'

'Yes?' said Rosanna.

'If you're divorcing Roberto, how would you feel about marrying me sometime in the future?'

'I . . . can't I just divorce Roberto first?'

'Of course. I only wanted to know if it's a possibility.'

Rosanna gently stroked his cheek. 'It is, *caro*. Goodnight.'

Before Luca left for Naples the following morning, he went into the sitting room and dialled Abi's number in London. He was nervous, as he hadn't spoken to her since the day they'd parted so painfully at The Manor House.

'Hello?' her voice sounded sleepy.

'Abi, it's Luca.'

'Luca, darling, how are you?' Her tone was warm, concerned, and he breathed a mental sigh of relief that she wasn't angry with him.

'I'm . . . okay. I'm sorry I haven't called before, but things have been complicated.'

'Don't worry. You've called now, that's what matters.'

'I wanted to tell you I'll be away for some weeks. I'm going with Carlotta to a convent hospital near Pompeii. I'll be there for as long as it takes.'

'Of course. It's just so awful. Poor Carlotta and poor you. How are you feeling?'

'Devastated, Abi, as you can imagine, but I must gather my strength for my sister. She'll need all I can give her.'

'She's lucky to have you.'

'I'll be in touch when it's . . . over.'

'Yes,' Abi said softly. 'But Luca' – she was unable to stop herself from asking – 'are you . . . missing me?'

He recalled those halcyon days of summer when the two of them had laughed and loved together. Then he thought of what he had to face in the next few weeks.

'More than you will ever know. *Ciao, cara.*'

42

'Well, Mrs Rossini, you'll be pleased to know that your husband is not going to contest the divorce.'

'Oh,' Rosanna replied sadly. She had hoped somewhere inside that he would.

'As you're divorcing him on the grounds of adultery, and Mr Rossini's not going to contest, we can petition for a *decree nisi* immediately.'

'What about The Manor House?'

'As you said, he bought it for you as a present and the deeds are already in your name. Mr Rossini will keep the house in London, as you suggested to him. He'll continue to pay you a generous allowance every month – until you remarry, that is. He has also agreed to pay the sum of two hundred and fifty thousand pounds to be put into a trust for Nico until he's twenty-one. In addition, he will bear the cost of Nico's education.' The solicitor paused. 'I really do think that we should have gone for a lump-sum cash settlement for you as well, Mrs Rossini. Your husband is a very wealthy man and—'

'No. We've been through this. All I want is the house and enough for Nico and me to live comfortably,' Rosanna replied definitively.

'Well, it's your decision.'

'Did he . . . did he ask about visitation rights?'

'No. I have the feeling, Mrs Rossini, that your husband is as eager to make a clean break as you are. But that doesn't stop him asking to see his son in the future. You must be aware of that.'

'And what about the things I have at the house in London?'

'You still have a key, don't you?'

'Yes.'

'Anytime you want to collect them will be fine. Mr Rossini lives in New York now, so he's rarely there. But if you don't wish to see him, ring and check before you go,' the solicitor suggested. 'If only every divorce was as easy as this. Your husband is being most accommodating.'

'He's being accommodating because he cannot wait to get me and Nico out of his life.' Rosanna stood up. 'Thank you for all your help.'

'Right. Well, as long as the terms are to your satisfaction, I'll write to your husband's lawyer and we should have this settled very quickly. Goodbye, Mrs Rossini.'

Rosanna left the solicitor's office and made her way through the busy Cheltenham streets to Stephen's gallery.

'What happened?' Stephen ushered her through to his office at the back and sat her down. 'What's he sticking on?'

'Nothing. Roberto has agreed to everything.'

'Then surely that's wonderful news? In a couple of months you'll be free, darling. I thought that was what you wanted, so why do you look so miserable?'

'You're right, it *is* what I want.' Rosanna forced a smile

and checked her watch. 'Could you call me a taxi? I must be getting back. I told Ella I'd only be a couple of hours.'

'Yes, of course.' Stephen searched for the relevant number on his rolodex. He dialled and booked the taxi, then replaced the receiver slowly and studied her. 'Are you *sure* this divorce is what you want, darling?'

'Yes, Stephen,' she repeated.

'Well then, when I come back from New York, why don't we take Nico and Ella away somewhere for Christmas? We could all do with a break.'

'Maybe, but we must wait and see what happens with Carlotta. Luca is telephoning me tonight to tell me how she is.' Rosanna saw the taxi draw up outside the gallery.

'Shall I come round later?'

'Yes, please.'

'Right, darling. See you then.'

Luca's footsteps echoed along the draughty stone corridor of the convent. He opened the door to Carlotta's room and walked quietly towards the bed. He sat down and gently took his sister's frail hand in his.

'How's Papa?' Carlotta murmured, opening her eyes.

Luca's eyes managed a twinkle. 'You were right.'

'About what?'

'Papa has proposed to Signora Barezi and she's accepted. They're to marry as soon as possible. He just told me on the telephone. He asked us both for our blessing.'

'You gave it?'

'Of course. You're a clever girl, Carlotta. It seems your plan has worked.'

She breathed a sigh of relief and closed her eyes. 'I knew he wouldn't last long alone.'

'Also, I telephoned England. Rosanna and Ella send their love.' Luca sat down in the chair next to Carlotta's bed. 'Rosanna sounded very miserable.'

'Why?' Carlotta's eyes were still closed.

'Because Roberto has agreed to the divorce. He won't contest it and has granted all Rosanna's requests. It seems that in two months' time, our sister will finally be free of him.'

Carlotta's eyes flickered open. Luca noticed that they shone with a light he hadn't seen there for many days.

'That's very good news. She should be happy.'

'I know, but I'm afraid she still loves him.'

'She'll forget him.' Carlotta struggled to sit upright. 'Luca, I wish you to do something else for me. Can you telephone my lawyer and ask him to come and see me? There are some details I still haven't organised.'

'It's best if you tell me, then I can see him. It will be too tiring for you.'

'No,' Carlotta said sharply. 'I wish to see him myself.'

A day later, the lawyer arrived at the convent. Carlotta insisted Luca leave them alone. When the door was closed, they talked. Finally, she handed him an envelope.

'You understand I wish no one to know of this? And it must not be posted until after my death.'

'I understand, signora,' the lawyer replied.

'Please ensure that the letter is marked "confidential" and sent care of the Metropolitan Opera House in New York. They will know the address to forward it to.'

'Don't worry. I promise I will carry out your wishes.'

'Thank you.'

When the lawyer left, Carlotta sank back onto her pillows, all her energy spent.

It was a decision she had agonised over for the past few months. She didn't wish to cause her sister any pain, and yet she felt it was important he was finally told.

The imminent divorce had finally decided her.

Soon, Roberto would know he had a daughter.

And she could at last find peace.

'Now, you have my number in New York. If there are any problems, ring me.' Stephen kissed Rosanna on both cheeks.

'There won't be,' said Rosanna.

'Two weeks seems like a long, long time to be away from you,' Stephen whispered as he held her close.

'It'll pass quickly. You'll be busy working and I'll be busy preparing for Christmas. You must go, *caro*, or you will miss your flight.'

Stephen got into his car and started the engine. 'Bye, Ella. Bye, Nico. See you soon.'

'Would you mind taking care of Nico for a few hours, Ella? I must go and collect all my things from the house in London. My solicitor has written to tell me that next week would be suitable, as Roberto is in New York. And it would be much easier alone.'

'No, of course not. We'll be fine,' said Ella.

'If you're sure. I can go on Saturday, so you won't miss any school.'

'Of course I'm sure. Nico loves his Auntie Lala, doesn't he?' Ella cuddled Nico, who wriggled in pleasure.

'Thank you, Ella. I appreciate it very much.'

'Are you okay?' Ella asked, noting the tense expression on her aunt's face.

'Yes, I'm okay.' Rosanna left the kitchen and went into the study to write out a list of the belongings she wanted to collect.

On the train on the way to London, to keep her thoughts from what she had to do in the next couple of hours, Rosanna pondered over the way Ella seemed to have adapted so very well to her new life. She'd enrolled her in a small private school in a neighbouring village. In the past two months, with the help of a tutor, Ella's English had improved immeasurably and she'd begun to make new friends. The coursework was difficult for her, but the teachers were being very accommodating by giving her extra tuition. They were confident that her English was good enough to pass a handful of exams in the summer. If she wanted to take more, they'd said she was welcome to stay on the following year. Next week, Rosanna and Nico were going to watch her school carol concert. Ella had been given a solo and had come home, eyes shining, to tell her aunt the good news.

Rosanna had grown extremely fond of her niece and admired her courage and tenacity. The twice-weekly telephone calls from Luca relaying news of Carlotta were a low point and usually resulted in a bout of tears, but for the most part, Ella seemed to have accepted the situation and was doing her best to come to terms with it. Rosanna found it comforting to be able to tell Luca how well Ella was doing.

She knew it helped Carlotta, who Luca said had been slipping in and out of consciousness for the past two days. Luca had warned Rosanna last night that he thought the end was close now, but that he felt their sister was ready.

The train pulled into Paddington station and Rosanna walked along the platform to find a telephone box. And, hands shaking, she dialled the number of the Kensington house. Even though she knew Roberto was in New York, she still wanted to double-check. The line rang for a good two minutes before she replaced the receiver and smiled her apologies at the irate businessman waiting to use it. She walked outside and caught a taxi from the rank.

'Campden Hill Road, please,' she said.

'Right you are, miss.'

Even though she knew Roberto was not in residence, Rosanna's heart began thumping as the taxi drove along Kensington High Street, turned left and drew to a halt in front of the house.

'That'll be six quid, love.'

Rosanna paid the driver and stepped out of the taxi. She stood for a moment looking up at the graceful white house. Then, taking a deep breath, she walked up the steps to the front door.

The familiar and once comforting smell of the house hit her as she stood in the hall. She felt suddenly dizzy and sank onto the bottom stair, as her breathing accelerated and she struggled to control it.

Come on, Rosanna, she told herself, *an hour is all you need and then you can go home.*

She got to her feet and felt inside her handbag for the list. It was very short and included mainly odd trinkets she'd bought and treasured as they'd travelled around the world. She walked up the stairs of the silent house, wanting to get the worst over with first. She pushed open the door of the bedroom she'd shared with Roberto and stepped inside.

Everything was exactly as it had been – even her photograph was still standing on the table next to Roberto's side of the bed. The entire house felt unlived in and Rosanna wondered how often Roberto had stayed here since they'd separated. Perhaps not at all, by the looks of it. She went to the wall-length wardrobe and opened it. There, hanging side by side with her clothes, were a number of his suits; by her shoes, his larger ones. She reached to remove the first dress, then stopped. She didn't want it or any of them; she had plenty at home. Besides, she'd never wear them – they'd be too painful a reminder.

Rosanna sat down abruptly on the bed and put her head in her hands. This claiming of her possessions had just been a poor excuse, a reason to allow herself to step back into the past. But this emptiness was the brutal reality and there was no turning back the clock.

Just one hour of remembering, then I must forget – forever, she thought.

Rosanna wandered through the house, picking up a framed programme cover of *La Traviata* at Covent Garden, crystal glasses she'd bought in Vienna, a candelabra she'd found in a flea market in Paris and placing them in the holdall she'd brought with her. Each item evoked a moment for her, a special feeling. She relived the joy, throwing herself wholeheartedly into the past, finding no pain, only pleasure.

In the drawing room, there was a photograph of the three of them just after Nico had been born. Her own eyes were alive, her face vibrant. Rosanna went across to the mirror that hung above the fireplace and studied her reflection. She knew she looked different now. Her eyes were sad and dead.

'I love you, Roberto. Whatever you have done, I will always love you, always love you,' she murmured to herself.

She walked downstairs to the kitchen and called a taxi to take her to the station. She sat down to wait, and almost without thinking switched on the cassette machine that sat in its usual place on the table. Her own voice streamed into the room, taking her by surprise.

Rosanna closed her eyes as she listened. Then she began to sing. Quietly, hesitantly at first, then as she gained the confidence of privacy, her voice drowned out the one coming from the machine. Her eyes still closed, she sang '*Sempre libera*', Violetta's heart-rending aria from *La Traviata*, as though her life depended on it.

When she finished, the silence was shattering.

Then she heard someone clapping.

She opened her eyes, the kitchen spinning a little as she did so.

There, in front of her, stood Roberto.

43

Rosanna didn't know how long they remained silent, staring at each other. His face was fuller, less angular than she remembered, and his figure bulkier, but he was still the same Roberto and her traitorous heart skipped a beat.

'*Ciao*,' he said eventually.

'*Ciao*.' She blushed. 'I didn't know you were here.' Rosanna stood up, the moment she had dreamt of, *known* would happen, now upon her. 'I must go. I was collecting a few things.'

'It's still your house too, at least for the next couple of weeks,' Roberto shrugged.

His casualness, the way he was obviously so unruffled at seeing her after all this time, tore at her soul. She desperately tried to pull herself together.

'My solicitor said you were in New York.'

'I wasn't planning to be here, but I arrived at Heathrow from a concert in Geneva and there's an eight-hour delay on my flight back to New York. There's fog at Heathrow, so I thought I'd come back here and sleep for a few hours.'

'Don't let me stop you,' she said abruptly. 'I was just leaving.'

'You're going back to The Manor House?' he asked.

'Yes. I have a cab on its way to collect me.'

'How is Nico?' Roberto was watching her intently.

'He's fine.'

'He's probably grown a lot since I last saw him.'

'Yes,' she answered as coolly as she could manage.

'You're still not intending to return to the stage?'

'No.'

'You should.'

'I have your child to care for, remember?'

'Of course. I apologise. I remember your strong feelings on the subject.'

She could take no more. 'I must go.' Rosanna walked towards the kitchen doorway in which he stood. 'Excuse me.'

Roberto made no attempt to move aside.

'Let me pass. Let me *pass*!' She hit out at him and he grabbed her by the elbows to restrain her.

'Stop it, Rosanna, stop it!'

'Just let me go . . . let me . . .' Despite herself, tears began to stream down her cheeks. 'You weren't meant to be here! You weren't meant to be here!' she repeated hysterically.

'Rosanna, *cara*, I'm sorry. Please don't cry. I can't bear to see you cry.' Roberto released his grasp on her elbows and folded her into his arms.

For a few seconds she remained taut, then her body gave up the struggle and relaxed against him as she continued to sob helplessly. He stroked her hair gently. 'Please forgive me. I was a pig just then. I'm sorry. You know it's my way of coping, *principessa*.'

The sound of him calling her by her pet name, smelling his familiar aroma and feeling his arms around her was unbearable. With enormous effort, she pulled away from him and wiped her eyes with the back of her hand.

'I'm sorry for being silly and emotional. We're grown-ups now.'

'You'll never be a grown-up in my eyes,' he murmured. 'You will always be that thin little girl in the cotton dress who sang "*Ave Maria*" at Mamma and Papa's anniversary party. Come, Rosanna, shall we have a drink while we wait for your car? For old times' sake.'

She stood, knowing with every fibre in her body she should leave now, but found that her legs refused to take her. She watched, silently, as Roberto peered into a cupboard and brought out a half-full bottle of brandy.

'This hasn't been touched since we left here. Luckily, it's one of the only things that improve with age.' He found two glasses, sat at the table and poured some brandy into them. 'Come, sit down.'

She finally persuaded her legs to move and joined him at the table.

'Rosanna, if nothing else, today has given me a chance to say how sorry I am.' Roberto took a mouthful of brandy. 'This has all been my fault. I was a bastard to do what I did. I know you can never forgive me, but I wished to say it anyway.'

Rosanna sighed, having found her voice. 'It's the way you are, Roberto,' she whispered numbly. 'It was stupid of me to think that you could be any different.'

'And the way you are,' he countered. 'Some wives would tolerate their husband's . . . *peccadilloes*.'

'While they're giving birth to their husband's child? I

doubt it,' retaliated Rosanna, feeling some reality return to her jumbled senses.

Roberto had the grace to blush. He shook his head. 'It meant nothing. I didn't love her.'

'Do you now?'

'No.'

'Then why are you with her in New York?'

'It's convenient, that's all. And Trish St Regent tells me you have someone in your life too?'

'Yes.' Rosanna berated herself for blushing.

'Are you in love with him?'

'It's too early to tell. I think perhaps in the future I could be.'

'You'll be lucky if you find love again. Me, I will not,' he shrugged.

'I don't think you know what love is, Roberto.'

'Yes I do. I know because, when you made me leave that night, I spent a week here at the house alone, crying. I've thought about you every day since we parted. There's barely an hour that goes past when I don't miss you. But what does it all matter now?' Roberto sighed, refilling his glass with brandy.

He's a consummate actor, Rosanna reminded herself. *I cannot,* must *not, believe what he's saying*. 'Then why didn't you ever contact us? Why have you not tried to see your son for eighteen months? Because you loved us?' She shook her head. 'I don't think so, Roberto.'

'I told you that night, if you made me leave without giving me a chance to explain, I would never return. Think back, Rosanna. Try to remember how angry you were. I shall never forget the way you looked at me on the doorstep. Your face was filled with such disgust, such hatred. I thought you would prefer it if I left for good. Was I wrong?'

'No, of course not,' she lied bravely. 'It was what I told you I wanted. But I thought you would contact me, if only to see Nico.'

'But don't you understand that I couldn't bear to see you or our child, knowing that I'd have to leave you both after an hour, two hours? You know how we are, Rosanna. With us, it's all or nothing. I understood you didn't want me back, so, for all our sakes, I made a complete break. Even so,' he admitted, 'I've tried to call you several times. You were obviously not at home.'

'Even I have to leave the house sometimes, Roberto.' *He's lying, he's lying*, she told herself firmly. *He's hardly thought about us at all.*

'Please, Rosanna. This might be one of the last times we talk. I'm being honest with you. I swear I have called you. At the very least, believe I still love Nico, if nothing else.'

'It's hard when you've made no effort to see him,' she countered, at last glad to feel genuine anger on behalf of her son. 'But I will try to believe it for Nico's sake, if not for my own.'

'Oh *principessa*.' Roberto swept a hand through his hair. 'Why did it turn out like this? We were so happy, the three of us. We've both lost so much. And it's all my fault, I know, I know.'

The doorbell rang, a shrill noise penetrating the tension.

Rosanna stood up. 'My taxi is here. I must go.'

'Of course.' Roberto stood up too. 'You know, *cara*, that I will never stop loving you,' he said softly.

Say it back, Rosanna, say *it*, she urged herself. *You know you belong with him, no matter what he is and how he might hurt you.*

But she didn't reply, and instead, with a huge effort of will, walked upstairs to the front door, Roberto following behind her.

'Goodbye, Roberto.' She walked down the steps, then turned back and looked up at him. 'If you want to see your son in the future, please let me know.'

Then she turned and hurried to the cab, the world a blur through her tears.

Roberto watched the taxi leave. Then he shut the front door and slowly made his way back down the stairs to the kitchen. He sat down at the table and poured himself another brandy. He could still smell her perfume hanging in the air. He felt devastated and completely empty.

Another six hours and he'd be leaving for New York, back to Donatella and a life that had everything, yet meant nothing. Roberto opened his eyes; every time he shut them, he saw her sitting in the kitchen, her lovely face still wet with the tears he had forced her to shed.

Two hours later, Roberto closed the front door behind him and stepped into the back of the car. As the driver set off, he looked behind him as the house disappeared in the fog; a dream that had become a living nightmare.

Rosanna arrived home three and a half hours after she'd left London. The fog had been dreadful and the train had been delayed. She stepped into the hall feeling emotionally and mentally drained.

'*Ciao*, Rosanna. Are you okay? You look very pale.' Ella appeared from the sitting room.

'It was a bad journey back. Is Nico okay?'

'He's fine. I've just put him to bed. Can I get you something to eat?'

'No thank you, Ella. I think I'll go upstairs and take a bath.'

'Okay. Where are your things?' asked Ella.

'What things?'

'The things you went to London to collect.'

'Oh, I . . .' Rosanna shook her head, realising that she'd forgotten all about them. 'I decided it was best if I left them there after all. Too many memories.'

Ella nodded as Rosanna slipped off her shoes and began to walk up the stairs. 'Stephen called from New York.'

'Did you tell him where I was?'

'Yes.' Ella looked confused. 'I'm sorry. I didn't realise I wasn't meant to.'

'No, it's fine, Ella.'

'He sent his love and said he would call again tomorrow.'

Rosanna nodded wearily. 'Thank you. Goodnight.'

It was past midnight and, although Rosanna had tried, sleep would not come. Eventually, she got up and rifled through the bathroom cabinet for the sleeping tablets that the doctor had prescribed when Roberto had first left her. She'd never dared to take one in case Nico was ill in the night and she didn't hear him. Knowing pills were not the answer, she replaced the bottle in the cabinet, and padded downstairs to the kitchen to make herself a hot drink. Switching on the kettle, Rosanna gazed out of the window. The fog was so thick she couldn't see the tree that stood a few feet from the house. She took her mug into the sitting room and switched on a lamp.

Then she heard a knocking sound.

Rosanna froze in fear. This was the moment she had always dreaded. Two women and a baby alone and defenceless against intruders.

The knocking came again from the front door.

But surely burglars wouldn't knock? she rationalised as she crept into the hall to try and see who it was.

'Rosanna. It's me. Let me in,' called a voice through the letterbox.

Her hands fumbling with the bolts and the chain, her heart racing, she opened the door.

'You said I was to let you know if I wished to see my son. Well, I do, so here I am. I love you, my *principessa*.'

Roberto gazed at her and held open his arms, his tired eyes filled with uncertainty.

She hesitated for a few seconds, but, unable to fight any longer, Rosanna walked tentatively back into them.

The Metropolitan Opera House, New York

So, Nico, that was how your father reappeared in our lives. When he'd arrived at Heathrow he was told his plane to New York had been cancelled due to the fog. He said later that he knew then it was fate.

Our reunion was passionate and emotional. We were two people in love who had been denied each other for over eighteen months. There were no more recriminations that night. We simply drowned in the relief of finally being reunited.

The following morning I studied my face in the mirror and knew I would not be asking Roberto to leave. I saw the sparkle had returned to my eyes. I looked genuinely happy for the first time in a year. Whatever had gone before, Roberto was my husband, and your father. We belonged together and that was all that mattered.

Nico, when I tell you what happened after this, I ask you please to try and understand how I felt about your father. The love I had for him overtook everything else. Having him back was so joyful that I was blind to the pain it would cause everyone else around me. I behaved selfishly, hurt people by actions that, under any other circumstances, I would never have contemplated.

On reflection, I've realised that we can love someone with all our hearts, but that does not mean that person is good for us. Roberto did not bring out the best in me. When I was with him, I was never in control. His very presence was like a drug. I now see clearly that it changed me for the worse.

I had Roberto back, but in having him, I lost myself.

It must be hard for you to read what I'm telling you. I've wondered many times if it's right to share these things with you, or whether I'm simply trying to assuage my own guilt. But my heart tells me you have the strength to understand. All I can say is that I always tried to do my best for you, protect you and bring you up in an atmosphere of love and security. And yet, when you really needed me, I wasn't there. And I will never forgive myself for that. Never.

44

Gloucestershire, December 1982

Rosanna awoke the following morning and turned over, hardly daring to look in case it had simply been a dream.

He was there, really there, beside her. The nightmare was ended. Life could begin again.

She lay watching him for a few moments longer, relishing the thought of their lovemaking, which had continued until just before the dawn broke. She didn't feel in the least bit weary. Every cell inside her tingled with a new energy.

Desperate to feel his arms around her again, to confirm he *was* there, that he did love her, she rolled closer and gently put a hand on his arm. There was no response. He didn't even stir. *Poor Roberto*, she thought, *he must be exhausted.*

Rosanna crept quietly out of bed and put on her robe. Unusually, there were no noises from Nico's nursery. She opened her bedroom door and padded along the corridor to his room. The cot was empty and she realised Ella must have already taken him downstairs for breakfast.

Ella . . . she must go and try to explain Roberto's presence.

Nico was sitting happily in his high chair being fed toast and honey.

'Good morning, Ella.' She greeted her niece with a smile. 'What time did he wake up? I'm so sorry I didn't hear him. Hello, darling.' She gave Nico a kiss and a hug and he painted his sticky fingers across her face.

'About half an hour ago. I knew you were tired, so I got him up.'

'Thank you, you're an angel.' Rosanna sat down at the table.

'Would you like some coffee? I've just made some.' Ella stood up and went to the machine that stood on the counter-top.

'I'd love some. Ella, there is something I must tell you.'

'Yes?'

'Come and sit down and I'll try to explain.'

Ella brought two cups of coffee over to the table and sat back down, looking expectantly at Rosanna.

'You know my husband, Roberto, and I were going to be divorced?'

'Yes. That's why you went to your old house in London yesterday, to collect your things.'

'Yes. Well, when I was there, completely by coincidence I saw him. He arrived just as I was about to leave. We talked, and late last night he came here to see me.'

'Oh. Where is he?'

'He's upstairs asleep.'

Ella nodded silently. Then she said, 'So, now you will not divorce him?'

'No, well, that is . . . I shouldn't think so. He's going to stay here for the next few days. Obviously, we have many things to discuss. And he wants to see his son.'

'Of course. What about Stephen?'

Rosanna shook her head guiltily. 'Ella, I really don't know. Roberto is my husband and Nico's father. If there's a chance we can become a family again, surely it's worth trying, don't you think?'

Ella nodded again, her face expressionless. 'Yes, I understand, but I like Stephen. He'll be hurt, no?'

'Yes, but . . .' Rosanna shook her head. 'To be truthful, I can't think about that now. I'll take some coffee up to Roberto. And tomorrow, as a thank you present for caring for Nico yesterday, I think we should go into Cheltenham and buy you a dress for your concert,' she offered as a weak, conciliatory gesture.

'Thank you, but I must wear my school uniform like the others.' Ella's tone was formal and distant.

'Well, for Christmas then.'

'That would be nice,' Ella agreed stiffly.

Rosanna lifted Nico out of his chair. 'Now, let us go upstairs and see your papa.'

Twenty minutes later, Rosanna came out of the bathroom and walked along the corridor to the bedroom. She stopped in the doorway and watched father and son curled up in bed together reading Nico's favourite Winnie the Pooh storybook. The picture was one she had dreamt of on so many occasions that it brought a lump to her throat.

'You must come down soon and meet my niece, Ella,' she said as she walked into the room.

'Of course.' Roberto looked at her over Nico's head. 'He's

so beautiful, Rosanna, and so bright. I'd forgotten how wonderful it is to spend time with him.'

'Don't forget again, will you?' she whispered.

Roberto shook his head. 'Never.'

'Papa?'

Roberto winked at her. 'See? He didn't forget me.' He bent his head forward. 'Yes, Nico?'

Nico pointed to the book in Roberto's hand. 'Read again, thank you, please.'

Ella turned as Roberto came into the kitchen an hour later. Rosanna followed behind him, carrying Nico.

'So, you are Ella,' Roberto said.

'Yes. I'm pleased to meet you,' she replied warily.

'Your aunt is treating you well, I hope?' he asked.

'*Sī*, I mean, yes, thank you, signor.'

'Please, call me Roberto. After all, I'm your uncle.' Roberto turned to Rosanna. 'Today, I've decided we will all of us go out to lunch at that wonderful restaurant we used to go to in Chipping Campden.'

'But, Roberto, you have to book weeks in advance,' objected Rosanna.

Roberto turned to her patiently. '*Cara*, you seem to have forgotten, there is always room for Roberto Rossini and his wife and family. I will call the *maître d'* now.' Roberto walked across to use the phone. He made a reservation, then came to sit down at the kitchen table. Rosanna bustled around the kitchen, making fresh coffee and toast.

'Whose are those?' Roberto pointed to a large pair of wellington boots standing by the kitchen door.

Rosanna blushed. 'They are my friend Stephen's.'

Roberto stood up and marched across the kitchen, picked up the boots, then opened the bin and dropped them unceremoniously inside. 'Now, lunch is at one o'clock. Will you bring the coffee and toast through to the study, Rosanna? I must call Chris and tell him where I am.'

'Of course, Roberto.'

As Ella watched this exchange, she knew things would be very different at The Manor House from now on.

Over lunch, Roberto was on top form, entertaining the three of them – and the rest of the restaurant – with operatic anecdotes. Ella sat quietly, watching the happiness on Rosanna's face with trepidation.

Later that night, Roberto and Rosanna lay on the rug in front of the fire.

'She's a strange one, your Ella,' commented Roberto.

'No, she's very sweet and kind, but a little shy, especially of you,' said Rosanna, running to Ella's defence.

'Am I that frightening?' he grinned.

'You can be a little . . . overpowering, yes.'

'Then I'm sorry.'

'You must treat her gently. Although she has come to terms with Carlotta being so ill, she still waits every day to hear the worst, as I do. Please don't forget that.'

'Of course. It must be hard for both of you.'

'It is.' Rosanna gazed into the fire. 'Roberto . . .' – she had to ask him – 'will you be staying?'

He reached for her hand and squeezed it. 'Of course, *principessa*. I belong with my wife and my child, unless you wish to continue with the divorce?'

'No, of course not.'

'Good. Then I will let my lawyer know.'

'We'll have many things to talk about, organise. I mean—'

Roberto put a finger to her lips. 'Hush, Rosanna, don't spoil this moment with thoughts of the future. You always did worry too much. I have no engagements until after the New Year. Why don't we simply enjoy Christmas together and then talk?'

'Will you tell Donatella?'

'Will you tell your "friend"?' Roberto countered.

'I will have to. He's expecting to spend Christmas here with us.'

'Then he'll be disappointed, but it can't be helped,' he replied lightly, but the muscles in his jaw betrayed his tension. 'I am your husband, the only man who truly loves you and understands you.' As his lips sought hers and a hand caressed her breast, Rosanna knew there would be no further talking tonight.

The following Tuesday afternoon, Roberto, Rosanna and Nico drove to Ella's school to watch the carol concert. Every head turned towards Roberto as he entered. He smiled graciously as the three of them took their seats towards the back of the hall.

'Mrs Rossini.' A flustered headmistress approached them. 'I had no idea you were bringing your husband. Please, there are seats available in the front row.'

'Thank you for the offer, but we can see very well from where we are. I don't wish to put any of the artistes off,' Roberto whispered.

'Well, I do hope you'll both be staying for a cup of coffee afterwards?'

'Of course,' Rosanna nodded, and the headmistress hurried off to see if the local paper could send a photographer immediately to take a photo of the *coup* that was taking place at her school.

The concert began. Roberto looked at Nico, who had fallen asleep on Rosanna's lap, and wished he could do the same.

Then he heard the voice. A low, deep sound, full of colour, and he looked up with interest at the stage. There stood Ella, her shoulders hunched with nervousness, her thin body almost disapproving that such a strong, powerful sound should be coming out of it. Ella reminded Roberto of the first time he had seen Rosanna – all arms and legs and huge dark eyes. One day, like her aunt, she would be a beauty.

'. . . All is calm, all is bright,' she sang. Roberto looked at Rosanna, who was also gazing up at her niece in amazement, and nodded at her in approval, then turned his attention back to Ella. There was no doubt she had an exceptional voice. It was very different from Rosanna's: it was a mezzo, or possibly even a contralto.

When Ella had finished singing, Rosanna turned to Roberto, her eyes bright with tears. 'If only Carlotta could have heard that.'

After the concert, Roberto and Rosanna did their duty and chatted to other parents and teachers over coffee.

'Ella has a voice that must be trained.' Roberto put his hand proprietorially on his niece's shoulder as he talked to her headmistress.

'Well, with your gift and your wife's, it's of no surprise, is it?' The headmistress smiled.

'Unfortunately, this has nothing to do with me. I'm only related to Ella by marriage,' corrected Roberto.

'Of course, we spotted her talent as soon as Ella came here,' the headmistress burbled on, her face growing pinker by the second. 'She was so shy when she arrived, but we've worked very hard to bring her out of her shell.'

'And you've done a remarkable job, has she not, *cara*?' Roberto turned to Rosanna.

'Yes.' Rosanna was trying to stop Nico from grabbing the chocolate biscuits the headmistress was holding.

'Do you have an ambition to be a singer, Ella?' Roberto looked down at her.

'Oh yes.' Ella smiled shyly, unused to being the centre of such attention and praise.

'Then we must find you the finest teacher in England. It is never too early to begin training, is it, Rosanna?'

'Oh no, absolutely not,' she agreed.

'Well, we can arrange private lessons here, Mr Rossini, and . . . oh, would you all mind very much having your photograph taken with me? It's just for the local paper,' the headmistress encouraged.

Roberto put his arm around the woman's shoulders and smiled as the camera flashed, Nico wriggling in Rosanna's arms. 'And now we must go home,' he stated. 'My son has had enough.'

'A Merry Christmas to you all,' the headmistress called, as the four of them walked towards the door.

The next day, Roberto declared he wanted to take Rosanna into Cheltenham to do some Christmas shopping.

'Would you mind looking after Nico for us, Ella? We

want to buy him his presents from Santa Claus,' Rosanna asked her.

'Of course not.'

'We shouldn't be more than a couple of hours,' she added, not wishing her niece to feel left out, or as though she was being used as an unpaid babysitter.

'Don't worry. I like looking after Nico,' Ella smiled, still on a high from the night before.

After Rosanna and Roberto left, she went into the kitchen to tidy up from breakfast and hummed along to the carols on the radio as Nico played with some toys on the floor. When Roberto had burst unexpectedly back into Rosanna's life, Ella had feared the worst – that she would no longer be welcome as part of the family she'd grown so fond of. But this morning, she felt happier than she had for a long time. The great Roberto Rossini had said she had talent. He was finding her a singing teacher and had suggested that next year she try for a place at the Royal College of Music in London. Although thoughts of her mamma were never far from her mind, even those couldn't dampen her spirits today.

She heard a car pull up in the drive and went to the front door to see who it was. Her heart dropped to her boots as she watched Stephen climb out of his Jaguar.

'Hello, Ella.' He smiled at her as he opened the passenger door and retrieved two carrier bags full of parcels. 'How are you?'

'I'm well. We didn't expect you back until Friday,' she replied nervously.

'I finished my business in New York faster than I thought, so I flew back early.'

There was a crash from the kitchen and the two of them

ran inside to see what had happened. Nico had pulled a biscuit tin onto the floor and the contents had spilt out. He was collecting the broken biscuits one by one and stuffing them into his mouth with relish.

'I see Nico's fine then.' The child gave a shriek of delight as Stephen picked him up and kissed his crumb-covered face. 'How are you, little chap?' he asked. 'And where's your mamma?'

'She's gone shopping. For Christmas presents, I think,' said Ella cautiously.

'Oh, then we'll wait for her to come home. She won't be that long, will she?' Stephen said, sitting down at the table with Nico in his lap. 'Did she take a taxi?'

'Er, no. She got a lift.'

'Who from?'

Ella did not reply. 'Would you like some coffee, Stephen?'

'I'd love some, yes. Ella, what's happened?' he asked her gently as she filled the machine.

'Nothing.'

'Look, I know something's up. I called on Sunday and there was nobody here. Then when I phoned from Heathrow this morning, the receiver was picked up and then put down again as soon as I spoke.'

'Stephen' – Ella's voice was low and she did not turn round – 'you had better talk to Rosanna. It's not my place to tell you.'

'I'm sorry, Ella, but I think I can guess: when Rosanna went to the house in London, she met Roberto. He's back, isn't he?'

Ella turned round, her eyes wide, her face pale. 'I didn't tell you, Stephen, please. You guessed.'

'And I guessed right, too. I knew it, I knew it.' He shook his head and sighed despairingly. 'I told her not to go to London without me.'

Ella wondered if he was about to cry. The misery on his face was obvious. 'Come, Nico.' Ella took the child from his arms, placed him on the floor by his toys and put a cup of coffee on the table in front of Stephen.

'I'm sorry.' She patted his arm mechanically, not knowing what else to do.

'No, *I'm* sorry,' he sighed. 'This isn't fair on you. Do you know if Roberto's staying?'

'For Christmas? Yes, he is.'

'I see.' Stephen looked down at Nico. Then he stood up, leaving his coffee untouched.

'Look, it's best I leave. There's a pile of toys in the hall for Nico, and a couple of presents for you and Rosanna.' He knelt down and kissed the top of Nico's head. 'Bye-bye, little chap. You be good now.'

'Bye-bye.' Nico looked up at him and smiled obliviously.

'What shall I tell Rosanna?'

'Just tell her I called in. Goodbye, Ella. Take care of yourself. Merry Christmas.' He kissed her lightly on the cheek and left the kitchen.

Ella went to the window and watched him as he walked to his car, his devastation palpable in his hunched shoulders and lowered head.

'Goodbye, Stephen,' she murmured sadly.

45

Christmas passed in a haze of happiness for Rosanna. During the festive week they stayed at home, enjoying lazy days sitting by the fire watching Nico play with the extravagant toys Roberto had bought him. In the evening they settled down to supper, a film and languid lovemaking afterwards.

The only thing that spoilt the tranquillity for Rosanna was thoughts of Stephen. Ella had told her of his visit, and she'd immediately hidden the presents he'd left for them all, not wanting Roberto to know he'd called round. Rosanna knew she should telephone him, arrange to meet and explain things to him in person, but just now, with the euphoria of Roberto's return, she simply couldn't face a showdown. The guilt of her inability to do so ate away at her.

At the end of the week, on New Year's Eve, Roberto took Rosanna and Nico into Cheltenham for lunch. Ella had declined to join them, saying she had a headache and didn't feel up to it. The three of them arrived home at four o'clock to a silent house.

'Ella? Ella?' Rosanna called from the hallway.

Getting no response, she ran up the stairs. Ella's bedroom door was closed. She knocked, but there was no reply so she pushed the door open. Ella was sitting on the window seat. Her knees were curled up to her chest and her arms were closed tightly around them. She was looking out of the window, motionless as a statue.

'Ella, what is it?' The girl did not acknowledge her presence. Rosanna walked over to her. '*Cara*.' Rosanna sat down next to her. 'Tell me, please.'

'Luca called. Mamma died at eleven o'clock this morning.'

With a supreme effort, Rosanna fought back her own devastation at the news for Ella's sake. 'Oh *cara*.' She reached out a hand to her niece. 'I'm so, so sorry.'

'She is all I have . . . *had* . . .'

Rosanna moved closer and put her arm round her shoulders, feeling her tension. 'You have us, Ella, really.'

'But you don't want me. I'm an intruder here. Now you have Roberto back, I'm in the way.'

'Ella, please don't say that. I love you and Nico adores you. You're an important part of our family.'

'I just . . . I thought I had prepared myself. I knew it would happen, but now it has, I . . .' She looked up at Rosanna with anguished eyes. 'She didn't want to see me when she was dying and now Luca says she doesn't want me at her funeral! Why? *Why?* Rosanna, did she not love me? Was that it?'

'No, Ella! Listen to me. The reason she has done these things is because she loved you so very much. She wanted to spare you the pain of watching her suffer, and now she doesn't want you to stand by her graveside and weep. Her plans for you meant she was prepared to lose you sooner than she needed to. She did it for you, Ella, can't you see?'

'She was my mamma. I want to say goodbye to her, I want to say goodbye . . .' Ella crumpled suddenly and sobbed onto Rosanna's shoulder. 'What will become of me now? I can't stay with you forever. I must go back to Naples.'

'Oh Ella.' Rosanna stroked her hair. 'Do you hate it so much here?'

'No, of course not, but it isn't my home.'

'Ella, Roberto and I, and most importantly your mamma, want you to make your home here with us. You know she wrote me a letter asking me to take care of you until you were old enough to take care of yourself. And in that letter, she said she thought you stood a better chance of developing your singing talent here, where we can help you.'

'So' – Ella looked up at her – 'you will do this because it's your duty? Because Mamma has asked you to?'

'No.' Rosanna gently smoothed the long dark hair back from Ella's face, understanding her vulnerability and wanting to reassure her. '*Cara,* when you first arrived here, I hadn't seen you for many years. We were strangers, and we had to get to know one another. But since then, you've become like a daughter to me, and a good friend too. I'd hate to see you leave. Really, *cara*. I have grown to love you.'

'You are sure you're not just saying these things, Rosanna?'

'You know I'm not. But it must be your decision, Ella. If you wish to return to Naples, no one will stop you. Remember, though, your mamma sent you away because she didn't want you to end up running the café for your grandfather as she did. If there's one thing I know Carlotta wanted, it was to give you your chance, your future, at whatever the cost to herself.'

'Because she never had hers,' murmured Ella. 'She was so beautiful, I've often wondered why she didn't want more from life.'

'She did once,' mused Rosanna. 'Then something went wrong, Ella. I'm not sure what it was, but she changed. If you want to make Mamma happy, then you must use your talent and the opportunity she planned so carefully to give you.'

'You really think I have talent, Rosanna?'

'Oh yes, *cara*, and so does Roberto.'

'And you honestly don't mind having me here?'

'No, I honestly don't.' Rosanna kissed the top of her niece's head tenderly. 'Now, why don't I go and get us both a cup of tea?'

Later that evening, when Rosanna had sat with and then soothed an exhausted, distraught Ella to sleep, she came downstairs. Roberto was watching a film in the sitting room, a half-eaten sandwich on a plate in his lap.

'How is she?' he asked, without looking up.

'Much calmer. The poor thing.' Rosanna slumped onto the sofa. 'I remember only too well what it's like to lose your mamma very young.'

'At least your sister was lucky she has you to take care of Ella for her.'

'It's the least I can do,' said Rosanna. 'I'm family.'

'Ah, the Italian way,' said Roberto, glancing at her briefly.

'No, the *human* way. And remember, I too have lost a loved one today.'

Roberto didn't respond to her comment. He took a bite of his remaining sandwich. 'I made myself a snack as there was nothing else for dinner.'

'Roberto, stop it! What's wrong with you? Why are you behaving so selfishly?'

'Because, my darling, I have to go away in two weeks' time. I have a concert in Vienna. I wanted you and Nico to come with me, but now I suppose you won't be able to.'

Rosanna stared at him in disbelief. 'No, you know I won't. How could you even imagine that I would leave Ella alone at the moment?'

Roberto said nothing and continued eating.

'How long will you be away?' Rosanna was outwardly calm, but anger was beginning to smoulder inside her.

He shrugged. 'Three weeks, I think, maybe more. I must call Chris and finalise the itinerary tomorrow morning. Maybe you could join me in Vienna later?'

'I doubt it very much,' Rosanna replied coldly. She stood up. 'I'm going to bed now. Goodnight, Roberto.'

Rosanna was awoken later by Roberto gently nuzzling her neck. '*Cara, cara*, I'm so sorry for being selfish. You're grieving for your sister and I behaved like a complete bastard.'

'Yes, Roberto, you did,' she agreed with feeling. 'How could you be so insensitive?'

'It's only that I hate the thought of us being apart so soon. It made me react badly. Say you forgive me. Please?'

Even though she was still furious with him, Rosanna rolled over and let him kiss her.

'Please try to think of others occasionally, Roberto.'

'I will. *Ti amo*, Rosanna.'

And then, as always, the last vestiges of her anger disappeared as he began to make love to her.

*

'Stephen?'

'Yes?'

'It's Luca. How are you?'

Stephen paused before he answered. 'I'm . . . okay. How is your sister?'

Luca hesitated for a moment before answering quietly: 'She died two weeks ago. Did Rosanna not tell you?'

'No. I . . . I've been busy recently and haven't seen her. I'm very sorry for your loss, Luca.'

'In many ways it was for the best. At the end, she was in so much pain. And now Carlotta has been laid to rest, I must begin to get on with life and make some decisions of my own. Stephen, now you've visited New York, have you any further details on the drawing?'

'Yes, I have, as a matter of fact. I've been waiting for you to call me. We need to talk, Luca, but not on the telephone. Will you be coming over to England soon?'

'Yes. I want to see Ella, but I have a few things to organise here in Naples for Carlotta before I fly over.'

'Then give me a ring when you know when you're arriving.'

'I shall see you at Rosanna's, surely?'

'I'm afraid quite a few things have changed since we last spoke,' replied Stephen brusquely. 'So no, you won't. But I'll leave Rosanna to tell you all about that. Goodbye, Luca.'

Donatella opened the door to Roberto's apartment. She picked up the pile of mail that lay on the doormat and took it over to the table.

She marched through the sitting room into Roberto's bedroom and flung open the wardrobes. Her first instinct was to get a knife from the kitchen and slash every item of his clothing that hung inside. But that was childish, and too ineffectual. He deserved far, far worse.

She pulled out several of her suits, skirts and cocktail dresses and threw them onto the bed. She emptied out two drawers of lingerie: the black suspenders Roberto had liked her to wear, the silk stockings that his hands had caressed as they made love . . . Donatella swallowed hard. She would not shed a tear. Oh no. She would take her emotion and turn it into anger, just as her therapist had suggested.

'I hate you, I hate you,' she muttered under her breath as she pulled a large suitcase out from the top shelf of a cupboard and began throwing her clothes inside it. 'I will punish you, I will punish you,' she repeated as she closed the suitcase and left the room.

It took her barely fifteen minutes to collect the few things she had in Roberto's apartment. Then she sat down at the table and took a pen from her handbag.

Should she leave him a note? What could she say to him? Was there *anything* that might frighten him? Shake the unbearable arrogance from him just for a few seconds?

When Roberto had not returned from the concert in Geneva, and she'd heard nothing from him, she had called Chris Hughes. He'd told her that Roberto was in England, but that he had no idea where he was staying or how long he'd be there. Donatella had screamed at Chris, telling him that she could guess exactly where Roberto was staying. Chris had not denied it. She'd slammed the telephone down and, later, she'd gone out to a cocktail party and got very, very drunk.

The following morning, she'd woken up hung-over and

reflected that there was every chance Roberto would turn up in the future, brazen it out and expect her to accept the situation. She'd made herself a Bloody Mary and asked herself whether she *was* prepared to accept this too.

It had taken a long time to come to the conclusion that she wasn't. He'd used her for almost ten years, treating her like a piece of rubbish that he could throw away whenever the mood took him. She'd kidded herself for years that he would one day forget Rosanna and marry her instead. Donatella knew now this had been a fantasy.

She'd packed her Louis Vuitton bags and spent Christmas with some old friends in Barbados. Every night when she was alone in bed, her resolution had become stronger and stronger. And, slowly, the love began to turn to burning hatred.

Donatella bit her lip. It was hard to keep that feeling going, sitting amongst Roberto's things, in an apartment where they'd shared so much. Had she meant anything to him? *No*, she answered herself brutally, and knew it was the truth.

She wanted to punish him, make him hurt, as *she'd* hurt so many times; make him feel the true pain of loving and losing.

She'd wracked her brains over the past month to try to think of some way she could teach him a lesson he'd never forget. But the man was seemingly invincible. She could go and sell her story to the newspapers, but that would only give him the attention he relished, as well as demeaning herself. There seemed to be no skeletons in his closet that he hadn't already revealed.

Donatella tapped her pen on top of the table and picked

up one of the envelopes from the pile of post to write her farewell message on. It was a bank statement. On impulse, she opened it, looked at the amount at the bottom and saw he had over two hundred thousand dollars in his current account. Disinterestedly, she tossed the piece of paper aside. It wasn't financially she wanted him to suffer.

She pulled the pile of post towards her and began to work through it methodically. She opened bills, party invitations and several Christmas cards from females she'd never heard of, discarding them on the floor after a cursory glance. Then she came to a bulky envelope of thick cream vellum. The postmark was Italian. It was marked 'Private and Confidential' in the left-hand corner and had been forwarded from the Metropolitan Opera House. Donatella tore it open. Inside was a letter and another envelope. She began to read.

Castellone Solicitors
Via Foria
Naples

Dear Signor Rossini,

I enclose a letter to you from my client, Signora Carlotta Lottini. She instructed me to send this letter to you on her death. Sadly, Signora Lottini died on 31 December 1982. I would ask you to confirm you have received it. If you need my assistance, do not hesitate to contact me.

I look forward to hearing from you,
Marcello Dinelli
Lawyer

Donatella picked up the second envelope, addressed to Roberto in spidery writing. Without further hesitation, she ripped it open and began to read.

Several minutes later, after she had reread the letter twice, Donatella began to laugh. She laughed so much that her stomach muscles began to hurt.

Eventually, wiping her eyes, she stood and looked above her.

'Thank you, Lord, thank you.'

46

'Did you ask Abi, *principessa*?'

'Yes, Roberto. She says she's too busy editing her book to come here for the weekend.'

'But I *must* see you. Can't you leave Nico with Ella for two nights? You know how he adores her.'

'No, Roberto. I know she's almost sixteen, but it isn't fair to give her that level of responsibility. Besides, I wouldn't like to leave Ella alone yet either. She's still grieving, remember.'

'I am so lonely here, *cara*. I have this big hotel suite with a large bed. I need you with me,' he moaned.

'Don't do this to me, Roberto, please.' Rosanna was on the verge of tears.

'I think you love your son and niece more than you love your husband. Well, I shall go and leave you to them.'

'Roberto, that is so unfair. I—' Rosanna heard the click of the receiver being replaced. 'Damn you!' She slammed the telephone down hard and slumped into a chair at the kitchen table.

'What is it, Rosanna?' Ella asked from the doorway.

'Oh, nothing,' sighed Rosanna. 'Just my impossible husband. Take no notice. Would you like a cup of tea? You look half frozen. How was school?'

'Fine, and yes, please, I'd love a cup of tea, I'm getting quite a taste for it! It's very cold indeed out there. It may snow.' Ella took off her coat, her school hat and gloves. 'Roberto wishes you to go to Vienna, yes?'

'Yes.' Rosanna miserably threw two teabags into the pot. 'I thought my friend Abi might come up for two nights and take care of you and Nico, but she's too busy.'

'Rosanna, you know I can take care of Nico. If you wish to go to Vienna, we'll be fine.'

'No, Ella.' She added water to the pot and stirred it disconsolately. 'I couldn't ask you to do that. It wouldn't be fair.'

'But for two nights? We would be okay, really.'

'You're nearly sixteen, Ella, and—'

'Yes, old enough to be a mother myself,' she countered. 'I was often left alone for the night when I babysat in Naples. It would cheer you up to see Roberto, wouldn't it?' Ella continued.

Rosanna poured the tea into two mugs, added milk and sat down at the table. 'When he came back, I understood that we'd be separated, but I'd forgotten how hard it was. It's the same nightmare as the old days all over again. I'm sorry, I shouldn't be telling you my problems.'

'You've listened to mine many times. You've been a friend as well as an aunt. I hope I can be your friend too.'

'You are, Ella, and I'm very glad you are here. Honestly, I would have gone mad without you.'

Ella smiled. 'I'm happy you feel that way. You've helped me, Rosanna, so please let me help you. Telephone Roberto and say you'll go to him in Vienna this weekend. I'll at least feel I'm repaying some of your kindness.'

'Thank you for offering, Ella. I appreciate it and I promise I'll think about it. Now, I must go and wake Nico.'

Rosanna stood up and left the kitchen. As she walked upstairs, she thought about what Ella had said. She was so tempted. Roberto's absence had put her yet again on an emotional roller coaster. She picked Nico out of the cot as the telephone rang. Ella must have answered it, for the sound ceased after two rings.

'How would you like to be a cosmopolitan little boy and travel round the world with me and your papa?' she asked Nico as she laid him on his mat and changed his nappy.

Carrying Nico back downstairs, Ella smiled at her. 'That was Roberto. He called to apologise.'

'Oh, did he now?'

'So I told him that you've changed your mind and are flying to see him this weekend. He was very pleased. He said you should let him know what time you would be arriving in Vienna.'

'But Ella, I—'

'It is all arranged. And you cannot let him down now, can you?'

Rosanna looked at her niece in an agony of indecision, then smiled gratefully. 'Thank you, Ella, thank you.'

On Saturday morning, Rosanna was awake at six o'clock. She showered and dressed, then went down to the kitchen and prepared some vegetables. She fried them with some minced beef and garlic, then added herbs and chopped tomatoes to make a bolognese sauce. She wanted Ella and Nico to have something tasty to eat that evening. While the mixture was simmering, she sat at the table and wrote down a lengthy set of instructions for Ella, starting from breakfast in the morning, right through to bedtime.

Feeling silly because, after all, Ella was involved in Nico's routine every day, she set them by the telephone, then added the Imperial Hotel's number in Vienna, along with those of the local doctor and Abi's flat in London. That done, she took the pan of sauce off the stove, put a lid on it and left it on the worktop to cool. She checked her watch and went upstairs to finish packing.

Rosanna touched one of Nico's cheeks. 'He feels a little hot,' she said, frowning.

'He's fine, aren't you?' Ella cuddled Nico to her as they stood together in the hall an hour later. 'He's been running around a lot this morning, that's all. Now go, Rosanna, or you'll miss your flight.'

'Bye-bye, *angeletto*.' She kissed Nico again, then picked up her overnight bag. 'Any problems, please ring me at the Imperial, or call Abi or—'

'I will! Go now, Rosanna. Please!' Ella laughed.

Rosanna sat in the back of the taxi and waved until the car turned out of the drive and she could see them no longer. What if Nico was sickening for something? He had felt hot, she was sure of it. She comforted herself that it was probably a tooth coming through, which always made his cheeks red. It was only her guilt making her paranoid. Besides, what was the point of going to Vienna if she was going to worry about Nico all weekend?

With an effort, Rosanna turned her thoughts from her

child and concentrated instead on the pleasure of seeing her husband in a few hours' time.

'Stephen, it's Luca. I'll be flying into London tomorrow morning.'

'Ah, right. What time?'

'My flight gets in to Heathrow at ten o'clock. I'll catch a train to Cheltenham and I should be at Rosanna's sometime after lunch. Could you come over tomorrow evening?'

'Best that I don't.' Stephen was amazed that Luca still seemed unaware of Roberto's return and his own subsequent departure from Rosanna's life. 'Look, I'm in London tonight. I'll pick you up from Heathrow tomorrow morning and give you a lift up to Gloucestershire. We can discuss the situation on the way.'

'That's most kind of you, Stephen. I'll call Rosanna and tell her what time I'll be arriving.'

'Right you are. Goodbye.'

Luca put down the receiver and picked it up to call Rosanna. The line rang and rang. He put it down and decided he would try later.

Ella heard the telephone ring, but Nico was having a rare screaming fit, banging his small knuckles into the floor and refusing to turn over so she could change his nappy. By the time she reached the telephone in Rosanna's bedroom, it had stopped ringing.

Nico had at last quietened in her arms. She felt his forehead. He did feel warm. Ella carried him downstairs to feed him some junior paracetamol as Rosanna had instructed.

*

'*Principessa*! You are here, you're really here!'

Rosanna dropped her bag as she was swept off her feet and into Roberto's arms. He carried her inside the suite and threw her onto the bed.

'How I have missed you, how I love you,' he moaned as he smothered her face in kisses and began undoing the buttons of her coat.

'I must telephone Ella first,' said Rosanna, pulling away from him.

'Later, *cara*, later.' His lips silenced her and she gave in.

Afterwards, they drank a glass of champagne in bed and Roberto filled her in on his plans for the weekend. 'Tonight there is a grand ball at the Hofburg Palace. We'll go straight there from the performance.'

'But, Roberto, I've brought nothing with me to wear! You should have told me.'

'Go and have a look in the wardrobe, *principessa*,' Roberto said.

Rosanna got out of bed and walked across the room. There, next to his dinner jacket, was a dress sheathed in polythene.

'I would have wrapped it but I thought it would crease. See if it fits you,' he urged.

Rosanna removed the polythene to reveal a shimmering black ballgown. It had a dramatic full skirt, fashioned from layers of floating tulle, and the strapless brocade bodice was covered in thousands of tiny beads.

'Roberto, it's the most beautiful dress I've ever seen.' Rosanna took it off the hanger and stepped into it. 'Can you do me up?' she asked.

'Most certainly, signora, if you promise to let me *undo* it later.' Roberto hooked the delicate seed-pearl buttons into their fastenings and Rosanna surveyed herself in the mirror. 'It could have been made for you.' Roberto nodded approvingly.

Rosanna turned round and, as she did so, the skirt caught the air and flew out. 'Oh, it's so wonderful. Thank you, Roberto. Thank you.'

'You will be the most beautiful woman at the ball.' He smiled. 'And you'll come to watch me sing Don José tonight, won't you?'

'Yes, of course.'

Roberto kissed her neck and began to undo the buttons he had so painstakingly fastened only minutes before.

An hour later, Rosanna was putting on her make-up and Roberto was getting ready to leave for the theatre. 'Oh Roberto!' Her hand suddenly flew to her mouth. 'I didn't call home.' She reached for the telephone and dialled The Manor House.

'Ella, it's Rosanna.' A frown crossed her forehead. 'Why can I hear Nico crying?'

'He's a little tired, I think. And he has a slight temperature, Rosanna.' Ella's voice sounded tense.

'Is he sick?'

'He's not eaten much today. I think he's okay, but he's not quite himself. I'm just going to put him to bed.'

'Then I must come home immediately.'

'What?' whispered Roberto, overhearing the conversation.

'Hold on one moment, Ella.' Rosanna covered the receiver with her hand and looked at Roberto. 'It's Nico. He has a temperature. I—'

'Let me speak to Ella.' Roberto grabbed the telephone. He talked fast in Italian, nodding occasionally. Then he said goodbye and put down the receiver before Rosanna could retrieve it from him.

'What do you think you're doing? I wanted to speak to her again, to find out whether—'

'Rosanna, please. I've talked to Ella and she says Nico has a temperature, but that is all. It's nothing to worry about, *cara*. It could be teething, a little cold perhaps, but you running all the way home to England won't help him. He'll be fine in the morning, I'm sure.'

Rosanna shook her head. 'But, Roberto, what if he's really sick? I've rarely known him to have a temperature before.'

'*Principessa*, Nico has you twenty-four hours a day. I have you for forty-eight hours, then you will go home to him. Please, can you not put your son out of your mind and give yourself to me for the time we have? I'm beginning to think you're paranoid about that child of ours.'

Rosanna hesitated for a moment, fighting her maternal instincts, which were telling her loud and clear that something was wrong. But she didn't want Roberto thinking she was being overprotective. Finally, she nodded. 'You're right. I'm sure he will be fine.'

'Come now,' he whispered. 'Put on your beautiful gown and let us show the world we are reunited.'

Ella rubbed Nico's back until he finally fell asleep. Then she crept out of his room, doing her best not to disturb him. She went down to the kitchen clutching the baby monitor, and made herself a sandwich. She ate it without even tasting it, then went up to her bedroom and fell into an exhausted sleep.

Rosanna sat in the box and surveyed the glittering spectacle beneath her. The Vienna State Opera House was one of her favourite theatres, perhaps because the ornate golden balconies reminded her of La Scala. She looked down into the pit where the orchestra was warming up. The usual frisson of excitement ran through her as she waited for the performance to begin.

Tonight, the opera was *Carmen*. Don José was a role she had never seen her husband play and Carmen was a role she had yet to tackle. As the overture finished, the curtains swung open to reveal a Spanish town square. Rosanna sat back and prepared to be entertained.

The role of the handsome, fiery Spaniard suited Roberto to perfection. His performance was electrifying and the audience were on the edge of their seats.

'*Ah, Carmen! Ma Carmen adorée!*' Roberto sang at the end as his lover's dead body sank to the ground.

Tears were spilling freely down Rosanna's cheeks. She stood with the rest of the audience, who were stamping, clapping, throwing flowers and cheering 'Bravo!' They would not allow Roberto and his lovely Carmen to leave the stage.

Roberto looked up at Rosanna and blew her a kiss.

It was then she knew what she wanted.

It would take a lot of hard work and a lot of sacrifice, but she would do it because she *had* to.

*

'*Principessa*, you look radiant. Rarely have I seen you so happy recently.' Roberto spun her round on the crowded dance floor of the Hofburg Palace's magnificent ballroom.

'I feel it.' She smiled up at him. 'I'm so glad I came.'

'And I'm glad too. We are no good apart, Rosanna. You know that, don't you?'

'Yes.' The music finished and Roberto stood for a moment, still holding her in his arms. 'Roberto, before we go back to the table, I want to tell you that I . . . I've made a decision.'

'And what is that?' Roberto looked at her expectantly.

'I want to sing again.'

'Rosanna, that is the best news I could have heard. Just think! No more separations. Things will be as they once were.'

'No, they won't be the same, because we have Nico. But I'm sure we can make it work somehow.'

'Of course we can. Now, let us go and drink champagne and toast to your return.' He took Rosanna's hand and walked her across the floor. 'I'll tell Chris tomorrow. I'm sure that he'll want you to sing Butterfly with me at the Met in July and . . .'

Rosanna listened to Roberto's excitement, knowing he was going too fast but not caring.

She had done what he wanted and given herself back to him completely.

47

Ella awoke early the following morning and lay listening for noises from the baby monitor by her bed. There were none. She sighed with relief, hoping that yesterday's problems were a burst of teething and that after a good night's sleep Nico would be better. She got up, walked along the corridor and pushed his door open. She crept inside, went to the cot and leant over. Nico's eyes were closed, but his hair was wet, his cheeks were bright red and his skin blotchy. She put a hand on his forehead and felt the heat. Swiftly, she pulled the covers from him and saw that his pyjamas were soaked through. She removed them, her heart beating a slow *tom-tom* against her chest, and Ella gasped as she saw the bright red rash that covered his body. Nico opened his eyes, gave a moan, then closed them again.

She ran along the corridor, down the stairs and flung open the kitchen door. She looked down Rosanna's list until she came to the hotel number. Picking up the receiver, she dialled the Imperial Hotel and waited for someone to answer.

'Yes, hello. Could I please speak to Rosanna Rossini?'

'I'm sorry, madam, but Mr Rossini requested that no

telephone calls are to be put through to his room until further notice.'

'But this is an emergency! His son is sick. I must speak to him or to Mrs Rossini.' Ella was almost weeping with frustration.

'All right, madam. I'll try and put you through.'

Ella waited in an agony of tension.

'I'm sorry, madam, but there is no reply. Mr Rossini may have barred the phone in his room. I'll ask someone to go up and knock on the door of his suite.'

'Please, immediately,' urged Ella. 'Ask Mrs Rossini to telephone Ella at home. Say Nico is sick.'

She replaced the receiver and then dialled Abi's number. There was no answer there either. 'Please let him be all right,' Ella moaned as she called the doctor's number.

'Hello?'

'Can I speak to Dr Martin?'

'I'm afraid he's out on a call. I'm his wife. Can I help you?'

'Yes. I'm looking after Rosanna Rossini's little boy, Nico. He has a high temperature and a bad rash all over his body. I . . . I don't know what to do.'

'I see. Right, well, Dr Martin should be home in a few minutes. If you give me your address, I'll send him straight over.'

Ella did so.

'Now, my dear, until the doctor arrives, sponge Nico with lukewarm water. That should help keep his temperature down. And try to get him to drink a little water. If he starts to deteriorate, or becomes unconscious, call an ambulance immediately.'

'I will. Thank you.'

Ella put the receiver down. She filled a bowl of water and climbed the stairs in trepidation, wishing with all her heart she'd never suggested that Rosanna go to Vienna to see Roberto.

The journey from Heathrow to Gloucestershire took less than an hour and a half. The roads were empty and Stephen pulled the Jaguar off the motorway and headed for The Manor House.

Luca sat in silence, staring out of the window. His mind was in turmoil. Not only had Stephen told him the upshot of his visit to New York, but then, calmly and without emotion, he had told him the reason he was no longer seeing Rosanna.

Roberto was back.

The ramifications of this news were so far-reaching that Luca couldn't begin to put his thoughts into any kind of order.

'Are you happy they're reunited?' asked Stephen. 'Part of you must be. I mean, he is Rosanna's husband and Nico's father.'

Luca shook his head vigorously. 'No, Stephen. Even though he's Rosanna's husband, the things that Roberto has done, I . . .' He sighed deeply as Stephen took the road that led to The Manor House.

Stephen pulled the car to a halt on the drive. 'You'll understand if I don't come in, won't you?'

'Of course.' Luca could see Stephen was itching to leave. 'Okay. Thank you, Stephen, for everything.'

'It was nothing. I'll be at the gallery all day if you want to talk further.'

'*Ciao*.' Luca opened the door, then stopped and turned back. 'I'm so sorry, Stephen. Rosanna does not realise what she has lost.'

Stephen shrugged sadly as Luca closed the passenger door behind him.

Ella was pacing the floor in Nico's nursery when she heard the doorbell ring. She ran down the stairs expecting to find the doctor on the doorstep. She unlocked the door, her hands trembling.

'Luca! Oh Luca!' She threw herself into his arms, sobbing hysterically.

'Ella, Ella, what is it? What is the matter? Come now, calm down.'

'Nico, it's Nico. He's very sick. I think he may even be dying! We must not leave him alone.' Ella pulled Luca inside and hurried back up the stairs.

'But where is Rosanna? And . . . Roberto?'

'In Vienna. I thought you were the doctor. I'm doing as his wife said, but she said I should call an ambulance if he got worse and . . .' Ella entered Nico's room and pointed to the cot. 'See, he has this rash and he won't wake up properly and . . . Help me, Luca, help me!' she gabbled hysterically.

Luca leant over the cot and immediately took in the seriousness of the child's condition. 'The doctor is on his way?'

'Yes, but I'm sure he is getting worse.'

'Then I think we must take no chances. We must call an ambulance.'

At that moment they heard the doorbell ring.

'Thank God,' said Ella, choking back a sob. 'That must be the doctor.'

'You go,' said Luca. 'I'll stay with Nico.'

Ella nodded and ran from the room. Luca stroked Nico's forehead. 'It's okay, *angeletto*. You're going to be all right. I think your mamma must have gone mad to leave you, but she'll be back soon, I promise.'

While Dr Martin examined Nico, Ella and Luca stood together by the window in the nursery.

'You say Rosanna is in Vienna with Roberto?' Luca confirmed.

'Yes.'

'Have you telephoned them?'

'Yes, but they haven't called back yet.'

'She shouldn't have left you alone with Nico, Ella. It was very wrong of her,' Luca sighed.

'Please don't blame Rosanna. I begged her to go. She was so unhappy, missing Roberto so much. I thought . . . I thought it would be fine. And it would have been if . . .' Ella wrung her hands in despair and Luca put an arm round her shoulders. 'She telephoned last night and I told her he was not well and—'

'Still she did not return?'

'No, but—'

Dr Martin broke into their conversation.

'I'm going to call an ambulance. I want to admit Nico to hospital. He has a very high temperature and we must get some fluids into him to stop him getting dehydrated.'

'What is it? What's wrong with him?' Ella asked, holding her breath.

'Nico has a nasty attack of the measles. It's a common childhood illness, but some children can get it very badly and there can be complications if we don't treat it quickly. Can I use the telephone?'

'Of course.' Ella led the doctor into Rosanna's bedroom.

Luca stared out of the nursery window, wondering what had possessed his sister – usually such a devoted mother – to leave her son with an inexperienced fifteen-year-old girl. He shook his head ruefully, knowing the answer.

'Okay, the ambulance will be along shortly.' The doctor reappeared. 'And if I were you, I'd get Mrs Rossini back fast from wherever she is. I'm sure she'll want to be with her son.'

At that moment the telephone rang.

'I'll get it,' said Luca and ran to the bedroom to pick up the receiver.

'Ella?' bleated a panicked voice.

'Rosanna, is that you?'

'Luca? What are you doing there? I didn't know you were coming.'

'It was short notice, but that doesn't matter now. You must catch the first flight back from Vienna, Rosanna. I'm sorry to tell you, but Nico is very sick. The doctor is here and we're taking him to the hospital in Cheltenham. The doctor says he has measles.'

'Oh, please God, no! I . . .' A strangled sob came from the other end of the line.

'Rosanna, I'm sure he'll be okay. The doctor is here and Nico is in good hands. Try and get on a flight home as soon as you can.'

'Yes. I'll get a taxi from Heathrow and come straight to the hospital. Please, Luca, give my baby a kiss and tell him his mamma will be with him soon.'

'Of course. Try not to worry. Goodbye, Rosanna.' Luca

put the telephone down as the ambulance pulled into the drive.

Five minutes later, the three of them were on their way to the hospital.

48

'Well, Mrs Rossini, you'll be glad to know that Nico is going to be all right,' the consultant informed Rosanna.

She put her head in her hands and sobbed in relief. The past forty-eight hours had been the worst of her entire life. She'd arrived at the hospital in the early evening on Sunday to find Nico wired up to a drip. Luca had taken an exhausted and drained Ella home and Rosanna had sat, hour after hour, as her child passed through what the nurses had called 'the crisis'. The following morning, Nico's temperature had fallen and he'd slept more peacefully. And today he'd actually opened his eyes and smiled at her. The drip was removed after the doctors had pronounced that Nico was over the worst.

Rosanna pulled a tissue from her sleeve. She wiped her nose. 'I'm sorry. After the last two days, it's such a relief.'

'I understand, Mrs Rossini. It's unusual for a child to get the measles so badly, but it does happen. I take it he hadn't been vaccinated?'

'No.' She reflected miserably that it was something that had never occurred to her in those dream-like months at The Manor House just after Nico's birth.

'Well, it might be an idea to arrange for anyone else in your household who hasn't had the jab to get it done. Measles can be contagious for several days after the rash appears. Best to be on the safe side. As for Nico, he'll obviously need some special care for the next couple of weeks, but he's a tough little thing. He'll be up and about sooner than you think. Another day here for observation and you can take him home. Now, I suggest that you go home and get some rest. Come back later this afternoon. We want to do a few routine tests this morning.'

'Okay. I'll go and kiss him goodbye. And thank you, Doctor, thank you.'

'No need to thank me. It's what we're here for. And try not to punish yourself, Mrs Rossini. There's little more you could have done, even if you had been with him.'

Rosanna shook her head. 'I'm his mother. I would have known how sick he was sooner,' she said quietly, and left the consultant's office.

Nico was in a side ward by himself. He was lying in a cot, his back facing her.

'Hello, darling,' she said. 'Mamma's back.'

The little boy did not respond. Rosanna walked over to him, thinking he must have fallen asleep. She leant over the cot and saw that no, he was wide awake. When he saw her, he rolled towards her and gave her a big smile.

Rosanna picked him up and cuddled him. 'Oh my darling, I swear I will never leave you again.'

An hour later, Rosanna arrived home in a taxi and wearily let herself into the house.

'Ella?' she called, but there was no reply.

'She's in her room taking a nap.' Rosanna looked up and saw Luca standing at the top of the stairs.

'Of course. She must be exhausted.' Rosanna wiped a hand across her brow.

'It's hardly surprising after what she's been through the last few days,' he said as he walked slowly down the stairs towards her. 'How is Nico?'

'The doctor says he'll be fine.'

'That's good news.' Luca spoke in a tone devoid of its usual warmth. He joined her at the bottom of the stairs. 'Would you like something to eat, Rosanna?'

'No, thank you. I'll just have a coffee. Then I'll shower and try to catch some sleep. I must get back to the hospital this afternoon.' Rosanna walked towards the kitchen and Luca followed her. He stood in the doorway and watched her as she filled, then switched on the kettle.

'Rosanna, I'm leaving tonight.'

'Of course. Thank you, Luca, for all your help.'

'But before I go, I must talk to you.'

She looked at his face. He was pale, with dark smudges under his eyes, and his mouth was drawn into a line of tension. 'Then sit down. Coffee for you too?'

'Thank you.'

Rosanna put some coffee into two mugs and added boiling water and milk. She stirred them and joined her brother at the table. 'What is it? I've rarely seen you look so serious. You're scaring me.'

Luca put his hands under his chin and took a deep breath. 'I have thought long and hard about whether I should say this. Rosanna, I love you very, very much, you know that, don't you?'

'Yes, of course.'

'And I would never interfere or question the way you live, or the decisions you take, if it were not that I feel a responsibility towards Ella. I promised Carlotta I would watch over her—'

'Luca, before you go any further, please,' Rosanna interrupted, 'I know what you are going to say. I was wrong to leave Ella with Nico, very wrong. I will never do it again, I promise. Haven't I been punished enough for what I did?'

'I know what a good mother you are to Nico and how kind you've been to Ella, but' – Luca shook his head – 'I worry that this . . . obsession, this love you have for Roberto, clouds your judgement sometimes.'

Rosanna's face turned pink with indignation. 'No! You're wrong! Roberto is the best thing in my life, apart from Nico. He loves me and supports me and—'

'Then why isn't he here now? When his child is in hospital? When his wife needs him by her side?'

'You know why, Luca! Roberto has commitments. He can't drop everything to be here. I accept it is the way his life is.'

'But he had no performance on Sunday or Monday night. You told me that yourself, Rosanna. He could have easily flown back from Vienna with you and returned in time for Tuesday evening. Or maybe he was worried about catching such an infectious disease and—'

'Stop it, Luca! Please, you're being unfair. By the time Roberto arrived home, he'd have had to turn round and go back. He can't let his audience down.'

'But surely he was letting his wife and son down?' Luca challenged. Then he sighed. 'Rosanna, I'm sorry, I don't mean to pass judgement on anyone, least of all you. But Roberto, well, I think he changes you, influences you.'

'Yes, for the better! I love him, Luca. And he loves me and Nico and . . . it is none of your business! You don't know him like I do.'

'You're wrong, Rosanna. I know him far better than you think,' he said quietly. 'Do you really believe he always tells you the truth?'

'Yes.'

'Then what about his affair with Donatella in New York?'

'Why are you trying to make me hate him, Luca? Why?'

'I'm not. I know that it would be pointless. All I'm trying to say is that sometimes we can love people, but that doesn't mean they bring out the best in us.'

'Luca' – Rosanna was angry now – 'you talk about the love between a man and a woman with such authority, and yet you're training to be a priest. How can you claim to understand how I feel when you've never known that kind of love yourself?'

Luca looked suddenly weary. 'Rosanna, I don't want to argue with you. I only say these things because I love you and I wish to protect you from things you do not, *cannot* know.'

'What "things", Luca? Tell me what you mean.'

'No, Rosanna, forget I said that. I'm being stupid, over-protective.'

'Luca, if you have something to tell me, then you must do so. I'm not a little girl any longer. So please don't treat me like one.'

'Okay.' He paused before he spoke. 'Roberto has things in his past that make me wonder if he is a good person. And he has such a hold over you, he influences you – sometimes I think, not for the better. Are you sure you know everything about him?'

'Yes, I know everything!' Already at the edge of her emotional limits from the past two days, Rosanna could take no more. 'I know what he was, what he is! You hate him, Luca, you've always hated him. Well, I love him and it doesn't matter what you say to me, I don't care what you think!'

'Rosanna, can't you see? Roberto has lost you your family in Italy, your career, and sometimes, I think, your sanity. Now *we* are fighting over him! Do you not realise how destructive he is?'

'You have no place telling me how I must live my life!' She was shouting now, out of control, tears spilling down her face. 'Please leave!'

'Rosanna, I'm sorry. I shouldn't have—'

'*Leave!*' She pointed at the door.

'Don't let us part like this.'

'I will not have you in my house for a minute longer!'

Luca looked at her then shrugged sadly. 'Okay, if that's what you want.'

'It is. And you needn't worry, I'll take care of Ella, not because I have to, but because I *want* to! Now go!'

Rosanna stormed out of the kitchen, ran up the stairs and into her bedroom. She slammed the door behind her.

Half an hour later she heard a car arrive in the drive and the doorbell ring. She went to the window and watched Luca climb inside a taxi. With a swirl of gravel, he was gone.

'Ah, Mrs Rossini, come in, come in.' The consultant ushered her into his office.

'Is anything the matter? I've just been with Nico and he seems so much better.'

'He's recovering well, yes, but our tests this morning have shown up a problem.'

'What? Tell me, quickly.'

'Sometimes, in bad cases of measles, the hearing of the child can be impaired.'

Rosanna looked up at the doctor, her face anguished. 'What are you trying to tell me?'

'Mrs Rossini, there's no easy way to say this. I can't be certain, but I'm afraid that Nico's hearing has been severely damaged.'

'Oh God . . . no!' Rosanna moaned.

'I know, Mrs Rossini. It's a shock, but you're going to need to be brave for your son.'

'Yes.' Rosanna galvanised her courage from somewhere deep inside. The doctor was right. She had to be strong. 'How bad is it? Will he be completely deaf?'

'It's too early to know the full extent of the damage, but as to his hearing in the right ear, very probably. His left ear is damaged too, but, it seems at this stage, not as seriously. We'll obviously be conducting further tests. I'm going to introduce you to Mr Carson, our ENT specialist, and . . .'

The words of the doctor blurred into background noise as Rosanna stared past him. She could think of only one thing. Her son was the child of the great tenor, Roberto Rossini, without doubt the owner of one of the most beautiful voices in the world.

And now Nico might never again be able to hear his papa sing.

49

'Mr Rossini?'

'Yes, speaking.'

'I have a telephone call for you.'

'Thank you.' Roberto, dripping from a shower, sat down on the edge of his bed. 'Hello?'

'Roberto.'

His heart sank. 'Donatella, how are you?'

'I'm well.'

'Good.' Roberto was eager to get her off the line. 'Now—'

'The weather is fine in Vienna for the time of year, is it not?'

'How would you know that? Where are you?'

'Downstairs in reception. We must talk. I'll come up to your room.'

'Donatella, this isn't a good time. I must rest for my performance tonight. I think I have a cold coming on.'

'What I have to say will only take a few minutes.'

The line went dead. Roberto sighed, donned his silk dressing gown and distractedly combed his hair.

There was a knock at the door and he went to open it.

'*Ciao*, Roberto.'

'Come in, Donatella,' he said brusquely.

'Thank you.' She walked past him and sat down on a large chintz sofa.

'How are you?' he asked.

'Never better.' Donatella reached forward and took a large grape from the brimming fruit bowl on the table in front of her.

'Good. You look very well.' Roberto didn't understand it. The woman was positively sparkling with happiness.

'Thank you, I feel it.' Donatella bit lasciviously into the grape, then eyed Roberto. 'You, on the other hand, look terrible.'

'Our son is in hospital. He's been very ill.'

'Yes, Chris told me you had family problems.'

'I have.' Roberto paced the room. 'Look, what is it you want? Have you come to shout and scream, tell me what a bastard I am? If so, please let's get it over with.'

'No.' Donatella shook her head and reached for another grape. 'You *are* a bastard, Roberto, but you don't need me to tell you that. Yes, I was angry with you for not returning to New York, for crawling back to Rosanna without even bothering to contact me, but' – Donatella shrugged – 'you are the great maestro, Roberto Rossini. You don't have to answer to anybody, is this not true?'

Her ebullient mood was unsettling him. 'Look, I apologise for what happened, Donatella. Rosanna forgave me and I went back to her. She's my wife. And I never made you any promises.'

'No. It's true, you did not. And as it happens, I've since realised that I'm no longer in love with you.' She waved her hand languidly. 'The infatuation has run its course. If you begged me now, I wouldn't take you back.'

'Well then, what is the problem?' Roberto hovered over her. 'I really must rest, Donatella.'

'Of course. Nothing must disturb you before you go in front of your adoring audience.' Donatella stood up, then drew out two envelopes from her handbag. She laid the first one on the table. 'The keys to your apartment in New York. I've removed my things from it.' She fingered the second envelope before holding it out to him. 'Oh, and this recently arrived for you there. Naturally, I read its contents.'

Roberto snatched the envelope from Donatella's hand. 'You shouldn't have done that.'

She shrugged carelessly. 'Well, no matter, I did. I think you had better open it, Roberto. Discover why it will be that your wife asks you to leave again.' Donatella smiled sweetly at him.

'What are you talking about? Rosanna and I are very happy. There is nothing she doesn't know about me.'

'Then maybe there is something *you* do not know about *yourself*.'

'Whatever it is, it doesn't matter. We have no secrets from each other. I tell her everything.'

'Good, then you won't mind if I send a copy of the letter to your wife, just in case you forget?' Donatella walked towards the door. 'I'm at the Astoria Hotel. *Ciao*.'

As the door shut behind her, Roberto sat down, his heart beating uncomfortably fast. He opened the envelope.

Convent Santa Maria, Pompeii

Dear Roberto,

Do you remember a long time ago, one hot night in Naples, we danced together in my papa's café at your parents' wedding anniversary? Then afterwards, we went for a walk along the seafront. Later, we made love. It was my first time, and a very beautiful night, one I have never forgotten.

I discovered I was pregnant six weeks later. The only person I could talk to was my brother, Luca. We decided that, for the sake of our family, I should claim the baby was my boyfriend's. So I did what I had to do with him to make this plausible. Then, a month later, I told my boyfriend and my father I was pregnant. Papa hastily arranged our wedding and I married a man I did not love to give our child a chance and avoid bringing disgrace on my parents. I knew you would never marry me, that at the time you may not have even believed the child was yours. I swear to you now it is the truth.

Ella, your daughter, was born five weeks earlier than expected. My marriage began in a web of lies and I should have known it had little hope of lasting. I'm still married, but I have not seen my husband for over ten years and neither has your daughter.

There have been many occasions on which I have wanted to tell you about Ella, but when you married Rosanna, I knew I could not, for her sake. However, Luca tells me you are soon to be divorced and this news decided me.

I tell you this, still trusting and praying Rosanna will never learn the truth. I know how she loved you and I don't wish to hurt her further.

As for Ella, I beg you not to turn her life upside down by confronting her with this knowledge. I ask only that you watch over her, discreetly, be there to help her if an occasion arises in the future when she needs it. This will be a simple process as I have sent her to live with Rosanna. You see, Roberto, she has a beautiful voice. I know Rosanna will know how to nurture and encourage her niece's talent, and believe it was inherited from her.

Luca does not know I've written to you. He advised me against it, saying it was dangerous. But if you ask him, he will tell you I speak the truth. And if you heard Ella sing, you would know I do not lie.

Goodbye, Roberto.

Carlotta

Roberto allowed the letter to fall from his hands and flutter to the floor. He sank back onto the sofa and emitted a low groan. Was it true? Or could Carlotta be lying?

He closed his eyes and pictured Ella singing '*Silent Night*' at her school carol concert. He recognised the deep mellow sound as his own, transmuted into the voice of the young girl who was apparently his daughter.

Roberto's eyes snapped open as his mind issued a clear picture of her face. The black hair, the pale skin, the eyes. *Mamma mia!* Even the smile was his.

Standing up, Roberto began to pace the room.

No wonder Donatella was so happy. She knew that if

Rosanna discovered the truth, he stood to lose not only the woman he loved, but his son *and* new-found daughter too. Given his track record, Rosanna would never believe he hadn't known about Ella. Besides, he had slept with her sister and never told her about that. She'd hate him, and have every right to do so.

He sat down heavily and realised that he'd do anything to keep his wife – give up his career, his fame, his fortune. It wasn't important. He needed *her*.

Roberto picked up the receiver and dialled reception. 'Get me the Astoria Hotel.'

'Yes, sir.'

Roberto waited, feeling sick with fear.

'Putting you through, sir.'

'Astoria Hotel. How may I help you?'

'Donatella Bianchi's room, please.'

'Roberto, that was quick,' Donatella purred. 'I have only just walked in.'

'What do you want? Whatever it is, you can have it. Money, the apartment in New York, anything.'

'No, Roberto. There is nothing I need in the way of material possessions; remember Giovanni left me a wealthy woman. However, I've been thinking a trip to England this weekend might be a pleasant distraction. Maybe to the Cotswolds. It's somewhere I've always wanted to visit – I've heard it's very beautiful. And, of course, I can drop off the letter personally at the same time.'

'Donatella, do you really want to destroy me? And what about Rosanna? She has done nothing to deserve this. You know this will devastate her too.'

'Ah, so you do have feelings,' she murmured. 'It is a

dreadful thing, is it not, to love deeply and have that love threatened?'

'I've told you, *anything*, Donatella. Name it. Just don't do this, I beg you.'

There was a long silence, then finally Donatella spoke.

'So, at last you understand.'

'Understand?'

'What it is like to be powerless.'

The line went dead in Roberto's ear.

50

Rosanna opened the front door and stumbled into the hall. Even though it was only half past five, darkness had already fallen. Without turning the lights on, she walked up the stairs and went into Nico's nursery. She stared miserably at the pale moonlight shining on his empty cot.

Her beautiful child, disabled for the rest of his life. And it was all her fault. Because of her selfishness, she had unwittingly passed a life sentence on her young son. Unable to look any longer at the empty cot, Rosanna left the room, calling for Ella, but receiving no reply, remembered she'd gone to stay with a friend for the night. She was here in the house alone.

Desperate now to speak to someone, she went back down the stairs and into the study. Picking up the receiver, she dialled Roberto's hotel. The receptionist informed her that Mr Rossini had left for his evening performance. Rosanna replaced the receiver, thought for a few seconds, then dialled again.

'Hello?'

'Abi, oh Abi, it's Rosanna, I . . .' Rosanna began to sob as she told her friend what had happened to Nico.

'Oh my God, I don't know what to say,' said a shocked Abi. 'I'm so sorry.'

'He's so little, and so defenceless. What has he done to deserve this? It was me who left him and didn't return when Ella told me he was sick. Maybe if I'd been here, I might have seen how serious it was and caught it before he got so bad. Oh Abi, Abi, how can I ever forgive myself?'

'Rosanna, you're going to have to calm down. Nico is alive and otherwise recovering, that's the most important thing. He's still your little boy and although he might need a bit more help now, he's very bright. He'll cope. And you don't know quite how bad the damage is yet. His hearing may improve over time.'

'Maybe. I just have to pray. But . . . oh Abi, I've had the most terrible row with Luca as well.'

'Yes, I realised something had happened between you.'

'What do you mean?'

'Luca turned up here at my flat in London a couple of hours ago,' said Abi.

'Oh.' Rosanna bit her lip. 'Has he said anything?'

'You know what Luca's like, he hasn't said a word so far, but I knew something was up. He's staying here tonight, but more importantly, Rosanna, have you told Roberto about Nico yet?'

'No. He's at the theatre but he'll be back at the hotel soon.'

'Well, if I were you, I'd tell him to get his ample backside on a plane,' Abi said vehemently. 'You need him, Rosanna, and so does Nico.'

'You're right, Abi, but you know the way things are,' Rosanna sighed.

'Yes. Unfortunately I do. Look, do you want me to drive up to be with you? You shouldn't be alone. I can come first thing tomorrow morning.'

'No. When I've spoken to Roberto, I'm sure I'll feel better, and Ella will be back tomorrow, but thank you anyway.'

'Okay. Now remember to eat something, Rosanna. And get an early night. You're obviously exhausted.'

'I am. Thank you, Abi. Goodnight.'

Rosanna replaced the receiver, walked to the kitchen and sat down numbly at the table. Luca had run to Abi because *she* had thrown him out of her house. Luca, who'd worked in Papa's café all those years to pay for her lessons because he believed in her, then had put his own future on hold to care for her in Milan.

Roberto . . .

Luca had said he should be here with his wife and son . . . Even she had struggled to justify why he couldn't have accompanied her home to be with his sick son when he'd not had a performance. Abi had sounded equally disgusted that he wasn't there with her. Roberto had barred the phone to their hotel room, making it impossible for Ella to contact them, even knowing that his son was unwell the night before.

Were these the actions of a 'good' man? Rosanna asked herself.

A glimmer of doubt about her perfect love began to form in her mind.

As for her own behaviour, was Luca right? Was she obsessed with Roberto? Had she changed? Rosanna remembered with a shudder how easily she'd been persuaded not to return home when she knew instinctively her son was sick.

She thought back to the innocent girl she'd been before their love affair had begun. She remembered Paolo and all he had done for her. And felt physically sick at the way she had betrayed him because of Roberto.

Then there was her career: she doubted if there had been another young opera singer more dedicated or determined to reach the top. Until Roberto had appeared in her life. She'd allowed him to stop her going back to Milan, and then to make all the decisions from the moment they were married. It was Roberto who'd chosen where and what they had sung. And, if she was brutally honest, her husband had chosen the roles *he* wanted before considering her.

She'd sacrificed her career, not just for Nico, Rosanna realised, but for Roberto too. He had a great gift, but then, so did *she* . . .

Rosanna's heart began to thud as she thought of Stephen and what she'd done to him. All that love, patience and understanding he'd so unselfishly given her when she'd needed it, and what had she given in return? Nothing. No . . . worse than nothing. Rosanna forced herself to face the truth. She had used him and then tossed him away without a backward glance. And she'd not even had the decency to contact him and explain her decision to him in person.

And finally – worse than anything else – she had left her child when her instincts had been on red alert that something was wrong. Her love for Roberto had even managed to overpower *that*.

As Rosanna sat watching the clouds scudding across the moon, she finally accepted that Luca was right. Her love for Roberto *was* unhealthy, unnatural. She *was* obsessed with him; he changed her, blinded her to everything else.

Where was he now? Not with her watching over their sick son, but standing on a stage pleasing an audience.

And that was the way it would always be.

Rosanna rose and went to pour herself a glass of water to ease her dry mouth. Something was happening to her, she could feel it.

Who was she? What was she?

She hated the person she'd become.

Roberto's face appeared in her mind, as it always did. And always would. She knew that.

The love would remain. But, as if she had been asleep for the past fifteen years of her life, she now felt as though she was awakening.

The world would turn. Her life would continue; she would be happy.

Without Roberto.

It was possible.

For the first time, Rosanna knew it was possible.

A little later, the telephone rang. Rosanna rose slowly and went to answer it.

'*Principessa*, it is me.'

'Hello, Roberto.'

'Are you okay? You sound strange.'

'No, I'm okay, but Nico is not.'

Calmly, Rosanna told him what had happened to their son.

'Oh my God. Please tell me it isn't true.'

'Sadly, it is, and I should never have left him, Roberto. It was very wrong of me to let your feelings on the matter persuade me otherwise. I don't blame you – I take responsibility.'

'Rosanna, we will take care of Nico together. He will have the best doctors, anything he needs.'

'When are you coming home? I need to talk to you.'

'I wish I was by your side now. I promise I'll be home with you within forty-eight hours. There are some . . . things that I must organise.'

It was the last time she would wait for him to return to her. 'I must go now,' she said. 'I'm very tired.'

'Rosanna, is Luca there? I want to speak to him.'

'No. He's gone to Abi's flat in London.'

'Do you have her number?'

She repeated it from memory, so exhausted she didn't even bother to ask why he wanted it.

'Rosanna, are you sure you're all right? You sound . . . distant.'

'I'm fine, really.'

'*Ti amo*, my darling.'

'Goodbye, Roberto.'

Roberto looked at the number he'd scribbled on the pad and, with trembling fingers, dialled it. It was answered immediately and Roberto recognised her voice.

'Hello, Abi. It's Roberto Rossini.'

'Hello, Roberto. This is a surprise. Rosanna's not here. She's at home.'

'I know. It's Luca I wish to speak to. Urgently,' he added.

'Okay. Hold on.' She put down the receiver. Two minutes later, Luca picked it up.

'Yes?'

'Luca, I apologise sincerely for disturbing you, but I must ask you something. I've received a letter written by your sister, Carlotta. Is it true that I am Ella's real papa?'

There was a pause on the line before Luca replied. 'Carlotta wrote you a letter that told you of this?'

'Yes, Luca. I understand it's difficult for you to talk now, but we must meet.'

'I don't see why,' Luca replied coldly.

'Someone else has read the letter. And is threatening to tell your sister. For Rosanna's sake, *please*, Luca. I am desperate. Maybe if you could tell this person it's not true, she might believe you.'

'I will not lie for you, Roberto.'

'I understand, but I'm at this person's mercy. There must be a way. If Rosanna finds out, she won't believe I didn't know of this until now. Whatever you think of me, Luca, I love her and don't want her to be hurt again. I lied to her before, you see – I wasn't honest about my past. If she discovers the truth about Ella, I'm scared that she'll believe I've deceived her again. And that it will be the end for us.'

Luca heard the desperation in Roberto's voice. 'When do you want to see me?'

'I am flying to England tomorrow. Can you meet me at Heathrow? My flight gets in to Terminal 3 at eleven o'clock.'

'All right, but I don't really see what I can do to help.'

'Thank you, Luca, from the bottom of my heart. I'll see you tomorrow. *Ciao*.'

Roberto put down the receiver and lay back on the bed. He knew he was grasping at straws. If Luca refused to cooperate, then he would have to tell Rosanna the truth himself.

The following morning, Luca stood uncertainly in the arrivals hall and suddenly heard his name being called over the tannoy. He went to make himself known at the enquiry desk as requested, and was led by a security officer through a maze of corridors to a small hospitality lounge. It was deserted, apart from Roberto, who was pacing the floor.

Luca walked towards him. Roberto's arrogance, his easy self-confidence had disappeared. He looked like any overweight, middle-aged man with a problem.

'Thank you, thank you for coming, Luca.' Roberto nodded at the security officer, who left the room. 'I thought it would be better to talk in private. Please, sit down.'

Luca sat and prepared to listen.

'I . . .' Roberto scratched the unkempt stubble on his chin. 'First, I want to say I understand that you have every reason to dislike me. You've known for all these years that I was the father of Carlotta's child. When I married Rosanna, it must have been hard for you both.'

'Neither of us wanted to hurt Rosanna. We knew she loved you,' Luca replied coldly.

'I swear, I didn't know about Ella until I got the letter yesterday. Donatella Bianchi, a woman who I've known for a considerable length of time, was at my New York apartment and opened Carlotta's letter without my permission. Donatella has told me she intends to take a copy of the letter to Rosanna personally.'

'Donatella Bianchi,' murmured Luca.

'You know her?'

Luca nodded. 'Oh yes. I know her. But why would she want to do this terrible thing to Rosanna?'

'To punish *me* for leaving *her*. She realises Rosanna is the only woman I've ever truly loved. It's the perfect revenge. Donatella knows your sister will almost certainly leave me when she hears the news. Or that at the very least it will drive a terrible wedge between us. And we have had enough problems recently.'

'Roberto, have you ever told Rosanna you had a liaison with Carlotta?'

'No. I didn't think it was important. Rosanna was a young girl when it happened and . . . yes, I was too frightened of Rosanna's reaction. Luca, please, help me.' Roberto fell to his knees. 'I'm desperate. I beg you, if you can think of a way, I promise before God I will be the best, most loving husband in the world. I love Rosanna, I can't live without her.' Roberto bowed his head and his shoulders began to shake.

Luca looked down at the man before him. He could see Roberto was broken, humbled in desperation. He finally knew that, selfish or not, at the very least the man loved his sister with all his heart.

And, of course, he now knew of a way to stop this, to keep Donatella quiet forever. On the other hand, had there not been too many lies already? Was it not better that Rosanna knew the truth? It would cause her pain, but she would get over it in time.

Then he pictured his sister's face, in their parents' café, staring at Roberto for the first time.

Whatever he was, she loved him. However he behaved, she wanted him. He was Nico's father *and*, Luca asked himself, who was he to play God? Surely all he could do was act with integrity, and give Roberto the information he needed. What happened beyond that was not up to him.

Luca looked at Roberto and took a deep breath.

'Roberto, I know of a way we can end this.'

51

Donatella walked into the lobby of the Savoy hotel.

When Roberto had called her in Vienna, begging her to meet him in London before she went to see Rosanna, she hadn't been able to resist. To watch him plead and squirm for mercy one more time would be most enjoyable. She had absolutely no intention of changing her mind. Nothing he could do or say would help him now.

He was waiting for her in the American Bar. She greeted him with a kiss on both cheeks.

'How are you? You look a little pale, Roberto.'

'Drink?' he asked, ignoring her question.

'Yes. Campari and soda, please.' Donatella sat down and crossed her long legs as Roberto ordered drinks from the waiter. 'So, Roberto, what is it you wished to see me about?'

'I wanted to ask you if you would reconsider. I wanted you to know that if you show that letter to Rosanna, it will not only destroy me, but her also. She has done nothing to you. Why would you punish her?'

'Do you really expect me to care? I loved you very much, Roberto, but now' – Donatella flicked her hand – 'it has gone.

In fact, I have a new boyfriend. I'm moving back to Milan and we're thinking of getting married.'

'Congratulations,' murmured Roberto as the drinks arrived.

'Now, what shall we drink to? Freedom maybe?' Donatella's green eyes sparkled venomously over the rim of her raised glass.

'You're enjoying every moment of this, aren't you?' Roberto took a sip of his mineral water.

'It was about time someone treated you the way you've treated everybody else. Do you realise that if it wasn't for me you would never have got your first big break at La Scala?'

'What are you talking about now, Donatella?' Roberto asked wearily.

'I gave Paolo de Vito an enormous cheque for a scholarship fund at his precious school on the condition that you were given your first leading role. You see, Roberto, others have cared about you, helped you. It's a pity you have never cared about them.'

'I don't believe you.'

'No matter,' Donatella shrugged. 'Ask Paolo one day.'

'Well then, if it's true, I thank you for your help,' he nodded.

'A meek Roberto,' she commented acidly. 'My God, you must love her very much.'

'He does,' said a voice from behind her.

Donatella turned round to see a slim, dark-haired young man standing behind them. He looked familiar but she couldn't place him.

'Luca, come and join us.' Roberto nodded to a chair.

'Thank you.' He sat down.

'Oh, of course, you're Rosanna's sainted brother. Have you been employed to come here and make me search my soul?' Donatella said dismissively. 'You'll sink to any level, won't you, Roberto?'

'Signora Bianchi, I'm here to see you for a completely different reason. It's only coincidence that Roberto told me of your knowledge of Carlotta's letter at a time when I was about to contact you anyway.'

'And why would you need to speak to me?'

'It's about this, Signora Bianchi.' Luca pulled an envelope out of his pocket, opened it and then laid a polaroid photograph on the table.

Donatella picked it up and studied it. Both men watched the colour drain from her face.

'What is this?' she asked.

'I think you know perfectly well what it is,' said Luca calmly. 'You once paid Don Edoardo, *il parroco* at La Chiesa Della Beata Vergine Maria, three million lire to buy it.'

'If you'll excuse me, I think I'll go outside for some air.' Roberto stood up, nodded at Luca, and left.

'I . . . yes, of course. Now I remember it.' Donatella looked distinctly flustered.

'A friend of mine took this photograph at an apartment recently in New York.' Luca spoke quietly, unhurriedly. 'A Mr John St Regent, the current owner of the drawing, told my friend he paid several million dollars for it.'

'*Mamma mia!* Well, that is an amazing coincidence. We . . . had a burglary at our palazzo just after I bought the drawing, you see. It was stolen, along with several other paintings. I had no idea it was worth that much. What is it, a Leonardo?' Donatella laughed nervously.

'Yes, I think that's exactly what it is, Signora Bianchi. You say it was stolen from your home?'

'Yes.'

'Then that is most odd, as John St Regent told my friend that it was your husband who sold it to him.'

'I . . . no.' Donatella shook her head. 'Your friend got it wrong. He made a mistake.'

'Well, it's a simple matter of a telephone call, Signora Bianchi. I am sure the Italian police will be able to ascertain the truth,' shrugged Luca equably.

'My husband is dead. The authorities can hardly question him now.'

'No, they can't. But they can question you. I believe you knew how valuable that drawing was when you paid Don Edoardo a pittance for it. I also know that if the police found out you had conspired with your husband to take an artwork of national importance out of Italy, you could end up in prison.'

A flicker of fear crossed Donatella's face. 'Luca, I swear, I didn't know the truth. My husband appears to have deceived me too,' she answered desperately.

'Roberto tells me you are very good friends with the St Regents. It's unlikely they have not told you about – in fact, *shown* you – their most precious possession.' Luca shrugged. 'But I'm not here to judge your innocence or guilt. As I said, I can simply tell the police what I know, and they can discover the truth, or . . .'

'Yes?'

'You can change your mind about telling Rosanna who Ella's real father is. Then we can all continue our lives as normal.'

Donatella looked outraged. 'You're blackmailing me!'

'I don't believe I have committed any crime, Signora Bianchi, whereas you clearly have. I love my sister, that's all.'

Donatella drained her glass and banged it down on the table. 'And loving your sister means saddling her with a child that she doesn't know her husband sired? You call that love?' she mocked.

Luca said nothing, just watched her calmly.

Donatella sat in silence, still trying to think of a way to salvage her perfect plan to ruin Roberto's life. But nothing came to mind. At last she sighed resentfully and looked at Luca. 'All right, you win. I don't wish to take the chance of being implicated, especially as I'm soon to move back to Milan. So I agree I will not tell your beloved Rosanna about her husband's illegitimate daughter.'

'I must also ask you for the copy you have of the letter.'

Donatella nodded sulkily and opened her handbag. She pulled out an envelope and handed it to Luca.

'This is the only one?'

'Yes, I swear.'

'Thank you.'

'Well, once again, Roberto has got away with his misdemeanours. You aren't stupid enough to think Ella's conception will remain a secret forever, are you? Or that this will mean Roberto will stay faithful to Rosanna? If you do, you are deluded.'

'Signora Bianchi, I can only do what I think best for now. The rest I must put in God's hands.'

Donatella stood up. 'I will leave before Roberto returns. I know he'll be looking self-satisfied and I couldn't stand that. I know him better than anyone, even his precious wife. We were meant to be together, you know,' she murmured wistfully.

'I think you're right, Signora Bianchi. The two of you deserve each other. Goodbye.'

Luca watched Donatella stalk across the bar and disappear, but the sense of relief that she'd agreed to the bargain did not arrive. Instead, a great wave of sadness closed around his heart.

Roberto appeared round the corner, his eyes hopeful. Luca nodded at him. 'It's okay, she's gone,' he said quietly.

'She agreed?'

'Yes. Here.' Luca handed him the envelope.

'Thank God.' Roberto wiped his sweating brow. 'Luca, can I buy you a drink? Anything, *anything* I can do to thank you.'

'No.' Luca shook his head and stood up. 'I must leave. Just look after my sister and your son. Goodbye.'

Luca arrived at Abi's flat forty-five minutes later. Abi appeared to let him in, fresh from the shower in her robe.

'Hello, darling,' she smiled at him.

Luca stood, silent and unmoving in the doorway. His face was white and his eyes were haunted.

'What on earth's the matter?' she asked him. 'Come and sit down, Luca.' She walked towards him and touched his hand. It was ice cold. 'Luca, for goodness' sake, tell me, where have you been? What's going on?'

His arms hung limply at his sides as he stood there. Abi stepped forward and put her own arms around him, then reached up and stroked his hair. 'Please, Luca, whatever it is, it can't be as bad as you think.'

She led him into the sitting room, sat him down on the sofa and took his hands in hers.

'Listen, my darling, you must tell me what has happened, what's upset you. I love you, you know that. Just this once, let me be *your* confessor.'

Luca looked up at her. 'Abi, it's all so complicated, such a muddle in my head. I feel, I feel . . .'

'Well, I feel like a brandy.' Abi stood up and went to the kitchen to collect a bottle and two glasses. She poured some into each glass and handed one to Luca as she sat down. 'Now, drink up, then we can talk, okay?'

Luca swallowed the glass of brandy straight down. And then he began to tell her. Abi sat there, her eyes growing wider and wider.

'Do you see, Abi, that at every step, Roberto is the perpetrator? And what have I done today? Sent him back to Rosanna, when I had the perfect opportunity to rid her of him forever.'

'Luca, she loves him. Whatever he's done, or might do, that will never change. Love has nothing to do with sense.' Abi looked at him and smiled sadly. 'I above anyone know that. And you can't – *mustn't* – punish yourself. You've done what you thought best to protect your family.'

'Yes, I can look at it that way, or I can say that I'm no better than Roberto, since I too have deceived Rosanna. And once again, Roberto has escaped without punishment. I, like everyone else, did as he requested and lied for him.'

'But it was a lie told with the very best of intentions, Luca, and one that was necessary, I think. I must admit, there is one part of the whole saga that I find funny . . . several million dollars for a drawing that, however lovely to look at, is virtually worthless. Stephen was sure about that, was he?'

'Well, he's the Renaissance expert and he took the drawing through a thorough authentication process,' Luca confirmed. 'He told me he understands why Donatella's husband was convinced it was a Leonardo. There are strong similarities and he thinks the drawing would still fetch a few thousand dollars at auction because it's so old and in such immaculate condition.'

'What did Stephen actually say to the owner when he was asked whether it was the real thing?'

'He took the decision not to tell Mr St Regent his true opinion; he told him he wasn't qualified at such a high level to make a definitive judgement and that he would have to seek a second opinion from the world's leading Leonardo experts. Which, of course, Mr St Regent won't ever do, as the drawing was removed illegally from Italy in the first place. As Stephen said to me, he gets enormous pleasure from the drawing, so why spoil it for him? And of course,' Luca added, 'the less Donatella knows about its real provenance, the better.'

'But all that money, Luca. It doesn't seem fair on our Mr St Regent.'

'A few million dollars to him is like a few pounds to you and me, believe me, Abi.'

'Well then. Come on, Luca, stop being so hard on yourself. You couldn't have done any more and you can't keep beating yourself up about it.'

'But Roberto is such a bad influence on Rosanna, Abi. The way she left Ella and Nico alone . . . that wasn't my sister. She becomes a different person when she's with him. And now she hates me because I told her so.'

'It's her life, Luca, and you must let her live it.'

'I know, I know. But listen, Abi, I've come back here tonight not only to tell you the outcome of the meeting with Donatella, but because I have something else I must talk to you about.'

'Really? And what is that?' she asked him warily.

'I had expected that the past six months might give me the time I needed to help me decide about the future. As it's turned out, I've had little time to think about myself. Carlotta, then Rosanna and Nico and now Roberto and Donatella.' Luca shook his head. 'I'm so very confused, about myself, my God. And you, of course.' He looked at her and smiled at her tenderly. 'At present, with all my uncertainty, it would be wrong to return to the seminary, but also I cannot make the kind of commitment to you that I wish to, until I am absolutely sure that I can say goodbye to all I've wanted and believed in since I first walked into La Chiesa Della Beata Vergine Maria in Milan over ten years ago. So' – Luca paused to gather the strength to tell her – 'I've spoken to my bishop and he made a suggestion which I think might be the answer. I'm going to Africa, Abi. There's a church being built in a village outside Lusaka in Zambia and I'm to be a lay preacher and assist the priest. Maybe there, away from everything, I can finally make sense of my life.'

'I see.' Abi's shoulders sagged in disappointment.

'I can understand if you feel angry. I realise I've never done anything to earn your love and you've offered so much to me. But, Abi, please don't wait for me any longer. I can promise you nothing just now because I don't know myself what the answers are.'

Abi took a gulp of her brandy, then licked her lips. Her hands were shaking slightly.

'Luca, do you still love me?'

'Of course, *amore mio*. I have no control over that. You know I adore you.'

'But you still love your God more,' she said slowly. 'Well, I could sit here and try to persuade you to stay, to tell you that *I* am what you need. But I know from bitter experience it's pointless, so I won't try.'

'Do you hate me? Have I used you? Oh Abi, the thought of hurting you makes me feel so terrible.'

'No, I don't hate you, Luca. How could I? I love you. I knew from the beginning you were promising nothing, but it was a chance I was prepared to take. I've lost and God's won yet again. When are you leaving?'

'I must go tomorrow.'

Abi nodded silently. Then she looked at him, her eyes bright with tears. 'If you really love me as you say you do, then you'll grant me one last wish.'

'Anything you want, *cara*.'

'Give me one night. For us, for the love we have.'

She leant towards him and put her lips to his questioningly. This time, he didn't protest. Instead, he took her face between his hands and responded with equal passion.

'For us,' he murmured, as he stroked her cheek gently. 'Even God can't deny me this.'

The following morning, Abi watched Luca as he stepped out of her bed. When he left the room to take a shower, she lay staring up at the ceiling.

All those years of wanting him, dreaming of his touch and, last night, it had finally happened.

And today he would walk away from her and – she had

to accept this – almost certainly it would be forever. She knew she couldn't go on hoping and wishing. For her own sake, she *had* to finally move on.

Abi swallowed hard and steeled herself not to cry. She rose from the bed that had been the scene of their lovemaking and began to dress hurriedly, then headed to the sanctuary of the kitchen before Luca emerged from the shower.

'I must leave now.' Luca's eyes searched hers as he appeared at the door.

She stood up and went to him, and he cradled her in his arms.

'Did it make a difference?' she asked. 'I thought perhaps . . .'

'Yes, it made a difference. I love you and I have no guilt about what we have done.'

'Then stay. Stay here with me. Please, Luca, I need you.' Her tears fell onto the roughness of his coat. 'Ask me to wait for you, please. I will, I will . . .'

Luca, too, was seconds from breaking down. 'No, *cara*, I can't and mustn't give you any false hope. However much I wish to ask you to wait for me. I must tell you no. I've asked too much of you already.'

'Yes, I'm sorry, I promised myself I wouldn't make a scene. You need to be going, I know.' She peeled herself away from him, brushed away the tears hastily and followed him to the door.

'*Ciao, amore mio*.'

Abi watched in silence as he walked down the steps. He turned and smiled up at her. Then, with a small wave, he was gone.

52

Rosanna heard the Jaguar sweep into the drive. She watched from the sitting room window as he walked across the gravel, then she went into the hall to open the front door.

'*Principessa*.' His arms went around his wife and he cradled her head against his chest. 'Rosanna, *cara*, I'm sorry, I'm so very sorry.'

'Roberto, let us go and sit down. We must talk.'

'What is wrong? Is it Nico?'

'No.' Rosanna led him into the sitting room and indicated the sofa. 'It is me.'

'You are ill?'

'Maybe in a way, yes, I have been,' she agreed.

'Then you must tell me what's wrong.'

She sat down next to Roberto and took his hands in hers. 'Roberto, have you any idea how much I have loved you – adored you – since I was eleven years old?'

'I know, *principessa*. I'm the luckiest man in the world. I do not deserve you, I never have. But I'm a changed man, you will see. Nico's illness and . . . other events have made me realise what I have been. I am going to cancel all my commitments for the next few months. A complete sabbatical, time to be with you and Nico, to get him well again.'

Rosanna smiled sadly, remembering the last time Roberto had made a similar promise. Then she shook her head.

'This is not about *you*, Roberto. It's about *me*, what I want,' she said gently.

'You want me here at home with Nico, don't you?'

'I used to think that might be the answer, and yes, you could take a sabbatical, but then, after a while, you will long to return to your other world. It's the way you are, the way it will always be. We . . . our love, it can never work.'

'What are you trying to say to me, Rosanna? That you wish me to leave?' He looked incredulous, half believing it was a joke.

'Yes, Roberto. That is what I wish. And if you love me, then you will do as I ask.'

Roberto ran a hand through his hair. 'No, no, Rosanna, you don't mean this. You love me, you need me. You know we are meant to be together.'

'Maybe we were once, but not now, not in the future.'

Roberto stood up and began to pace the room. 'You cannot mean this, you cannot. Not after what I have just . . .' He shook his head and slumped back down into a chair.

'What is it you have just done?'

'I meant I've taken a decision, the most important decision of my life. From now on, I will put you and Nico first. Nothing else matters to me. Only you, only Nico.'

Rosanna tried to gather her thoughts, to explain to him as rationally as possible how she felt.

'Roberto, everyone who cares for me has always been worried about our relationship. At first I thought it was only jealousy, that they couldn't bear to see us together and so happy.' She sighed softly. 'But now I understand. They saw how you changed me, how I became selfish, how my love for you overtook everything else. It wasn't your fault, it was mine. I didn't see this clearly until I put our child's life at risk. He might have died, Roberto, and I wouldn't have been there.'

'*Cara*, you cannot let go of our love for one mistake!'

'Roberto, don't you see that was just a symptom, not a cause?' she begged him. 'When I'm with you, I'm not myself. I drown in you and the love I have for you. Please, try to understand – it isn't because I don't love you that we must part, but because I love you too much.'

'No! No! Please, no!' Roberto put his head in his hands and began to sob. 'I cannot live without you. I cannot!'

She cradled him in her arms. '*Caro*, if you love me as you say you do, then you will go, give me a chance to have a future as the person I think I can be, *want* to be. Roberto, if you care for me at all, you must see what I am saying is right. For once I want you to be unselfish. Don't make this any harder than it is already.'

He looked up at her, utter devastation in his eyes. 'It is really what you want?'

'Oh yes. I don't think I have a choice.'

'Maybe you just need some time, *principessa*. The shock with Nico, it has confused you, made you overreact.'

'No, it hasn't. It's made me see things clearly for the first time. I've seen who I've become and I don't like her. My obsession with you has damaged many people's lives. And now, I want to be me again. Or at least to find out for the first time who I am.'

Slowly, he began to understand what she was trying to say.

'And what of Nico? You will deprive him of his papa?'

'Roberto, I have thought long and hard about Nico and whether I'm being selfish to ask you to leave. But we owe it to him to give him at least one parent who will put him first. And I can't do that when you are with me.'

'You'll let me see Nico?'

'Of course. Whenever you want, as often as you wish. We can organise it, I'm sure.'

'Is this . . . forever?'

'I think it must be.'

'I . . . When do you want me to go?'

'As soon as possible. The longer you are here, the harder it will be.'

Roberto gulped back the tears as he stood up. 'Rosanna, if I could find the words that would change your mind, I'd give up everything, my career, *everything*.'

'You may think that now, but you know as well as I do, deep down, that is not the answer. It would create more problems in the future than it solved. And it wouldn't be fair for me to ask it of you. Tell me you understand, Roberto. It's important to me that you do.'

He walked towards her, held out a hand and she stood up. He traced the contours of her face with trembling fingers.

'Yes, *principessa*, I understand. I understand now that it was *you* that I should have put first. It was our love for each other and for Nico that really mattered. And the tragedy is, I've learnt all these things too late. Don't blame yourself, Rosanna. It's my fault we've come to this, all my fault.'

'We must both take equal responsibility for the mistakes we've made.'

'Rosanna, I must tell you one thing. If you ever change your mind, please, all you have to do is tell me and I will be back by your side.'

Rosanna walked with him out of the sitting room and towards the front door.

'I will go and say goodbye to Nico at the hospital,' he muttered.

'Of course.'

'Anything . . . anything you need for him or yourself, just ask. I will not let my pride get in the way, as I did in the past.'

'Thank you, Roberto.'

'I must feel you in my arms one last time.'

She went to him, and they stood holding each other as if it was impossible for either of them to let go.

Rosanna felt that her heart might actually break in two. 'Thank you for understanding. I will never stop loving you. Never,' she whispered.

'Nor I you.' He tipped her chin up towards him and they kissed for the last time, their tears mingling. 'I will be waiting for you, *principessa*. Always.'

The Metropolitan Opera House, New York

So, Nico, that was how Roberto left us for a second time. It will be very hard for you to understand how your mamma could love someone the way I loved your papa, yet know I had to let him go. I had sent him away, after all those times I'd been alone and desperate for him. But I knew it was my only chance.

We saw each other occasionally over the next two years. I was determined I would not deprive you of your papa, however hard it was for me. I knew how much you loved spending time with him. Roberto insisted on sending you to all the best specialists to see if your hearing could be improved, but there was little they could do – the damage was irreversible.

It was ironic, Nico, as, when I did see your father, I really felt he had *changed for the better. It was as if, after all those years of behaving like a child, he'd finally grown up. There was a quietness, a wistful quality about him that seemed to have replaced the arrogance of the past.*

Then one day, as we watched you playing in the garden, he told me he was going to curtail his heavy work schedule. He would still sing, but he'd had a mild heart attack and the doctors had recommended a strict diet and a much quieter lifestyle. He was going to live at the villa in Corsica and any time we wished to visit, we were welcome. I knew, of course, that while I would send you, it was wrong to go myself. Any more than a few hours with him and I'd be back to where I started. And yet, we never discussed divorce. It was unimportant to me. I knew I would never marry again and he knew he wouldn't either.

I won't say that period was easy for me, but I'd spent so much of my past living for Roberto, I was determined to make the most of each second I had in the present. That is why I tell you now, Nico, to hold on to and appreciate every moment. Never let a day slip by without taking the most from it, because you will never have that day again.

And I was so lucky I had you. I was very proud of you, Nico, the way you adapted to your disability. With the help of the best hearing aid, it was possible for you to continue a relatively normal life. There was frustration, but there was a lot of laughter as well. And what you couldn't hear, you made up for with your eyes. You missed nothing.

And Ella, my dear, sweet Ella. The summer after Roberto left, she won a place at the Royal Academy of Music. Roberto not only insisted on paying her fees, but we also agreed she could use our house in Kensington, where he visited her whenever he was in England. He was so very caring towards her and the two of them struck up a close friendship.

As for my own career . . . well, after what had happened to you, I couldn't bear the thought of ever leaving you again.

There was only one thing that troubled me. I hadn't heard directly from Luca since our argument, apart from a number of postcards from Zambia all written to you. There was never a forwarding address. And Abi, too, was distant. At the time, I believed it was because she was so wrapped up in her successful career as a novelist and I didn't give it much thought . . .

53

Gloucestershire, March 1985

Rosanna left the church hall, hating the moment when she left Nico at playgroup. But it was important for him to socialise with other children, to live as normal a life as possible. He loved going there and the organiser had assured her that he was getting along just fine.

She checked her watch. She had three hours to kill. Usually, she'd drive home and spend the time doing domestic chores. But today Rosanna decided she'd do some shopping instead.

Entering a small boutique, Rosanna picked out a new outfit for Nico and a scarf for Ella. She emerged carrying her parcels and walked down the bustling Cheltenham street. Ambling past a bookshop, she paused and looked in the window. It was filled with a large display of Abi's new book.

'Aria'

The title filled her with curiosity. She'd bought a couple of Abi's books before and had read them with enjoyment.

Rosanna pushed open the door to the shop and walked across to the table on which a pile of Abi's books were stacked.

'Personally signed by the author,' read the banner above the pile. Rosanna wondered why, if Abi had been in the area for a signing event, she hadn't popped in to say hello. She picked up a copy and read the blurb on the back.

> From the author of *Sometime Soon* and *Forever* comes a stunning new bestseller to delight her many fans. Taking a world she knows intimately, Abigail Holmes brings us a story set in the world of opera; a tale of forbidden love, ambition and the sins of the past that weave an intricate tangle of emotions.

Rosanna took a copy up to the desk and paid for it. Then she strolled along the street to a small teashop she was fond of. She ordered a coffee, sat down at a table, opened the book and began to read.

'Hello.'

Rosanna looked up, startled.

'Stephen, hello.' Rosanna knew she was blushing.

'How are you?'

'Fine, very well.' She felt awkward and embarrassed, but reasoned with herself that Stephen must have wanted to speak to her. He could easily have walked straight past.

'How's the family?' he enquired.

'They're well, although I don't see Roberto very often. He lives in Corsica these days.'

'Does he? I had no idea. I thought you two were back together.'

'We were, but then . . . well, it's a long story,' she shrugged. 'Can I buy you a coffee?'

Stephen looked at his watch. 'I'm meeting someone here in ten minutes, but yes, that would be nice.'

Rosanna ordered a coffee for both of them as Stephen sat down.

'Stephen, I've been meaning to apologise to you for the past two years and, to be absolutely honest, well, I've never plucked up the courage to do it. Anyway, now we've met, I must say it: I behaved very badly and very selfishly and I'm terribly sorry, Stephen, really. Especially after all you did for me and Nico.'

'Thank you, Rosanna. That means a lot.' Stephen took a sip of his coffee. 'I was devastated when Ella told me, and I have to admit I was pretty angry you didn't even contact me to explain what had happened yourself. But,' he shrugged, 'it's all water under the bridge now.'

'I'm so sorry, Stephen. Can you forgive me?'

'In my heart of hearts I always knew you'd go back to him. I knew I could never compete with the great Roberto Rossini. But I don't regret our time together and I hope you don't either. And yes,' he added, 'I forgive you.'

'Thank you. I suppose all I can say is that I did come to my senses shortly after Roberto returned.' Rosanna sighed. 'It wasn't only you I hurt, Stephen, and I'm ashamed of the way I behaved then. I ended up cutting myself off from many people who had cared for me.'

'So tell me, just out of interest, after reuniting with Roberto, why are you now separated?'

'Oh, it's very complicated, but something happened to make me realise I was unhealthily obsessed with him.'

'What was that?'

'Nico became sick while I was abroad with Roberto. As a result of acute measles, he now has badly impaired hearing.'

Stephen looked stunned. 'Oh Rosanna, I really am sorry. The poor little chap.'

'Yes. It was hard for all of us. But I'm happy to say he's now doing well.' Rosanna took a sip of her coffee. 'Anyway, how are you? How's the gallery?'

'Fine, and yes, the gallery's going very well. I've just bought an old house on the other side of Cheltenham. It's being renovated at the moment, so I'm out antique-hunting. Maybe you and Nico would like to come over and see it sometime? I'd love to see him again. I really was awfully fond of him.'

'That's kind of you, Stephen, but—'

'Rosanna, there's no reason why we can't be friends, is there?'

'No, of course not,' she agreed.

'Ah, there she is.' Stephen looked up as the teashop door opened. A willowy blonde walked towards them and Stephen stood up.

'Rosanna, this is my wife, Kate.'

'Rosanna Rossini! Oh, I'm so pleased to meet you. I don't know much about opera, I'm afraid, but Stephen's talked about you often.' There was no edge to Kate's voice, just genuine warmth as she held out her hand.

'And it's lovely to meet you, too,' Rosanna replied.

'I think I told you that Rosanna has a lovely little boy, darling. I've invited them over to the house for a cup of tea.'

'Great, we'd love to have you,' smiled Kate. 'Now, I'm

sorry to drag him away, but we've got heaps of shopping to do. Houses don't decorate themselves unfortunately.'

'Yes, darling, we must get on.' Stephen stood up. 'Thanks for the coffee, Rosanna. We'll give you a ring and make a date. Take care of yourself.'

'Goodbye, Stephen. Bye, Kate.'

Wistfully, she watched Stephen wrap a tender arm round his wife as they left the teashop. But there was no point in dwelling on what might have been, and she was glad to see him happy and settled. She glanced down at her watch and saw she was already ten minutes late picking up Nico.

Rosanna ran up the path to the church hall. Nico stood peering out of the front door.

'Ah, Mrs Rossini, we were wondering where you'd got to,' said Mrs Price, the playgroup organiser.

'I'm so sorry, I bumped into an old friend and lost track of the time. Come on, darling.' Rosanna picked Nico up in her arms and walked towards the car park.

At three in the morning, Rosanna finished Abi's book. She had enjoyed it immensely and it had made her feel very nostalgic for the world she'd left behind. She turned off the light and lay in the dark, thinking how much she missed Abi. She decided that next time she was in London she would drop in on her. It had been too long.

Two weeks later, after a visit to the ear, nose and throat specialist in London, Rosanna stood on the pavement outside the hospital and turned to Nico.

'Shall we catch a taxi to see Auntie Abi?' she asked him,

exaggerating the words, which the specialist said would help him as he learnt to lip-read.

Nico nodded excitedly at the thought of a ride in a big black cab. 'Yes please, Mamma.'

Rosanna hailed the next taxi that passed.

'Fulham Road, please,' she said as the two of them climbed inside.

Rosanna rang the bell of Abi's ground-floor flat. And two minutes later, Abi opened the front door. She was wearing a pair of old jeans and a grubby T-shirt and her face had black smudges on it.

'What are you doing here?' she said in astonishment.

'Oh, that's nice, Abi. Your old friend drops in for a coffee and you're obviously not pleased to see her,' Rosanna teased her.

'No, I . . .' Abi looked flustered. 'It's just that it's not an awfully good time at the moment. I'm moving tomorrow.'

'We won't stay long, will we, Nico?' Rosanna smiled. 'Will you make us stand on the doorstep forever, Abi?'

'No.' Abi shrugged resignedly. 'You'd better come in.'

Rosanna and Nico followed her down the hall and into the flat. The sitting room was full of tea chests and newspaper.

'Where are you moving to?'

'A house in Notting Hill. I needed somewhere for . . . well, somewhere bigger.'

'The writing must be paying off then! That sounds exciting.' Rosanna watched as Abi knelt on the floor and began to wrap up a glass. 'Abi.' Rosanna knelt next to her and put a hand on her arm.

'Yes?'

'Why have you done your best to avoid seeing me for the last two years?'

Abi concentrated on her packing and didn't look up. 'Oh, you know how it is. We've both been so busy and . . . it's just one of those things. It's good to see you now, though.'

'You don't seem like you mean that. I read your latest book, by the way. It was wonderful. It evoked so many memories.'

Abi finally looked up and smiled. 'Thank you. Look, Rosanna, I really don't want to be rude, but could we arrange a time to meet for lunch or something? I have so much to do this afternoon.'

'Okay.' Rosanna stood up. 'Come on, Nico,' she sighed.

Abi followed them to the door.

'It was good to see you, Abi. I really hope we can get together soon.'

'And so do I . . . but the thing is . . .'

A high-pitched cry came from one of the rooms at the back of the flat.

'I have to go. She's crying again.'

'You have a baby?' Rosanna looked at her in amazement.

'Yes, well . . .'

'Abi, why didn't you tell me? Oh, I must see her!'

Before Abi could stop her, Rosanna was back inside the flat and walking down the corridor. She led Nico through the door and into a small but pretty pink and white nursery. There, sitting up in the cot, was a child of about eighteen months.

'Hello, little one, it's your Auntie Rosanna come to visit you.' She went to the window, drew back the curtains and turned back to the cot. '*Cara*, come to—' Rosanna stopped speaking abruptly as she stared at the baby.

Abi was standing at the door of the nursery, her face expressionless.

'Now you see why I haven't been in contact?' she sighed.

Rosanna took in the baby's olive skin, dark hair and eyes. 'I think I need to sit down.'

Ten minutes later, they were perched amongst the boxes in the sitting room drinking tea.

'We were only together once, I swear, Rosanna. It was Luca's last night in England and we both threw caution to the wind. And yes, it was an enormous shock to find myself pregnant, but I've wondered since if, subconsciously, I wanted it to happen. If I couldn't have Luca, at least I'd have part of him forever.' Abi stroked her baby's downy head as she bounced her on her knee.

'And you've never tried to contact Luca, to tell him he has a daughter? What's her name, by the way?'

'Phoebe. I named her after the heroine in my first book,' she grinned. 'No, Rosanna. I don't want him to know. He has written to me from wherever he is out in the bush in Africa, but I haven't responded. To be honest, I don't trust myself not to say anything,' she sighed. 'It would put him in a dreadful position and could ruin his future if he's still intending to become a priest. His beloved church preaches forgiveness of sins, but they don't seem to apply that very freely to their own clergy. So, that's why I've stayed away from you as well. I'm sorry, I should have told you sooner. Are you horrified?'

'No, Abi.' Rosanna shook her head wearily. 'I'm simply hurt that you didn't trust me enough to tell me. You know I would have been there for you.'

'I think that maybe I was ashamed,' Abi admitted. 'After all, I knew when it happened there was no future for us. And it was me who instigated it, not Luca.'

'Goodness, Abi, after what's happened in my life, I hardly think I have any right to be narrow-minded,' Rosanna chided her. 'I'm also sorry that I was so wrapped up in my own world, that I didn't take the time to notice what was happening between you and Luca.'

'Well, Luca and I were never as dramatic as you and Roberto, but, in our own quiet way, we loved each other as much. He made me a better person,' she said sadly. 'Anyway' – Abi took a sip of her tea – 'I'm so glad you know, Rosanna.'

'And Luca must know one day, too.'

'Maybe,' shrugged Abi. 'Only time will tell.'

After they'd arrived home and Rosanna had put Nico to bed that evening, she paced up and down the kitchen. She looked out onto the terrace and remembered Abi and Luca together that summer. The private jokes they shared, the way they would talk for hours, long after everyone else was in bed . . . She remembered Stephen had once remarked that he thought they were in love.

Could it be that Luca had spent his life searching for something that had been staring him in the face for all these years?

By the following morning, Rosanna had reached a decision. She'd asked Abi yesterday for Luca's forwarding address in Zambia. And now, it was *her* turn to play God. She would find him and bring him home.

*

The flight from Lusaka landed on time. Rosanna stood nervously, scanning the faces as they came through the sliding doors into the arrivals hall.

Finally Luca emerged, thinner than she remembered, a deep suntan etched on his handsome face. Rosanna went to greet him and flung her arms around him. 'Luca, it is so good to see you.'

'Rosanna.' He returned her hug, then pulled back and studied her carefully. 'You look very well for someone who's supposed to be in the middle of a crisis. I'm glad you said in your letter that it was nothing to do with Nico or I'd have been worried sick. How is he, by the way?'

'He's gorgeous.' Rosanna smiled.

'Then what is it that has dragged me all the way back from Africa?'

'I'll tell you as we drive,' she said, taking his arm. 'Do you know, it must have taken two weeks for you to get my letter? I was beginning to despair of a reply,' she said as she steered him towards the car park. 'I thought maybe you didn't want to ever speak to me again.'

'Rosanna, I only get into the town to pick up my mail once a week or so. I promise that I telephoned you as soon as I received it. I've missed you, *piccolina*, so very much.'

'And I you. The main thing is that you're here now. Hop in.' Rosanna unlocked her Volvo and Luca got into the passenger seat.

'You've passed your driving test at last?' he commented.

'Yes. Living out in the country with a young child, it became rather essential. Anyway, you must tell me all about Africa. It looks as if you haven't eaten for weeks, Luca.' Rosanna started the car and reversed it out of the space.

'That's an exaggeration, but you're right. I admit I've begun to dream about pizza recently.'

'Has it helped you, though, being so far away?'

'You mean, made up my mind whether I still wished to become a priest?'

'Yes.'

'Well, now I can tell you what happened. You see, I'd seen Carlotta suffer so, and there were other things too that confused me at the time. Then, when I arrived out in Africa, I witnessed such poverty and sickness that I had a complete change of heart about the priesthood. I realised that God had a different plan for me. To help those in need, yes, but not by conducting Mass, taking confession and dealing with Church bureaucracy. I wrote to my bishop and told him of my feelings, and I gave up my official position with the Church soon after.'

'Well, that's wonderful that you were finally able to make a decision, Luca. But why then did you not come back home?'

'Where was my home, Rosanna? I felt I didn't have one any longer. I received no reply from Abi when I forwarded her my address originally and I knew I'd upset you terribly. So I decided to stay on in Zambia and joined a British charity working over there. For the first time in my life, I really began to feel I was of use, practically as well as spiritually.' Luca stared out of the window. 'I can't begin to tell you what it's like there. The people and the landscape are so extraordinary, but the hardship, the deprivation, I . . .' He looked at her suddenly. 'Are you disappointed in me, Rosanna?'

'Of course not. I know only too well how much courage it takes to admit you were wrong,' she replied, desperate not to reveal her relief at Luca's news.

'But please, enough of me. Tell me what it is that has brought me back here?'

'I will. It's nothing bad, I promise,' comforted Rosanna. 'But first, let me tell you about Roberto.'

Luca sat in stunned silence as Rosanna explained the circumstances of their separation of two years ago. When she'd finished, he exhaled slowly. 'Rosanna, I never believed you would leave him. If I had known this at the time, well, many things might have been different.' Luca stared out of the window as he remembered. 'You must know, *piccolina*, that I desperately regret the argument we had. I should not have interfered. I might not have liked Roberto, but I should have respected what you felt for him.'

'No, Luca, you were right to say what you did. It forced me to make a decision. Thanks to you, I'm much happier now, though occasionally a little lonely,' she admitted.

'Loneliness is sometimes the price we pay, Rosanna,' he said sadly. 'Who is looking after Nico while you collect me?'

'A close friend,' she replied lightly. 'So tell me more about Africa . . .'

Abi heard the car on the gravel. She picked up Phoebe with one arm, held Nico's hand with the other and went out to greet Rosanna.

'Mamma, Mamma!' Nico let go of Abi's hand and ran towards Rosanna as she climbed out of the car.

Abi watched the passenger door open and a familiar slim figure emerge. He turned and saw her, and they gazed at each other, both rooted to the spot in shock.

'Luca,' Rosanna prompted softly. 'Go and say hello to Abi. And your baby daughter.'

'My daughter? I . . .'

'*She* is the reason you had to come home, Luca. I promise you, Phoebe needs your love and protection more than anyone else.'

'Abi too,' Luca choked out. And finally, he began to walk hesitantly towards them.

'Oh God, Luca, oh God,' whispered Abi, her eyes glittering with tears as he reached her side.

Rosanna hugged Nico tightly to her, her own eyes streaming, as Luca stretched out his arms and embraced his family.

The Metropolitan Opera House, New York

I took a chance, Nico, a big chance, but it was the right thing to do. And maybe I felt as though I had finally repaid Luca for all he had done for me by reuniting him with Abi and their baby. After that, Luca never did return to Africa, but instead took a position in the London office of the charity, fund-raising as though his life depended on it. They were a joy to be with, all those years of pain and searching finally washed away. Abi, between novels, produced another two children and they all lived in ordered chaos in the house in Notting Hill.

But what of me, Nico? What of your mamma?

When you were six years old, you started at the small private school Ella had attended. The teachers there were wonderful, taking your disability into account but ensuring that you took part fully in all the school's activities. I'm sure you will remember how much you loved it there and how many friends you made. But for me it was difficult. I was used to being with you all the time, and the hours while you were at school dragged by interminably.

So, to fill the silence, I began to play my old recordings and found myself singing along to them. Much to my amazement, my voice had not vanished.

If anything, it had mellowed, matured. I was, after all, only thirty-one years old. And the passion I had once been driven by began to build inside me again.

I found a lovely young woman in the village who looked after you while I attended twice-weekly sessions with a singing coach in London, and after four months of hard work and a great deal of practice, I picked up the telephone and called Chris Hughes, my old agent.

I started tentatively, singing at small recitals to build up my confidence. I had to prove my talent all over again, not just to a new audience, but to myself. And the offers slowly began to come back in. The only stipulations I made were that I would never again sing with Roberto and that my schedule was not so taxing as to take me away from you for long periods.

But when Paolo de Vito offered me Mimi in La Bohème *at the beginning of La Scala's new season, as you can imagine, I couldn't say no. You went to stay with your beloved Uncle Luca and Aunt Abi and I flew off to Milan. There were no recriminations from Paolo; he welcomed me back with open arms. And, ten years later than scheduled, I sang Mimi on the stage of La Scala. I blush to say it, but I was a sensation. Even your grandfather was in the audience, with Signora Barezi, his wife, hearing his daughter sing live for the first time since Luigi Vincenzi's soirée.*

In retrospect, the best thing I could have done was to have the break I did when you were small.

When I returned to opera, I was far more mature and able to cope with the fame and the attention that surrounded me. And my experience has meant I have been able to guide Ella through some of the pitfalls that befell me. You know how well she is doing at Covent Garden, her roles growing along with her confidence, but then again, she has not yet fallen in love . . .

I've now had eight years of being back at the top of my profession. The life I lived with Roberto seems a universe away. I won't say I didn't think about your papa, for that would be a lie. I never tried to stop myself, for I knew he was as much a part of me as my arms or my legs, and nothing could ever change that.

And then, two weeks ago, I got a telephone call. It was from a doctor in Corsica. Roberto had suffered another heart attack. His condition was very serious and he was asking to see me . . .

54

Corsica, June 1996

Rosanna arrived at the nurses' station and smiled with trepidation at the nurse on duty.

'I'm here to see Roberto Rossini,' she said quietly. 'I'm his wife.'

'I'm glad you're here, Mrs Rossini. He's been asking for you. But I must warn you, he had another attack last night and has been slipping in and out of consciousness ever since.'

'Oh God.' Rosanna gulped down a sob. 'Is he . . . ? Is it . . . ?' She could not voice the words, but the expression on the nurse's face told her everything she needed to know.

'I'll take you to see him. Please, try to prepare yourself, Mrs Rossini. And say what you would like to if he regains consciousness. I'm sorry to tell you, but there isn't much time.'

Desperately trying to prepare herself and gather strength, Rosanna followed the woman along the corridor and into a private room. A collection of monitors and tubes were bleeping and pumping. Amongst all the mechanical paraphernalia lay Roberto. His eyes were closed, his skin grey.

The nurse smiled sympathetically at Rosanna, then left her alone.

She walked over to the bed and stared down at him. She reached for his hand, took it in hers and stroked it. 'Roberto, Roberto, I'm here,' she said softly.

Eventually, he stirred and opened his eyes. The sun shone out of them as he looked at her.

'Rosanna, my *principessa* . . . I . . .' His eyes filled with tears. His trembling fingers moved towards her cheek. 'Let me touch you, make sure you are real. Oh my love, my love.'

They stared at each other for a long time, drinking each other in.

'I've heard you sing many times since your comeback. You are wonderful, wonderful. Your gift was always exceptional, but now you sing with such maturity and integrity.'

'I learnt that thanks to you, Roberto.'

'Did you?' His eyes brightened.

'Oh yes. I was still a little girl when I met you. I've grown up in the past few years.'

'Are you happy, my Rosanna? I want you to be happy.'

'Not in the same way as when we were together, but I'm content, yes.'

'I was at my happiest with you,' he murmured. 'Please, my darling, don't live the rest of your life on your own. Find someone to love you, give Nico a papa. Apologise to him for me, won't you?'

'You have nothing to apologise for, Roberto, but I promise I will try to explain to him what it was his parents shared.'

'And what was it?' Roberto's eyes brimmed with tears once again.

'Love. A love so powerful and obsessive it blinded me to

everything else. But I will be forever glad that it happened to me.'

'Yes. I . . .' She watched as pain seared through Roberto's eyes and held his hand tighter, trying not to show her despair.

'You won't have to divorce me now,' he said a few seconds later. 'You can be my widow. It's much more dignified.' He managed a hoarse chuckle.

'Roberto, please don't say that,' she begged him.

'No, *cara*, I feel this body has lived enough. And now that I have seen you, I can die in peace. Rosanna' – Roberto beckoned her nearer to him so she could hear him clearly – 'there is something I want to tell you, one thing that you do not know. I cannot bear for you to think I deceived you, or wanted to hurt you. I didn't know at the time, you see. Please, you must believe that.'

She could see he was becoming agitated. 'Tell me, Roberto. I promise I will understand.'

'It is . . . it is . . .'

Rosanna watched as Roberto's face contorted in pain and he gripped her hand. 'Tell Ella, tell her she must sing for her papa. Ask Luca, he will understand. I . . . kiss me, Rosanna.'

Her head bent to his and she kissed him gently on the lips.

'There was never anyone else. Never. Tell me you love me, tell me you—' His body jerked upwards, then relaxed.

Rosanna put her arms round him as the monitors began to sound a single, monotonous tone. The room was suddenly full of strangers, but she was oblivious to them.

'*Ti amo*, Roberto, I love you, I love you . . .'

The Metropolitan Opera House
New York, July 1996

Rosanna dabbed at the tears that had spilt on the page she had just written. It was nearly over. One more page and she could at last find peace. The story had been told and she hoped one day Nico would understand. She picked up her pen and began to write.

So, Nico, since your father died three weeks ago, I have spent every spare moment writing to you. I promised your papa I would try to explain our love and I hope that, as you read this, you will forgive both of us. I love you very much and I know, in his way, so did Roberto.

After my last meeting with your father, Luca told me about Ella, about the secret he and Carlotta had kept for so long. I broke the news to Ella a few days after Roberto's funeral and she took it in that calm, controlled way she has. She loved Roberto very much; in his last few years she saw how he had tried to make up for the past.

So your papa is gone, Nico, and in a few hours' time, I will stand on the stage of the Metropolitan Opera House in New York and sing an aria especially composed in memory of Roberto Rossini. On the last chorus, Ella will join me, take my hand and we will sing together, for him. We will forget the bad things and only remember the good, for we are human and that is how we survive.

I have also decided that all I have written to you will be kept by my solicitor until I too am gone. Only then will you know the truth of the passion from which you were born.

Death is not frightening, Nico. For now Roberto waits for me there. And our kind of love never dies.

I see him, I see him everywhere.

Your loving mamma

Acknowledgements

I would like to thank my editor, Jeremy Trevathan, for persuading me that the story should see the light of day again. Susan Moss for helping me with the extensive re-edits and her dogged search for the tiniest detail. (When I first wrote *The Italian Girl*, there was little in the way of Internet, especially on the south-west coast of Ireland, so it was left to me to conduct all the research in the British Library.) Catherine Richards, Jonathan Atkins and all the team at Pan Mac for their hard work on the book's behalf. Olivia Riley, Jacquelyn Heslop and Stephen Riley for their constant support behind the scenes.

And of course, my children. Harry, now 21, to whom this book was originally dedicated and Isabella, now 17, who decided to make her entrance into the world two chapters from the end of this book. Leonora, who hadn't appeared yet, and Kit, my 'baby' son, who has sworn he won't ever read this, as he prefers cricket bats to books, even if it is now 'his'! I love you all.

The Midnight Rose

by LUCINDA RILEY

Spanning four generations, *The Midnight Rose* sweeps from the glittering palaces of India to the majestic stately homes of England, following the extraordinary life of Anahita Chavan, from 1911 to the present day . . .

In the heyday of the British Raj, eleven-year-old Anahita forms a lifelong friendship with the headstrong Princess Indira, the privileged daughter of rich Indian royalty. Becoming the princess's official companion, Anahita accompanies her friend to England just before the outbreak of the Great War. There, she meets the young Donald Astbury – reluctant heir to the magnificent, remote Astbury Estate – and his scheming mother.

Eighty years later, Rebecca Bradley, a young American film star, has the world at her feet. But when her turbulent relationship with her equally famous boyfriend takes an unexpected turn, she's relieved that her latest role, playing a 1920s debutante, will take her away from the glare of publicity to the wilds of Dartmoor. Ari Malik, Anahita's great-grandson, arrives unexpectedly, on a quest for his family's past. What he and Rebecca discover begins to unravel the dark secrets that haunt the Astbury dynasty . . .

An extract follows

Prologue

Anahita

I am a hundred years old today. Not only have I managed to survive a century, but I've also seen in a new millennium.

As the dawn breaks and the sun begins to rise over Mount Kanchenjunga beyond my window, I lie on my pillows and smile to myself at the utter ridiculousness of the thought. If I were a piece of furniture, an elegant chair for example, I would be labelled an antique. I would be polished, restored and proudly put on show as a thing of beauty. Sadly, that isn't the case with my human frame, which has not mellowed like a fine piece of mahogany over its lifetime. Instead, my body has deteriorated into a sagging hessian sack containing a collection of bones.

Any 'beauty' in me that might be deemed valuable lies hidden deep inside. It is the wisdom of one hundred years lived on this earth, and a heart that has beaten a steady accompaniment to every conceivable human emotion and behaviour.

One hundred years ago, to this very day, my parents, in the manner of all Indians, consulted an astrologer to tell them about the future of their newborn baby girl. I believe I still have the soothsayer's predictions for my life amongst the few possessions of my mother that I've kept. I remember them saying that I was to be long-lived, but in 1900, I realise, my parents assumed this meant that, with the gods' blessing, I would survive into my fifties.

I hear a gentle tap on my door. It is Keva, my faithful maid, armed with a tray of English Breakfast tea and a small jug of cold milk. Tea taken the English way is a habit I've never managed to break, even though I've lived in India – not to mention Darjeeling – for the past seventy-eight years.

I don't answer Keva's knock, preferring on this special morning to be alone with my thoughts a while longer. Undoubtedly Keva will wish to talk through the events of the day, will be eager to get me up, washed and dressed before my family begins to arrive.

As the sun begins to burn off the clouds covering the snow-capped mountains, I search the blue sky for the answer I've pleaded with the heavens to give me every morning of the past seventy-eight years.

Today, please, I beg the gods, for I have known in each hour that has ticked by since I last saw my child that he still breathes somewhere on this planet. If he had died, I would have known the moment it happened, as I have for all those in my life whom I've loved, when they have passed over.

Tears fill my eyes and I turn my head to the nightstand by my bed to study the one photograph I have of him, a cherubic two-year-old sitting smiling on my knee. It was given to me by my friend, Indira, along with his death certificate a few weeks after I'd been informed of my son's death.

A lifetime ago, I think. The truth is, my son is now an old man too. He will celebrate his eighty-first birthday in October of this year. But even with *my* powers of imagination, it's impossible for me to see him as such.

I turn my head determinedly away from my son's image, knowing that today I deserve to enjoy the celebration my family has planned for me. But somehow, on all these occasions, when I see my other child and her children, and her children's children, the absence of my son only feeds the pain in my heart, reminding me he has always been missing.

Of course, they believe, and always have, that my son died seventy-eight years ago.

'Maaji, see, you even have his death certificate! Leave him to his rest,' my daughter, Muna, would say with a sigh. 'Enjoy the family you have living.'

After all these years, I understand Muna becomes frustrated with me. And she is of course right to. She wants to be enough, just her alone. But a lost child is something that can never be replaced in a mother's heart.

And for today, my daughter will have her way. I will sit in my chair and enjoy watching the dynasty I have spawned. I won't bore them with my stories of India's history. When they arrive in their fast Western jeeps, with their children playing on their battery-operated gadgets, I will not remind them how Indira and I climbed the steep hills around Darjeeling on horseback, that electricity and running water in any home were once rare, or of my voracious reading of any tattered book I could get my hands on. The young are irritated by stories of the past; they wish to live only in the present, just as I did when I was their age.

I can imagine that most of my family are not looking forward to flying halfway across India to visit their great-grandmother on her hundredth birthday, but perhaps I'm being hard on them. I've thought a great deal in the past few years about why the young seem to be uncomfortable when they're with the old; they could learn so many things they need to know from us. And I've decided that their discomfort stems from the fact that, in our fragile physical presence, they become aware of what the future holds for them. They can only see, in their full glow of strength and beauty, how eventually they will be diminished one day too. They don't know what they will gain.

How can they begin to see inside us? Understand how their souls will grow, their impetuousness be tamed and their selfish thoughts be dimmed by the experiences of so many years?

But I accept that this is nature, in all its glorious complexity. I have ceased to question it.

When Keva knocks at the door for a second time, I admit her. As she talks at me in fast Hindi, I sip my tea and run over the names of my four grandchildren and eleven great-grandchildren. At a hundred years old, one wants to at least prove that one's mind is still in full working order.

The four grandchildren my daughter gave me have each gone on to become successful and loving parents themselves. They flourished in the new world that independence from the British brought to India, and their children have taken the mantle even further. At least six of them, from what I recall, have started their own businesses or are in a professional trade. Selfishly, I wish that one of my extended offspring had taken an interest in medicine, had followed after me, but I realise that I can't have everything.

As Keva helps me into the bathroom to wash, I consider that my family have had a mixture of luck, brains and family connections on their side. And that my beloved India has probably another century to go before the millions who still starve on her streets gain some modicum of their basic human needs. I have done my best to help over the years, but I realise my efforts are a mere ripple in the ocean against a roaring tide of poverty and deprivation.

Sitting patiently whilst Keva dresses me in my new sari – a birthday present from Muna, my daughter – I decide I won't think these maudlin thoughts today. I've attempted where I can to improve those lives that have brushed against mine, and I must be content with that.

'You look beautiful, Madam Chavan.'

As I look at my reflection in the mirror, I know that she is lying, but I love her for it. My fingers reach for the pearls that have sat around my neck for nearly eighty years. In my will, I have left them to Muna.

'Your daughter arrives at eleven o'clock, and the rest of the family will be here an hour later. Where shall I put you until they come?'

I smile at her, feeling much like a mahogany chair. 'You may put me in the window. I want to look at my mountains,' I say. She helps me up, steers me gently to the armchair and sits me down.

'Can I bring you anything else, Madam?'

'No. You go now to the kitchen and make sure that cook of ours has the lunch menu under control.'

'Yes, Madam.' She moves my bell from the nightstand to the table at my side and quietly leaves the room.

I turn my face into the sunlight, which is starting to stream through the big picture windows of my hilltop bungalow. As I bask in it like a cat, I remember the friends who have already passed over and won't be joining me today for my celebration.

Indira, my most beloved friend, died over fifteen years ago. I confess that was one of the few moments in my life when I have broken down and wept uncontrollably. Even my devoted daughter could not match the love and friendship Indira showed me. Self-absorbed and flighty until the moment she died, Indira was there when I needed her most.

I look across to the writing bureau which sits in the alcove opposite me, and can't help but think about what is concealed inside its locked drawer. It is a letter, and it runs over three hundred pages. It is written to my beloved son and tells the story of my life from the beginning. As the years passed, I began to worry that I would forget the details, that they would become blurred and grainy in my mind, like the reel of a silent black-and-white film. If, as I believe to this day, my son is alive and if he were ever returned to me, I wanted to be able to present him with the story of his mother and her enduring love for her lost child. And the reasons why she had had to leave him behind . . .

I began to write it when I was in middle age, believing then that I might be taken at any time. There it has sat for nearly fifty years, untouched and unread, because he never came to find me, and I still haven't found him.

Not even my daughter knows the story of my life before she arrived on the planet. Sometimes I feel guilty for never revealing the truth to her. But I believe it is enough that she has known my love when her brother was denied it.

I glance at the bureau, viewing in my mind's eye the yellowing pile of paper inside it. And I ask the gods to guide me. When I die, as surely I must soon, I would be horrified for it to fall into the wrong hands. I ponder for a few seconds on whether I should light a fire and ask Keva to place the papers onto it. But no, I shake my head instinctively. I can never bring myself to do that, just in case I do find him. There is still hope. After all, I've lived to a hundred; I may live to a hundred and ten.

But whom to entrust it to, in the meantime, just in case . . . ?

I mentally scan my family members, taking them in generations. At each name, I listen for guidance. And it's on the name of one of my great-grandsons that I pause.

Ari Malik, the eldest child of my eldest grandson, Vivek. I chuckle slightly as the shiver runs up my spine – the signal I've had from those above who understand so much more than I ever can. Ari, the only member of my extended family to be blessed with blue eyes. Other than my beloved lost child.

I concentrate hard to bring to mind his details; with eleven great-grandchildren, I comfort myself, a person half my age would struggle to remember. And besides, they are spread out all over India these days, and I rarely see them.

Vivek, Ari's father, has been the most financially successful of my grandchildren. He was always clever, if a little dull. He is an engineer and has earned enough to provide his wife and three children with a very comfortable life. If my memory serves me, Ari was educated in England. He was always a bright little thing, though quite what he's been doing since he left school escapes me. Today, I decide, I will find out. I will watch him. And I'm sure I'll know whether my current instinct is correct.

With that settled, and feeling calmer now that a solution to my dilemma is perhaps at hand, I close my eyes and allow myself to doze.

*

'Where is he?!' Samina Malik whispered to her husband. 'He swore to me that he wouldn't be late for this,' she added, as she surveyed the other, fully present members of Anahita's extended family. They were clustered around the old lady in the elegant drawing room of her bungalow, plying her with presents and compliments.

'Don't panic, Samina,' Vivek comforted his wife, 'our son will be here.'

'Ari said he'd meet us at the station so we could come up the hill together as a family at ten o'clock . . . I swear, Vivek, that boy has no respect for his family, I—'

'Hush, *pyari*, he's a busy young man, and a good boy, too.'

'You think so?' asked Samina. 'I'm not so sure. Every time I call his apartment, a different female voice answers. You know what Mumbai is like; full of Bollywood hussies and sharks,' she whispered, not wishing any other member of the family to overhear their conversation.

'Yes, and our son is twenty-five years old now and running his own business. He can take care of himself,' Vivek replied.

'The staff are waiting for him to arrive so they can bring in the champagne and make the toast. Keva is concerned your grandmother will become too tired if we leave it much longer.' Samina sighed. 'If Ari's not here in the next ten minutes, I'll tell them to continue without him.'

'I told you, there will be no need for you to do that,' Vivek said, smiling broadly as Ari, his favourite son, entered the room. 'Your mother was in a panic, as always,' he told Ari, smiling as he clasped his son in a warm embrace.

'You promised to be there at the station. We waited an hour! Where were you?' Samina frowned at her handsome son but, as always, she knew it was a losing battle against the tide of his charm.

'Ma, forgive me.' Ari gave his mother a winning smile and took her hands in his. 'I was delayed, and I did try to call your cellphone. But, as usual, it was switched off.'

Ari and his father shared a smirk. Samina's inability to use her cellphone was a family joke.

'Anyway, I'm here now,' he said, looking around at the rest of his clan. 'Did I miss anything?'

'No, and your great-grandmother has been so busy greeting the rest of her family, let's hope she hasn't noticed your late arrival,' replied Vivek.

Ari turned and looked through the crowd of his own blood to the matriarch whose genes had spun invisible threads down through the generations. As he did so, he saw her bright, inquisitive eyes pinned on him.

'Ari! You have thought to join us at last.' She smiled. 'Come and kiss your great-grandmother.'

'She may be a hundred today, but your grandmother misses nothing,' Samina whispered to Vivek.

As Anahita opened her frail arms to Ari, the crowd of relations parted and all eyes in the room turned to him. Ari walked towards her and knelt in front of her, showing his respect with a deep *pranaam* and waiting for her blessing.

'Nani,' he greeted her using the affectionate pet name that all her grandchildren and great-grandchildren addressed her by. 'Forgive me for being late. It's a long journey from Mumbai,' he explained.

As he looked up, he could see her eyes boring into him in the peculiar way they always did, as if she were assessing his soul.

'No matter,' she said as her shrunken, childlike fingers touched his cheek with the light brush of a butterfly wing. 'Although –' she lowered her voice to a whisper so only he could hear – 'I always find it useful to check I have set my alarm to the correct time the night before.' She gave him a surreptitious wink, then indicated that he was to stand. 'You and I will speak later. I can see Keva is eager to start the proceedings.'

'Yes, Nani, of course,' said Ari, feeling a blush rising to his cheeks as he stood. 'Happy birthday.'

As he walked back towards his parents, Ari wondered just how his great-grandmother could have known the exact reason why he was late today.

The day progressed as planned, with Vivek, as the eldest of Anahita's grandchildren, making a moving speech about her remarkable life. As the champagne flowed, tongues loosened and the peculiar tension of a family gathered together after too long apart began to ease. The naturally competitive edge of the siblings blurred as they re-established their places in the family hierarchy, and the younger cousins lost their shyness and found common ground.

'Look at your son!' commented Muna, Anahita's daughter, to Vivek. 'His girl cousins are swooning all over him. It will be time for him to think of marriage soon,' she added.

'I doubt that's how he sees it,' grumbled Samina to her mother-in-law. 'These days, young men seem to play the field into their thirties.'

'You will not arrange anything for him, then?' enquired Muna.

'We will, of course, but I doubt he'll agree.' Vivek sighed. 'Ari is of a new generation, the master of his own universe. He has his business and travels the world. Times have changed, Ma, and Samina and I must allow our children some choice in picking their husbands and wives.'

'Really?' Muna raised an eyebrow. 'That's very modern of you, Vivek. After all, you two haven't done so badly together.'

'Yes, Ma,' agreed Vivek, taking his wife's hand. 'You made a good choice for me.' He smiled.

'But we're swimming against an impossible current,' said Samina. 'The young do as they wish these days, and make their own decisions.' Wishing to change the subject, she glanced across to Anahita. 'Your mother seems to be enjoying the day,' she commented to Muna. 'She really is a miracle, a wonder of nature.'

'Yes,' Muna sighed, 'but I do worry about her up here in the hills with only Keva to care for her. It gets so cold in the winter and it can't be good for her old bones. I've asked her many times to come and live with us in Guhagar so that we can watch over her. But, of course, she refuses. She says she feels closer to her spirits up here and, of course, her past too.'

'Her *mysterious* past.' Vivek raised an eyebrow. 'Ma, do you think you'll ever persuade her to tell you who your father was? I know he died before you were born, but the details have always seemed sketchy to me.'

'It mattered when I was growing up, and I remember plaguing her with questions, but now,' Muna shrugged, 'if she wants to keep her secrets, she can. She could not have been a more loving parent to me and I don't wish to upset her.' As Muna glanced over and looked at her mother fondly, Anahita caught her eye and beckoned her daughter towards her.

'Yes, Maaji, what is it?' Muna asked as she joined her mother.

'I'm a little tired now.' Anahita stifled a yawn. 'I wish to rest. And in one hour I want you to bring my great-grandson, Ari, to see me.'

'Of course.' Muna helped her mother to stand, and walked her through her relations. Keva, as ever hovering close by her mistress, stepped forward. 'My mother wishes to have a rest, Keva. Can you take her and settle her?'

'Of course, it has been a long day.'

Muna watched them leave the room and went back to join Vivek and his wife. 'She's taking a rest, but she's asked me if Ari will go and see her in one hour.'

'Really?' Vivek frowned. 'I wonder why.'

'Who knows the workings of my mother's mind?' Muna said, sighing.

'Well, I'd better tell him, I know he was talking about leaving soon. He has some business meeting in Mumbai first thing tomorrow morning.'

'Well, just for once, his family will come first,' said Samina firmly. 'I will go and find him.'

When Ari was told by his mother that his great-grandmother wished an audience with him in an hour's time, he was, as his father had predicted, not happy at all.

'I can't miss that plane,' he explained. 'You must understand, Ma, that I have a business to run.'

'Then I will ask your father to go and tell his grandmother that on her hundredth birthday, her eldest great-grandchild could not spare the time to speak with her as she had requested.'

'But, Ma—' Ari saw his mother's grim expression and sighed. 'Okay,' he nodded. 'I will stay. Excuse me, I must try and find a signal somewhere in this place to make a call and postpone the meeting.'

Samina watched her son as he walked away from her, staring intently at his cellphone. He'd been a determined child from the day he was born, and there was no doubt that she had indulged her firstborn, as any mother did. He'd always been special, from the moment he'd opened his eyes and she'd stared at the blueness of them in shock. Vivek had teased her endlessly about them, questioning his wife's fidelity. Until they'd visited Anahita and she'd announced that Muna's dead father had also been the owner of eyes of a similar colour.

Ari's skin was lighter than that of the rest of his siblings, and his startling looks had always attracted attention. With the amount of it he had received over his twenty-five years, there was no doubt he had an arrogance about him. But his saving grace had always been his sweetness of character. Out of all her children, Ari had always been the most loving towards her, at her side in an instant if there was a problem. Up until the time he'd taken off for Mumbai, announcing he was starting his own business . . .

Nowadays, the Ari who visited his family seemed harder, self-absorbed, and if she were being frank, Samina found she liked him less and less. Walking back towards her husband, she prayed it was a stage that would pass.

'My great-grandson may come in now,' Anahita announced, as Keva sat her up in bed and fluffed the pillows behind her head.

'Yes, Madam. I will get him.'

'And I do not wish for us to be disturbed.'

'No, Madam.'

'Good afternoon, Nani,' said Ari as he walked briskly into the room a few seconds later. 'I hope you are feeling more rested now?'

'Yes.' Anahita indicated the chair. 'Please, Ari, sit down. And I apologise for disrupting your business plans tomorrow.'

'Really,' Ari felt the blood rushing to his cheeks for the second time that day, 'it's no problem at all.' He watched as she gazed at him with her penetrating eyes, and wondered how she seemed to be able to read his mind.

'Your father tells me you're living in Mumbai and that you now run a successful business.'

'Well, I wouldn't describe it as successful right now,' Ari said. 'But I'm working very hard to make it so in the future.'

'I can see that you're an ambitious young man. And I'm sure that one day your business will bear fruit as you hope it will.'

'Thank you, Nani.'

Ari watched as his great-grandmother gave the ghost of a smile. 'Of course, it may not bring you the contentment you believe it will. There's more to life than work and riches. Still, that's for you to discover,' she added. 'Now, Ari, I have something I wish to give you. Please, open the writing bureau with this key, and take out the pile of paper you'll find inside it.'

Ari took the key from his great-grandmother's fingers, twisted it in the lock and removed an ageing manuscript from inside it.

'What is this?' he asked her.

'It is the story of your great-grandmother's life. I wrote it to keep a record for my lost son. Sadly, I've never found him.'

Ari watched as Anahita's eyes became watery. He'd heard some talk from his father years ago about the son who had died in infancy in England when his great-grandmother had been over there during the Great War. If his memory served him right, he thought she'd had to leave him behind when she returned to India. Apparently, Anahita had refused to believe that her son was dead.

'But I thought—'

'Yes, I'm sure you've been told I have his death certificate. And I'm simply a sad and perhaps mad mother who is unable to accept her beloved son's passing.'

Ari shifted uncomfortably in his chair. 'I have heard of the story,' he admitted.

'I know what my family think, and what you almost certainly think too,' Anahita stated firmly. 'But believe me, there are more things in heaven and earth than can be explained in a man-made document. There is a mother's heart, and her soul, which tells her things that cannot be ignored. And I will tell you now that my son is not dead.'

'Nani, I believe you.'

'I understand that you do not.' Anahita shrugged. 'But I don't mind. However, it's partly my fault that my family don't believe me. I've never explained to them what happened all those years ago.'

'Why not?'

'Because . . .' Anahita gazed out of the window to her beloved mountains. She gave a slight shake of her head. 'It isn't right for me to tell you now. It's all in there.' She pointed a finger at the pages in Ari's hands. 'When the moment is right for you – and you will know when that is – perhaps you will read my story. And then, you will decide for yourself whether to investigate it.'

'I see,' said Ari, but he didn't.

'All I ask of you is that you share its contents with no one in our family until I die. It is my life I entrust to you, Ari. As you know –' Anahita paused – 'sadly, my time on this earth is running out.'

Ari stared at her, confused as to what his great-grandmother wished him to do. 'You want me to read this and then make investigations as to the whereabouts of your son?' he clarified.

'Yes.'

'But where would I start?'

'In England, of course.' Anahita stared at him. 'You would retrace my footsteps. Everything you need to know you now hold in the palms of your hands. And besides, your father tells me you run some kind of computer company. You, of all people, have the webbing at your disposal.'

'You mean the "web"?' Ari held back a chuckle.

'Yes, so I'm sure it would only take you a few seconds to find the place where it all began,' Anahita concluded.

Ari followed his great-grandmother's eye-line out to the mountains beyond the window. 'It's a beautiful view,' he said, for want of something better to say.

'Yes, and it's why I stay here, even though my daughter disapproves. One day soon, I'll travel upwards, way beyond those peaks, and I'll be happy for it. I will see many people there whom I've mourned in my life. But of course, as it stands –' Anahita's gaze landed on her great-grandson once more – 'not the one I wish to see most of all.'

'How do you know he's still alive?'

Anahita's eyes reverted to the skyline, then she closed them wearily. 'As I said, it's all in my story.'

'Of course.' Ari knew he was dismissed. 'So, I'll let you rest, Nani.'

Anahita nodded. Ari stood up, made a *pranaam*, then kissed his great-grandmother on each cheek.

'Goodbye, and I'm sure I'll see you soon,' he commented as he walked towards the door.

'Perhaps,' she answered.

As Ari made to leave the room, he turned back suddenly on instinct. 'Nani, why me? Why not give this story to your daughter, or my father?'

Anahita stared at him. 'Because, Ari, the story you hold in your hands might be my past, but it is also your future.'

Ari left the room feeling drained. Walking through the bungalow, he made for the coat rack by the front door, underneath which his briefcase sat. Stowing the yellowing pages inside it, he continued into the drawing room. His grandmother, Muna, approached him immediately.

'Why did she want to see you?' she asked him.

'Oh,' Ari replied airily, 'she doesn't believe her son is dead and wants me to go and investigate in England.' He rolled his eyes for full effect.

'Not again!' Muna rolled her own eyes equally dramatically. 'Listen, I can show you the death certificate. Her son died when he was about three. Please, Ari,' Muna laid a hand on her grandson's shoulder, 'take no notice. She's been going on about this for years. Sadly, it's an old woman's fantasy, and certainly not worth wasting your precious time with. Take my word for it. I've listened to it for much longer than you. Now,' his grandmother smiled, 'come and have a last glass of champagne with your family.'

*

Ari sat on the last plane from Bagdogra back to Mumbai. He tried to concentrate on the figures in front of him, but Anahita's face kept floating into his vision. Surely his grandmother was right when she'd told him Anahita was deluded? And yet, there were things his great-grandmother had said when they were alone – things she couldn't have known about him, which had unsettled him. Perhaps there was something in her story . . . maybe he would take the time to glance through the manuscript when he arrived back home.

At Mumbai airport, even though it was past midnight, Bambi, his current girlfriend, was there at Arrivals to greet him. The rest of the night was spent pleasantly in his apartment overlooking the Arabian Sea, enjoying her slim young body.

The following morning, he was already late for his meeting, and as he packed his briefcase with the documents he needed, he removed the papers Anahita had given him.

One day I will have time to read it, he thought, as he shoved the manuscript into the bottom drawer of his desk and hurriedly left his apartment.